THE FIEND QUEEN

What Reviewers Say About
Barbara Ann Wright's Pyramid Series

"...a healthy dose of a very creative, yet believable, world into which the reader will step to find enjoyment and heart-thumping action. It's a fiendishly delightful tale."—*Lamda Literary*

"Barbara Ann Wright is a master when it comes to crafting a solid and entertaining fantasy novel. ...The world of lesbian literature has a small handful of high-quality fantasy authors, and Barbara Ann Wright is well on her way to joining the likes of Jane Fletcher, Cate Culpepper, and Andi Marquette. ...Lovers of the fantasy and futuristic genre will likely adore this novel, and adventurous romance fans should find plenty to sink their teeth into."—*The Rainbow Reader*

"*The Pyramid Waltz* has had me smiling for three days. ...I also haven't actually read...a world that is entirely unfazed by homosexuality or female power before. I think I love it. I'm just delighted this book exists. ...If you enjoyed *The Pyramid Waltz*, *For Want of a Fiend* is the perfect next step...you'd be embarking on a joyous, funny, sweet and madcap ride around very dark things lovingly told, with characters who will stay with you for months after."—*The Lesbrary*

"This book will keep you turning the page to find out the answers. ... Fans of the fantasy genre will really enjoy this installment of the story. We can't wait for the next book."—*Curve Magazine*

Visit us at www.boldstrokesbooks.com

By the Author

The Pyramid Waltz

For Want of a Fiend

A Kingdom Lost

The Fiend Queen

THE FIEND QUEEN

by
Barbara Ann Wright

2015

THE FIEND QUEEN
© 2015 By Barbara Ann Wright. All Rights Reserved.

ISBN 13: 978-1-62639-234-2

This Trade Paperback Original Is Published By
Bold Strokes Books, Inc.
P.O. Box 249
Valley Falls, NY 12185

First Edition: January 2015

Credits
Editor: Cindy Cresap
Production Design: Susan Ramundo
Cover Design By Sheri (graphicartist2020@hotmail.com)

Acknowledgments

Ross and Mom, you know who you are. Thanks to Writer's Ink for always buying my books. Matt Borgard, Natsu Carmony, Deb de Freitas, and Erin Kennemer, you are the bestest beta readers since you okayed the use of bestest. Pattie Lawler, you always go above and beyond.

Thanks to Radclyffe, Bold Strokes, and Cindy Cresap for slogging it out with me.

I love you, pets.

And I love you, wonderful readers, for continuing with me all the way to the end. Cheers!

Dedication

For my grandma, Sadie Fox, a life well lived.

CHAPTER ONE

KATYA

Pounding echoed down the corridors of the secret passageways. Katya's eyes strained against the blackness, and she closed them rather than face the dark. She pictured bright, sun-filled halls, safety around every corner, anything but being bent double, knife wound screaming in her back as she dragged Brutal's unconscious bulk.

"Come on, Redtrue. Keep going," Castelle said from beside her. "You can do it, dearheart. I know you can."

Katya clamped her lips together, swallowing the urge to tell Castelle to shut up. The huffing and puffing of Redtrue's breathing kept pace with them. After they'd fought Averie in the pyramid room, Redtrue had fallen, blood trickling from her nose. The Fiend energy in the palace had overpowered her. Katya had heard her collapse several times, and Castelle's words got her moving again.

Even with two people pulling Brutal down the corridor, they barely moved. Katya had lost track of whether the trickling sensation down her spine was blood or sweat. She kept her shoulder against the wall, anxious to feel the first turn that would take them deeper inside the castle walls.

"Come on, Red," Castelle said. "One foot in front of the other."

Katya ground her teeth. The syrupy quality to Castelle's voice, the certainty that everything would be okay, made Katya want to drop Brutal and leave them there. She could charge into battle where she belonged, confront Averie, and meet her death. At least then she wouldn't have to be in the dark anymore.

"That's enough." Katya lowered Brutal to the cold stones, dug a candle from her pocket, and lit it. She'd hoped they'd only need Redtrue's pyramid for light, but she never went anywhere unprepared.

Now she was reminded of why.

Redtrue sagged down the wall, her mouth smeared with blood from her nose, turning her reddish-brown skin black. She rolled her shaven scalp against the wall until she rested on her one braided lock of black hair. Her dark eyes went half-lidded as she struggled to breathe.

Castelle knelt and tucked her own curly dark hair behind her ears. She watched Redtrue with concern in her turquoise eyes, the tattoo around the right eye wrinkling. Redtrue drew a pyramid, and light flickered inside before it went dark again.

"Leave it," Castelle said, "until your strength returns."

They were a sorry, bleeding group. An arrow stuck out of Brutal's chest like a flagpole. They hadn't dared remove it. Brutal had taught her not to pull an arrow or blade unless she was ready to treat the wound, and they couldn't stop long enough to treat any of them.

Katya stalked past them, her body aching with every step. Away from their noise, pounding filled the corridor again. Averie and Roland's thugs would be on them soon. Katya pushed herself to hurry until she spotted her mother lying in the gloom.

As Katya bent and scooped her mother into her arms, she praised the spirits that Ma was petite instead of tall and muscled. She could have easily carried her mother before, but her arms now felt as if they were filled with porridge, and her back burnt like the sun.

She cradled her mother's blond head against her shoulder while settling the weight on her hips. The comforting rise and fall of Ma's chest made Katya's own breathing come a little easier. Katya held the candle between two fingers, tilted away, the wax dripping onto the stones.

When she approached the others, Castelle held out her arms. Katya passed Ma and the candle over, and Castelle started down the corridor, the queen of Farraday snug against her chest.

"Take the first left," Katya said, "and then straight on."

"I won't go far."

Katya knelt next to Redtrue as the candlelight faded. "How are you feeling?"

"Useless." She mumbled something Katya didn't catch. The worse Redtrue fared, the thicker her Allusian accent became. She'd muttered as she followed them, and Katya was tempted to ask if she also wished Castelle would shut up.

Katya snaked an arm around her and lifted her. "Come on. We'll get a head start on Brutal." In the dim light, they could see enough to step around him.

"You're supposed to be resting," Redtrue said.

"I'll rest when I'm dead." She winced, recalling a time Crowe had said those same words.

"The Fiend magic," Redtrue said. "We have to stop it."

That wouldn't be possible, not when the palace was built on the prison of a greater Fiend, Yanchasa the Mighty, the monster that had allowed ancient Farradains to conquer this land and had forced Katya's ancestors to carry its Aspect in order to keep their power.

With her Aspect stripped away, Katya had been able to keep the secret of the Umbriels from Redtrue, but time spent with Katya's mother undid all her work. Ma had already transformed into her Fiendish self in order to save Katya's life.

But no pyradisté had ever been sickened by the great capstone under the palace. Redtrue couldn't even blame her mysterious illness on the fact that she was Allusian. After all, the capstone had never affected Starbride.

Katya told herself not to wander there. Starbride was in the city fighting a rebellion, the same thing Katya was supposed to be doing from inside the palace. Katya had seen Roland venturing into the city as well. She had to destroy his pyramids, cripple his power before he could use it against anyone else. Instead she was crawling through the dark, looking for a place to hide her wounded while Starbride was entangled in the fight of a thousand lifetimes.

"It's in that direction," Redtrue said, pointing ahead. "The pyramid with the Fiend magic, I can feel it."

Katya frowned. "Not down?"

"Is there something beneath us I should know about?"

"Not now." Maybe not ever.

Redtrue made a disgusted noise. "You and your secrets."

It was so close to what Starbride said on a regular basis that Katya didn't know whether to laugh or cry.

They couldn't stop anywhere obvious. Averie knew the palace as well as Katya, and she knew the secret passageways twice as well. Katya hadn't called her a first class lady-in-waiting just for her sewing skills. But Averie was gone, just as dead as Roland's other victims. He'd stripped her mind and made her his puppet. At least it gave Katya a reason to focus on anger rather than grief.

Averie might look in their old bedrooms or any of the Order's meeting places, but the secret passageways connected more than just the royal apartments. As a young rake, Katya had taken great delight in maneuvering her lovers into certain rooms along the secret routes.

After they'd dragged Brutal a little farther, Katya pressed her ear to a stone door. Nothing moved in the room beyond. She peeked out. An unmade bed and various objects scattered about said the occupant had left in a hurry, probably when Roland had taken over. Katya hurried to the door that led to the hallway and locked it.

She and Castelle hauled the others inside. "Do you think we can get Brutal in the bed without hurting him?" Castelle asked.

Katya shook her head. "Do you know how to stitch someone?"

"No."

"I wouldn't attempt it then," Brutal said softly.

Katya knelt by his side. "Are you back with us?"

"I passed out, don't remember when." His baby face, usually so ruddy, was the gray of old stone. He waved weakly toward his chest. "I think it's in my lung."

She brushed his short brown hair away from his slick forehead and fought the tears swimming in her eyes. "What can we do?"

"Can you talk us through fixing you?" Castelle asked.

"If it were you," he said, "I'd bandage you and take you to a chapterhouse."

"The bandages we could do." Katya clenched her fist. Before Roland, she couldn't remember feeling so helpless. "We could stitch you up, but if you're wounded inside…"

"Leave me here."

"Brutal—"

He captured both her hands in one of his. "Finish the mission. I trust in Best and Berth. Fortitude will see me through. Kill Roland, destroy his pyramids."

Katya made her voice as steady as she could. "I will come back for you."

"I know."

The faith in his eyes made her want to weep anew, and she could almost hear the echo of unspoken words: he knew she would come back, but he might not be alive to greet her.

Katya's mother began to stir as they were draping blankets around Brutal, curling them around the arrow shaft. Before Katya could help her, Ma sat up, inhaled sharply, and grabbed hold of her pyramid necklace.

Her blue eyes locked with Katya's. "What did I do?"

"You took your necklace off—"

"After that."

"You can't just take it off, Ma. It's not why you came."

"Is it not?" She stood, using the wall as support.

"Ma…"

"Did I kill Averie, or is she still hunting us?"

"She's still out there."

Redtrue watched them like a hunting hawk. "We must find the source of this Fiend magic. If it is a pyramid, I shall cleanse it and recover."

Katya and her mother exchanged a glance.

Redtrue sighed long and loud. "Is now the time for secrets?"

"Does she mean the capstone?" Ma asked.

"I don't think so. She didn't think it was below us."

"Again you mention down," Redtrue said. "What are you keeping below this place?"

"Farraday is built on the backs of Fiends," Castelle said.

When Katya glanced at her sharply, Castelle shrugged. "Like she said, what good are secrets now? She's seen her Majesty's darker side."

"There is a great Fiend trapped under the palace," Ma said in clipped tones. "If you cleanse its prison, you could release it."

Redtrue closed her eyes and sagged in Castelle's embrace. Exhaustion or despair, Katya couldn't tell. "I can feel it."

"From all the way up here?" Katya asked. "That's impossible."

Redtrue gestured toward her shoulder as if she might throw her braid over, but her arm dropped to her side. "Impossible or not, I can sense it, and it is not the pyramid I believe is sapping my strength."

"Fiendish magic." Ma stared into space.

"Something new?" Katya asked. "Something Roland made?"

"Not a prison," Ma muttered. Katya was reminded of how often she thought out loud. Maybe she'd gotten it from her mother instead of her father.

"These wild Fiends," Ma said, "we thought Roland might have summoned them."

"And how else but through a pyramid?" Katya asked. "This call must be doing something to Redtrue."

"Poisoning me," Redtrue said.

But Starbride hadn't seemed sick, and she'd been in the city longer, closer to this pyramid. She hadn't reported any of the pyradistes being afflicted, either, so why affect Redtrue and none of the others? Maybe it was one of those differences between Farradain and Allusian magic that Katya was starting to suspect were fundamental.

"Can you walk?" she asked Redtrue.

She nodded, but Castelle had to help her to her feet.

"You're going to have to lead the way," Katya said.

"We'll be faster now that we've found Brutal a place to rest," Castelle said.

"If Averie's broken into the secret passageways, we could find ourselves fighting in close quarters in a hurry."

"If we go via the hallways," Castelle said, "we might have to fight every step of the way."

"Passages it is." Katya's body demanded she rest and let someone else take care of Farraday's problems, but there were too many people depending on her. If the wild Fiends were fighting the army or protecting Roland, Katya had to do something about them.

After Castelle changed Katya's bandage, they took to the secret passageways again. Ma and Castelle helped Redtrue limp along. Katya took point, rapier drawn and holding a lantern they'd found in the abandoned room. Her back ached with every step, but that didn't alarm her as much as the numbness inside, as if someone had hollowed her out.

Katya heard the hint of footsteps over Redtrue's labored wheeze. She set her lantern down and backed away, staying low and hoping the flickering flame would mask her presence. The footsteps paused before they clattered into a run. Castelle took her place at Katya's side, sword out. A corpse Fiend barreled around the corner and leapt for them, its gray lips pulled back in a snarl.

Katya tried to catch its charge, but her shoulder gave, and she fell to one knee. Castelle grunted as she tried to bear the corpse Fiend's weight alone. She staggered, tripped over Katya, and then rolled away. Katya hacked at the corpse Fiend's knees while Castelle aimed for its pyramid. It ducked to the side and let out a ghastly howl.

The howl echoed in the corridors, and a heartbeat passed before a number of Fiendish throats took up the cry. Desperation and adrenaline pushed Katya up. As the corpse Fiend dodged Castelle, Katya thrust with all her strength and shattered the pyramid in its forehead. It dropped lifelessly to the stone.

Katya grabbed her lantern as Castelle hauled Redtrue upright.

"We need to get out of here," Ma said.

Castelle chuckled, though it had little humor. "Nice of the corpse Fiends to make our decision for us."

The closest door led into a storeroom cluttered with furniture. It would have to do. After everyone was inside, Ma and Castelle stacked furniture against the passageway door. It wouldn't stop anyone determined, but it might convince a near mindless corpse that Katya and her friends had gone another way. Katya only hoped that if Averie heard the howls, the furniture would fool her, too. "Not likely," she muttered.

The door to the hallway creaked as Katya opened it, but no one lingered in the hall. The unadorned walls and uncarpeted floor indicated the servants' section. Maybe Katya had gotten lucky for once and found someplace Roland wouldn't bother to guard.

CHAPTER TWO

STARBRIDE

The silence seemed to close around Starbride until nothing distracted her, not the pain that pounded through her temples, nor the distant sounds of fighting. She'd stuck a knife in Roland's puppet, the last of the Sleeting brothers. If she turned, she'd see him dead in the street behind her.

No one spoke. It felt like an invisible wall separated her from Dawnmother, Hugo, Pennynail, and Master Bernard. After everything, were they afraid of her? Or maybe they just worried. She'd never know if they said nothing.

"Say something!" she cried as she whirled around.

Hugo and Master Bernard took a step back. Dawnmother's dark brown eyes creased with concern. "Star, are you all right?"

"It's war! You've all killed people!"

"It's not the killing." Hugo spoke slowly and smoothed his brown curls away from his forehead, looking younger than his fourteen years. "We do what we must, but you didn't have to…"

Pennynail pushed his laughing Jack mask onto his head and became Freddie again. "We don't have time for this. What's done is done." Anger burned in his green eyes and the taut line of his lean body. He loosened the collar that hid the pink scar around his neck. Combined with his raspy voice, no one could mistake the fact that he'd been hanged and lived to tell the tale.

Dawnmother and Hugo gawked at him. Master Bernard just blinked, clearly not recognizing him as the Dockland Butcher.

"Starbride," Freddie asked, "can you keep fighting? Because we have to move faster than this. Talking can come later."

"I feel…oh." She pressed her forehead with the heel of her palm as pain roared in her ears.

"Your headache?" Master Bernard asked. "From days ago?"

"Stress is—" Dawnmother started.

Starbride walked away. It didn't matter what the cause was. Freddie was right. They had to keep fighting. She headed toward the nearest echoing cries of pain.

Two groups of townspeople fought one another in the neighboring square. One side was easy to identify, all red-robed strength monks. Starbride picked out the first monks she'd freed from Roland's mind control, Scarra and Fury, fighting near the front, both using staves along with kicks and punches. She knew the leader of the chapterhouse, Ruin, was probably somewhere in the press.

Starbride had hoped their opponents would be corpse Fiends, an enemy they'd taken the measure of, but these looked like ordinary people. None sported Starbride's colors—the hawk of Farraday clutching a pyramid—the only way the citizens of Marienne had to tell friend from foe.

Still, that didn't mean these people were helping Roland willingly. As Hugo and Freddie charged into the fight, Starbride pulled a pyramid from her satchel, one that could detect other pyramids in use. Beside her, Master Bernard did the same while Dawnmother kept watch.

Starbride's skull screamed as she concentrated, the pressure so great she felt as if it might crack in two. The world faded to grays in her augmented sight, and she spotted the golden glow of Master Bernard's pyramid, but little forks of lightning flashed across her vision. Her concentration began to crumble. She snarled and focused harder, but the gray edges of the world began to blacken.

"I see something," Master Bernard said.

"Where?"

He tried to tell her, but she could barely hear. With a curse, she shoved the detection pyramid back in her satchel. She couldn't focus with the pain, and if she couldn't use her pyramids, what good was she?

Since the onset of her headache days ago, only two events had made her feel better: being with Katya and killing Alphonse. And, a small voice inside her said, she still had destruction pyramids. She didn't have to focus to use them.

Starbride marched closer to the fighting, dipped into her satchel, and threw a flash bomb into the midst of the mind-controlled enemies. She closed her eyes against the bright flash and then opened them to see several people fall, but the residue from the flash made her pain spike. She dragged another pyramid out and threw without thinking, and fire bloomed in the attackers' midst.

Her headache quieted, leaving room for guilt to punch her in the gut. These people weren't beyond help like Alphonse had been. Master Bernard had said he'd seen something, maybe the pyramid responsible for their behavior. The smell of burning flesh washed over Starbride, and she fell to her knees in the street.

The attackers didn't scream as they burned. Those hypnotized by Roland were always happy, sublime even, no matter what they did. When she'd first seen them, they'd strolled happily and fought happily, and now they died the same way. They probably would have starved to death while grinning like fools.

Dawnmother's arms went around her, pulling her away from the fighting. Master Bernard stepped around her as he threw a flash bomb. She could feel the pain creeping up on her again.

"Did you free them?" Starbride asked.

Master Bernard glanced back at her. "I found an explosive pyramid and cancelled it. I don't know where these people were hypnotized, but it wasn't here."

It didn't bring her any comfort. "What's wrong with me, Dawn?"

"Maybe we should stay away from the fighting."

"But the *pain.*" It wasn't enough to say it. No words could explain. With the agony lessened, she knew one truth. "I can't abandon everyone, Dawn."

The look in Dawnmother's eyes said it all. It wasn't abandonment if they had to divide their time between helping her and fighting for their lives.

"Wait here," Dawnmother said.

Before Starbride could speak, Dawnmother ran toward the fighting. With pyramid magic on the monks' side, the fight was over within moments. Dawnmother hurried back, dragging Scarra and Ruin. Both monks peered anxiously into Starbride's face.

"You said she was hurt," Scarra said. She tilted Starbride's face up. "Where?"

Ruin looked her up and down.

"You know pain," Dawnmother said. "Her head has been splitting open for days."

"Let's get off the street," Ruin said.

Starbride tried to pull away. "I can't leave!"

Ruin snatched the satchel from his shoulder and passed it to Dawnmother. "Are you sick enough that I'll have to carry you?"

Starbride pictured herself being hoisted through the street like a sack of flour. If he was willing to take her seriously…

"I'll get the others," Master Bernard said. Ruin led her through a storefront, Scarra and Dawnmother just behind. He made her sit on a countertop, the contents of which had been looted, and the owners of the shop were nowhere to be seen.

"Tell me what's wrong," Ruin said, and even though they looked nothing alike, he reminded her so much of Crowe that she nearly burst into tears. Freddie had been right when he'd said that leaning on someone was intoxicating.

"My head, there's so much pain, and I've been hurting people."

He peered closely into her eyes, and she focused on his gray hair. "Were you hit in the head recently?"

"Not that I recall."

He glanced at Dawnmother. She shook her head. Ruin dragged his lower lip through his teeth. "If it's not from an injury, I don't know what I can do for you."

"There are herbs," Scarra said.

Starbride felt like shouting, but Ruin shook his head before she could. "If the pain on her face is any indication, I think we're beyond herbs."

Starbride could have hugged him, but the agony spiked, taking her breath away. She heard voices, but it sounded like hundreds, thousands, screaming all at once. Someone touched her shoulder, and she clawed blindly before her hands were captured in a grip like stone. When she tried to jerk away, different pain sang through her shoulders across old scars caused by Fiendish claws.

It dwarfed the feeling in her head, and she opened her eyes. Fury had hold of her arms. Behind him, Scarra held Dawnmother, saying, "He won't hurt her," over and over.

"Are you yourself again?" Ruin asked.

Starbride could only blink at him.

Ruin let her go. "You had the most monstrous expression on your face. Like when the young lord turned."

Starbride's eyes widened, and she felt over her face for horns or fangs.

Dawnmother wormed out of Scarra's grasp. "You did *not* turn into a monster, Star." She glared at Ruin until he backed away. "You were out of your mind with hurt, nothing more."

"But it makes sense," Scarra said. "You haven't busted your head, you've never felt this before, and we know the spirits' bedamned power of the Fiend king's fuc—um, pyramids."

"Master Bernard is not affected," Dawnmother said.

"And I don't have a Fiend," Starbride added.

Scarra shrugged. "Perhaps it only nails Allusian pyradistés."

"Adsnazi," Starbride mumbled. Redtrue hadn't seemed in pain, but Starbride hadn't been around her long, and she was newly come to Marienne. At the moment, Redtrue might also be in agony.

In the palace, leaving Katya without a magic-user.

Starbride pressed her forehead and tried to think. When Master Bernard led the others inside, Dawnmother filled them in on the discussion. Scarra and Ruin stared at Freddie without his mask on, but he spoke too quickly for them to ask questions.

"Starbride," Freddie said, leaning close to her ear, "you set those people on fire."

Did she? She barely remembered anything except that the ache had stopped for a short while. "I…"

"I can knock you out," he whispered.

One quick blow to the head and she'd have merciful darkness. No more chances of hurting people; she wouldn't even be awake for her splitting skull.

Katya would never do it. Katya would call it cowardly. She might urge Starbride to do it out of love, but she'd never take that path herself.

As if reading her mind, Freddie said, "Better to miss the fight than to make it harder on your allies."

He was right, she knew he was, and the pain built in her head again, ballooning behind her eyes. "Hurt me," she said.

"What?"

"Just do it! Pinch me or something."

She felt the pressure on her leg, but it was tiny compared to the swells cresting in her brain. "Harder!"

She heard shuffling feet, and then a hot pinpoint bloomed just above her elbow. Her eyes jerked open as the rage in her skull subsided Ruin pressed her arm with his thumb and forefinger.

"Pressure point," he said as he released her. "Other pain dulls the one in your head, does it?"

She nodded, and hope seemed to appear before her. "I can fight."

"If someone else is hurting you?" Hugo asked. He frowned as if the very idea appalled him.

Starbride hopped down from the counter. "Show Dawnmother, please."

Ruin had a quick word with Dawnmother, showing her the points on his body and hers. Starbride stepped to the front of the shop. The other monks milled, waiting for Scarra and Ruin. She'd kept them talking too long. They needed to get out in the street again.

"Miss Starbride—" Hugo started.

"They're wearing my colors, Hugo. I can't let them fight without me."

"But you're injured."

"Time enough to settle it when this fight is done. Once Dawnmother knows what she needs to know, I'll be myself again." It might serve as fitting punishment for the people she'd killed. With the hurt dulled, she remembered it more clearly now: the light fading from Alphonse's eyes, the screams of those she'd set aflame. Their smoking husks littered the street even now. How did Katya do it, kill without remorse? The thought that they were enemies didn't give her any relief, and she realized that every time she'd seen someone killed she'd been thankful it hadn't been her that had ended them.

A bit of Alphonse's blood still clung to her fingertips, around her nails.

"Maybe, um, maybe you did them a favor," Hugo said.

Starbride squeezed his arm. "Don't throw away your principles for me, Hugo."

"No, I mean it."

"You don't, but thank you for saying it."

"This isn't worth debating," Freddie said as he joined them.

Scarra stepped closer. "I agree. Death is the whore that gives us all the clap eventually." When they stared at her, she blushed. "Well, that's what my da used to say."

Different mindsets, different upbringings. They could argue around and around forever. Master Bernard patted Starbride's shoulder. "Time heals all," he offered.

Starbride supposed that would have to do. After the battle was won, they'd have time for both joy and sleepless nights filled with guilt. Time enough for all things, healing, too.

Dawnmother curled her fingers around Starbride's elbow, ready to do what needed to be done, though Starbride could see that it pained her.

They split off, Ruin leading his monks down another street, the better to cover more ground. Master Bernard went with them, while Scarra stayed at Starbride's side.

"Just in case you need more pressure points," she said, giving them a wide grin.

Thick and muscular, she was as tall as Freddie and probably stronger, quite an asset, never mind that she seemed to take most of her speech from Darkstrong himself. She'd recently cut her blond hair close to her head, though it didn't make her angular features any less striking.

"Your eyes are straying," Dawnmother said.

Starbride barked a laugh. "I can admire anyone I want."

"She does cut a nice figure."

"Now whose eyes are straying?"

"I don't have a princess waiting for me. Perhaps you have a weakness for blondes."

"Just one." Dwelling on Katya, even for a moment, helped keep the pain at bay. She just hoped the pressure points would continue to work. She couldn't fight while stabbing herself in the leg. If it got that bad, she supposed she'd have to take Freddie up on his offer.

A boom sounded a few streets over, the same as they'd heard just before Alphonse. Starbride shook the thought away. Before they'd killed the corpse Fiends, Dawnmother had been convinced the creatures had called something with their otherworldly howls. Now it appeared that whatever it was had caught up to Starbride again.

Everyone looked to her. They weren't out here to avoid a fight. With renewed purpose, they headed toward the sounds of the explosions now peppered with screams and the rumble of collapsing masonry.

"Those have to be explosive pyramids," Starbride said.

"Well, maybe there's a spirits fuc—forsaken rogue pyradisté running around." Scarra said.

"It's Roland," Starbride said. She could almost feel him, and the thought of fighting him made the pain fly from her mind. The thought of killing him carried no guilt. Maybe it would even cure her. Starbride left her mind open to that possibility, and she smiled as the screams drew nearer.

CHAPTER THREE

KATYA

It was a hard choice between caution and speed. With Katya's wound and Redtrue's malady, avoiding confrontation seemed safest, but the fact that they were being hunted in the palace halls—and that the rest of the town depended on them to defeat Roland's pyramids—cried out for speed.

Katya had to settle for something in the middle. Ma supported Redtrue and crept along slowly, led by Katya, who held her blade ready while Castelle ranged ahead of them, scouting.

Castelle paused at a corner. Her athletic body tensed, and she leaned far back against the wall on the balls of her feet. After listening for a few seconds, she hurried to Katya's side.

"There's noise in a room ahead of us," she said. "Voices and someone moving around."

Not corpse Fiends, at least. "Could you hear what they said?"

Castelle shook her head and looked to Redtrue, worry lining her features.

"We must go…right," Redtrue said. Standing and speaking seemed harder for her now. By the time they reached the pyramid that affected her so, Katya worried she'd no longer be able to keep her feet.

As it was, right was the only direction available, past the voices. Katya and Castelle could take any of Roland's living creations. After all, few guards had practiced with the sword from an early age by the best trainers money could buy. Of course, it might not come to that. If the troublesome room stayed shut, Katya and her party could just sneak by.

"Let's go," Katya said.

They paused at the corner and listened. Katya heard voices behind one door, though it sounded as if some endeavored to be quieter than the others. An argument, then, by the rushed tones. But Roland's guards didn't argue; they were hypnotized into obedience. Maybe some of them had found a way to free themselves? If these were enemies of Roland, they could be friends.

Katya waved everyone ahead just as the door cracked open, and a pale face peeked out. Katya met a wide, green-eyed glance before the door slammed shut. The voices grew louder before silence fell. Katya glanced at Castelle. She seemed torn between the desire to laugh and frown.

Katya stepped lightly to the door. "We're not here to hurt you."

Silence reigned for a few seconds before the door cracked open again. "You're not guards."

If Katya read these people right, bold was the way to go. "We've come to kill the usurper."

The door flew open, and a slight, dark haired woman confronted them. She was dressed in servants' livery, but her posture spoke of nobility. Without all the frippery, it was a heartbeat before Katya recognized her. "Baroness Jacintha."

Jacintha bowed deep. "Highness." When she straightened, she had tears in her eyes. "You've come to rescue us at last." She looked at the rest of them, and her mouth fell open. "M…Majesty?"

At least eight people had crammed into the room behind the baroness, probably what was left of her household, as well as a few courtiers. "You've been living in the palace since the usurper took over?" Katya asked.

"Hiding, Highness." She glanced up and down the hall. "We shouldn't talk out here."

Katya hesitated, torn between caution and haste again, but if the baroness had been in the palace since Roland had taken over, she was an invaluable source of information.

When the door shut behind all of them, it was cramped indeed. The narrow chamber had been a servants' bedroom, made to sleep at least six in narrow bunk beds without much room for anything else. Several people began speaking at once, but Jacintha lifted a hand, and they stopped mid-word.

"Highness, Majesty, surely you did not come alone?"

"Our tale can wait, Baroness. You've been living as servants?"

Some nodded shamefully, but the baroness shrugged, far from the flippant woman Katya remembered. It seemed she'd finally found the forge that would make her into a blade. "We do what we must." She sounded wistful, as if the privileged noble still lurked in there somewhere.

When Katya described her mission, Jacintha promised to send someone to tend to Brutal. They couldn't heal him, but they could look after him until help arrived. It warmed Katya's heart that he wouldn't be alone, even if the worst happened. Small comfort, but Katya had learned to live on those.

"You'll need to keep hidden until the fight is won," Katya said.

"Of course, Highness." The looks that the others exchanged spoke volumes, as if they wondered how stupid she thought they were.

"The guards don't come here," Jacintha said. "We've seen some looters in the regular halls, but no one's bothered with the servant quarters."

"There's nothing to steal here," one of the courtiers said softly. "And most of the servants fled when the palace fell."

"We forage for what we need." Jacintha took the hand of a man beside her without seeming to think about it. His bearing and deference screamed courtier, and Katya bet that before Roland had taken over, the baroness wouldn't have looked at him twice. Maybe when the fight ended, everyone would have lost a few of their prejudices.

"Sometimes, when we've encountered the guards," Jacintha said, "we've pretended to be hypnotized, and they've let us be."

"It's harder with those things," the man beside her said, "the dead things."

"But it can still be done, Highness."

Katya glanced at Redtrue. From what Starbride had told her, the corpse Fiends could sense pyradistés. Perhaps they could do the same for adsnazi. She carried a pyramid that protected them from mind control but not one that hid them from a corpse Fiend's unnatural sight.

"Some have gone out and never come back," someone said. "Or we've seen them later, sweeping the halls and sporting that smiling, dead-eyed look."

"They erase your mind," another said, "and put whatever they need in its place."

Ma reached for Jacintha's arm. "You have done well, keeping everyone safe."

Jacintha beamed as if she'd forgotten any courtly training she'd ever received. "I thank your Majesty."

"Will you take the kingdom back soon, Majesty?" one of the courtiers asked. All of them leaned close as if they lived for her answer.

"Soon," Ma promised, and Katya was glad she didn't have to say it.

"Any information you can give us would be helpful," Castelle said.

"Especially if you know where any of the usurper's pyramids are kept," Katya added.

Rumors and conjecture were all they had to offer. As a rule, they tried to stay away from Roland's pyramids. They'd heard of one near the library, and rumor painted it as something other than a mind pyramid, though they hadn't been close enough to see for themselves.

It sounded like it could be the one causing Redtrue's illness. Katya was embarrassed to admit that she didn't know how to get there from the servants' corridors. She didn't know them as well as she should have, but she'd never had much reason to go there. Jacintha and her fellows were happy to give directions, seeming both grateful to be useful and eager to see the Umbriels return to power.

"I think even those who occasionally voiced displeasure will welcome you back with open arms, Majesty, Highness," Jacintha said.

"The freedom to grumble is infinitely preferable to a ruler who changes your mind for you."

"I hope they all see it that way, Baroness," Ma said. "And if they do not, we would be grateful if you could remind them."

Jacintha bowed, and after making sure they had memorized the route, Katya set out again with Castelle scouting ahead, and Ma helping Redtrue behind them.

After two or three turns, Katya was certain that stopping had been the right decision. The rest of the palace was a maze, but there were clues if you knew where to look. Carpets, paintings, alcoves, and statuary provided signs pointing to which part of the palace you were entering.

The servants' quarters, though, were featureless. Maybe each new servant was partnered with an older one until they had the place memorized. Maybe it was also the servants' way of keeping those they served out of the way and out of their business. They couldn't very well do their jobs with nobles blundering into the linen closets.

Averie or Dawnmother could have led them through in a flash. Katya tried to banish thoughts of both. Averie would only bring her grief, and thoughts of Dawnmother would slide toward the oblivion of worry for Starbride.

At last they found the door they were looking for. Castelle pressed her ear to it. Katya paused with the others and waited. Castelle turned and shrugged, signaling that she'd heard nothing, but that didn't mean there was nothing to hear. Corpse Fiends didn't become bored and wander around making noise.

Katya moved closer and readied her rapier. Castelle opened the well-oiled door and peeked out. Seconds stretched on as she watched and listened. Katya strained to hear over Redtrue's labored breathing. Castelle widened the door until she had enough room to poke her head out.

When she waved behind her, Katya rushed forward, eager to see for herself. The hallway stood empty, but it wouldn't remain that way forever. The pyramid was undoubtedly guarded, and they still had some ways to go before reaching the library. Even then, they didn't know if the pyramid was in the library or just nearby. They'd need time to search.

Katya couldn't help but think of the time she'd led Starbride down these halls, just after they'd first met. She'd let Starbride think her a guardswoman, someone anonymous who could flirt with impunity, someone who didn't have to wear a courtly face.

Tension spread across Katya's shoulders, pulling at her wound. When they reached a junction, she looked to Redtrue who waved them to the left. They would have left her with Jacintha, but they didn't know exactly where this pyramid might be and didn't have the luxury of opening doors at random. Castelle peeked around the corner then skittered back.

"The Guard!" she whispered.

Katya opened the nearest door and ushered everyone inside. According to Starbride, all members of the king's Guard had been mind-warped. They weren't peasants who'd been hypnotized into loving Roland; they were trained fighters, and Katya would avoid them if she could. She shut the door noiselessly and waited. It was a larger room, some salon or study for use by the courtiers or nobles. The fine furniture had been overturned, cushions slashed and books and papers scattered. Looters had turned their anger on the furnishings when no valuables presented themselves, though Katya couldn't believe no one had carried off the tables or chairs. Perhaps it was just more satisfying to smash them.

She heard the tread of boots go past and counted to twenty before she looked out. If it was a patrol, they'd have to hurry or be caught when it came back. They piled into the hall and took the left. Redtrue's eyelids had begun to flutter, and her nose dribbled blood. Katya waved at Castelle to help while she took the lead.

The hallway before the massive library doors stood empty. Redtrue gestured into the library itself. When Katya pressed her ear to the thick doors, she heard a thump. Someone moved around inside, and she knew in her bones that it wasn't a helpful baroness.

Katya hurried back to the others. "Is there any way you can do something about the pyramid from out here?"

Redtrue could barely keep her eyes open. She shook her head.

Katya pressed her lips into a thin line. They couldn't barrel in like they had before. That was how they'd gotten to their current injured state. Well, it had been going all right until Averie had shown up.

Katya forced herself to focus. "We need a distraction."

Castelle frowned. "Something that would bring everyone in there out into the hall would be as bad as charging in."

"Then we need someone to go in there and draw their attention," Ma said. She gripped her pyramid necklace.

"No, Ma," Katya said. "With Redtrue hurt, there's no guarantee we'd get you back." And no guarantee that once they were inside, Ma would spare her daughter.

"Destroy this pyramid, and Redtrue will regain her power," Ma said.

"That's a big gamble, Highness," Castelle said.

"And yet no other ideas present themselves, and haste is still our ally."

Katya's stomach turned over at the thought that she might have to fight her mother. And turning into a Fiend more than once a day couldn't be healthy. "Ma…"

"Wait a few seconds and then sneak inside." She caught Katya's chin. "Do not catch my eye." She removed her necklace and pushed it into Katya's grasp.

Castelle offered her hand. "Do you need an angry thought to get you going?"

Ma pressed Castelle's fingers once before letting go. "Oh, I've enough for an entire army." The gravel of the Fiend roughened her voice as she moved toward the library. Before Katya could run after her, Ma was through the doors, and Katya heard a high-pitched screech.

She leapt up as Castelle dragged Redtrue behind her. A crash boomed within the room, and Katya caught the door before it shut. Forms darted past, too fast for the eye to follow, and a bookcase slammed over, knocking into one of its fellows and throwing it into another until a row of them collapsed. Katya slipped inside, staying low. Her mother had been gone but an instant, and the room was already in chaos, or perhaps the looters had been here, too. Katya hobbled over books and scattered papers. She scurried under the cover of a table, keeping Castelle and Redtrue close behind.

Shrieks rang through the air, and the howls of corpse Fiends echoed as they fought Katya's mother, but there was another sound: high tittering laughter that Katya recognized from the forest. Cold, paralyzing fear settled around her. There were wild Fiends inside with them.

Castelle pushed her on, but the aura of the wild Fiends pressed in from all sides, stunning her. Katya gritted her teeth and sought to drag her limbs forward. Castelle kicked her in the rump, and she got moving again, cheeks burning in shame as she hurried to a bookcase.

"There, it's there!" Redtrue said, her voice barely audible above the shrieks and howls. Something thudded into the bookcase they leaned against, and books shuddered from the shelves and rained around them. Redtrue pointed them deeper into the stacks, and they hurried on.

A pyramid the size of a large dog crouched like a spider at the back of the library. It sat on a bed of frost that climbed the shelves beside it in a jagged, splintery web. So cold it stole Katya's breath, it seemed to pulse, and black oil oozed across its surface like a living thing. With trembling hands, Katya drew her knife and stepped forward.

She lurched sideways as something yanked her right leg out from under her. She fell to one knee, fighting to pull her leg back. Blue and white mottled hands gripped her from the shadows between the shelves, and claws as long as knives dug into her calf.

Katya stabbed at the shadowy Fiend, but it leaned away from her attacks as a blur. It never lost its grip. She sliced at where it caught her, but it released and then grabbed her again before she could blink.

Still, it didn't seem to want to hurt her. Castelle moved close, but Katya called, "Wait!" The Fiend's courtesy wouldn't extend to anyone else, Katya was certain. She fought her fear and forced herself to study what she could see. The creature seemed the same size as a person, but she could dimly see horns, over-large eyes, and a mouth filled with fangs. Her blood pounded in her ears, and the commotion in the room faded.

"Let me go," Katya said.

It tilted its head and said a word, the sound like a saw grinding across a blade and filling her mouth with the coppery tang of blood.

Katya summoned the only memory she had of being a Fiend, when Roland had first attacked them under the palace, and Starbride had saved her. She'd wanted to kill and maim and destroy. She would have enjoyed it. This creature didn't seem to share the one other feeling she remembered: she'd wanted to try her strength against other Fiends. This one seemed to want to communicate, and the more she thought of her past Aspect, the more she sensed its interest.

"Go, Castelle," Katya croaked. She surrendered to the feelings of cold and dread and embraced what it had once felt like. She stared at eyes like liquid silver and reached for the kinship she found there.

Dimly, she heard a crunching sound behind her, what could only be the pyramid repeatedly smashing against the floor. It shattered at last with the skittering sound of scattered crystal, and before Katya could breathe again, the Fiend was gone.

Katya climbed to her feet. Castelle's hands were bright red, the fingertips pale blue as if she'd plunged her hands into icy water.

Redtrue leaned against a bookshelf, but as Katya watched, she wiped the blood from her nose and pulled herself to her feet. Even with tears streaming down her face, she seemed triumphant. "Let's go get your mother."

CHAPTER FOUR

STARBRIDE

Between the pain spiking in her head and the sharp ache of Dawnmother pressing above her elbow, Starbride barely held in the urge to scream. Freddie and the others had engaged a group of corpse Fiends. They depended on her for pyramid support, but her Darkstrong-cursed head wouldn't leave her be, and the pressure point was helping less and less.

"Is it working?" Dawnmother asked, her fingers digging into Starbride's flesh.

"Yes," Starbride said through her teeth. She held a cancellation pyramid and tried to focus, tried to gain the corpse Fiends' attention like she had before, but she couldn't concentrate past both sets of pain. Her fingers inched toward her destructive pyramids. She wouldn't feel bad about killing corpse Fiends by fire, and maybe that would give her a break from the agony.

Blinding misery roared through her temples, and her vision went white. Her legs turned to water, and someone shouted in her ear. Before she could hit the ground, her strength returned, pain gone, unruly thoughts vanished as quickly as if someone had pulled a bag off her head.

"Star!" Dawnmother shouted.

Starbride threw back her head and laughed. "It's gone!"

"What?"

"The pain's gone, Dawn. I'm free!"

Dawnmother smiled, looking confused but still happy. Starbride whipped toward the fighting and focused on her pyramid as easily as slipping into warm water.

When the corpse Fiends had to divide their attention between her and their attackers, the fight progressed quickly, leaving only scratches and bruises on her side and a host of unmoving bodies on the other.

Starbride leapt among her comrades and hugged everyone in reach. "The pain's gone!"

"Just like that?" Hugo asked.

"Who cares?" Freddie gripped Starbride's shoulders. "As long as it's over."

"But aren't you a little curious—" Hugo started.

"Princess Consort!" Captain Ursula called from up the street. "Have you found any—"

Starbride couldn't help turning toward the familiar voice. Unfortunately, that left Freddie with no one to hide behind and with his face plain as day.

"Freddie Ballantine!" Ursula roared. She pointed her sword.

"Oh shit," Freddie said.

"Stand where you are!"

"Freddie Ballantine," Scarra muttered. "Wait, *the* Freddie Ballantine? The Dockland Butcher Freddie Ballantine?"

"It's not what you think," Freddie said.

Ursula stomped toward them, eyes unblinking, mouth set in fury. Her sword didn't even tremble, though her arm had to be getting tired. Her dark blond hair was slicked back with sweat, and her Watch uniform and chain shirt were smeared with soot, including the hawk and pyramid badge pinned to her sleeve.

"Captain, wait," Starbride said. "You don't understand."

"Death just can't hold you," Ursula said.

Starbride grabbed back for Freddie. "Stay behind me."

"I *knew* you looked familiar!" Scarra cried.

Freddie twisted out of Starbride's grasp. "I don't need you to protect me."

"Darkstrong can take your ego." Starbride stepped into Ursula's path. "I know there's a lot to explain." Ursula just stared over Starbride's shoulder. Starbride caught her by the waist, making her look down at last as she lowered her sword. "You've been a good friend to me, Captain, to all of us, and you're owed an explanation, but there isn't time."

"I warned him what would happen," Ursula said, "if I found him in my town again."

"That was Dockland," Starbride said, "and it might as well have been the moon, not to mention long ago. Circumstances have changed."

"He's the masked man, your ex-thief," Ursula said. "No wonder he ran from me."

"Ursula," Freddie said, and Starbride heard him step closer.

"That's Captain to you!" Ursula shouted. She gestured to her squad. "Take him."

"You can't!" Starbride said.

"Don't worry about the charges," Ursula said to her squad. "I'm sure there are more than a few."

"This is madness." Starbride backed up and felt the others close ranks with her, even Scarra, the pack of them facing off against the Watch.

Freddie stepped to Starbride's side, a sad smile on his face. "I told you once that I'd never be taken again."

"And I gave you the choice between leaving my city for good and spending your life in a cell," Ursula said.

Freddie shrugged. "That's before you thought I was dead."

"You should have stayed dead!"

Starbride drew a pyramid. "Please, don't make us fight you."

Ursula gaped at her. "Do you know what this man did?"

"I know he's innocent of the crimes he was nearly hanged for. He's no Butcher."

Ursula paused before understanding passed over her face. "He hasn't told you anything."

"I'm sorry I hurt you," Freddie said.

"The spirits curse your apologies." Ursula looked back at her squad. "What are you waiting for?"

They stared at Starbride. "Isn't she the…" One man waved toward the colors decorating his own uniform.

"There will be time to sort this out," Starbride said. The booms they'd been chasing erupted one street over, and Starbride had never been so glad to see conflict coming for them. "Are you with us, Captain?"

The tendons in Ursula's jaw stood out like steel bands, and Starbride thought she might launch herself at Freddie and damn the consequences. "Form up!" she called. Together, she and her squad turned toward the commotion and moved off as a unit.

Starbride and the others trailed in their wake. "That was a near thing," Hugo said.

"One that's not over," Freddie grumbled.

When Starbride turned the corner, time seemed to slow. Bodies littered the street like scattered blossoms, torn or shredded or blown apart. Her eye fell upon one boy no older than Hugo, her emblem fluttering upon his still chest and the remains of his lower half spread across the ground. She followed the line of bodies to a few people still on their feet, holding their own against a line of corpse Fiends, and across the street…

The air left Starbride's lungs in a rush. Roland stood before them as boldly as he'd once appeared in the palace. "Hello there." He gave a cheery wave before lobbing a pyramid over the corpse Fiends' heads.

"Get down!" Starbride cried. She dove with the others and covered her head as the resulting boom shook the ground. Mud and brick rained atop them along with wet things best not thought about. Starbride struggled upright. Some of the corpse Fiends had been blown apart along with the townspeople, but more of them were regaining their feet, some missing arms while those who'd lost a leg crawled forward.

"Scatter!" Captain Ursula called, and the Watch left large gaps between them as they advanced on Roland.

He laughed, and his features melted into those of a Fiend. Horns curled over his head, and fangs pressed down against his lower lip. His eyes turned all blue, deep and rich like Katya's. He raced to the side in a blur and tore the face from one of Ursula's officers. Before the others took two steps, he reappeared on the other side of the street, his eyes on Starbride. There had to be some way they could get close to him. Maybe she could get him talking.

Starbride drew her cancellation pyramid. "Getting your own hands dirty? Isn't that a bit beneath you?"

"Oh, entertain me with your taunts, please!" he said. "How will you play this? Dare me to fight you one-on-one? Do you like that better than threatening me? Or playing a beggar on her knees?" When Freddie threw a knife, Roland plucked it out of the air. Several of the Watch darted for him, and he planted the knife in one of their chests before moving again. Scarra fought the corpse Fiends along with others of the Watch.

"I had hoped for something craftier from you," Roland said, "more romantic. Like, say, your assurance that if I kill you, my son will challenge me to a duel."

"You're not my father," Hugo spat.

Roland rolled his eyes. "Oh, I know! My daughter will challenge me in a lovesick haze if I dare to ruffle your hair, hmm? My already besotted niece will no doubt oblige me. How about my nephew? No! The entire kingdom is in love with you and will fight me to the death for the merest insult!"

Starbride focused on her pyramid. If he'd keep talking, she'd cancel as many of his weapons as she could. Before she could even detect the tell-tale glow of his pyramids, her mind lurched sideways, and her scalp ached as if someone had yanked her hair. Her pyramid had gone dark, cancelled. Starbride threw it to the ground and snarled.

Roland wiggled his fingers, a tiny pyramid in his own grip. "Do you want a Fiend of your own, Starbride? I think you'd enjoy it."

Starbride lobbed a fire pyramid at him, but he blurred out of the way. "And who would give it to me now that I have your daughter?" she asked.

He winked. "I'm sure I could accommodate you, dear lady."

Starbride shook her head. She'd been half wondering why he hadn't given Lady Hilda a Fiend himself, why he'd had his daughter do it instead. "I think you're far too dead to manage it." She threw another pyramid while he scowled, and this time, it singed him a bit.

He got his smile back quickly. "Why don't we do this?" He blurred again and appeared next to Hugo. Before Hugo could turn, Roland reached inside his collar and yanked his pyramid necklace loose. "And this!" Roland shoved him hard, and Starbride knew it wouldn't be Hugo who got up again. "And see what happens."

Hugo's Fiendish form barreled forward, reaching for his father, but Roland's blur stayed just out of reach. Hugo's eyes had become wholly light blue. A spike jutted from his chin, and two crow's wings sprouted from his back. Fangs from his upper jaw plunged well past his chin, forcing his lips into a snarl as he chased his father across the street.

"Shoot them both!" Ursula called, and some of her people lifted crossbows.

"No!" Dawnmother called, but Starbride knew the bolts wouldn't hurt either of them unless they were hit over and over, and both moved too fast for the bowmen to track. Starbride dug out her Fiend suppression pyramid. If Roland wasn't concentrating, she might be able to use it, but she'd have to get closer.

Hugo slammed into what seemed like an invisible wall. He whirled around, tracking something. When Roland appeared just behind him, his eyes still followed something Starbride couldn't see.

"Hugo, turn around!" Dawnmother cried.

He paid her no mind, nor did he look over his shoulder. Starbride searched for whatever had entranced him and caught the hint of a blur, dust cascading down a brick wall, an awning flapping in the breeze, something moving too fast for the eye to track, always just on the edge of her vision. Hugo moved too slowly to catch it, even as fast as he was.

"He can't resist it, you see," Roland said. "It's hard for me not to follow them as I am."

"Wild Fiends," Starbride whispered.

"There's nothing quite like their pull." He watched his son caper around the square.

Before he could look her way again, Starbride focused on her Fiend suppression pyramid, and he shrank back from her, hissing. Freddie came with her as she advanced, and two of the crossbowmen took aim and fired. Roland leapt away from one shot, but the other caught him in the side. He wrenched the bolt out and threw it to the ground, trailing freezing blood in its wake. Starbride whipped her second cancellation pyramid from her satchel and focused, catching the one he carried before he could use it on her Fiend suppression pyramid. He crushed his cancelled pyramid in his fist.

Starbride tried to push him into a corner where he couldn't retreat. He lobbed a flash bomb at the Watch officers. Starbride shielded her eyes and heard several cries from those who weren't quick to take cover. Roland barked a word in the Fiend tongue, and Starbride flinched to hear it. Still, she didn't lose her focus even as she tasted blood.

"Look out!" Dawnmother pushed her, but not before something sliced across her arm. The deep ache of severe cold set her back teeth together. Starbride's pyramid tumbled from her grasp, and before she could reach for it again, Roland's boot smashed it into nothingness.

Freddie lunged for him, but he sidestepped, grabbed Freddie's collar and chucked him across the street into Ursula's crossbowmen.

"You really don't learn, do you?" Roland asked.

"I have." Now she kept a duplicate of every pyramid she carried. Before Freddie landed, Starbride grabbed her second Fiend suppression pyramid and focused.

Roland staggered back with a cry. The Fiendish Aspect that made him so powerful was the very thing that made him vulnerable. Hopefully, it would keep the wild Fiends away, too. Hugo tried to grab them from the rooftops, leaping in their wake. Starbride tried to back Roland into a corner again, leaving Dawnmother to keep lookout.

The corpse Fiends who'd kept their feet before were now lying motionless in the dust. Roland dashed behind a Watch officer and threw him at Scarra before she got too close. Captain Ursula tried for a stab, but Roland flung a fire pyramid. Quick as a blink, Starbride switched focus and cancelled the pyramid before it smacked against Ursula's chain shirt. Ursula threw her arms in front of her face, but the deadened crystal only shattered on the ground.

Starbride didn't wait for Roland's reaction before she switched focus again and used her suppression pyramid. Roland grabbed one of the injured corpse Fiends and threw it in her direction. It howled as it neared the pyramid, but it couldn't stop itself. Dawnmother tried to pull Starbride out of the way, but the corpse Fiend landed atop them in a tangle of moldy limbs. Starbride's focus slipped, and she pushed at flesh that felt like an old, hide-covered bundle of sticks. Dawnmother grabbed a broken piece of wood and shattered the corpse Fiend's pyramid.

Something knocked into Starbride from behind, that same, bone-aching cold, and she flew face forward into the dust. She locked her arms over her chest, protecting her pyramid and put all her energy into focusing.

The cold withdrew. Starbride sat up, her forehead and nose aching where she'd slammed into the ground. Hugo, still following the wild Fiends, blundered toward Dawnmother. Starbride lifted her pyramid in his direction. He staggered away with a hiss. Dawnmother's eyes widened as she stared over Starbride's shoulder, and Starbride whirled around.

Roland stood only a few feet away when he met the invisible bubble of Starbride's suppression pyramid. He drew up short, sliding, before he hopped backward. "Pesky little gnat!"

She flung a fire pyramid at him, but he batted it away without breaking it, and Ursula had to leap from its path.

A great cry went up, several streets over, and a worried look passed over Roland's face. Whoever was coming, they weren't allies.

"For Dockland and Marienne!" someone yelled, and a great many voices answered.

"Is that who I think it is?" Dawnmother asked.

Freddie limped to their side. "It's got to be Maia and Prince Reinholt."

Starbride didn't take her eyes off Roland. She could see him calculating the odds. Maia's Fiend would have to stay locked inside her, but Reinholt's was free to come out if he let it. Two royal Fiends could keep his wild Fiends occupied, and then who would keep Starbride from backing him into a corner? Even he would die if stabbed over and over and over.

"You shouldn't have killed all your pets," she said.

He drew two pyramids. Starbride switched focus and pounced on one, but not before he threw them both. People leapt out of the way, both from the pyramid that smashed harmlessly on the ground, and the other that bloomed into a sphere as black as ink. A deep, hollow sound echoed across the street, rattling Starbride's teeth. The sphere winked out, taking a perfect half-sphere from a building's side. Part of a chair fell out of the hole, leaving a view of the terrified people huddling at the back of a shop.

Even as Starbride switched her focus to her suppression pyramid, she knew Roland had gone, taking the wild Fiends with him.

"Coward," Dawnmother said.

"Or smart." He'd seek more easily defended ground. Like the palace. Starbride glanced in that direction before watching the Docklanders charge toward them. "We need to catch Hugo before they get here."

CHAPTER FIVE

KATYA

The commotion from the other side of the library stopped as suddenly as it had started. Katya crept in that direction, keeping her rapier out. Redtrue followed, walking under her own power for the first time in hours. She took deep, steady breaths and smiled as if that simple act pleased her. Castelle watched their backs, her own weapon drawn and ready.

Katya stepped over books and scrolls, straining to be quiet in the cavernous space. As she emerged from between the shelves, she paused before the tables that dominated the middle of the room. The bodies of corpse Fiends and human guards sprawled among overturned chairs and splintered planks of wood. Light poured in from a window high on the wall.

The shelves on the other side of the library leaned against one another, their contents scattered across the floor. The heavy wooden doors stood closed, and Katya couldn't recall hearing them open and shut again. Her mother was still in here somewhere, waiting perhaps, but for what?

Or maybe she was stalking them. Katya couldn't help a shiver. Slight movement caught her eye from the leaning shelves. She nudged Redtrue and pointed.

As they drew closer, Katya recognized her mother's small silhouette even with the crow's wings sprouting from her shoulders. Her back was to them as she stared at something. Katya squinted. Someone else knelt in the shadows, barely visible, and Katya's eyes went wide as she caught a glimpse of mottled skin.

The Fiend lifted its head. When it scuttled farther into the shadows, Ma stepped after it.

From Katya's time as a Fiend, she remembered having to resist attacking her own family, Fiend drawn to Fiend. She took a step forward, ready to leap on her mother, but soft yellow light blossomed behind her, and the energy from Redtrue's pyramid flowed over her, warm as a summer breeze. Ma stiffened as if struck by lightning, and her wings receded through the tears in her shirt and into her back, leaving only bloody trails. She collapsed, and the way stood clear for the radiance to reach the Fiend.

It shrieked, long and loud. Katya's rapier fell from her nerveless fingers, and she clapped her hands over her ears. The noise clattered through her skull and up and down her spine like shards of pottery rubbing together combined with that metal-on-metal squeal. She tasted so much copper she was certain she'd bitten her tongue.

A bang cut through the noise, and the shriek faded. Katya tottered to her feet and bent to reclaim her rapier.

"What in the spirits' names?" Castelle asked.

The glow from Redtrue's pyramid faded. "It fled rather than be cleansed."

One of the library doors had been knocked clean from its hinges. The noise was bound to attract some attention. Katya slid her rapier into its scabbard and picked up her unconscious mother. "Let's get moving."

Katya hated to backtrack, but the servants' halls had been the safest place they'd seen. They didn't try to find Baroness Jacintha again but stopped in the first room they came to.

The small chamber had been a storeroom, but someone had picked it clean. A few empty sacks littered the bare stone floor. Katya laid her mother on them and settled against the wall, her wound praising her for getting off her feet.

"Should we not leave your mother with the baroness and continue our pyramid hunt?" Redtrue asked.

Katya had thought of that, but leaving her unconscious mother with people she didn't know rankled. They'd had no choice with Brutal, but Katya at least wanted her mother awake for the decision.

"She's too powerful a weapon," Castelle said.

"We can't let her transform again if we can help it," Katya said. Still, Castelle was right. And Ma had been right about her presence attracting the wild Fiends' attention. Katya had been able to keep the Fiend from harming her friends, but once the pyramid was destroyed, it had gone straight to the only other Fiend in the room. "You said the wild Fiend didn't want to be cleansed, Redtrue. What did you mean? How can a pure Fiend be cleansed?"

"With its Fiendness stripped away," Castelle asked, "wouldn't it be nothing?"

Redtrue frowned hard. "The energy I felt from that pyramid was akin to the Fiends. Since the one who grabbed your leg fled once the pyramid was destroyed, I think it was calling them. The question is, why was the pyramid affecting me so?"

"Because of your purity," Castelle said.

Katya rolled her eyes and caught Redtrue doing the same. "Now that you're well," Katya said, "can you sense any other pyramids nearby?"

Redtrue took another pyramid from her bag and focused. After a moment, she nodded.

As much as Katya craved rest, she knew they couldn't linger. The fight would still be raging in the city, and she didn't know when Roland might return. Of course, with Redtrue free from her affliction, Katya thought their odds against Roland were pretty good. Redtrue seemed to have a knack for overcoming Fiend energy. As Katya tried to wake her mother, she hoped that Roland *would* come back soon. Maybe they could end the fight sooner than anyone thought.

It usually took an hour to recover from turning into a Fiend, but Katya shook her mother gently, trying to hasten the process. She began to think that leaving Ma with Jacintha was the only cause left to them when her mother blinked and tried to open her eyes.

"Oh," Ma said as she struggled upright, "my head."

In the past, Katya had awakened from her Aspect feeling tired but never with the fatigue on her mother's face. Powerful weapon or not, could they risk her transforming again? Would they even be able to wake her?

"I trust we got what we were looking for?" Ma asked.

Katya told her of the battle.

"I don't remember any of that, but I'm glad I was useful." She climbed shakily to her feet. "What's next?"

Katya hesitated, afraid that if she suggested her mother stay behind, she'd be in line for a scolding. And if her mother wanted to risk her life, who was Katya to say no? It was just a question of putting one more person she loved in danger.

Ma glanced up, and something in Katya's face must have betrayed her thoughts. "You want me to stay behind." There was no hurt in her words, just a statement of fact.

"If you turn into a Fiend again…"

"I feel the difference now compared to before," Ma said. "But I still might be able to distract any wild Fiends while remaining human."

"I can do that, too."

"Let me distract. You do the stabbing."

It was a good argument, but Katya couldn't quite give her blessing.

"You are the leader here," Ma said. "If you order me to stay behind, if you think I've done as much as I can, I'll stay."

Her own mother taking her orders; it boggled the mind. But in the end, it wasn't a question of safety and danger. Nowhere in the palace was safe. "No, you come with us."

Ma squeezed Katya's arm. "I had every faith that you were as brilliant as I thought."

Katya barked a laugh, and when they piled into the hallway again, her heart was a little lighter.

They found another of Roland's hypnosis pyramids on the floor above them. Redtrue cleansed it through the wall. Katya's earlier excitement came rushing back, even with all they'd suffered. The faster they could cleanse these pyramids, the faster they could regroup with Starbride and then the army outside the walls of Marienne.

As soon as they'd disabled the pyramid, they moved on, taking the secret passageways when they could and sneaking past any guards. In the halls, Katya kept everyone close to the walls, ready to dive for cover. When they reached one of the grand staircases that spiraled up into the third floor, Katya took the lead as they climbed single file along the outer wall. Long tapestries hung almost to the floor as they ascended the staircase, each suspended by ropes tied to hooks hidden behind the black iron rail. Castelle kept her blade out; Redtrue held her pyramid. Ma clutched her long knife, but her other hand hovered in front of her chest, ready to remove her pyramid necklace.

Katya caught a hint of movement above them, just around the curve. "Down!" she whispered.

The air whooshed above her head, and an arrow *thunked* into a tapestry where her head had been.

"Back, back!" Katya said. They scuttled down the stairs and moved to the inner rail where the archer would have to move closer to see them.

The arrow didn't bear Averie's signature green fletching, but it had to be her. Katya lamented again that the adsnazi didn't use destructive magic and that she hadn't brought Pennynail.

Averie didn't call down the stairs. Mind-warped into a killer for Roland, she had no use for taunts. And she held the high ground. Katya could picture her waiting, bowstring half drawn, ready to pull at the first sight of them. They could find another way up, Katya supposed, circle back down, then cross over several hallways, and up another staircase.

And then Averie would know they had gone and would wait for them at another point. She could call for more guards. Time was on her side.

"Follow close behind me," Katya said in Redtrue's ear. "When I give the word, throw a pyramid."

Redtrue balked. "I do not use—"

"Any damned pyramid! It doesn't matter what it does."

Redtrue frowned but stayed on Katya's heels as they tiptoed up the stairs, just at the edge of the well-worn carpet.

When Katya saw a shadow ahead, she crouched. "Now."

Redtrue's pyramid sailed upward, and Katya raced behind it, hoping Averie's instincts weren't completely lost. Averie leapt out of the pyramid's path. The crystal smashed harmlessly on the wall.

Averie managed to fire an arrow, though only at a quarter draw. It clipped the leather at Katya's shoulder, but she pushed through, swinging as she came, trying to catch Averie on one knee. Averie blocked with her bow and launched backward, into the steps, using the incline to push herself up.

A man in chainmail darted around her and swung at Katya. She ducked out of the way and then leapt for Averie as Castelle barreled into the chain man.

Katya drove her rapier into Averie's thigh. Her face creased in pain, but she jerked her leg clear. Averie thrust inside her coat pocket and dragged forth a pyramid to drop at Katya's feet.

Katya leapt backward, hoping she wouldn't be caught by her own trick. "Look out!" Her foot snagged the carpet, and she slipped. Redtrue caught her arm before she could roll down the steps. Fire roared to life on the carpeted staircase, catching one tapestry alight and giving Averie time to scamper upward, the flames between them. She nocked another arrow.

Castelle and the chain man were caught on Katya's side of the fire. Katya dragged Redtrue behind the two, and Averie's arrow thudded into the back of her own man. He yowled in pain, and Castelle took him through the neck. Katya helped hold his body like a shield, but they couldn't walk him through the flames.

When Averie's next arrow clipped Redtrue's sleeve, she ducked, cursing. Beyond the crackle of flames, Katya thought she heard the clatter of more feet on the stairs.

"We have to rush her or retreat," Castelle said.

"Push the body toward her on my mark." Before Katya could give the order, the flaming tapestry above Averie's head dropped like a wet blanket, engulfing her in pounds of burning fabric. Katya looked to where Ma still held the frayed end of the rope.

"Castelle, cover my back!" Katya dropped the body and ran through the patch of burning carpet. She kicked at the struggling lump under the tapestry. Steel rang behind her, and Katya looked long enough to see Castelle fighting a woman in boiled leather. The howl of a corpse Fiend came from above, but as soon as it rounded the corner, Redtrue's pyramid flared, turning it into an empty puppet. The lifeless body rolled down the stairs.

Ma joined Katya, and they put the fire out by beating at the flames and at Averie still struggling inside the tapestry. Soon the fire was just a smolder, and the lump an unmoving, smoking hulk. Castelle had beaten the guard, but not without a jagged wound down the side of her face. Redtrue pressed a bandage to Castelle's cheek and forehead, trying to staunch the bleeding.

Ma pulled the tapestry aside while Katya waited with a ready blade. Averie still breathed, her nose bloody, face bruised, and hair and clothes burnt and blistered. Her bow had been broken across her body, and one of her arms lay unevenly beneath her.

Tears came unbidden to Katya's eyes. In sleep, Averie was still the lady-in-waiting who'd served her faithfully for many years, the hunter who'd supplied game for her hunting princess persona, and the dear friend and confidante who'd helped her through her darkest, loneliest moments. Katya couldn't hold in a sob as she sank down at Averie's side.

"Jewel of my heart," she said, the absurd nickname she'd given Averie so long ago. They'd never been lovers, never would have been, but Averie had been so constant and loving yet respectful of the distance that had to remain between them.

Lost in desperation, Katya looked to Redtrue. "Can you do anything for her?"

"Not unless she needs a bandage," Redtrue said as she tied a cloth around Castelle's head. "And I know she was once your friend, but should we even think of healing her now that she is your enemy?"

"Roland poisoned her mind. Can you cleanse her?"

"There is no pyramid to cleanse."

Katya was tempted to ask if Redtrue could undo the mind magic, but of course she couldn't; she wouldn't even if she were able. And Starbride had already told them that there was nothing of Averie to reclaim. Roland hollowed out some of his puppets, those he found most useful, and left nothing but what he wanted in their places. Averie hadn't been hypnotized; she'd been remade.

"Katya, we have to go," Castelle said.

Given time, Averie would recover and dog their steps again. She wouldn't stop until she was killed. Katya pictured the pained expression of shock on Averie's face as Katya's blade sank into her heart. A look like that would live with her forever. But if they captured her, she'd be executed eventually, and Katya bet that however she went to her grave—stoically quiet or cursing their names—she wouldn't bear the peaceful expression she wore in sleep.

Katya kissed Averie's soot-stained forehead. "You died long ago, jewel of my heart, in a battle bravely fought. Whatever awaits us after death, I hope you find peace, with no ungrateful royalty bossing you about." Katya smoothed the hair from Averie's cheeks, curled a hand around her chin, and pinched her nose and mouth shut.

Ma gasped, but no one spoke. There were faster ways to kill someone, but Katya couldn't bear the thought of slitting Averie's throat. She remembered Crowe telling her that he had killed Roland in nearly this same fashion. Of course, if Crowe *had* slit Roland's throat, Katya suspected that even the Fiend couldn't have saved him.

Crowe would have agreed, but he still would have said something like, "If we must kill those we love, best we do it softly."

Averie shuddered once, and then she was gone, her eyes not even opening before the end.

CHAPTER SIX

STARBRIDE

Hugo lay unconscious at Starbride's feet. It had taken Scarra, Freddie, and Starbride's Fiend suppression pyramid to subdue him, and even then he'd managed to claw Scarra's arm. One of Ursula's men gave her a bandage as Starbride tried to field a hundred questions at once.

Luckily, the pack of Docklanders who'd charged their position included Prince Reinholt and Maia, two people well versed in keeping Fiendish natures secret.

"Did the Fiend king do that to him?" one of the Docklanders asked, gesturing toward Hugo.

"No doubt," Reinholt said in a drawl eerily reminiscent of Katya. Either he'd been taking lessons from his sister, or she'd based some of her court persona on him. He made some joke about Hugo's Fiendish nature not helping with the ladies, and a few of his followers laughed.

Those who didn't looked to Maia, but she waved their questions away as, "Something to worry about later."

"Let's hope none of these people have long memories," Ursula said in Starbride's ear. "Pretty soon there won't be a war to put off their questions."

"I like your confidence, Captain."

Ursula's light touch on Starbride's shoulder turned her around. "I won't be put off, either. Freddie Ballantine will be gone from here after the dust settles, or he'll be a guest of the city Watch."

Starbride sighed. "You're talking about events that happened *ten* years ago."

"Crimes don't just vanish, Princess Consort. Those who died don't disappear from memory."

"But he wasn't the Butcher!" Starbride was louder than she planned, and several of the Docklanders glanced her way. Freddie had faded to the background, not wanting to be recognized by anyone from his old haunting ground.

Ursula barked a laugh, but it had no humor in it. "There were more deaths than just those killed by the Butcher. I meant what I said. If he's still here when the fight is done, he belongs to me. Form up!" Her squad piled around her, and Ursula led them off in another direction.

"What was that about?" Maia asked.

"Dawn," Starbride said, "will you keep the Docklanders occupied?"

When Dawnmother nodded, Starbride gestured for Maia and Reinholt to join her out of earshot of the others. Several of the Dockland group catcalled to Reinholt about keeping all the women to himself. He just shrugged as if it couldn't be helped. Scarra joined them and helped move Hugo to the side of the street.

"Having fun?" Starbride asked Reinholt.

"Can I help it if they love me?" He'd dressed all in black with his coat undone at the neck, the black prince in repose. His dark blond hair was untidy, but his smiling blue eyes and the shadow of stubble on his cheeks were more in line with hard partying than hard living. He'd taken to the disgraced noble persona like an old horse put to pasture.

Starbride just kept from rolling her eyes. She had asked him to win the Docklanders over. She couldn't mock him for doing as he was told.

"What was the captain upset about?" Maia asked again, too accustomed to deflecting questions to have her own dismissed. Color had returned to her once pale face, and she looked much healthier than when they'd first freed her. She'd managed to put on a little weight, or maybe it was just her heavy coat that made her bulky. As a Fiend, she'd been painfully thin.

"It's about me," a voice said over Starbride's shoulder. Freddie emerged from the shadows of a ruined storefront, managing to keep his back to the Docklanders.

Reinholt blinked at him, but Maia looked him up and down, frowning hard at his leather outfit and the knives sheathed about his person. "Pennynail?"

"I'm glad to see you up and around." He dipped his head. "And to finally speak to you at last."

"You're different than I pictured," she said.

"Bit more red in my cheeks?" He held his palms to his face as if blushing, reminding Starbride so much of his pantomimes as the masked Pennynail that she grinned.

Maia did, too. "I thought you must be horrifically ugly."

"Thanks."

She put a fist on her hip. "But you're *not*, I was about to say. You do have a scratchy voice."

"Again, thanks."

"*But*," she said with a laugh, "that's not a good enough reason to cover your face and never speak, so why did you?"

"I know you," Reinholt said. He pointed to the scar around Freddie's neck. "You're a criminal."

Freddie turned his nose up. "I'm *the* criminal."

"What do you mean, what criminal?" Maia asked.

"Dear little Maia," Freddie said, "I'm glad you never had the stomach for horror stories."

Reinholt took Maia's arm and made her retreat a step. "You're that murderer."

"Which murderer?" Maia asked, looking back and forth between them

"I'd never hurt you," Freddie said to her.

Reinholt sneered. "What's that worth, the word of a killer?"

Freddie gave him an up and down glance. "I wasn't speaking to you."

"Enough," Starbride said. "The short of it is this: people were murdered years ago in Dockland. Freddie took the blame. They tried to hang him; Crowe rescued him. The real murderer died, but Freddie was never exonerated. Yes?"

"Couldn't have said it better myself," he said.

"So, you didn't murder anyone?" Maia asked.

"No," Freddie said just as Reinholt muttered, "Probably."

They exchanged glares, and Starbride had to wonder how much animosity was from Reinholt's remembrances of the Butcher and how much was for how he'd been treated by Pennynail while in Starbride's care.

Maia wriggled out of Reinholt's grasp and stepped forward to peer into Freddie's face. She put her hands up, covering his features from her perspective. "Seems like the same old Pennynail to me."

He grinned so hard it was like the sun had come out, and when he turned away from Maia, Starbride thought she saw tears in his eyes.

"You might be a tad better looking *with* the mask," Maia said.

He gave her a tickle. "You ought to wear it all the time, then, if you think so much of it!" He pulled it out of his belt and tried to put it on her head, but she danced out of the way.

"I don't see what the fuss is about," Scarra said. "No matter his past, he's covering our asses now."

"An enviable position from any angle," Reinholt said with a wink.

Scarra snorted. "Go ahead and try your luck, Prince, but I'd sooner charm the trousers off the princess consort than you'd talk your way into mine." She knelt and lifted Hugo in her arms. "I've got skinny here. Let me know when you want to move out." She crossed the street to join Dawnmother.

"So, the battle is going well for you?" Starbride asked Reinholt.

He shrugged. "We've lost some people. We collected some pyradistés who were hiding in Dockland. They helped destroy this pyramid a few streets over." He sniffed. "I thought you were supposed to be doing that."

"I've been busy fighting your uncle."

Maia leapt back to their side. "You've seen my father?" Before Starbride could say anything, Maia bit her lip. "I mean *him*. He's not my father anymore."

Reinholt wrapped an arm around her shoulders. Maia seemed to banish his snottier side as easily as shooing a fly. "You've got plenty of family left, dearheart."

Maia shook her head. "We heard he was out fighting the army."

"What else have you heard?" Starbride asked.

"All rumor, apparently," Reinholt said. "We heard that the Fiend king, those corpse things, and even some wild Fiends were tearing through the army. But if you've seen Roland, it can't be true unless he can be in two places at once."

Starbride told them of what Roland had done to Alphonse, turned a pyradisté into a copy of himself.

And then, a voice inside reminded her, she'd killed him, stuck the knife in, felt his blood on her hands. And then she'd lit those people on fire, and she'd enjoyed it.

"Starbride," Freddie said, "are you still with us?"

She buried the thoughts again. "He's probably heading back to the palace. If we're winning in the streets but his forces have the army pinned down, he'll want to gather more resources."

"How can you be sure?" Reinholt asked.

She couldn't, but it was as good a guess as any. "He knows now that Katya isn't with me. He might know she's not with the army. He led the Order of Vestra. He knows what kind of jobs we're best at. He might have guessed that Katya will go for the palace."

"You just want to ride off to be with your lover," Reinholt said.

Maia said, "Rein—"

Freddie cut her off. "Watch your mouth, princely."

Starbride put an arm between them before they could burst into argument. "I've made my decision. We're heading for the palace."

"As I was going to say," Reinholt said loudly, "I'm glad. If we can, we should all be with the people we love right now."

Starbride didn't know what to make of any supposed sincerity on his part. "Can you send groups sweeping toward the palace and the wall? If the army is in trouble, they'll need your help."

Reinholt nodded, but Maia shook her head. "I'm coming with you, Starbride," she said. Reinholt looked as if she'd just punched him in the gut. "You don't need me out here, Rein. You've got enough soldiers, but I'm sure Starbride could use an archer."

"Glad to have you," Starbride said. She exchanged a glance with Reinholt, one that promised she wouldn't let anything happen to his dear cousin. He didn't seem convinced.

"Reinholt," Maia said, "I'm in the Order of Vestra, too, you know."

After a sigh, he said, "Take the greatest care with yourself."

They split then, Reinholt taking the Docklanders in one direction while Starbride, Dawnmother, Freddie, Maia, and Scarra bearing Hugo moved off in the other.

"Should we stash skinny somewhere?" Scarra asked.

"He'll wake in about an hour," Starbride said. "Not to worry." She hugged Maia around the shoulders. "I'm glad you decided to come with us."

"Like old times," Maia said "Well, almost."

Starbride sensed that Maia was hiding something. She never could resist a secret, and someone else's problems would give her something to think about besides what she'd done that day. "It's not just the fighting that's upsetting you."

Maia chuckled. "Spirits know it would be enough."

"Even so."

Maia sighed and leaned so close her head almost touched Starbride's shoulder. "I missed my monthly."

Starbride waited for more and finally said, "Your monthly what?"

Maia rolled her eyes. "You know. What happens to all women every month?"

"You haven't bled, you mean?" When Maia nodded, Starbride sighed. Maia could be sick, she supposed, or it could be some after-effect of being a Fiend for so long. But no, she knew what it meant. "Oh, Maia."

"When I was a Fiend, I didn't notice if I bled or not. Such things seemed beneath me. But Darren, before he went chasing Katya, he and I..." She pressed her lips together so hard they turned white. "The Fiends liked it with each other once we'd merged with them." She looked up as if she could make the tears sink back in her head.

"Is everything all right?" Freddie called.

"We're fine." Starbride pulled Maia closer. "But it's been months."

"I know."

The weight she'd put on, Starbride had taken it as a sign of health, and Maia's loose coat would conceal any small bulge. "Perhaps—"

"If you say I shouldn't be coming with you, I'll shoot you."

"Does anyone else know?"

Maia shrugged. "When I suspected, I talked to an herbalist, but he says it's too late to get rid of it. Anything he could give me might kill me, too."

"I'm so sorry, Maia."

"I can't hide it forever."

"You won't have to. Katya will understand. And you have a long time to decide what you wish to do after it arrives. Focus on today." Good advice if she could only continue to follow it herself.

❖

They fought through two more groups before Starbride saw the palace in the distance. She hadn't realized how far from it they'd come. She hadn't been this close since they'd decided to sneak inside.

They didn't have the muscle to break down the front door and charge in. Starbride briefly regretted that she didn't have Roland's talent with mind pyramids. Maybe she could have hypnotized a few people over to her side instead of simply freeing them.

She shook the thought away, blaming it on any lingering feelings leftover from her headache. Roland had always said he wanted his people to be happy. That's why he'd claimed to have taken over the kingdom and hypnotized the populace. And people were happy under his rule, whether they liked it or not, even when they were on fire.

Starbride doused that thought and wondered if anyone lamented the loss of bliss when she freed them, if they preferred it to the fear and anguish that accompanied war, if even false peace was better than horror.

No, better to be free, she decided. She couldn't really consider losing Katya—the thought was just too painful—but she'd always want to keep her memories. No doubt the populace of Marienne largely agreed with her, though she'd never have known it by how hard they struggled against freedom. The desire to remain hypnotized and to press others into it was another *gift* of Roland's. He wouldn't have to watch the entire city if it was also watching itself.

By the time they reached the palace, Hugo was awake again, his fatigue lifting with every step. The royal stables were abandoned, just as Starbride hoped. She'd decided to take the same route Katya had planned on, increasing the chances that they might stumble upon each other in the palace's great jumble. They scaled the gate and hurried into the barn nearest the palace walls. Redtrue would have had to cancel a pyramid to get inside the secret passageways, so Starbride knew the way was safe, but when she saw what now guarded the door, she paused.

She'd expected to see the darkened side of a cancelled pyramid, but this one was a soft, milky white. Starbride whipped out her cancellation pyramid, hoping she wasn't too late to catch a trap. The world faded to grays, and she looked for the golden glow of an active pyramid, but this one emitted a pure white radiance. Power flowed through it, shining like a beacon, but there was no purpose behind it.

"What is it?" Dawnmother asked. "What's wrong?"

Starbride had to shake her head, and they kept moving. Anything Redtrue had done was a puzzle to figure out later.

Freddie led them to the ballroom Katya had wanted to visit first. Light spilled into the secret passageway, the door clearly open.

Freddie crept toward it and peeked around the corner before hurrying to Starbride's side. "Someone broke down the door into the passageway."

"Is there anyone left in there?"

"Just bodies."

Starbride moved before he could say more. People lay scattered across the floor. Some bore small, bloody stab marks; others appeared to have been ripped apart, but by what, Starbride didn't know. She recognized none of them and couldn't help a sigh of relief, even with death all around her. Two corpse Fiends sprawled on the floor near a large chair, and the pyramid that dominated the room had turned the same milky white as the one before.

Starbride ran a finger down the pyramid's smooth side. "What is she doing to them?"

"As long as she's disabling them, does it matter?" Dawnmother asked.

"I suppose not." But she planned to work it out soon.

"Someone broke in here, too," Hugo called from the door to the hallway. He pointed to the splintered edge next to the lock. "They bashed in from the other side."

Starbride looked back to the bodies, most of them in a line from the secret passageway to the pyramid. "Katya had to fight when she came in here. She barred those doors, but someone broke them down and chased her into the passageways."

Dawnmother gestured to one of the ripped bodies. "And the corpse Fiends did this?"

"Why would they attack their own?" Scarra asked.

Freddie waved from the passageway entrance. "You need to see this."

By the light of her pyramid, Starbride stared at the dried brown stains streaked across the stone underfoot. "They're hurt," she said softly.

"We don't know anything yet," Freddie said. "This could have been caused by someone following them."

But why would Roland's mind-warped guards drag their fellows along? They were more likely to leave the wounded behind, and corpse Fiends didn't bleed.

Hugo squeezed Starbride's shoulder. "We won't know until we follow."

They followed the bloody drag marks. When they ended at a door that led into the palace, Starbride nearly crashed through.

Freddie grabbed her arm. "Let's get ready first."

"Any idea where we are?" Scarra asked. "I had no idea the palace was so much fun for sneaking."

"We're somewhere in the courtiers' quarters," Freddie said. "Everyone ready?"

They readied weapons or stood clear. Starbride tried to banish the image of a pile of bodies on the other side.

When Freddie toggled the switch, they barreled through, ready for anything but the sight of two courtiers who shrank back, screaming as Hugo and Scarra burst into their midst.

Starbride lifted her hands to quiet them, but Maia pushed past her, crying, "Brutal!"

Starbride followed her to a blanket-wrapped mound on the floor, torn between staring at Brutal's too-pale face and the arrow sticking out of his chest.

CHAPTER SEVEN

KATYA

After she covered Averie with the tapestry, Katya numbly fought another group of guards at the top of the stairs. Luckily, her opponents weren't that skilled, and she could let her body react from memory. Spirits knew she didn't remember the fight after it was over.

Ma shepherded them into some noble's former apartment. Katya sat on a slashed footstool and just watched the others. Castelle had bled through her bandage. She winced as Redtrue peeled the sticky fabric away. An oozing line led from her hairline to her jaw, the skin around it puffy and angry. She'd have quite the scar.

The room's furniture lay overturned, the art smashed. One survivor hid in a corner: a slender wingback chair upholstered in pale blue damask. Katya wondered if the looters had missed it, or if they'd thought the shiny silk too beautiful to destroy.

"Let me look at your wound," Ma said.

"It's fine."

"It'll give me something to do with what's left of this shirt." She slipped the ruined garment off. Even with the tears in the back, her coat provided plenty of coverage.

Katya took her own coat off, and her mother tugged her shirt up. Obeying came easier than arguing, but Katya found it difficult to care about the wound, the war, anything. She tried to summon anger again, tried picturing Averie's dying face and Roland's smirking one, but… nothing.

"You did what you had to, Katya," Ma said.

Yes, what Roland had *made* her do, but her brain refused to be goaded. "I don't feel guilty."

"Then what?"

"I'm waiting to fly into a rage." If she'd still possessed a Fiend, her pyramid necklace wouldn't even be tingling.

"And that would help us how?"

Katya could only shrug.

Ma sighed. "Time enough for rage and remorse later. You need your wits. Try being cold and calculating if your emotions won't support you."

But Katya had always depended on passion. She let her feelings guide her just as much as her thoughts, just like her father, her brother, her uncle. "Be like Lord Vincent, you mean."

"He gets results."

But he was always the one taking orders, not giving them. "Redtrue, where's our next target?"

"Close." She pointed down the corridor. "In that direction. There is another I did not sense before, and there are many above our heads in the opposite direction."

"Those will be guarding the royal apartments," Ma said.

"Best we pick off these isolated ones first," Katya said. "They're more likely to be Roland's handiwork." Cold and calculating. But the image of Averie's face wouldn't be banished so easily, though it brought her no feeling at all.

Their next target stood in the middle of a large alcove, with floor-to-ceiling windows and stone benches lining the walls. Redtrue cleansed the pyramid from around a corner while Katya hid and watched. As the pyramid turned milky white, the handful of guards milling around it stopped and stared at each other, brows drawn in confusion.

It could be that these hadn't been permanently mind-warped, only hypnotized. And since Redtrue had cleansed so many pyramids already, the hypnotized people might awaken.

The guards looked at one another and at their weapons with shock or suspicion. One woman in leather let her sword clatter to the floor and touched her armor as if she'd never seen it before. "What in the spirits' names is going on?"

The others murmured. Katya backed up, ready to leave them to it, but Castelle stepped around before Katya could grab her.

"What are you all doing here?" Castelle barked. "Put down those weapons and get out of here, double time, or it'll be the cold comfort of the Watch for you!"

Metal clanged against stone, and footsteps hurried away. Katya couldn't help but smile.

Castelle had only half a grin, and it seemed to pain her. Her eye hadn't swelled shut, but it might yet. "I've had to roust enough thief catchers out of taverns in my time."

"I wonder if that's where Einrich learned the art of bellowing as well," Ma said.

They headed downstairs, targeting the lone pyramid Redtrue had felt from above. Katya sometimes felt as if they were going in circles, but Redtrue needed to be within a certain distance to detect the pyramids, even if that distance was over or under where she stood. And the more powerful the pyramid, the easier she sensed it. When she was close, she didn't need her detection pyramid at all.

Once they'd defeated the next target, Redtrue searched again and shook her head. "I sense many above us and the very powerful one far below. No, wait, there is one more, in the path of the powerful one. I missed it before."

"We'll cut back across near the library," Katya said, but she hoped it wasn't so far below them that it was in the caverns. She wanted to keep Redtrue as far from the capstone as possible.

In the hallway past the library doors, someone moved. Katya hurried her party back around the corner. "Is it Fiends?"

"There is something." Redtrue's pyramid went dark, and she gasped, clutching the wall for support.

Katya recognized cancellation when she saw it, and Roland had no pyradistés besides himself. But if he was alone...

Redtrue muttered and dug in the bag slung across her body. Katya peeked around the corner and caught someone on the other end of the hall doing the same, a red haired man. So, Roland had some guards after all. She ducked back and considered charging forward. No, better to let Roland come to them.

"Princess?" someone called, a young voice, but one she recognized, though she hadn't heard it in months.

"Lord Hugo?" She looked around the corner again, and he stepped out, *waving* to her, of all things.

Her mind raced. If he'd been captured, he'd be mind-warped.

Starbride turned the corner, a pyramid held out in front of her as she searched the hallway.

"Star." Katya leapt out of hiding, and the block in her head dissolved, her emotions tumbling through like water. Sheathing her rapier, she strode down the hall, not noticing that there was anyone else present until she put her arms around her beloved.

Starbride chuckled into her shoulder. "I missed you, too."

Katya kissed her quickly and winced as Starbride's embrace caught the wound on her back.

"You're hurt?" Starbride asked.

"Nothing that won't heal. How did you find us?"

"Tracking skills and a helpful baroness."

When Katya turned, the others were saying their hellos, all except Redtrue, who held her darkened pyramid in Starbride's direction. "Did you do this?"

Starbride's mouth worked for a moment. "I'm sorry. When I sensed a pyradisté—"

"Adsnazi," Redtrue said through clenched teeth.

Starbride dipped her head, but Katya could read her less-than-pleased expression. "I apologize again."

Before Redtrue could open her mouth, Katya said, "Why don't we step into one of these rooms?"

Redtrue turned stiffly, muttering, "Cancelling pyramids," as they all shuffled into a room just down the hall from the library.

Katya's gaze locked with Starbride's as they moved, and Starbride's hand didn't leave her own before they were behind closed doors. Then Starbride shifted out of the way and revealed Maia standing behind her, a soft smile on her young face. "Hello, coz."

Katya's breath left her. Here was another balm to drive bad thoughts away. She swallowed Maia in an embrace. "I thought I might never see you again, cousin."

Maia held her hard, making her wound ache, but Katya didn't protest. "I'm trying not to cry," Maia said into Katya's chest.

Katya pushed her gently to arm's length. The tears made her seem the same old Maia, but there were dark circles under her eyes and a permanent line between her pale brows that spoke of hard times. Katya squeezed her once more before letting go. Ma took her place, grasping Maia's shoulders.

Dawnmother greeted Katya with a nod. Katya clapped Hugo on the back, welcoming the sight of his grinning face. "If you've met the baroness," Katya said, "then you know about Brutal."

They all nodded. Katya squeezed Maia's shoulder. "I'm sorry, coz, but he, he might not—"

"Later," Maia said, but she didn't seem as agonized as Katya would have thought. Well, they all had a lot to think about.

"And who are these others?" Katya said, nodding toward the strength monk and the red-haired man. "And where's Pennynail, skulking about?"

"Well," Starbride said.

Katya whirled on her, her heart sinking. "He hasn't been killed?"

"No! It's just, well, Freddie, do you want to…"

Katya turned to the red-haired man. The closer she looked, the more familiar he seemed. "Freddie, did you say?"

He nodded, his face deadly serious, and a memory popped into Katya's mind: searching the library at the command of one of her tutors. She'd been ten? No, eleven, and sent to fetch some dry volume on the history of Farraday. She'd wandered between the shelves, bored, wasting time. One of the knowledge monks who were always prowling around had asked if he could help her find something.

"No," she'd said with a dramatic sigh. "Books are so *boring*."

He'd chuckled and pulled a small, soft-bound volume from a high shelf. "You might like this better."

She'd taken a peek. It was important to be *polite*, her mother was always saying. And then she'd spent the next few hours immersed in *Murderers and Scoundrels: A Bloody History of Farraday*. When her tutor had scolded her, she'd said she *was* researching history, just like he'd told her. He'd ordered her to put the book back, but she'd hidden it under a heavier tome and carried it to her room where she read it over and over until she'd lost it, or one of the servants had spirited it away.

"Freddie Ballantine," she said, "the Dockland Butcher." Excitement and anger and a tingle of fear raced through her. It was him down to the scar. All he lacked was the feral snarl from the illustration, that and the sharpened teeth, the better to eat his victims with. "You're not as terrifying as I imagined."

Pieces tumbled together in Katya's head. Why Crowe would never tell her who Pennynail was and why Starbride had done the same. Why he'd had to wear a mask and cover the ghastly scar at his throat.

"Will someone tell me what is going on?" Redtrue said loudly, spoiling the mood. Castelle whispered to her.

"You're Pennynail," Katya said. "Why would you serve the crown? Did you think it would get you a pardon?"

"I won't turn down a pardon if you're offering," he said, his voice not much more than a rasp. He watched her as if waiting for something, maybe for her to kill him.

But her mind was still working. She stepped close and touched his ragged scar with one finger. "You've been fighting by my side for three years, and in all that time, you didn't trust me enough to tell me who you are? Did you think I'd cut you down?"

He swallowed, and her finger jumped, but she didn't remove it.

"Crowe and Starbride would never work with the Butcher," she said, "the animal who sneaked into the bedrooms of random citizens and cut them to pieces. Crowe would say that such a creature would never help anyone but himself. Therefore, you cannot be the Butcher. Did you think I wouldn't be smart enough to figure that out?"

"Katya—" Starbride said.

"Please, Star. I want to hear it from him."

He took her touch from his throat, that simple reminder that she could have him hanged all over again. He didn't toss her hand away but held it between his gloved fingers. "I was afraid at first, of mobs looking for retribution, of children who'd run from me, of Watch officers who'd kill me on sight. I needed to remain hidden to separate myself from the Butcher, mostly in my own head, but then you got to know Pennynail, respected him. Perhaps even liked him?"

Katya nodded.

"I didn't want to risk losing that, not from you. Crowe knew me from the beginning, before I started wearing the mask, and I didn't tell the others in the Order because I thought it might hurt you to be left out. I might not have told Starbride if she hadn't stumbled on my room."

Katya smiled. "No secret is safe from Star."

He grinned crookedly. "So I've found out. I should have told you."

Dawnmother cleared her throat. "As Horsestrong said, the past is a horse dead and buried. Why dig up what you can no longer ride?"

"I was just thinking the same," Redtrue said. "And we might all be dead and buried if we linger here much longer."

Katya slipped free of Pennynail's, no, Freddie's grasp. Betrayal beat within her, but she would deal with that later. She was just happy that some of herself had come back. Averie's face still lurked in her mind, but Starbride and her friends didn't know about that. Katya didn't have to tell them for a long time to come, giving her room to pretend it hadn't happened.

"Redtrue was just leading us to our next target," Katya said.

Starbride and Maia exchanged glances. "If we want to save Brutal," Starbride said, "we have to hurry."

"You know a healer in the palace?" Katya asked.

"I did what I could," the strength monk added. When Katya glanced at her, she made a very awkward bow. "Highness. I'm Scarra, by the way." She bowed again.

Katya waved at her to stop. "But you know someone else who can do more for him? Or are you offering to get him out and to a healer?"

When Maia and Starbride shared another secretive glance, Katya almost shouted at them to get on with it. Her face must have betrayed her because Starbride squeezed her arm. "We need to get to Crowe's office. I'll explain on the way, but we can save Brutal and cause more problems for Roland at the same time."

CHAPTER EIGHT

STARBRIDE

Starbride wondered how silly it would look if she and Katya sneaked through the palace hand in hand. But maybe it was better to throw pride out the window and be silly. After months apart, they'd had one night together, and it hadn't been enough. And now Katya was *right there*, and it took every ounce of Starbride's will not to touch her at every opportunity.

"Focus," Hugo whispered. When she glanced at him, he winked.

"I wasn't doing anything wrong."

"You were staring," Dawnmother said from her other side.

"What's this?" Katya asked, looking back at them.

"They're just pointing out that I'm admiring you when I should be watching where I'm going," Starbride said.

Katya squeezed her hand. "Admire away, just as long as someone tells me what we're up to and soon. Brutal doesn't have much time."

Starbride pulled on Katya's arm, slowing her and letting Dawnmother creep between them and Redtrue. "Not everyone is going to like it." She didn't care about any objections, just what Redtrue would do to back those objections up. Starbride would sooner marry Darkstrong than cease using the powerful weapons she'd learned from the Farradains.

"Just tell me," Katya said.

There was no way to sneak up on it. "Maia is going to give Brutal a Fiend."

Katya's grip tightened, and she stumbled, her court persona blown away by surprise.

Starbride laid a finger over her lips. "He'll die if we don't."

Scarra had said she'd seen a wound like Brutal's before, and the victim had only been saved because the monks had a surgeon close by. With the bubbling sounds in Brutal's breath, Scarra feared the arrow had lodged in his lung. By his pallor, she was certain he was bleeding inside, maybe to drown in his own blood, especially if they tried to move him anymore.

While Maia had cried over him, Brutal's eyes fluttered open, and he muttered her name. Starbride had thought to leave Maia there, but she'd gone quiet at the sound of his voice, and Starbride knew she'd thought of a plan.

"If we find the pyramid we're looking for in Crowe's office," Starbride said to Katya, "I can perform the ritual while Maia passes the Fiend to Brutal."

"You know what 'passes the Fiend' means, don't you?"

Starbride shuddered at the images of Maia and Darren, Maia and Hilda. "Yes."

"And how is Brutal supposed to *perform* if he's half-dead?"

"Maia says the pyramid ritual heightens the experience. She said it's impossible not to perform under its influence."

"And how does she know unless…" Katya blanched. "Oh spirits, no."

"I'm afraid so."

"With Darren?"

"And Hilda."

Katya wiped at her mouth. "My poor cousin."

Starbride glanced back. Maia walked near the rear of their column with Scarra, too far away to have to participate in this conversation again. "I think she takes some comfort in the fact that Roland had already unlocked her Fiend. The creature was happy to do his bidding, at least in that respect."

"But her Aspect isn't out now! If she performs the ritual with Brutal, it'll just be her and him."

"She wants to do this, Katya. She'd rather he live."

"And after it's done? He hasn't Waltzed. How can his Aspect present and heal him?"

Starbride took a deep breath, less firm on that territory. "According to Maia's memories, Roland used a pyramid to make her Fiend come out without Waltzing, the same as he did with Darren and Hilda. I'll have to use the same kind of pyramid, and we'll find a way to restrain Brutal while he transforms. Then we wait until he heals, subdue his Fiend, and make him human again. The Aspect shouldn't be able to present again without help or unless he Waltzes."

"And people accuse me of planning around lots of ifs," Katya said.

"At this point, it's all we can do." Starbride had already gone through this conversation with Maia, already dealt with her shock, doubt, and distaste. And she'd brought up that the ritual itself might kill Brutal before the Fiend could be passed, but Maia had been right. He'd be just as dead if they didn't try.

"Our biggest obstacle is Redtrue," Starbride whispered.

Katya grimaced. "She probably thinks we're going to Crowe's office to cleanse all the pyramids."

"It's Roland's office now. That's what Maia remembers. And I think you're right."

"I can handle her, if it comes to that."

"By stabbing her?" Starbride asked, remembering all the times Redtrue had cut their mind conversations short.

Katya gave her a wry grin. "If she becomes a problem, we'll send her to take care of another hypnotizing pyramid while we heal Brutal."

Starbride squeezed her arm. "I knew you were in charge for a reason."

❖

The hallway leading to the royal apartments was just as Starbride remembered, complete with the Guard watching over it. As Castelle and Freddie reported, these guards didn't seem inclined to abandon their posts, which meant they'd been mind-warped instead of simply hypnotized.

"I'd have to enter their minds to free them," Starbride said. When Redtrue made a noise of disgust, Starbride tried her best to ignore it. "And I might not find anything to save."

"Knock them out if you can," Katya said, "but do it quickly. I've had enough death for today."

Starbride stepped into the hall, and when the eyes of one guard settled on her, she held her mind pyramid aloft and pounced on his thoughts, subduing him as the others piled on the remaining guard. Starbride pressed a pyramid to her guard's forehead, and he dropped to the carpet. The other lay unconscious from the blows he'd taken, but Starbride put her pyramid to his forehead anyway, guaranteeing he'd stay down.

"Leave them for now," Katya said. "They should stay asleep until our business is done."

"But now the difficult part begins," Starbride said. The entirety of the royal quarters, including the path to Crowe's office, was guarded by pyramids, both in the secret passages and in the halls. Starbride remembered what a pain it had been to break in the first time. They hadn't had time to defeat all the pyramids that led to the king's and queen's quarters or to Crowe's office, and she'd had three other pyradistés with her.

"Difficult part?" Redtrue asked. "How so?"

Starbride gestured at the hall. "If you use a detection pyramid, you'll see what I mean."

"I do not need a detection pyramid so close to a target." She spoke slowly, as if to a child, and Starbride almost chucked a pyramid at her. "And these trap pyramids go against the adsna. If you turn them to the adsna's natural order, they cleanse immediately. The adsna wants to flow as it should."

"Wants to flow?" Starbride said, just as slowly. "You think pyramid magic is alive?"

"Perhaps the philosophical debate can wait until later," Ma said.

"It's not philosophy!" Redtrue said just as Starbride shrugged.

Katya touched Redtrue's shoulder. "Just show them."

Redtrue turned toward the hallway. Starbride fumbled for a detection pyramid and fell into it just as Redtrue raised her pyramid.

In Starbride's augmented sight, waves of pure white radiance rolled from Redtrue's pyramid like the tide, curling and flowing to crash into the traps and alarms dotting the walls. Redtrue didn't strip the magic away like Starbride did. Her white tendrils filled the pyramids to the bursting point, pushing their natures aside and engulfing them until they were wells of power.

And she did it so fast! One after another, the waves rolled down the hallway and washed all the pyramids clean as far as Starbride's augmented sight could see.

She knew her mouth was open, and she shut it quickly. "Very impressive."

Redtrue dipped her head. "Later, I will teach you."

Starbride thought combining Farradain and Allusian magic seemed a fine idea, but she feared if she said it out loud, Redtrue might rescind the offer.

When they neared their destination, Katya said, "Don't cleanse anything in the office itself."

"Why?" Redtrue barked. "We do not need any of your usurper's pyramids."

"Until you get a chance to teach me," Starbride said, "I need those pyramids in order to be effective. You don't have to come inside if you don't want to."

Katya cast a glance Starbride's way. "I still don't get why Farradain magic is so wrong." When Redtrue began an impassioned speech, Katya waved behind her back, urging Starbride to go into the office without them.

As nonchalantly as she could, Starbride edged past the office door with Maia in tow. She scanned for traps, but found none in the office itself. Roland must have trusted what he had in the hall. And those pyramids would have been enough to stop them if not for Redtrue.

"She's really good, I take it?" Maia asked.

"At cleansing pyramids. At everything else?" Starbride shrugged.

Maia took a small box off one of Crowe's shelves. "He kept the pyramid for the ritual in here."

It was probably where Crowe had kept it, too. All the times Starbride had been in this office, she'd not had the time to nose around. After Crowe had died, she'd stripped the cabinets of most of his ready-made pyramids, but she hadn't gone poking through his scrolls and boxes. She supposed she would have at some point, especially if she'd stayed on as the royal pyradisté.

Inside the velvet-lined box sat two exquisite pyramids, their edges set with gold filigree that bore minute crystal pyramids along the surface. For something that passed on a creature as foul as the Fiends, they were beautiful. The insides were heavily faceted, all the way to the core, and cast hundreds of tiny prisms as the light struck them. Starbride used her detection pyramid and found them to be a delicate combination of Fiend and mind magic, but she'd have to fall into one and experiment to use it, and she couldn't do that until Maia and Brutal...

"Are you sure you want to do this, Maia?" Starbride asked.

Maia turned away. "I don't want to talk it to death."

"Understood. Do you know where your father, I mean, do you know where *he* kept the pyramids that helped you transform into a Fiend?"

Maia dipped into a pocket and pulled out a tiny pyramid, its small sharp edges bearing rust colored stains.

"Is that from your neck?"

"I kept it." She rolled it around in her palm. "For luck or something, I don't know."

"Maia, that could have turned you back into a Fiend!"

Maia hauled out the pyramid necklace Starbride had made for her. "Not while I wore this."

Starbride snatched the pyramid out of Maia's grasp. "Let's collect whatever else might be useful."

Roland had a few destructive pyramids left in the office, so they grabbed those. Starbride lifted the lid off a large chest in the corner. She gasped, remembering this pyramid as if she'd seen it yesterday, the device that let a pyradisté touch Yanchasa's essence. It focused the energy of the Umbriels' Aspects and used it to keep Yanchasa contained.

She let the lid drop slowly. After Roland had been defeated, they'd still need that particular pyramid for a long time to come.

When they stepped out of the office, Redtrue moved to confront them. "Find what you were looking for?"

Starbride gave her a bright smile. "We'd better be on our way."

❖

They'd cleared the small room except for Starbride, Maia, and a barely conscious Brutal lying on the floor, the arrow sticking out of his chest. It was the most unromantic setting Starbride had ever seen.

She was tempted to ask again if Maia was determined, but the way Maia stroked Brutal's cheek gave her all the answer she needed. In spite of that, Starbride wasn't certain it would work, not with Brutal so injured, but she had to try. She was glad Dawnmother had elected to wait just outside the door rather than down the hall with the others. At least someone could run for help if things took a horrific turn.

Brutal breathed wet and raspy bubbles. As Maia removed the blankets around him, his eyes fluttered open. He licked his lips and slurred, "Wha's goin on?"

"Brutal," Maia said. "I can save you, but I'll only do it if you want."

He frowned, pale face working. "Wha?"

"I can give you a Fiend. If you can hold on for a little bit, you'll have a Fiend and then you'll heal, but you have to say yes."

He stared at her with glassy eyes, and Starbride waited, wondering if he could even understand. "Maia." He reached one shaky hand and covered her fingers. "Wanna live, but can't ask you to, not like this."

"You don't have to ask. I do this to heal you, dearheart, and then we can begin from the beginning, pretend it never happened, but not without a yes."

"You can't. Not for me."

She pressed her lips to his forehead. "Let me save you."

His eyes closed, and tears dribbled down his cheeks. He paused so long Starbride thought he might have passed out again.

"Maia?" Starbride whispered.

Maia shook her head slightly, gaze not leaving Brutal.

"Yes," he said.

Starbride's thumbs had been working around the sides of the two pyramids, but now she clutched them and focused. Maia had told her what it had felt like under their influence, giving Starbride clues about how to work them. She closed her eyes, blocked out the slight sounds of fabric rustling, and gave her mind to the pyramids.

One didn't function without the other, two pyramids for two people, but they were easy to get lost in, and dipping further into them was as comfortable as slipping into silk sheets.

A warm current ran through Starbride, sensuousness flooding her limbs. The air itself seemed warmer, and Starbride felt how the pyramids' energy was designed to be focused outward, like any mind pyramid, but she didn't need to see her targets. She could feel them, the warmth of their bodies, the pounding of their pulses, though one was weaker than the other. As the pyramids' energy touched them, their heartbeats sped, and Starbride could feel the same warmth going through their limbs as coursed through hers.

She became a link in their triangle, a conduit for power that flowed from her to Maia to Brutal, three people, two pyramids—magic number five—the same as a pyramid's sides. As the power flowed back from Brutal into Starbride and the pyramids, it sped up before beginning the journey again, picking up speed each time.

Starbride's breath came faster, and she felt the pyramids' energy changing, turning darker. She'd thought that Fiend energy would be ugly, but the darkness was powerful, beautiful, and every bit as intoxicating as the sexual energy she felt. As the pulse traveled through her again, she knew that all it would take was one more round.

Even before she'd finished the thought, the pulse was back, and the dark energy of the Fiend came out in a burst, slamming into Maia where it paused. It seemed to drag something from her and tow it over to Brutal. Another pause, but when the pulse passed through Brutal, the dark energy was gone. When the pulse returned to Starbride again, it stayed, settling back into the pyramids.

Starbride kept her eyes closed as her heartbeat returned to normal.

"You can open your eyes now," Maia said, and they were both covered. Maia pressed two fingers to Brutal's neck. "He's alive, but barely. We have to finish it."

CHAPTER NINE

KATYA

Only a short time before, Katya had lamented her lack of feeling. It had felt as if Averie's death had brushed part of her soul away. As she waited for news of Brutal, she wished for a little of that distance. Relief over Starbride's safety, amazement at Pennynail's unmasking, and shock about Brutal and Maia fought for the chance to turn her innards to ashes.

With Starbride at her side, it had been easier to cope. It had been months since Roland had forced them apart when he'd taken the city, and Katya still felt guilty that she'd had to escort her family to safety rather than scour the city for Starbride. Now each small touch centered her, and it had been all she could do not to throw her arms around Starbride, the world be damned. Starbride waited down the hall, but it was too far away. Katya couldn't keep her eyes off the door.

She drew her knees up to her chest. Not long ago, the idea of Brutal with a Fiend would have consumed her, made her think of him as more royal than her, but they were drowning in Fiends lately. Corpse Fiends, wild Fiends, the late Hilda and Darren. If just having a Fiend made someone royalty, they'd have a surplus. She pitied anyone having to share a distinction with a cadre of villains and the dead. And if Katya had still had a Fiend, it might have burst forth during one of their many fights that day. Castelle would have had four people to drag around the palace.

They'd been gone so long that Brutal had to have agreed to take a Fiend. He wanted to live. More, he knew that his friends needed him, a powerful incentive indeed.

Around the room, the others talked in muted voices while they ate the meager fare that Baroness Jacintha's courtiers had found. After a round of good wishes, Jacintha and her followers had withdrawn to their hiding place, citing a need to stay out of the way but promising to pass on any news. Katya wondered if it would be as hard for them waiting to hear from her as it was for her waiting to hear of Brutal. Probably. She hated waiting however it came.

"Maybe we should go find that last pyramid," she muttered to her mother.

Ma kept her voice low. "They'll need your help tackling the Fiend."

Redtrue snorted from across the room. "More whispers. I don't know exactly what they're doing down there, but I can feel the evil."

"How can saving someone's life be evil?" Hugo asked.

Redtrue sneered. "How exactly do you think they're *healing* him? That is the horseshit story you concocted, yes? How stupid do you imagine me to be?"

Hugo stared her down. "Clearly, the healing story is a cover for the fact that they're saying *good-bye*. I'll also want to tell Brother Brutal how much I enjoyed his company, and well, that I hope he learned all about the universe, and that in death he will finally reach enlightenment."

"Wouldn't it be a little late by then?" Castelle asked.

"Horsestrong save us from the young and naive," Redtrue said.

Freddie scowled at her. "What crawled in your trousers and made a nest?"

"Yes," Hugo echoed, "I don't think you should question Miss Starbride's—"

"Enough." Katya stood. "We may not all have been fighting together for the past few months, but we're on the same side."

"So which is it?" Scarra asked. "Are they saying good-bye or trying to fix him? Because I could—"

"That's not necessary," Ma said.

"They are using perverted Farradain magic," Redtrue said. "Unless you neglected to tell me of any miraculous healing magic you possess?"

But there was no healing magic, Farradain or otherwise, and she knew that.

"Miss Starbride is undoubtedly using a pyramid to hypnotize Brother Brutal," Hugo said, "and make his transition easier on him."

Hugo to the rescue. Redtrue gave him a flat look.

Katya smirked. Time for the distraction part of their plan. "Since you seem so eager to be moving again, Redtrue, I'm sure you wouldn't mind cleansing that last pyramid we missed."

Redtrue narrowed her eyes.

"Now." Katya stepped aside, leaving the path to the door clear. "Castelle, will you go with her? And anyone else?"

"I'm in," Scarra said. "Better than sitting on my…" She glanced at Katya. "I don't know a polite way to say it in front of royalty."

Katya had to grin. "I get the idea. Anyone else?"

"I'll stay," Ma said quietly. That was good. If a rampaging Fiendish Brutal got away from them, Ma's Fiend would be a match for him.

"I'd like to stay near Miss Starbride if that's all right, Highness," Hugo said.

"Fair enough," Katya said. After all, he'd been guarding her for a long time. That only left one more.

It was hard to look at Pennynail without imagining the mask. Freddie, Freddie, Freddie. She tried to cement his name in her mind, but it was difficult, especially when it kept swinging back and forth from Pennynail to the Butcher.

He met her gaze, but she could read the worry in his shoulders, the slight lines around his eyes, as if he feared she would withdraw the slim approval she'd given. And she didn't know if she would or wouldn't. It all depended on his actions now that his identity had been revealed. He'd have to prove himself all over again, never mind if that was fair or not.

"I'll go," he said. "Four's a nice round number."

"Good to have you," Castelle said, her forced cheerfulness springing out once more. Katya passed over the anti-hypnosis pyramid Starbride had given them, just in case.

They trooped out, and Redtrue gave Katya a look that said there would be words between them again and soon. Katya stretched her neck and tried to soothe overtaxed muscles.

Moments later, a soft knock on the door had them all on their feet. Dawnmother stood in the hall, sweating slightly as if she'd been running. "It's time."

Katya, her mother, and Hugo followed her down the hall. "Were you in the room?" Katya asked.

"Just outside, in case Star needed me, but I felt something."

Brutal seemed even paler, if that was possible. Katya didn't know what she expected. A glow of health, maybe? But that couldn't be until he transformed.

"Did it work?" Katya asked.

Maia nodded, but the blush was gone from her cheeks just as it had retired from Hugo's. They'd all been through too much to be easily embarrassed anymore. Katya knelt at Brutal's side and pressed her fingers to his neck. His pulse beat weak but steady. "Brutal?"

He didn't stir. "We'll have to do this quickly," Katya said. She bound him hand to foot with tapestry cord. Katya wished they'd been able to find some chains, but Fah and Fay didn't smile upon them. All they could hope for was that he didn't break through the rope in an instant.

Hugo helped them, though no one had told him the plan.

"So, now you know that no one is saying good-bye," Katya said.

"I knew all along. No matter what Redtrue says, I'm not naive. And not stupid, either, though it helps us to let her think so."

Katya blinked away her surprise, wondering who had replaced Hugo the boy with the young man beside her.

They'd ripped Brutal's shirt open, and Katya pushed the fabric wide so they'd be able to see the wound as he transformed.

Starbride held up a tiny pyramid, stained around the edges. "I'll use this to make his Aspect present, then we have to pluck the arrow out, give him a few seconds to heal, and I'll subdue the Fiend."

"But in that time," Ma said, "he'll be trying to tear us apart."

"Perhaps we should have kept the others," Hugo said.

Katya shook her head. "We had to get rid of Redtrue. She might try to stop us rather than help."

Starbride gave her a sharp look. "I think I can manage, thank you."

Katya kissed her knuckles. "No offense intended, dearheart. I would take your power over an army of adsnazi."

Starbride smiled wryly. "Thank you."

"Perhaps if we put the bed over him?" Hugo said. "And then laid on it?"

It would give them a little more weight. They'd have to be careful how they timed it and not put their weight on Brutal until after his Aspect had begun to emerge. They dragged the bed over his legs sideways, ready to shove it forward and jump on top of it. Ma had taken her necklace out, ready to transform. Hugo did the same.

"Get ready." Starbride pressed the tiny pyramid to Brutal's forehead. When she closed her eyes, Katya grabbed the bed frame.

Seconds passed, a minute. Katya didn't take her eyes off Starbride. She could feel the tension thrumming from her mother, Hugo, and Dawnmother. They leaned forward as if ready to sprint.

Brutal continued to lie still, chest fluttering, color waxy and sallow. Perhaps the pyramid was broken, or the Fiend transfer hadn't worked.

"Star," Katya whispered. Brutal twitched, but in reaction to her voice or what Starbride was doing? Starbride didn't answer. "Brutal?"

His eyes slipped open, sure and even. Katya watched, rapt, as the iris expanded, bleeding into all parts of his eye until they were two pools of blue.

"Now!" Katya yelled.

They shoved the bed forward, stopping just short of the arrow shaft. They tumbled on top, pressing Brutal into the floor. He didn't flinch, and Katya watched his first transformation from only a foot away. A spike like Katya's father's jutted from the middle of his chin, joined by two others just under his cheeks. The horns that sprouted from his brow and continued over his crown were just like Katya's had been, or so she'd heard.

"Wait," Katya said as Hugo inched forward.

Brutal's lips pulled back in a snarl, showing off fangs. Katya's glance flicked to the arrow. The skin around the shaft inched together. "Hugo, now!"

Hugo grabbed for the arrow shaft as the bed jerked upward. Katya kept hold of the mattress, but her mother went flying. Hugo clutched the bed frame and Dawnmother. Starbride fell backward against the wall.

Katya grabbed for the arrow, but Brutal bucked again. He might have been tied, but that didn't stop him from thrashing. Katya slid toward his face, and his eyes fixed on her, teeth snapping at nothing. Katya pushed off his chest and back onto the bed.

Ma threw herself across all of them, sending the bed smashing down again. Katya made another grab for the arrow, but Ma's knee dug into her wound, making her cry out.

Dawnmother scuttled forward, under Ma, and grabbed the arrow. As the bed bucked again, the fletching slid through her fingers, but by the spurt of blood, she'd pulled it out a little.

Starbride pushed off the wall, shaking her head. She darted forward and gave the arrow another yank, but Brutal nipped at her, and she jerked away.

Katya heard one snap and then another. Brutal had broken his bonds. As his large hands grabbed the sides of the bed, Katya lunged forward and grabbed the arrow shaft.

Brutal heaved, and the bed seemed to fly upward, but Katya kept her grip. The arrow ripped from Brutal's chest with a sickening pop, and then Katya was weightless, sailing through the air in a tangle of limbs and furniture.

The bed *thunked* into the floor, and Katya slid off, banging her knees. She landed on top of everyone, the bloody arrow still in her grasp as the mattress fell on top of them.

Katya struggled to get up, but the bed flew to the side as if under its own power. Brutal stood over them, flexing his long claws. Katya fell back and kicked him, but her ankle threatened to buckle against his hardened skin. Brutal bent down for her. She shoved her feet against his chest. The arrow hole inched closed, the bleeding only a trickle of frozen droplets. The pile of people squirmed and cried out underneath Katya, and Brutal ignored her force as if she wasn't even there.

He jerked upright, eyes wide.

"Hold him!" Starbride cried.

Katya barked a laugh. She'd sooner push the palace five feet to the north. Still, she threw the arrow away and lunged, wrapped her arms and legs around Brutal, and held on. The others piled on him, looking for all the world like children climbing a tree. When Brutal turned in Starbride's direction, Katya lost her grip, certain she'd hindered him much as a fly did a bull moose.

But a fly could still bite. Katya yanked on his legs. Starbride had stabbed him with a pyramid as she'd once stabbed Katya, the blood contact making it easier for the magic to take effect. Katya punched Brutal in the knee, his frozen bone making her knuckles ache.

Brutal kicked, and Katya skidded across the floor. Ma climbed across Brutal's shoulders while Hugo and Dawnmother tried to pin his arms behind his back. He reached up, letting them dangle, but before he could reach Ma, Katya barreled into him.

He staggered a step under Katya's onslaught, so she backed up and rammed him again.

"Almost there!" Starbride cried.

Katya felt wetness trickle down her back and knew she'd bled through her bandages. Still, she slammed Brutal again. They'd come so close to losing him; she couldn't stop now. "Come on, Brutal!"

His head turned as she began another run, his eyes fading to normal and falling closed. She hit him hard, and he toppled, taking everyone with him.

Katya lay on his legs and gasped. Everyone followed suit amidst the remains of the furniture. Katya heard the clatter of wood shifting and glanced up to see Hugo peeking at Brutal's chest. "He's healed."

They all sighed so loudly it was like a shout. Katya couldn't help a chuckle, and as the adrenaline abandoned her, it turned into a guffaw until gales of laughter shook her. They all cackled like mad idiots who'd just turned their friend into a Fiend.

Soft hands pulled Katya to her feet, and she wrapped her arms around Starbride.

"You make a lovely battering ram," Starbride said.

"And you're my hero." Katya kissed her long and deep, as she'd wanted to every moment since they'd laid eyes on each other again. "Will he be all right?"

"Should be. The pyramid wound I gave him won't have healed, but it's far more manageable than a hole through his chest."

"We're lucky his Fiend didn't know what it was doing," Hugo said.

"Very lucky." Katya recalled how clumsy Hilda and Darren had been the first few times they'd transformed. Even without control, the Fiend had to get used to its new body. Katya pressed a kiss against Starbride's forehead. "He would have killed us without you."

Hugo snorted. "He would have died in the first place without her."

"Afraid I'm not giving my love enough credit, Hugo?" Katya asked.

He stammered, wide-eyed, but Starbride waved his protests away. "She's only teasing, Hugo."

When he looked to Katya, she nodded, granting him a reprieve. She wanted to stay in that room forever, to keep the giddy mood.

❖

Brutal awoke before the others returned. His eyes snapped open, and he bolted upright so fast, they all scrambled back. "Maia?"

"Here." She knelt, and they gazed at each other for a few seconds. What had passed between them seemed too large for words.

When he stood, he clasped both of Katya's arms. "See," he said, "I told you you'd come back for me."

"I'm glad you didn't have any doubts." Averie's face drifted past her mind's eye, and she had to swallow. "Brutal, I'm so happy."

He ducked close to her ear. "I understand now, about the Fiend."

"How? You can't remember. No one can unless they're joined with their Fiend!"

"It's just something that I feel, some enlightenment I received. I feel like I understand you more."

Katya breathed a laugh and had to chalk that up to the unknowable, at least by someone who'd never set foot on Best's and Berth's path. "And I learned that trying to knock you down is like trying to fell a tree."

He moved to shake Hugo's hand, and he bowed low to Ma, who gave him a gracious nod. Dawnmother waved away his thanks and hugged him, Starbride joining her.

"We're so glad you're all right," Starbride said as he wrapped his arms around both of them.

After the greetings were done, they stood in a silence that managed to be comfortable and strained, companions reunited yet still with hard tasks in front of them.

"Should we go looking for the others?" Maia asked.

"Best to stay put," Katya said. "We might miss them."

Brutal rubbed his hands together. "Any wounds need looking at?" He pointed at Katya. "I seem to remember you being stabbed in the back, and I see a new cut on your arm."

At the mere mention, her back started to throb. "The arm's not bad, but I think my back is bleeding again." Ma had taken Brutal's medical bag when they'd left him, and now she happily returned it. Katya grimaced as she saw the needle and thread come out. "Can't we just bandage it?"

"Not if it's going to keep reopening." When she didn't move, he gave her an uncompromising look. "Do I have to sit on you?"

She glared at him. "And there I was happy that you're well."

She shrugged out of her coat and lay face down on the mattress after the others had cleared it from the debris. Brutal lifted her shirt, undid her bandages, and clucked his tongue. "I wish we had some of the count's brandy, but water will have to do."

He sluiced some over her wound, and Katya cursed. Starbride sat at the head of the mattress and held her hands. Katya grunted and gnashed her teeth as the needle tore little holes in her flesh and dragged the thread through. Starbride smoothed her hair from her face, whispering loving words in her ear until Katya didn't know if she squirmed from the pain or the delights that Starbride promised.

When the others returned, Brutal saw to their wounds, Scarra hovering over his shoulder as he talked her through what he did. All the while, Redtrue glared and looked him up and down as if trying to determine what had been done to him.

Freddie remained in the hall, talking to Hugo. When Brutal took a final look around, he said, "I guess Pennynail's all right then. Skulking around?"

"Not exactly." Katya quickly told him of Pennynail's real identity. He'd had enough surprises for the day.

When she waved Freddie inside, Brutal said, "I know you."

Freddie smirked. "I get that a lot."

"No, not from the Butcher stories." Brutal's eyes narrowed. "We've met. In a tavern?"

Starbride burst out laughing. "The night we went out to see what the townsfolk thought of Appleton's murder, in your promised den of ill repute that was nothing of the sort, Freddie."

Freddie's grin made Katya think of the laughing Jack mask, even without the paint. "You thought I was giving Starbride some trouble, Brutal. You came after me in the crowd."

"But I got distracted by that other man." He pointed at Freddie's lean frame. "You're lucky, friend. I would have torn you in half."

"You would have *tried*."

Dawnmother tsked. "You said the same thing, boastful, right after we left the tavern."

"Knows when he's beaten," Brutal said. "A good frame of mind for a fighter, though being beaten teaches us just as much about the universe as winning, brother."

"The universe and I know as much of each other as we'd like, brother." Freddie opened his arms slightly, and Brutal moved in, lifting Freddie clear off the floor as they embraced.

Some of the tension left Katya's shoulders. Brutal had sparred with Pennynail, and to a member of the strength chapterhouse, that meant they knew one another. A handy trick if one could only believe in it.

CHAPTER TEN

STARBRIDE

While Katya asked Castelle and Freddie about the last pyramid they'd taken care of, Starbride took the time to sit. Yes, they still had work to do. Yes, Roland was still out there. But that morning they'd started a war, and that afternoon it was still raging, and they were wounded and tired. Pain had crept up Starbride's shoulders and to her head, recalling the headache that had plagued her earlier, though this pain was only a shadow.

Starbride pulled the bit of cheese and bread Dawnmother had given her from her satchel. She hadn't been hungry before Brutal, but ravenousness rolled over her as quickly as fatigue, and she had to force herself not to take huge bites.

In one corner, Brutal and Maia sat together, eating and sipping from their water skins. They didn't speak, but it seemed they didn't need to. She laid her head on his shoulder as she ate, and when Scarra and Hugo sat cross-legged in front of them, they both smiled. Dawnmother wandered over, touched Maia's shoulder, and whispered something in her ear.

Queen Catirin sat by herself, eyes closed, resting against the wall. Starbride thought she had the right idea: rest while they could. Still, Starbride didn't think she could sleep if she had a featherbed. Maybe if Roland were dead. And if Katya climbed in with her.

The fantasy faded as Redtrue settled next to her. "You know what I'm going to say," Redtrue said in Allusian.

"You want to know what I did or how or why."

"I don't care how or why. As for what, I have an idea. My question is, how could you let these people corrupt you so?"

"I happen to be in love with one of 'these people,' and I'm friends with a great deal more. I'm helping them fight a Fiendish madman."

"Fighting Fiends with Fiends." Redtrue sneered. "Those are words from Katya's mouth."

"I speak with my own voice."

"You should have come to the adsnazi."

Starbride fought not to squeeze her bread into crumbs. "The adsnazi never bothered to look for me. How many potentials have they missed?"

"We do not force ourselves on anyone."

"And what if a person would like to learn but just doesn't know she can?"

"Those who truly desire to learn the ways of the adsna always find us."

Starbride took a deep breath, determined not to get into an argument about her own feelings. But what was it that drew some to the adsnazi and not others? Was it more than just the call of power? From what Crowe had told her, she wasn't weak when it came to pyramid magic. He'd claimed she was as strong as him in some areas, just lacking in practice. Did only the exceptionally strong gravitate toward the adsnazi, and those with lesser gifts never felt the need?

"So they called to you?" Starbride asked. "What did they say they felt? What did you feel?"

Redtrue shifted, and Starbride could see the discomfort in eyes that wouldn't meet her own.

"You don't want to talk about it?" Starbride asked. "You seem so glad to talk of everything else."

"As Horsestrong said, knowledge is a guide, not a destination."

Starbride wished her hair wasn't braided up so she could throw it over one shoulder. "So guide me. Did you hear their voices in your mind?"

"Adsnazi do not—"

"Then how? Was your body nudged in their direction? Did they put a letter and some sweets under your pillow?"

"Nonsense."

"Curiosity. I'm known for it, ask anyone. I remember when the adsnazi came to Newhope. Were they testing the children who followed them through the streets? Did you get too close, and they found you out?"

"We do not haul people from their beds in the middle of the night."

Starbride thought of what Captain Ursula might say. "So you felt pulled to them in the middle of the night?"

"I did not—"

Dawnmother sat on the other side of her. "I heard Allusian and thought I'd come over. Maia seems much better now that Brutal is back on his feet." She looked back and forth between them. "Am I interrupting?"

"Redtrue was just telling me how she became an adsnazi."

"I wondered about that," Dawnmother said. "Did you leave your mistress, or was it before you were bound to one?"

Redtrue's nostrils flared, but she said nothing.

Starbride stared at both of them until her brain caught up. "Ah."

Dawnmother nodded. "I've known quite a few fellow servants with 'true' in their names."

"I am not a servant." She sounded as if she had to drag the words past her bile.

"What's wrong with being a servant?" Dawnmother asked.

Redtrue's mouth worked for a moment. "I have to..." She stood and moved to the other side of the room.

Dawnmother snorted. "That shut her up."

"That was rather mean, Dawn."

"I won't let her turn her nose up at you *or* me. I'm betting that any mystical calling she felt was only her running away from a life she didn't want."

"But if everyone who finds them is just seeking a new life, and yet everyone who finds them also becomes an adsnazi, that could mean there are many more adsnazi among our people than anyone has ever thought!"

Dawnmother shrugged as if it didn't matter.

Katya settled on Starbride's other side, and Starbride leaned into her without thinking. "What did you say to Redtrue?" Katya said. "I've never seen an Allusian turn so pale."

"Dawnmother guessed that she's servant caste. Evidently, it embarrasses her."

"When she told me in the adsnazi camp, she was surprised I didn't know. Something about the servant caste being better at quoting Horsestrong."

"Helps to keep your mistress on the right track," Dawnmother said. "I'll see how the others are doing." After a wink, she made the rounds again, stopping to speak with each person.

As Katya slipped an arm around Starbride's shoulders, she said, "Well, which of us is going to say which part?"

"You'll have to give me more of a hint," Starbride said. "We've said a lot over the..."

Katya chuckled. "Were you about to say years?"

"We haven't known each other a year yet."

"Hard to believe."

Starbride sighed. How could so much life be packed into such little time? "What did you mean about saying our parts?"

"Any little time we've gotten to be together, one of us says that we have to return to the real world, and the other one asks why we can't stay like this just a little longer."

"As I recall, most of the times, we were in bed—"

"Or the bath."

Starbride's belly warmed at the thought. "Not in a room full of our friends while wounded and exhausted."

"Makes it trickier, to be sure."

Starbride kissed her softly. "You are a scoundrel."

"I'm constantly surprised by our lives. Brutal's come back from the dead with a Fiend, given to him by Maia. Pennynail is a famous murderer."

"Falsely accused."

"A story I must hear at some point. My mother has become a Fiend twice today in order to save my life. And I'm supposed to be champing at the bit to get out there and fight some more, maybe take Roland down once and for all, but I can't bring myself to move from this spot."

Starbride knew how she felt. Even after they'd finished Roland, another challenge lay ahead of them. If she'd still been living in Allusia and the Farradains had come asking for help, Starbride would have had a list of conditions, and she bet the others did, too. She loved Katya, loved Katya's family and friends, but that didn't stop her from loving her homeland. The war would give the Allusians leave to stand their ground and not be pushed around by Farradains anymore.

"What are you thinking?" Katya asked.

"That it's going to be me who says we should move soon."

Katya held up her thumb and forefinger an inch apart. "You beat me to it by this much."

While they were repacking their gear, Queen Catirin approached Katya and Starbride, a slight smile on her tranquil face. Starbride envied that look even as she wondered what depths it hid.

Before Katya could ask, Catirin said, "I'm not going with you, dearheart."

Katya nodded. "You're tired. I understand."

"You better not be calling me old, Katyarianna, unless you want your mother to show you up in front of all these people."

Katya bowed. "I'd never dream of it."

Catirin waved the bow away. "You're right, anyway. And now that you have young Hugo's Fiend to come forth whenever you need it, you don't need me."

"I always need you."

Catirin squeezed her arm. "Dearest daughter, I know that's not true no matter how often I wish it was."

Starbride was afraid to move, to break the delicate bond, but she also didn't want to intrude. She tried to step away, but Catirin reached for her.

"I haven't forgotten you." To Starbride's astonishment, Catirin kissed her cheek. "I didn't make you as welcome as Einrich did, but that changes now." She took a hand from each of them. "I see the inexorable path the spirits have set you on. Your wedding is going to rival Reinholt's."

Starbride caught Katya's slightly crazed smile and returned it with one of her own. "I don't suppose we can just skip ahead to that," Starbride said, "like jumping ahead in your favorite book?"

"Soon," Katya said, "that I *can* promise."

Catirin drew herself up. "Now, I'm going to wait with the baroness, and if we see an opportunity to sneak out of the palace, we'll take it. In the meantime, I'll be asking all the spirits to watch over you."

All that was left to do was find Roland, and as they trekked into the halls once again, Starbride had to wonder how they could accomplish such a task. She'd thought he might come here, but he hadn't shown himself.

"We could clear the palace level by level," Hugo said. "See if there are any more corpse Fiends or wild Fiends, also see if my"—he coughed—"if he's hiding here somewhere."

Katya shook her head. "That might take too long."

"He'll want to protect the capstone," Starbride said. "It's the only thing in the palace he's got left."

"You think he can do something with it?" Katya asked.

Starbride shut out the sounds of Redtrue's muttering. "I don't know if he can until five years have passed again."

"Well, if he was going to try, now's the time." Katya glanced around her. "There's an entrance to the secret passageways in one of the basements nearby. That should get us close to the tunnels."

"The basement near the front doors of the palace?" Freddie asked. "Should we bar them while we're there? If Roland isn't in here, that'll slow him down."

Brutal shook his head. "The entire Guard couldn't keep Roland out the first time. He won't be stopped by a barred door."

"I can live with slowing him down," Katya said.

They'd been angling toward the front doors while they spoke. As they jogged down a long hallway that eventually led to the grand staircase, Redtrue cried, "Stop!"

Everyone skidded to a halt. Starbride took a deep breath as she turned. Maybe Redtrue had finally figured out what they'd done to Brutal and was taking her leave. Well, Starbride was through trying to explain herself. They'd seen a way to save Brutal, and they'd taken it. What more was there to say?

"I feel a pyramid," Redtrue said.

Starbride drew her own detection pyramid. "Can you tell where?"

"Don't," Redtrue said. "Can you not sense it?"

Starbride frowned, not ready to hear again about her deficient education. "I don't have your ability."

"That's not what I—"

Starbride fell into her pyramid, and the world burst apart as a deafening boom rammed into her like an invisible hammer. The hallway tilted back and forth from where she sat against the wall. When had she sat down? Dust rained from the ceiling, drifting like snowflakes. Dimly, she heard someone saying her name, but she couldn't hear over the ringing in her ears.

Redtrue's shaved head passed into her vision. "I told you not to!"

Starbride blinked and shook her head. She climbed to her feet as the world rushed back to her. An explosive pyramid like the one Roland had implanted in the strength monks, designed to go off if a pyradisté tried to detect it. The world threatened to spin, and she clamped her teeth on the little she'd eaten.

The hallway in front of them had collapsed, blocked by rubble. A gaping hole led to the floor above. If Redtrue hadn't detected the pyramid, they would have walked under it and been buried beneath the rubble or blown to pieces.

"Katya? Dawn?" Starbride turned until she found them. Dirty and confused, they were as deafened as her, but no one seemed badly hurt.

"We passed near here before," Katya said.

"And there was no pyramid," Redtrue added.

"So he is here." Starbride stared at the walls that might suddenly burst apart and batter them with stone.

Redtrue touched her shoulder, making her jump. "I would sense more pyramids were they near."

Starbride's cheeks burned as she scanned the destruction she'd caused.

Redtrue's head lifted. "Wait. I feel something else." When she pointed to the ceiling, everyone hurried to the sides of the hall, but Redtrue's finger shifted as if her target was on the move.

"Well, isn't this a fun new development?" Roland's voice called from the hole. "Someone who can detect my pyramids without setting them off."

Katya waved everyone back. "Come closer, Uncle. You're not afraid, are you?" She leaned close to Starbride. "Ready flash bomb."

"Something is—" Redtrue started.

A glittering object fell down from the hole. "Scatter," Starbride cried. She dug for her cancellation pyramid as the hallway exploded in flames, forcing them back from the pile of rubble.

Another pyramid flew after it, angled to arc down the hall, but Starbride focused on it, turning it dark as it spun through the air. Redtrue might be good at detecting pyramids, but how good would she be at cleansing them when they were on the move?

Katya led them away. No matter how good they were at cancelling Roland's arsenal, they wouldn't be able to catch everything raining down on their heads. They turned down another hall.

"There's something in the floor!" Redtrue shouted.

They scrambled to the left, the way they'd come from. Starbride couldn't detect the pyramid, not without risking setting it off. "Can you cleanse it?"

"It might explode," Redtrue said.

"Everyone, back," Katya said. "Redtrue, do it."

Redtrue held her pyramid aloft, but another hurtled their way from around the corner, and fire bloomed again. At the same time, an explosion rattled this hallway, too, blowing out a large chunk of the floor and exposing the basement.

Starbride coughed as the fire sucked the air from her lungs. She staggered back from flames so hot she felt them ten feet away.

"I've been following you, niece," Roland called, "listening in the walls, waiting, leaving my pyramids behind so your new asset couldn't detect them. She's a keeper, that one."

Starbride stood ready, her cancellation pyramid clenched in her fist. She couldn't try to detect Roland's pyramids with his explosive surprises lying around.

"Show yourself, Uncle, if you want a fight."

"Moron. This *is* how I fight." Two more pyramids sailed through the flames. Starbride pounced on one and cancelled it. The other burst into flames against the wall and caught two paintings alight. They were forced to retreat again.

Starbride saw a figure on the other side of the fire. Well, if he liked it so much; she took a fire pyramid from her satchel and flung it, following it with a destruction pyramid for good measure. The hallway shook again, but not as it had for Roland's traps.

"Almost, but not quite," Roland sang.

Maia fired into the flames, but the arrows hurtled back, their fletching smoking. Brutal and Scarra ducked out of their path.

"Now, now, daughter," Roland called. "Is that any way to thank me for teaching you how to share your Fiendish gifts?"

Maia only snarled and fired again. The arrow hurtled back at her and nicked her leg.

"Coward!" Brutal called.

"The stupid and brutish always confuse cowardice and tactics."

Starbride watched for the figure again and tried to focus. She got hold of something, but it moved too quickly, and she lost it. Another pyramid sailed forth, then another, and another. Starbride could always get one, but the others backed them down the hall. Soon, the entire palace would be alight.

"He's herding us," Katya said. She looked to Brutal. "Ready for a mad dash?"

"Always, but I'd prefer not to be on fire, thanks very much." He jerked his head back. "Let's get ahead of him and find a way around."

They ran instead of being backed up inch by inch. The sound of Roland's laughter grated on Starbride's nerves, but she told herself they were regrouping, not running away. Their best chance was to surprise him as he had surprised them and hit him before he knew what was happening.

CHAPTER ELEVEN

KATYA

"What about Fiend suppression pyramids?" Katya asked as they ran.

Starbride shook her head. "No good if he won't come near us. And it would be better if I could see him. He's more cautious than when we fought in the city."

"He must know you've cleared out the palace," Brutal said, "He can't have many resources left." He led them around a sharp corner. Getting anywhere quickly in the palace was always a problem, but if they could circle around, they could catch Roland before he had a chance to plant more traps. They could cut through the receiving hall and down another hallway, and that would take them close to the front doors again, maybe before he knew they were coming.

As they passed a set of stairs, Katya had the flash of an idea. "He might not expect us to come from above." She turned to Starbride. "Can you punch a hole in the floor like he did?"

She shook her head, eyes wide. "I don't have anything that powerful. I was afraid of it blowing up before I was ready."

Which was why Crowe never used such destructive pyramids. Katya couldn't blame Starbride for listening to her teacher. They'd have to use the hole provided by Roland to sneak up on him.

After they raced up the stairs, Redtrue shouted, "Stop!"

Katya skidded to a halt, arms out to catch anyone who staggered past her. "Another pyramid?"

"Somewhere ahead. In the floor perhaps."

"We could set it off," Starbride said.

"Do you sense any more, Redtrue?" Katya asked.

"It's difficult when they're small."

But they could set it off before Roland expected them to. "Do it."

The floor blew upward in shards of masonry and dust. An orange glow flickered from below, the fire raging just below them.

Freddie took a cautious look down. "Carpet and paintings are gone, but the fire's dying out. We're lucky stone doesn't—" He leapt away. "Get back!"

Katya dragged everyone she could reach and caught the glittery arc of a pyramid flying upward. It went dark before it could smash into the ground, Starbride's wondrous ability to cancel a pyramid in mid-air.

"Very clever, niece," Roland called. "But I've learned not to underestimate you. Shame you still can't say the same about me."

Katya cursed, though she'd suspected he might be ready for them. "Can you give us some cover so we can get down there?" she whispered.

Starbride nodded. "Flash bombs."

"Oh, I'd wait on that," Roland called. "Unless you want to blind your mother."

Katya's heart froze. She glanced at the others, but they all looked to one another.

"He's lying," Hugo said, "has to be."

Roland had already said he'd been dogging their footsteps. She thought it was a trick to unnerve them. He might have seen a little, but if he'd been watching the entire time, he would have struck when they were only four rather than wait until Starbride and the others had joined them.

But Ma had gone to wait with Baroness Jacintha *after* Starbride had arrived. Roland could have been watching then and waiting for an opportunity to pick them off one at a time.

"She won't call to you," Roland said. "She may be a queen, but she's also a mother. I so admire her for that, you know."

Katya crept toward the hole, Starbride just behind her with Redtrue. If they could get close enough, maybe they could cleanse Roland's pyramids before he could throw them.

The fire had died down, leaving only a small table smoldering. Katya coughed into her sleeve as she searched through the smoke. Roland stood at the edge of Katya's field of vision, Ma beside him, unbound. Part of her hair had come undone, and spatters of blood covered her clothing, but her serene expression would have fit in at any garden party.

She had a bit of metal twisted around her neck like a collar, and Katya guessed it was more to keep her pyramid necklace in place than to lead her around. She wouldn't run; she wouldn't see the point. Roland could catch her in an instant, and Ma would never do anything as undignified as screaming and running in fear.

"All right, Mother?" Katya called. She fought to keep her voice calm, but the anger she'd been missing mixed with her fear until her insides felt like a furnace.

"She's perfectly fine," Roland said. "I haven't laid a claw on her."

Ma's eyes locked with Katya's, all the gentility of court mixed with the iron of rule. "I'm all right, Katyarianna."

Her full name to remind her that no matter what happened, however Roland tried to use her mother to manipulate her, she must not yield.

"What do you want?" Katya called. If he asked for safe passage out of the palace, she'd let him go and catch him in the streets or out among the army. Their final battle didn't have to take place here.

"What if I said I wanted you to take her place?" Roland asked.

She could get close and then strike.

"Don't even think it," Brutal said.

But it wasn't his mother. Something slipped into her palm from behind. A pyramid. Katya slid it into her pocket. She'd throw it in his face, and then the others would be right behind her. "I'd say yes."

Ma's eyes narrowed.

"I don't sense any pyramids on him," Redtrue said, "only your mother's necklace."

All the better. "Get ready."

"I knew you would say that," Roland said. "What if I asked for the princess consort, our dear little Starbride, what would you say then?"

Katya's heart pounded. Starbride for her mother, one kind of love for another.

Starbride nudged her. "I can defend myself better than she can."

True, and Katya tried to say it, but no sound came out.

Starbride called, "I'll go," just as Roland howled with laughter.

"Keep her," he said. "I would play with you a little longer, go through all your friends, but I'm bored with this game. I just wanted you to see this."

He grabbed Ma's arm and turned her toward him. His transformation bled over him like a shimmer, and he lifted his claws toward her throat.

"No!" Katya dropped down the hole, rolling as she landed to absorb the shuddering impact. He moved slowly but inexorably as Ma struggled against him. Katya knew she'd be too late, that she'd get there just in time to catch her mother's body as it fell.

But Ma's eyes bled all blue, and her wings thrust through her coat. She grabbed Roland's arm as her lips pulled back in a snarl.

Katya got her feet under her as Ma and Roland careened down the hallway in a blur. They rammed into a wall, pausing long enough for Katya to see Ma's fangs sunk into Roland's wrist. Roland's ghastly howl echoed down the hallway, making Katya's ears throb and her mouth fill with the now familiar taste of blood.

She ran, hearing the others behind her, but the Fiends were too fast. Roland spun to a halt, still caught in Ma's mouth. She sank her claws into his arm and yanked, a sickening crunch of bone and bloody spray that tore hand from wrist.

Roland shrieked, and Katya stumbled as something deep in her ear popped. She leaned against the wall and tried to stagger forward. Roland ducked as Ma swiped with her claws, but before she could strike again, he stepped inside her reach and slammed his claws into her throat, between the metal collar and her chin. Her eyes jerked open, and she pawed for him, but he pulled away in a shower of her blood and flesh, and she crumpled to the floor.

Katya cried out, but her own voice seemed muted. Roland cradled his stump to his chest. An arrow and a knife streaked past Katya. He sidestepped the first and caught the latter, throwing it as Brutal charged. Brutal ducked out of the way. Roland ran away a few steps and then jumped farther back.

Redtrue cried, "Stop! There's another pyramid."

Katya didn't listen. She had to get to her mother's side. If they could stop the bleeding, her Fiend could heal her. Another shuddering boom filled the hall, but Katya paid it no mind as she skidded to a halt.

Ma's fingers twitched along the carpet, fanged mouth working, and her gaze fixed on the ceiling. Katya pressed into what was left of Ma's throat. The blood burned with cold, making little webs of frost across Ma's collar. "Brutal!"

He knelt beside her. "Let me see."

She couldn't take her hands away or more blood would jet out. It already flooded the carpet. "You have to give her time to heal."

"Katya, let me see!" He elbowed her over. She scrambled up as he pressed a wad of fabric to Ma's neck. "Someone hold her down."

Scarra knelt on one of her arms while Castelle held the other. "Strong as a damned mule!" Scarra said.

Strong enough to live. Tears filled Katya's eyes. She swiped at them, smearing her mother's cold blood across her cheeks.

Ma's legs had ceased moving. Castelle let one arm go, and it stilled on the singed carpet.

"Ma?" Katya said.

Starbride knelt at Katya's side. "He went down a hole."

"There's too much fallen stone blocking the way to follow," Freddie said.

Katya couldn't even wonder what they were talking about. She took her mother's frigid hand in her own. "Ma?"

"Katya," Redtrue said as she knelt at Katya's back. "Let her die as a human."

Katya rounded on her. "She can heal."

Redtrue shook her head, her eyes dry and hard.

Tears trickled down Brutal's cheeks, and he swallowed before he said, "She's right."

"No."

"The damage is too much," he said, "even for a Fiend."

"It wasn't too much for you!" Katya cried. "It wasn't too much for Roland when he died!"

"You can't make her into a monster like him." Starbride squeezed Katya's shoulder so hard, she felt it through her grief. "You don't want that, and neither does she."

"Let her *die* as a *human*," Redtrue said.

"Shut up!" Katya screamed.

Ma's mouth had stopped working, and her eyes seemed too heavy to keep open. She had never liked the idea that she had a monster inside her. She spoke of it only as a necessity, yet she'd used it that day more than any other because she cared about her family, her kingdom.

But she wouldn't want to die with it riding her.

"Do it."

Yellow light bloomed, but it brought no relief. Ma's eyes widened a final time, and when the light faded, they were back to human and still.

No final shuddering breath, no last glance between them. The Fiend had been the only thing keeping her alive, and now she lay as still as stone. Brutal took his bloody fingers from her throat and smeared crimson trails across his cheeks as he wiped his tears away. He stood, but Katya couldn't take her eyes off Ma's still face.

"Shift over," Brutal said.

Katya felt movement around her, and then Brutal lifted her to her feet. It was too soon; she couldn't stand, but he didn't let her try, cradling her against his massive chest.

It started as a sound deep within her, a growl that tore her throat into something raw and tight. Then the tears came, spilling from her along with sobs and screams. She thrashed, beat at Brutal, and pledged her revenge to all ten spirits in a language only she could understand. She watched Ma's death over and over, compounded by so many images: Averie; the guards in the palace; the young girl Roland had used as a bomb, her chest blown open; Maia; Crowe; even Brom and Lady Hilda, both of whom had welcomed a monster into their midst without knowing how far he'd take them into the abyss.

At last she shook and shuddered but without tears. "Put me down."

He set her on her feet. When Starbride's arms went around her, she was ready for them, but her grief was done for now. The pitying, loving look in Starbride's eyes would have to wait, but Katya kissed her forehead so she would know she was loved.

The others had moved a discreet distance away, peering down the hole Roland had made. "He's gone down there?" Katya asked.

"And the way is blocked," Brutal said.

"Then we keep for the basement, like we planned," Katya said.

"He's probably going to get in the secret passageways," Brutal said.

"He's missing a hand," Starbride said. "I don't know if even a Fiend can regrow a limb."

"You think he'll be looking for something to make up for lost strength?" Katya asked. "Do you have any traps?"

Starbride looked in her satchel. "Some that I took from Crowe's office, but nothing that Roland couldn't get around."

"We need to trap him down there where he's got fewer options. If we can get him into the caverns, even better."

"The capstone," Brutal said. "He'll want it more than ever now."

Katya started toward the hole in the floor, her mind already working, but her eyes sunk to her mother's body as if by anchor.

Hugo's coat covered her head and shoulders, and someone had folded her arms across her waist. A few feet away, Roland's severed hand lay upturned. Katya kicked it to the side with the rest of the rubble. Ma would have to wait for them to come back.

Katya knelt by her side, not brave enough to lift the coat. "I'll do my duty, Ma." Her eyes burned, but she was out of tears. "I'll kill him."

CHAPTER TWELVE

STARBRIDE

Starbride didn't know what she could say to ease Katya's pain. The sight of Queen Catirin lying in a pool of blood and staring at nothing, first as a Fiend and then as a woman, would haunt even Starbride's dreams.

Another horror to add to the list.

But Katya's look of cold determination troubled Starbride more than any memory ever could. That look was a lie. Katya had grieved, writhing in Brutal's arms like a wild thing, and then cold, deadly calm had washed over her. Grief couldn't be done after so short a display. Starbride had known Katya long enough, had been through enough at her side, to know that her grief would linger. And just as with everyone else, it made her do incredibly stupid things.

She could demand a Fiend from her cousins or Brutal. And would they do it? Brutal might, out of duty, and how would they live with each other? No, much more likely she would give in to rage and anger and just fly in Roland's face and make it easy for him to tear her apart.

Starbride clenched a fist. If she had to, she'd hypnotize Katya and endure the consequences later; anything that kept Katya from killing herself.

"Will she be all right?" Redtrue asked in Starbride's ear.

Starbride tried not to jump. "How well did you get to know her?"

"Well enough to know when she's angry."

Starbride smirked. That wasn't well at all. "No, she's not all right, but she might be someday if she doesn't get herself killed for revenge."

"We do what we must."

That sounded too much like a confession. "And what have you done that you had to do?"

"Many things."

"Not *you*, someone who holds her principles so close."

"You don't know me."

"Go ahead and think of yourself as mysterious if it helps you."

Redtrue bristled, then her shoulders sagged. "I've been around Farradains too long. They have infected me as they infected you."

"Another lecture?"

"I used evil to fight evil," Redtrue said between gritted teeth, though the only person who could understand them was Dawnmother, and she remained silent.

Starbride thought over the fight. She hadn't seen Redtrue use a single pyramid save when she returned the queen to human, when she'd *insisted.*

"The necklace." Starbride had guessed that the queen's collar had kept her from removing her Fiend-suppression necklace. She'd also thought the queen had broken the necklace's power using emotion, as Katya once had, but that didn't have to be true. "You cleansed her necklace so her Fiend could emerge."

Redtrue looked away. "I thought it might save her life."

"You did the right thing."

"No," Redtrue said with a snarl. "The fact that you're applauding me shows how far down their road you've traveled. And that it even crossed my mind to help someone become a Fiend shows that I've already set my feet on their path."

"Thanks to you, Roland is wounded. After the battle is joined, you'll be glad of that fact."

"When the battle is done, I'll speak to Leafclever, and if he will consent to still have me among the adsnazi, I'll introduce you to him. Perhaps he can save you."

Starbride rolled her eyes and moved away. Save her indeed. Couldn't he come early and save all of them? Maybe Redtrue could subject Roland to one of her speeches. Perhaps he'd retch until he died.

Dawnmother found the quickest way into the basement, leading them into the servants' halls and then down a wide stairway. Starbride trapped the sides of the stairs, but if Roland came this way, he wouldn't be stuck for long.

Huge vats dotted the large room, and by the smell of lye that burned Starbride's nostrils, she guessed they'd found the palace laundry. Dawnmother took the lead again as Katya blinked with obvious confusion, all of the royals oblivious to the work that went on under their feet. Starbride couldn't blame them, guilty of the same crime herself.

Dawnmother led them to where Roland had blown a hole in the ceiling. A trail of blood led into an adjoining room piled high with soiled linens. The trail quickly went from a trickle to a sprinkling of blood drops, and then to nothing at all. Roland's wound had closed.

In a back corner stacked with old furniture, they found what they were looking for: a hatch of stone, now ajar, a secret way from the cellars into the tunnels beneath the palace.

Starbride and Redtrue held light pyramids, one at the front of their column and one behind. Starbride stayed on Katya's heels as she took the lead again. This tunnel must have connected with the main path that led to the capstone, but how Katya knew which tunnel to take, Starbride had no idea. Quite a few tunnels branched off from this one, smaller paths that wound through the rock. Starbride began to hope the tunnels would slow them down enough to quench Katya's anger, but the tendons standing out in her jaw argued against that.

When the first corpse Fiend jumped at them from an adjoining tunnel, Starbride skidded back. Katya slid forward and ducked its attack. Starbride hauled a cancellation pyramid out of her satchel, but before she could focus, Katya bashed the corpse Fiend's pyramid with her rapier guard. It sagged to the ground, and Katya stepped over it without a glance.

Brutal moved to her side, and Starbride thought he might seek to calm her, but his eyes held the same steely determination. Starbride swore. Now she'd have to watch both of them. She didn't know if Brutal grieved for Katya or with her, but Starbride wouldn't let either cast their lives at Roland's feet.

They approached a fork in the tunnel, one route ending in a short dead-end, and the other joining the much larger path that had to lead to the capstone. Redtrue called, "Stop," from the back of the column, and Starbride hauled on Katya's and Brutal's shoulders, her light momentarily hidden.

The cavern shook out from under Starbride's feet, and stone rained from the ceiling. Starbride hacked up a cloud of dust and lifted her pyramid high. Katya and Brutal jumped to their feet. Steel rang against steel as they fought someone. Starbride tried to peer through the gloom and heard sounds of combat behind her as well. They'd walked into an ambush.

But had they set off a trap, or was Roland throwing pyramids? She pulled out her suppression pyramid and focused. Katya and Brutal advanced as their opponents shrieked. Starbride stayed on their heels, leaving those in the rear to Redtrue.

Starbride gasped as the swirling dust parted long enough to reveal corpse Fiends packing the tunnel in front of Katya. At the edge of the light, something glinted. Pyramid crystal. And it was moving.

She pushed her light and suppression pyramids into one hand, grabbed for her cancellation pyramid, and focused. Whatever Roland's pyramid had been destined for, she never found out.

"Star!" Dawnmother yanked her out of the path of a corpse Fiend that dodged around Katya. Starbride focused on her suppressor again, and the creature shrank back. Scarra slammed the butt of her staff into the pyramid in the creature's forehead, and it dropped.

"Get behind me!" Scarra called.

Starbride did as she was told, using her suppressor to drive the corpse Fiends back. She felt someone brush past her, and radiance filled the tunnel ahead. The corpse Fiends fighting Katya and Brutal dropped as Redtrue's cleansing reached them, their pyramids turning milky white. If Starbride took nothing from the adsnazi, she told herself, by Horsestrong she'd take that.

Redtrue reached Katya, pyramid still blazing. Starbride peered past them, looking for Roland, when the ground lurched again.

Huge chunks of ceiling tore loose in crumbling shrieks. Freddie dragged Hugo out of the path of one boulder, and they forced Starbride farther backward. Katya and Redtrue stood side by side, Katya killing what Redtrue couldn't cleanse. Starbride fought the tide of jealousy and told herself to be practical. One arm of Katya's coat hung open, blood dotting her shirt. She needed all the help she could get.

Starbride tried to press through the fighters. "Katya's hurt."

"I'll go." Dawnmother shifted past Hugo. If Brutal could take Katya's place at the front of the line, Dawnmother could see to her wound.

Another blast shook the tunnel. Starbride cursed and focused on her cancellation pyramid. Roland had to be throwing destruction pyramids at the tunnel walls, hoping to bury them.

She pushed ahead and caught sight of him again. Two pyramids launched into the air, quickly followed by a third. "Dawn, look out!"

Dawnmother leapt for Katya, knocking her into Redtrue and then to the ground. A bright flash filled the cavern as Katya fell on the flash bomb Starbride had given her earlier, the one she'd put in her pocket. Starbride focused through the pain that half-blinded her and cancelled one pyramid that arced for them, but another blasted nearly at their feet, making stone rain atop them as the cavern rocked and shifted. Dust billowed upward in waves. Before Starbride could blink away the spots dancing before her eyes, Roland's third pyramid exploded into a sphere, engulfing the space where Katya, Dawnmother, and Redtrue had fallen.

Starbride's stomach shrank to a hard knot. She staggered to her feet amidst swirling dirt and cries of pain. The tunnel had mostly collapsed, walls and floor only jagged hunks of stone, and the ceiling bearing a hole large enough to climb into. There, in the debris of the floor, was a perfect bowl cut into the cracked rock. The tip of Katya's rapier lay on the edge, cut as perfectly as if it had been snapped off. The rest had been consumed in the sphere of impenetrable blackness.

Sound died in that impossible instance. The two most beloved people in her life, gone, marked only by a hunk of metal barely longer than her palm. People shouted. Some called her name and fought to protect her. Starbride couldn't look away from that bowl, so like the one that had consumed Crowe.

Someone turned her around, and she stared into Freddie's face. Her light pyramid glowed, and her gaze lingered on it, the first pyramid she'd learned, and she'd been so happy.

Her head rocked as Freddie shook her. "Starbride!"

She blinked at him. "I'm busy."

"We've backed Roland down the hall, but we need your help!"

"I can't leave. I'm waiting for Katya."

He gave her such a look of pity and horror and sorrow that she laughed at him. "We have to finish this, Star, for their sakes."

Was he allowed to call her that? She supposed they'd been through enough, but Hugo wouldn't like it. "We can't leave Katya and Dawnmother here."

"Please don't go mad on me now, Star. They're not coming back, and all we can do is avenge them." He jerked his thumb over his shoulder. "Like Castelle. You have to be like Castelle."

His voice quavered as if it might break. Starbride heard Castelle shrieking as she fought. How silly. Did she think it would help Redtrue find them again?

Freddie picked up the broken bit of blade and shook it in her face. "They're *dead*."

She slapped him, hard. When he tried to speak again, she hit him so sharply her palm ached. "You can't...tell...lies," she said, banging her fists into his chest.

He locked his fingers around her wrists. "I'm sorry, Star."

The floor seemed to give way around her. She was falling while standing still. She tried to picture Katya's arms around her, to feel them as she'd often imagined during their time apart, but the feelings wouldn't come. Roland had killed them, too.

Dawnmother would never speak to her again, never brush her hair or comfort her, never share tales and hopes and wisdom. And Katya...

"What will I do?" Starbride had never contemplated life alone, and now the whole world opened up without the two people she loved the most, the long life ahead of her empty, miserable, and pointless.

Freddie shook her again. "Stop crying! Get angry. Fight. This is all Roland's fault!" He shoved her, and she felt rage and anguish ripening and spreading through her veins.

"Roland." Redtrue had been right. Starbride's feet had been set on a path, but not by all Farradains, just one, just *Roland*. Become evil to fight evil. At the end, even Redtrue had seen the necessity of it.

Katya and Dawnmother guided her steps but not toward Roland. That was still suicide, and she couldn't die until she had him.

Starbride focused on her light pyramid and commanded it not to stop glowing. It took longer, but it obeyed, never to darken again unless broken. She pressed it into Freddie's grasp and drew another, keeping it out along with a suppression pyramid. "Stay alive."

Starbride ran from the fight, ducking down another tunnel and bolting toward the capstone. She ignored Freddie's cries for her to come back. They were on their own. They were all on their own, now and forever.

Any corpse Fiends she passed, she suppressed long enough to run by. She heard someone chasing her and then the rattle of blades as whoever it was found the corpse Fiends.

When she reached the capstone cavern, she tore through Roland's traps, desperation and determination giving her the strength she needed. She stepped over the remains of the door that had once stood there, that she'd forced Roland to break down when she'd locked it from the inside. She could feel the capstone reaching for her, ready to give up its power.

The cavern's jaggy stalagmite teeth had always reminded her of some vast creature's maw, but now the creature seemed welcoming rather than threatening. The capstone glowed softly. In her mind, she heard Katya saying, "I'll do my duty."

Starbride knew her duty. She set her light and suppression pyramids on the floor. Raw power licked her palms as she placed them on the capstone's cool sides. She'd never fallen into this pyramid directly. That was only for those who Waltzed. She'd acted through another pyramid, wanting to stay as far from Yanchasa's foul essence as she could.

Now she sought that essence and gave her mind to the capstone, seeking the power that would let her kill Roland, tear his throat and rip out his eyes. *End* him.

Starbride sank into a world of white murk, the vast void that always accompanied absolute pyramid communion. A presence lingered in that void, and she felt its powerful attention turn upon her, pinning her spirit in place with terrifying knowledge.

"Welcome, daughter," it said in a voice made of two whispers, male and female. "I've waited so long for you."

CHAPTER THIRTEEN

KATYA

Darkness surrounded her, still as a grave. Katya's heart filled her throat, and she flailed, trying to beat against the coffin that held her. She opened her mouth, ready to roar that it had been a mistake. She wasn't dead.

Her right arm hit nothing. Her left arm was trapped. Beneath stone? Katya's head swam as she tried to remember. They'd been fighting corpse Fiends, and Roland had done something. Thrown a pyramid? The ceiling had come down on her head. Dawnmother had tackled her out of the path of falling stone, but then the flash bomb had gone off, and the floor had opened. They'd fallen. She felt the stones now, beneath her back, dotting her chest, everywhere.

"Star?" she said, a hoarse croak. The air was made of dust.

"Is that you, Princess?"

Katya turned toward the voice and sat up. The stones rolled away from her, and she pushed the larger one from her arm. "Dawnmother?" She rolled her wrist, sore but unbroken.

"Is Star here?"

"I don't know. Have you found anyone else?" They were both silent until Katya heard a groan from her left. "Who's that?" She stood and felt her way over. Under the debris, the floor seemed smooth. They must have fallen into another tunnel. Katya groaned at the thought of how much backtracking they'd have to do. She heard stones shifting. "Dawnmother?"

"Here," came from her side.

Light blossomed. Redtrue lay in front of them, grasping a pyramid and trying to shift a small block of stone off her chest.

Dawnmother and Katya helped free her, but she grasped her side and whimpered. "I think some of my ribs are broken."

"How about you?" Katya asked Dawnmother.

"Just bruised. How is your arm?"

Katya looked to where one of the corpse Fiends had gotten past her guard. "Stopped bleeding. Probably because of the dirt." Katya put her hands to the sides of her mouth. "Star?" When her voice didn't echo, she took her first good look around. "I don't know much about caverns, but I'm pretty certain they don't form in cubes." At least it was tall enough to stand up in. She looked up at what was undeniably a ceiling, though it sported the hole they'd fallen through, now packed with stone.

"We can't go back that way," Dawnmother said, a hint of fear in her voice.

"We'll find a way." They'd lost Roland for the time being, but she could still hope the others were giving him hell. The fall had robbed her of some of her rage.

Katya and Dawnmother helped Redtrue to her feet. She grasped her side and bent double only to straighten and groan in pain.

Dawnmother felt over her ribs and clucked her tongue. "No breaks that I can feel. Probably cracked or bruised. Princess, may I borrow your knife?"

Redtrue shrank away. "What do you intend?"

Dawnmother gripped Redtrue's shirt and cut a strip from the end. "Hold still." While Redtrue cursed and muttered, Dawnmother bound her ribs tightly. "There, that should help."

Redtrue shuddered. "We're in a room, a room underground. How can this be?"

The walls were pink in patches, once red, but the color had sloughed away. One wall held a rectangular opening, like a door, but it was jammed with rock and stone, and a window held the same, a small house buried in a landslide.

"Over here." Dawnmother knelt in a far corner, near a hole large enough for a person to crawl through. The room stood bare of all else, furniture or decoration, just rocks and stone that had leaked inside.

"Could this be a very deep cellar?" Redtrue asked.

Deep indeed. They were well under the palace. Redtrue lifted her pyramid high, scowling in pain as she did so. There was no way to climb up or dig through the hole that had sealed behind them. With only a few cracked ribs among them, Katya didn't think they'd fallen from too great a height. Starbride and the others could be digging for them right now, or they might have had to flee the tunnel as it collapsed.

Katya knelt in the rubble, searching for her rapier, but she must have dropped it as she fell. "Belt knife will have to do," she muttered.

"Come on," Redtrue called. "There's only one way to go."

"I'll lead the way," Katya said. "You keep the light behind me."

Katya knelt in front of the tunnel and crawled forward. Little pebbles cascaded around her, and she swallowed, trying not to notice. She emerged into a room similar to the first, though this had a connecting chamber. Katya thanked the spirits that she could stand again. A pile of wood lay in the corner, and these walls were muted blue instead of red.

Redtrue grunted as she crawled out, muttering what sounded like curses in Allusian until even Dawnmother tsked. "Are you the child of fishermen? Where did you learn such language?"

"Where did you, since you seem to know it?" Redtrue said.

"Knowing and repeating are two different things."

"Neither matters right now," Katya said. Both doors and windows in this room were packed with rubble, save the door to the adjoining room. If these were early cellars, what had made them such a shambles? Katya stretched, and the wound in her back ached, but she didn't seem to have torn her stitches.

"Here's another tunnel," Dawnmother said from the corner.

"And another," Redtrue said. "This one halfway up the wall, but it has collapsed." She shined her light down the one Dawnmother had found.

Katya hovered over her shoulder. "What do you see?"

"This one goes on." She grunted as she lowered herself to the floor. "My ribs say they are tired of going to all the trouble of standing if we just have to crawl again."

"Better get to it, then," Katya said. Forward toward getting hopelessly lost. She took the lead again and tried to keep her mind off such thoughts. They were moving, which was much preferable to sitting still. What torture it would have been to be stuck in that first room with no way out and nothing to do but think.

Ma would have kept going and gladly.

They emerged into another room, similar to the first. "It's a town or something," Katya said, "a group of buildings that have been buried." She pointed to the blocked windows. "I'm guessing these looked out on streets, but they must have all filled in when it was buried. These pockets remain because the rooms are made of stone."

"And these tunnels?" Redtrue asked. "They must be new. If they'd been built when the city was aboveground, they would have just been holes in the sides of houses."

Dawnmother turned a slow circle. "Someone has come down here since it was buried."

"No one that I heard about," Katya said. Everything had been coated in grime, turning it all the same grayish brown. The walls must have been bright once, though the floors and ceilings seemed paler. "Lemon yellow," Katya said, touching the dusty stone. Wooden doors and shutters had rotted away or been destroyed in whatever cataclysm had brought this place low. The bright mixed with the pale put Katya in mind of Newhope with its startling colors and dazzling whites.

Dawnmother picked up a bit of broken pottery. "Well, we know that whoever returned here wasn't thorough in their cleaning. At least they pushed any trash they found into the corners."

Katya had to shake her head. Maybe this was the original settlement her ancestors had founded, and they'd built on top of it? Why would they just abandon it?

Katya shivered and not just from the cool air in the subterranean room. Her ancestors weren't the first people to occupy this land. They'd conquered it, and they'd used Yanchasa to do it. She turned another circle. It made sense. If the capstone was the top of a huge pyramid, Yanchasa's prison, why wouldn't the rest of the city be down here, too? Maybe Yanchasa had destroyed it by burying it in dirt and stone. "It's the original city," she said.

"The conquered one?" Redtrue asked.

"Conquered and mostly destroyed, and there was a flood, if I remember correctly."

"And the Fiend." Dawnmother rubbed her arms.

Katya racked her brain for what history she remembered. Marienne used to be in a valley, and for a few seasons they had terrible weather—torrential rains—and the Lavine River flooded the entire countryside. And for years after her people came, they were hounded by disaster, a fire that destroyed what they'd built, and earthquakes. She thought of Reinholt's welcoming ball and the earthquakes caused by Roland trying to awaken the great Fiend.

Katya remembered reading about the city quaking for years after the Umbriels took over. It could have been Yanchasa. Her ancestors hadn't known what they'd have to do to keep the Fiend asleep. And maybe the shaking and flooding and fires had buried the original city far underground.

But who had come there since?

They continued through the tunnels, each leading to another room that sometimes held two or three tunnels branching off it. Some had caved in, but several times Katya and the others ran into a dead-end. That was the worst, backing through the dark with no way to turn around. Katya had to fight the urge to slide from the tunnels as quickly as she could. She'd only crash into those behind her, but the sight of a stone wall before her as well as all around her made her breath come quicker. The sweat that dripped from her forehead took on a cool, clammy feel.

In one room they paused, staring at a swath of wall where the smooth stone was interrupted by brick, less ancient but still impassable. Katya touched it lightly and wondered if this was how the tunnel builders had first broken into the dead city.

After the tenth room, the tunnels seemed to head in a straight line; their makers had finally gotten their bearings. Katya said a prayer to the spirits of luck for saving her from dead-ends.

She spoke aloud only when they were out of the tunnels and upright. The underground city kept silent except for the sounds of their boots clomping over stone, the rattle of rocks and debris shifting out of their way, and the hiss of their knees dragging as they crept along. When they stopped, Katya felt the urge to fill the silence with something besides the sounds of breathing.

"If floods and such buried this city," Dawnmother asked, "why did your people not dig it out?"

"Maybe it was easier to build anew," Katya said.

Dawnmother glanced around. "And they didn't want to be reminded of what the Fiend had done."

"I can feel it," Redtrue said softly. She gestured ahead. "It's in that direction, same as these tunnels. Will you tell me the rest of the story? Do I want to know?"

"Wise of you to ask," Dawnmother said.

"I'm not stupid," Redtrue added. "If you're thinking of lying to me."

"I wouldn't dream of thinking that," Katya said. "But do you want to hear it now?"

She stared at the next tunnel before answering. "There's no way to go but forward."

Katya didn't know how to interpret that until Redtrue knelt in front of the next tunnel. Everyone heaved a sigh before they began to crawl again.

Judging by the bricked-up passage and the fact that they had to fall to get down there, Katya imagined that even the tunnel-makers had stopped coming to this dead place. But Redtrue's assertion that they headed toward Yanchasa's prison gave her hope. If they could find the pyramid, they could climb it, maybe break out near the capstone.

After two or three more tunnels, Redtrue slowed, lagging behind.

"Are your ribs paining you?" Katya asked when they stopped.

Her eyes shifted across the floor. "Yes."

"If it's the Fiend that you're worried about, it can't hurt you. And its prison might be our only way out of here."

"I gathered that you think so."

"We have to try," Dawnmother said.

"You don't know what it's like. I can feel it in a way you never could."

"You won't have to commune with Yanchasa," Katya said. "It'll just be giving us a boost out of this place."

"I didn't know the creature had a name." She shook her head. "I want nothing from it."

"Horsestrong preserve us," Dawnmother said. "The 'boost' part is only a metaphor."

Redtrue shrugged but kept up with them. At the first two-story building they reached, they paused again, Dawnmother sharing around a skin of water. They trooped up the stairs to explore, anything to put off crawling again.

The upper level was a round room, dominated by ten columns. A wash of stone had caved in half of the ceiling, and unlike the bare rooms they'd seen, these walls were carved with letters Katya didn't recognize.

Dawnmother traced them with her finger. "It seems Allusian."

"Impossible," Redtrue said. "Unless the Farradains have imprisoned Allusians down here before."

"Well, we turn them into Fiends first," Katya drawled. "That's before we make them fight to the death for our amusement, enslave their children, and feast on their dead."

Redtrue simply sniffed.

Starbride had showed Katya Allusian writing, but this seemed different. "Maybe the original inhabitants of this land used to have contact with the ancient Allusians."

"Before Farradains killed them all?" Redtrue asked.

"Not all of them, I think." Katya hadn't paid much attention in history. She'd memorized the stories of heroes, like Vestra and her husband, both of whom had fought Yanchasa and won by taking some of its essence into themselves.

"Shouldn't you know?" Redtrue asked.

"Those in charge never memorize the history," Dawnmother said. "It's always the servants who remember."

Redtrue sneered at her. "Everyone should be responsible for his or herself."

"True," Dawnmother countered, "but some of us like to share in that responsibility. Star has never argued that I am responsible for her, but I enjoy being so, nonetheless."

"She always struck me as fairly responsible for herself," Katya said.

"We share that burden."

"She must be sick with worry." Katya hoped Starbride wasn't on her knees overhead, scrabbling through broken rocks. Well, better to hope for that than imagining her being torn apart by Roland. Maybe she could defeat him, and Katya would emerge to find him already dead. She just wanted it over with, wanted all those he'd killed to be peaceful in death. Nothing sounded as good as sleeping and grieving and then sleeping again, except for maybe…

"When all this is over," Katya said, "I'm going to have a bath."

"Not alone, I bet," Dawnmother said.

Katya barked a laugh. "I hope not."

"When all this is over, your leaders and mine will need to speak of a great many things," Redtrue said.

"I'm sure they wouldn't mind a bath," Katya answered. "Sounds good, no? A little food, some time alone with Castelle."

"Castelle, is it?" Dawnmother asked. "Not too proud to take a Farradain lover, Redtrue?"

Redtrue turned her back on them and studied the walls again.

"If you're feeling better," Katya said, "let's get moving."

As they entered the tunnels once more, Katya tried to focus on the future, how good it would feel to hold Starbride again, but after hours of nothing but crawling and worrying, the dead stone walls reflected her darker thoughts back on her. She couldn't stop herself from seeing Averie's final shudder or the blood pouring from her mother's throat.

Katya bit her lip. No, she would not think about that.

Focusing on her surroundings wasn't much better. Deserted and quiet, the underground city felt like it was waiting. Shadows made by Redtrue's pyramid seemed to move of their own accord, just at the edge of the light. Katya's thoughts turned to Yanchasa, trapped for hundreds of years, waiting for anyone to come looking for it

She told herself not to be silly. If the great Fiend could grab people, it would have eaten anyone who'd ever come to Waltz in the capstone chamber.

Unless it couldn't reach them. It might be able to now, when they walked where Yanchasa was the only living thing, alone in a sea of stone.

Katya told herself to focus on the rock, watching the cracks and lumps, the lines in the ceiling, the smooth stone of the rooms. Tons of dirt and rock, packed above her head, and the palace sitting on top of that. It was a marvel that this place had been able to survive this long. It all *wanted* to come down on top of her, to finish what it had started— the natural order of things. Just as it leaked through doors and windows, so it would through nostrils and throats. It wanted to crush and kill and be rid of the fact that there had ever been life here.

Katya clenched her fists. Since when had she been afraid of rocks or her own thoughts, for spirits' sake?

But she'd never been trapped far belowground with a monster for company and pain and misery waiting above.

She tried to focus on Roland, who was a far greater threat than Yanchasa or a bunch of stone. She tried to summon her anger, but fear wasn't so easily banished in this foul, dead place.

Maybe that was Yanchasa's doing, too; maybe the Fiend was affecting her the same way it seemed to be affecting Redtrue. "Dawnmother, are you feeling strange?"

"How?"

"Well, Redtrue's clearly uneasy being so near Yanchasa's prison."

"A wise reaction," Redtrue said.

"And I'm feeling…" Katya couldn't finish, ashamed. Some leader she'd become.

Dawnmother tsked. "You'd have to be made of stone to be able to relax in this place. The living were banished from here long ago. I would place a wager that even the famously rude Lord Vincent would break a sweat down here."

Katya had to grin. Sweat he might, but he'd never let anyone see it.

CHAPTER FOURTEEN

STARBRIDE

Starbride sank through the void, her spirit towed down as if through quicksand. The white faded to swirls of gray, and among them she saw a vague collection of shapes: a huge arm, the curve of a wing and a horn, the sharp glint of a fang. A slit of light tracked her spirit as it slowed to a halt, and she looked on an enormous, half-closed eye.

"I am not your daughter." Energy pulsed around Starbride's spirit, the dark power of the Fiends, but as with the pyramid that passed the Fiend from one person to another, she found beauty here. She sensed strength and hunger for battle, but there was also cunning and a protective urge that appealed to her. The scent of intrigue brought her closer. Here was a puzzle even Crowe didn't know, one that would be the instrument for her revenge.

The whispering voices chuckled, and images formed in Starbride's eyes: mountains, tall peaks tearing holes in the clouds and then jutting beyond. A snow-covered valley lay between those peaks as if nestled in a giant bowl. A city filled the valley from end-to-end, yet it seemed to float above the snow it rested upon.

Towers rose up from the jumble like fingers, spare minarets, intricately carved, almost too delicate to stand on their own. Five stood taller than the rest and were spread through the city in a rough circle.

"Belshreth," the two voices whispered in her ear. "Filled with inquisitive people who could do wonders."

Starbride gasped as she sped through the city. Each building bore the same sort of intricate carvings as the minarets, and all of them gleamed. Though snow blanketed the streets, the inhabitants wore thin coats that hung to their knees, brightly colored and standing out sharply against walls that shone like pearls. Their skin was dark like hers, and their hair black, but their features were a little different, broader faces and smaller noses, and each carried crystal pyramids at their belts.

Children used magic to light their rooms, to make their dolls dance. Adults used it to build, coaxing crystal from the ground, large groups meditating together upon a single pyramid to raise a tree from a seedling to a towering giant.

"How is this possible?" she asked.

"We were the people of the crystal. Born among it and so raised."

"You are *not* a person."

The whispering voices chuckled. "There was a time."

She soared among the five great towers and saw three women and two men, each with a tower to her or himself. They met in each other's homes or strolled among the streets to the adulation of the people. They talked and laughed and loved.

"Close as fingers on a hand," the whispers said. "The council of five: Layess the Wise, Fionette the Skilled, Edette the Beautiful, Daronee the Lucky, Yanchasa the Mighty. We ruled and led and transcended."

The faces flashed by too quickly for her to tell who might be whom, but that didn't matter as she watched the marvels they wrought. They created towers out of light and darkness, transformed ice into servants to do one's bidding. And their bodies! As the power of the five grew, they transformed themselves, taking fearsome shapes or those so lovely it made Starbride weep to see them. They cast off sex and could appear as women or men. They shucked their humanity to turn to crystal or smoke.

"Or what you call Fiends," Yanchasa said, still in dual whispers. "I led Belshreth's great army and thought it apt to be as fearsome as I could."

Fiends as people? Not possible. Animal, beast, monster, those she could believe. Fiends infected people like viruses. They did not create miracles. Only humanity could do that for them, and they corrupted whatever they touched.

But they had power she needed.

"If you became Fiends, where did the wild Fiends come from?" she asked. Crowe had told her that greater Fiends had a reputation for manipulation that they did not share with their lesser brethren.

Yanchasa showed her its fearsome form—winged, horned, fanged, scaled—huge as some of the peaks it walked among as it led Belshreth's army against any invaders. It took chunks of crystal and ice and breathed life into them, remaking them into copies of itself.

Malice molded by human hands, not the other way around. Starbride felt the truth in those visions. Redtrue had been right about one thing: only humans could corrupt, but power did not always equal corruption. Roland's desire to dominate had been within him the entire time, Fiend or no, based on what she'd heard.

"Show me more."

"At the pinnacle of Belshreth's dominion, the council of five discovered the secret to life in the adsna that flowed around us. We ruled for centuries but did not unlock our secrets for the people we led, seeing how that would lead to overpopulation and destruction."

"And they resented you," Starbride said.

She watched secret sects and cults meet in dark rooms, jealous of the council's powers. Rebellion followed. The council of five fell in a long, bloody coup. The jealous and the wrathful imprisoned them, but the city paid a great price. Belshreth crumbled without the power of the five, and the traitorous rebels fled southeast.

"Toward Allusia," Starbride said. And a thousand years spent in the harsher southern sun had changed them a little.

"And so I name you daughter," Yanchasa said. "More so than that pale copy who sought to merge with me before."

But did he mean Katya or Roland? Both names brought rage to Starbride's mind. The descendants of Fiends had founded Allusia. And wasn't that good news for her? If Roland was a pale copy, she could take what Yanchasa offered and use it for good. "I need power." She thought of Roland, of the Fiendish Darren or the mindless Umbriel Fiends. "I won't become a monster, no matter that it's one humans created."

Yanchasa laughed, a sound that skittered around in her mind. "When the Farradains imprisoned me here by stealing some of my essence, I *chose* what I gave them."

Starbride thought of what that could mean. The Fiends she'd known were cruel, malicious, barely cunning, seeking only slaughter.

"Any good general shows malice and cunning, daughter."

Starbride frowned. Had she spoken aloud?

"To share in power, one needn't be mindless or fanged. I gave the Umbriels the Aspects of myself that I wished. They thought me a monster, so I gave them one.

"When I was first summoned, I was not myself, drowsy from long captivity. I made do with mindless destruction, and so they called me animal, and still do. I hid my true self from them, but I will grant you my wisdom and so much more, daughter."

She sensed something else. "Well?"

Feminine laughter surrounded her, and a hazy silhouette formed inside the void, hovering in front of the horned, fanged creature that sat motionless inside the great pyramid. A tall woman strode out of the shadows, dressed in silver armor outlined in gold and adorned with tiny pyramids. She held her arms out, her form shifting from female to male and back again as she came closer. Her skin was reddish brown like Starbride's, her face longer and more angular, and her cheekbones high. Her brown eyes sparkled with knowledge. Her hair was hidden under a tall silver helmet with a gold ribbon cascading back from its peak.

"Embrace me, daughter, and I will show you everything."

Katya would not want this, Dawnmother either. It was not the way.

But what other way? She could worry what the dead thought of her once the fight was done.

And then what? Live forever as a Fiend? Shunned by her old family and her new one?

"They will not shun you, daughter," Yanchasa said. "They will see all the good you may do for them. With your help, they need never suffer, never hunger or want. Be as you wish, leader or helper, protector or god. You will be exactly what they need, and I will show you the way."

Ultimately, it didn't matter what else Yanchasa offered. Starbride could take the power, kill Roland, and then perhaps the power could also help her die.

Yanchasa's face softened, reminding Starbride so much of Dawnmother that her heart ached. "I will never leave you."

Starbride sobbed and reached out with spiritual arms. Yanchasa's cold armor chilled her all the way to the heart as his male form wrapped long arms around her, supporting her, lending his strength. His cold breath tickled as he whispered in her ear.

She gasped as knowledge flowed into her mind. The whole basis for Farradain magic was wrong. One didn't *use* pyramids but became one with them. Redtrue had been right about that, but the adsnazi were afraid of true potential.

"Work with the adsna," Yanchasa said, "let it flow through you, become its master, and the pyramid becomes a tool to shape your art."

As the adsna filled Starbride, she saw that calling anything done with it evil would be like labeling air or fire. It was simply power, and in the right hands, it was power that could raise a civilization or burn it to the ground.

"And only a mind that understands that is worthy of rule," Yanchasa said.

"Yes." Starbride saw it now, saw how the world worked and the adsna flowed with it, seasons falling into seasons, life and death, the sun and moon and stars, all of it wheeling together in the most intricate dance of all creation. How could anyone expect to call herself another person's master if she didn't understand this? Evil was pulling down the council of five, in laying low the greatest civilization in history. Their teachings would have spread to all corners of the world, to all peoples. They would have united humanity in the harmony of the adsna, as simply as they'd changed their bodies by its powers.

Starbride wept to see it. "Everything is so clear. How in the world did I miss it before?"

"Farradains like to do things the hard way."

"Roland thought so *small*."

"Indeed. Why stop at making his subjects eternally happy when he could make them better than they'd ever dreamed? When he could crush his enemies instead of toying with them?"

"The king of Farraday and the rulers of Allusia, I have to bring this to them," Starbride said.

"They'll thank you for it, daughter, I guarantee it."

There was something she had to do first, if only she could remember.

"Vengeance," Yanchasa said.

It burned in her again. "He stole my beloved."

"He will be made to see his error. You will teach him, daughter, so he does not forget."

"Show me more." She felt her spirit begin to withdraw from the capstone, but Yanchasa went with her, happy to be her guide. When Starbride opened her eyes, the capstone was alight, washing the cavern in a bright glow. Some corpse Fiends were sprawled on the ground, arms out in worship.

"Pale remnants of my children," Yanchasa said. He stood to her right, flickering, fading to female and back again.

"Should I destroy them?" It would be as easy as breathing. She'd turn their pyramids in on themselves.

"They could prove useful."

Starbride dipped into her satchel. Throwing pyramids, such an archaic practice, a thing for children. She needed only to have the crystal near, and she could shape it with her mind, no more sanding and chipping and carrying on. Yanchasa showed her how to transmute the pyramid to anything she wanted, how to undo its pathways and remake them by letting the adsna flow instead of trying to control it.

She gazed a long time at her suppression pyramid. "We called this Fiend magic."

"We call it flesh. It is the re-shaper, the most powerful magic that lets one"—she gestured at her body as it shifted to male—"control oneself. I'll show you." He pointed to the suppression pyramid. "There you have created anti-flesh. It repels anything created with flesh magic." He gestured to the corpse Fiends. "Simply tune it so."

Starbride shifted the pyramid to something more like Roland used. "Though not so crude," Yanchasa said.

It reminded her again of the pyramid that passed the Fiend from one person to another, dark but powerful. Yanchasa showed her how to focus it inward, to change herself, and she fashioned her hand into one strong enough to crush stone to powder.

Lightning tingles cascaded through Starbride's body, and she fought a giddy laugh.

Yanchasa showed her that all destruction pyramids came from the same base design, so all she had to do to access them was create that base. She re-tuned a small flash bomb, and Yanchasa guided her through using flesh magic to implant the small pyramid in her palm. In her other hand, she embedded a utility pyramid for disabling other pyramids or casting light. For mind magic, she crafted a tiny replica from a hypnosis pyramid and then pushed it into the thin skin of her forehead, all without pain. They set her nerves jingling, a constant reminder of the adsna that coursed through her. "I can do anything."

"Soon, daughter. Now you will only need to focus briefly upon each in order to use them."

"What about the flesh?"

Yanchasa cocked her head. "Where do you think it should go?"

Starbride pressed her small flesh pyramid over her heart. She stared at the soft glows in both her palms, in her chest, felt over the tiny cold patch on her forehead. "Why did the Belshrethen not continue to do wonders after they fled your city? Why do the Allusians not use flesh pyramids now?"

"Fear. They are the descendants of the rebels, after all. Fear rules all that they do."

She thought of Redtrue. If Katya hadn't come to the adsnazi, they wouldn't have learned anti-flesh magic, either. They'd let themselves become weak. She glanced at the corpse Fiends and focused on her flesh pyramid. "Get up."

They rose as one.

"Why would they obey me instead of Roland? He created them."

"I created them, daughter. I taught him how."

Jealousy roared through Starbride, and she rounded on Yanchasa's shade. "How long have you been talking to him? I'm your chosen one, no? Daughter and descendant?"

Yanchasa threw his head back and laughed. "One uses the tools one is given, daughter. Now that you have come to me, his presence is no longer required." Yanchasa laid hands on her shoulders, settling on feminine as she whispered in Starbride's ear. "If these corpse Fiends are remnants of me, he is but a ghost of you. He could not have taken to the pyramids as you have. He is not blood of my blood."

So that was why Redtrue used anti-flesh magic with such ease. She was also blood of Belshreth and hadn't had to learn from the Farradains, minds that barely comprehended it. What could she do with such wondrous power, one who'd grown up among it, though her people wouldn't use it?

"I have felt her," Yanchasa said, "bursts of power flying above my head, but she would never come to me, daughter. Power is nothing without creativity, without courage."

"Miss Starbride!" Hugo called from the entrance to the cavern.

The corpse Fiends turned his way and barred their teeth. "No," Starbride said, and they turned back to her.

Hugo stepped into the chamber, his mouth hanging open. "What happened here?"

Freddie skidded to a stop beside him. "Did you find her?" He quieted as he surveyed the room. When his eyes settled on her, he stared, but at her or Yanchasa?

"They cannot see me, daughter. I dwell within you."

Yanchasa's secret presence made her want to beam. Power, calm and confident, flowed through her. Hugo and Freddie would feel it soon enough when she mended their every woe.

As she came closer, Freddie's eyes fixed on the miniscule pyramid in her forehead. Hugo gawked at her from head to toe. She'd undone the first few laces of her shirt, and she knew the pyramid emitted a faint light, as did the ones in her palms and forehead.

"Starbride?" Hugo asked.

As if she could be anything else. "Where's Roland?"

"The others are harrying him through the tunnels. We thought he might have run in here," Freddie said.

"No doubt he intended to," Starbride said, "but first he wanted to see how many of you he could pick off."

"Even if he had come," Yanchasa said, "I wouldn't have given him what I gave you."

"What's happened to you?" Hugo asked.

She gave him a bright smile. "I've found the power to do what must be done." She pushed past him, focusing, feeling for Roland through herself like Redtrue did, as Yanchasa guided her. She detected the way he'd been shaped by the Fiend inside him.

"By the Aspect *I* gave him," Yanchasa said. "There are no such things as Fiends."

Starbride laughed aloud. She shaped her legs to carry her faster.

"What's going on?" Hugo asked as he tried to keep pace. "What power?"

"Follow me," Starbride commanded.

"We are," Freddie said. "We just want to—"

But it wasn't him she was talking to. The host of corpse Fiends— no, *remnants*—slinked in her wake.

"Starbride?" Freddie touched her shoulder. "What have you done?"

She felt along his body with flesh magic. She could make his arms drop from his shoulders with a thought. Why hadn't she seen how fragile he was before?

His grip tightened. "You did something with the capstone."

"Miss Starbride would never…" Hugo trailed away as she glanced at him. "Spirits above."

"Yanchasa is not what you think," she said.

"A giant monster the ancient Farradains used to conquer this land?" Freddie asked.

"Close," Yanchasa said.

"And so much more," Starbride added. "Now hush. I've got a Fiend king to find."

They babbled at her, but she blocked out their words, listening to Yanchasa instead. She turned the corner to the sounds of fighting. Scarra tried to keep a pair of remnants from tearing her to pieces. Beyond her, the tunnel boomed again as Roland threw an explosive pyramid.

Starbride felt for his other pyramids and cleansed them, letting the power of the adsna carry their purpose away. She waved, and the remnants fighting Scarra went still. Scarra used her staff to smash in the pyramid of one. When she turned to the other, she backed away, confusion on her face.

"What the f—" Scarra glanced around the still remnant to where the glow of Starbride's pyramids filled the tunnel. "Starbride?"

Starbride ignored her. Brutal stumbled around the corner, carrying Maia. She loosed an arrow back the way they'd come. Trickles of red flowed from both of them, and Starbride sensed wounds along Brutal's entire body. Maia's left leg hung crooked from the knee, her trousers soaked in blood.

Starbride closed the wounds on Brutal with a thought. He staggered as if she'd struck him, his eyes wide. "What?"

Before he could set Maia down, Starbride yanked her leg straight. As her howls filled the tunnel, Starbride mended the knee and closed the wound.

Maia gasped and sobbed in Brutal's arms, and they all gaped at Starbride.

"Wait here," she said.

Farther down the tunnel, Castelle lay in a pool of blood, unmoving. Starbride rolled her over and found a gaping chest wound, newly opened and still pumping, the edges singed.

"Explosive pyramid," Yanchasa said as he knelt beside her.

Starbride used flesh magic to knit Castelle's chest together, but the blood could replenish itself. When Starbride left her, the others rushed in to help as Starbride gathered the remnants in her wake.

Roland hid behind a boulder. Maybe he hoped she would pass him by.

"Come out."

He stood and tossed a bright white pyramid at her feet. "Is this your doing?"

"Seize him," she said.

The remnants leapt to do her bidding, but Roland dodged past them. The Aspect Yanchasa had given him bled over his features as he reached for her with the hand remaining to him. Starbride lifted her destructive arm, and the pulse of a flash bomb caught him full in the face.

He shrieked and staggered. The remnants piled on top of him. He thrashed and bit, but there were too many. When they dragged him close, he stared at Starbride with his all-blue eyes. The grating sound of his voice would have bothered her before, but now it was nothing. *He* was nothing.

"I see you, little fool," he said. "I know what you've done."

"What you couldn't."

"What I *resisted*! I wanted my people to be happy. You've killed them. Do you know that?"

"Take him to the capstone," Starbride said.

As they hauled him past the others, he shouted, "You're doomed, already dead. Don't you see? Farraday will be a pile of ash by the time you're through."

His panic sweetened her ears like music. Yanchasa hummed along. The others pressed around her, but she ignored them. "Don't follow if you don't want to see."

The remnants laid Roland on the floor of the great cavern. She took a suppression pyramid, anti-flesh, from her satchel. It burned her skin, but she ignored the pain and held the pyramid over Roland while he squirmed.

"You killed my love," she said and felt nothing. She saw Katya clearly in her mind, but Roland had killed all the feeling in her.

"And you've killed us all."

"Just you." She used flesh magic to open a hole in his belly and then dropped the suppression pyramid inside, leaving it to heave among his guts. She focused and made it permanent, like she'd done with the light pyramid, before she closed the hole. He screamed and screamed as it repelled what he was from the inside out.

"Keep him here," she said. The others had gathered at the mouth of the cavern, watching Roland writhe and shriek, their hands over their ears. Starbride smiled at them. "We've got an army to save."

CHAPTER FIFTEEN

KATYA

Katya paused as tiny stones cascaded down the sides of the cramped tunnel. Not since the first one had they found a tunnel so unstable. The floor became littered with debris, digging in to her palms and knees. She could almost feel the rock overhead straining to crush her, but she made herself breathe. "Go carefully here."

All the bending and crawling continued to take its toll on Katya's back and Redtrue's ribs, and the suffocating feeling of being buried alive frayed all their nerves. It became harder and harder to get back into the tunnels once they'd broken through to another room.

Whenever they encountered writing or the ruins of decorations and mosaics, Redtrue stopped and examined them. If they'd been in the palace halls, Katya would have chafed at the delay, but the prospect of another tunnel tempted her to say, "Take as long as you need."

At each pause, Katya lingered by the tunnel they'd come from, listening. If Starbride and the others came looking, Katya would have to crawl back the way she'd come, but she could deal with that as long as she knew Starbride waited at the other end. So far, she'd heard nothing. Maybe they hadn't been able to break through or were still trying to find their way back to where Katya and the others had fallen. It couldn't be easy with Roland dogging their steps.

Or maybe Roland had killed them all, and there was no one coming to rescue her.

Katya shook the thought away. "Let's get moving." She plunged into the next tunnel, trying not to think, keeping her eyes fixed on the gloom. After a few turns, though, she had to blink at what seemed like light coming from ahead.

"Redtrue, hide your pyramid."

When darkness descended, it was a relief not to have to look at the rock. Katya blinked to adjust her eyes to the meager light coming from ahead. Steady and unwavering, it couldn't be firelight, though it had a soft yellow glow. They crawled slowly until at last they broke into a large room. Light trickled up from a hole in the floor, but no sound came with it.

Four columns rose to a ceiling at least twenty feet high, and a stone balcony stretched along the left side and then through the far wall. A door guarded the entrance to the next room, old but intact, unlike the floor-to-ceiling windows which were filled with debris.

By the dim light coming from the hole, Katya noted an intricate mosaic under their feet, some fantastical beast that looked like a three-headed hillcat. She drew her knife as she tiptoed toward the hole, fighting images of what the people who lived in this dead city might look like as they dug their tunnels and whispered in the dark. They'd be huge moles with giant white eyes.

But moles wouldn't need the light.

Katya peeked down and saw a large pyramid implanted in the floor of the room below. She gestured Redtrue forward.

Redtrue stared at the pyramid before whispering in Katya's ear. "It feels old."

They knelt and listened. Dawnmother crept to the door and put her ear to it. Katya despaired of just dropping down and then not being able to find her way up again. She glanced at Dawnmother, who shook her head. Katya pushed the door open slowly. She froze as it shrieked on old metal hinges. Well, there went secrecy.

A large room lay behind the door, much like the first, but with a staircase that led to the balcony, and what had probably been a large front door now blocked with stone. Makeshift beds ringed this room, cloth-wrapped bundles of straw with furs sitting atop them. Katya doubted they had belonged to the original inhabitants but instead to the mysterious tunnel builders.

Redtrue commanded her pyramid to glow again as she bent over one of the beds. She picked up a piece of fur that cracked, yellow with age. She let it fall and wiped her fingers on the hem of her shirt.

Part of the staircase had been buried under debris spilling from the windows that ran its length, making it impassible, but a door underneath led back into the house. As they passed through, Katya stopped in surprise. The outer wall in this small room bore another tunnel, but this one reached a little more than half her height, and had been reinforced by thick wooden pillars. The remains of a torch lay at the mouth as if someone had tossed it there passing by.

Another wall in the small room had collapsed, but someone had cleared it out enough to punch a hole in the floor and reveal a stone staircase going down, wan light filtering up it.

Katya stepped carefully down into the five sided room that held the pyramid. When no mole people dashed from the shadows, she stopped and stared in wonder. Each wall had been carved with two intricate figures, surrounded by the same blocky characters Katya had come to think of as ancient Allusian.

Each pair stood joined at the back, the one facing left male, the right female, both faces tilted to look at the sky. The first pair was dressed in intricate plate armor, both with high, peaked helms, a halberd strapped to their shared back rising up between their heads. She had a sword at her waist, and he a knife at his thigh. A long ribbon led from the top of their helms and curled down to entwine near where their hands nearly touched.

The next pair wore robes that swept the ground. Their arms were angled over their chests, fingers curled protectively around books. Hats covered their hair completely before sweeping up over their skulls and leading to points over their faces.

Another pair wore tight clothing, and both balanced a ball on their fingertips while knives dangled from their nearly touching fingers. The next pair wore nothing but a gauzy ribbon draped over their bodies, and their fingers entwined. Their free hands turned upward toward the carved stars glittering overhead. By the time Katya turned to the last pair, she knew what she would see: each figure balanced atop a single egg, though the scales they carried and the masks on their faces were new to her.

"The ten spirits," she whispered. The spirits had no history that she knew of, not as real people; they existed as myth, as she suspected Horsestrong and his brother Darkstrong did. But how the people that had lived here before her people arrived had come to know them, she had no clue.

The pyramid in the middle of the floor seemed attached to the stone, and she bet it had sat there for a millennia, installed when the room had been built, though it had probably been brighter then.

"It's like a chapterhouse," Katya said, "a country chapterhouse where they don't have enough room or the population to build each pair of spirits their own space."

"Did your people only begin to worship them after you'd conquered this land?" Redtrue asked.

"No, Vestra spoke about them in her journals as if she'd worshiped them all her life."

"Then these people and yours communicated well before they fought," Dawnmother said. "Maybe they all came from the same place."

But Vestra's journals mentioned nothing of the people who'd lived here before the Farradains came. If they'd been trading partners or something, surely she would have said. Her journals spoke of the original inhabitants as if they were nothing except an obstacle to overcome.

"Can you read any of this?" Katya gestured to the words that surrounded every pair of spirits, encircling them like a frame. She had never seen the spirits carved this way, except for a few things commonly associated with them. Best and Berth did not normally go about armed and armored, but almost naked and always muscled. They wrestled or acted as pillars, holding buildings aloft.

And Jack and Jan were more playful than this dangerous pair. As Katya stepped closer, she saw that the balls were dotted with lines as if covered with tiny blades. And this representation of Ellias and Elody were almost interchangeable, both lithe and youthful. Each had long hair that mingled with the other. In the representations Katya had seen, Elody usually had wide hips and large breasts, but this pair were androgynous, told apart only by a slight difference in their jaws and shoulders. The only female spirits on this wall who seemed well endowed were the strength and wisdom spirits, and their male counterparts had barrel chests and larger bodies.

"The words are difficult to decipher," Redtrue said. "I'm no scholar, but I remember seeing something like this before."

"In school," Dawnmother said, nodding. "I remember it, too. It does look like ancient Allusian, though I remember nothing from those lessons save that they were only a small part of the history book."

Katya held her tongue. The prevalence of any books in Allusia was due to the Farradains' introduction. Before the Farradains came, only a few Allusians had lived in settlements like the one that preceded Newhope; most had been happy being nomadic. Moving frequently and quickly left books out of the question.

"I remember a bit of the alphabet," Dawnmother said, "though the writing was mostly pictographic." She pointed to the drawing of Best and Berth and the lettering closest to them. "But nothing in here looks like a B." She scratched a symbol in the dust that covered the floor. "This is our B now, and something like this"—she made another mark—"was a B then."

"So they called the spirits by different names," Katya said. "That makes sense, but I can see that they're the same."

"Perhaps." Redtrue pointed to the pyramid embedded in the floor. "But what of this? Your chapterhouses and your pyradistés remain quite separate, yes?"

"But anyone can hire a pyradisté," Katya said.

"Is that so? Hmm. The adsnazi have never been for sale."

"Maybe a long time ago," Dawnmother said, "the adsnazi were actually helpful. Maybe they just gave these people a pyramid for their chapterhouse."

"A *hidden* chapterhouse." Katya gestured toward the staircase. "Whoever unearthed this had to dig through the floor, which meant there was probably a secret way to get down here, like a switch that opened the staircase. Who would hide a chapterhouse?"

"You hide that which is forbidden," Dawnmother said.

"Or that which is reserved for the privileged, like your palace passages," Redtrue said.

Katya knelt by the pyramid as if it could give her some answers. "If this place was secret, they couldn't have just hired a pyradisté."

"Strange," Dawnmother said, "that we would have forgotten these spirits completely. If these people were early Allusians, then they were at one time joined with our ancestors."

"Perhaps we wanted to forget them," Redtrue said.

"Yes," Katya added, though she couldn't get past the feeling that everything in front of her was wrong. "Or maybe you had to."

"What do you mean?" Redtrue asked.

"We're not going to figure anything out just by staring at it, and this will still be here after we get out," Dawnmother said.

Redtrue glanced at the pyramid. "I could cleanse this."

"Why bother?" When Katya told her father of this, she wondered if he would let the knowledge monks descend on this place. That would put them close to Yanchasa, but as long as there were no adsnazi or pyradistés in their midst, she didn't see how they could detect Yanchasa's presence. The whole kingdom knew of Fiends by now, but they were still ignorant of the fact that most of the Umbriels bore one. Perhaps she'd have to stand guard at the capstone, letting the explorers see everything but that.

Her mother would have insisted upon such a thing. Katya's heart lurched, but she buried the grief as deeply as she could.

"We should leave a mark," Dawnmother said as they trooped back up the stairs. "In case the others come looking for us. Though they'll have a hard time tracing us if they're still dealing with the Fiend king, the usurper, whatever you want to call him."

Katya snorted, not caring what anyone called him until they could call him dead.

"Maybe when we climb up the pyramid, they'll hear us and help dig us out," Dawnmother said.

"If not, we're going to have to find a way through the stone." Katya glanced at Redtrue. "Can that pyramid you use to put out fire help us?"

Redtrue cocked her head, thinking. Katya hoped she wasn't about to have to listen to another diatribe, but finally Redtrue shrugged. "We will see."

Katya guessed that moving rock out of the way must not be against the world's natural flow. Spirits knew just about everything else was. Redtrue grew quiet, though, and Katya knew she was thinking about the room they'd just left. Once they started down the larger tunnel, having to stoop instead of crawl, Redtrue muttered to herself in a way Katya knew Castelle found charming, but at the moment was just annoying.

"Out with it," Katya finally said.

"I could not make out most of the writing," Redtrue blurted as if she'd been waiting for someone to ask. "Some of it, I could decipher, and it's not what I expected to see. The figure in armor had a Y in its name."

Katya shrugged. "So does mine."

"Maybe it's supposed to be you, then," Dawnmother added.

Katya gave her a wry look. "That must be it."

Dawnmother chuckled. "I knew a Youngstrong once. Perhaps it's him."

"The spirits holding the books had a name starting with L that seemed to have two parts. Do your spirits have two names?" Redtrue asked.

"Like surnames? I don't think so."

"Surnames are not an Allusian custom," Dawnmother said.

Katya shrugged. "I think we've proven that whoever lived here, they weren't typical Allusians, if we can even call them that."

"This second name was similar to 'smart' or 'wise,'" Redtrue muttered.

Dawnmother nudged Katya. "Perhaps we should just let her think out loud to herself. She'll tell us when she's ready."

"Perhaps it was an Allusian name," Redtrue said, "ending in wise. Somethingwise."

"The spirits' parents got their wish, then. Matter and Marla are the paragons of wisdom," Dawnmother said.

"The embodiment," Katya said. "And I don't think they had parents. They just are."

"Even Horsestrong had parents." Dawnmother said. "That's the way of things. I know your education is not that lacking."

Katya had to chuckle, but she kept to herself her doubt that Horsestrong even existed. The idea that the spirits had alternate, Allusian names was intriguing, though. Perhaps the Allusians weren't native to present-day Allusia either, and at one point, they'd come this way, leaving some of their fellows behind before finally settling. She wondered why they'd left the spirits behind, or maybe they'd left most of their history in their tracks and combined the ten spirits into two people who were far easier to remember, even if they were both men.

When they found another room with writing upon its walls, Katya called another break, a short one, though Redtrue spent it in study.

"Fiends," she said, tapping the stone.

Dawnmother and Katya peered over her shoulder. "Are you certain?" Dawnmother asked.

"Look? Has it changed much?"

Dawnmother traced the markings. "No, I remember from the books where Fiends were children's tales."

"Perhaps these people harbored Fiends just as some of the Umbriels do," Redtrue said. When Katya stared at her, she returned a haughty look. "Just because I didn't get the entire story from you doesn't mean

I didn't ask the others, especially since you seemed desperate to keep me blinded. Some of your fellows do not have lips as tight as yours or your mother's."

"Castelle," Katya said with a growl, but Castelle didn't know everything.

"And then later, the young lord."

"You badgered poor Hugo?" Dawnmother asked. "Shame on you."

"I pretended to know more than I did, and he was happy to have someone to talk to. The object of his affection was otherwise engaged "

"Devious," Katya said. "So based on one word, you've decided that these people knew about Fiends, creatures native to mountains thousands of miles away, and maybe bore their Aspect, as my mother does. Did."

Dawnmother gave Redtrue a sharp look, and Redtrue had the grace to grimace. "I'm sorry to bring up your pain, but I'd already guessed that your family is afflicted based on the necklaces they wear. Castelle and Hugo just confirmed it. Though why Brutal does not have to wear such a device, I do not know." Katya just stared at her until she rolled her eyes. "Not stupid," she said slowly.

"But this wall doesn't tell us anything except that these people knew about Fiends, just like both our peoples do."

"How was the great Fiend summoned?" Redtrue asked.

"I'm not a pyradisté."

"You said this Vestra kept journals. May I see them?"

Katya barely held a straight face. "Certainly. I'll ring for a servant."

"Some wine, please," Dawnmother said, "if someone's going." She gestured to the tunnel. "Shall we?"

"Why do you want to know how the creature was summoned?" Katya asked as they walked.

"Because I wish to know if the Farradains used the pyramid they found here to summon the Fiend, or if they brought another with them. If they used the capstone, then I must ask, what was its original purpose? Did the Farradains have to retune it in order to use it, or did it have something to do with Fiends in the first place?"

"From the stories," Katya said, "the original inhabitants of this land seemed surprised to see a big monster stomping around in their midst. If they knew of Yanchasa, why didn't they summon him first to repel the invaders?"

"Perhaps they tried, but the Farradains' corrupted magic beat them to it. As for the surprise, who wouldn't look shocked when they were being trodden on?"

Katya waved her arguments away. "One word on one wall proves nothing. And it does not bear arguing about when there's nothing we can do about it."

Redtrue sighed. "Still, I can't help but think there's something there."

"After everything is done," Dawnmother said, "perhaps both our peoples could come down here and lose themselves in study."

"Starbride will like that," Katya said, her heart warming at the thought.

Even through the loving feelings generated by those thoughts, an itch settled between Katya's shoulders. Who were the people who'd settled this place? Could it be that they were another version of her own people, or some strange blend of Farradain and Allusian? Vestra's journals were few. There hadn't been much time for writing in her life. First she'd been embroiled in battle and then consumed with the foundation of Marienne. Of her life before, there was no record, save what she'd spoken of later, and she hadn't lived to old age but was killed in an accident during Marienne's construction, plagued as it was by flood and fire.

Maybe the knowledge monks and the Allusian scholars could figure it out together. And maybe that would stir up old feelings of a conquered people, as Redtrue said, if the Allusians had fought the Farradains twice and lost. Or it could unite them in the spirit of exploration.

If the politics of uniting two peoples became as hairy as Katya expected, news of the ancient city might distract everyone. She hoped her father would see it that way. He'd need something to distract him, too.

Katya stumbled. Oh spirits! *She'd* have to be the one to tell her father that her mother had died. Da was going to have to unite two kingdoms while mourning his beloved wife, while bereft of her advice and comfort. Da would want Roland dead, and Katya would give him that. If he could take some satisfaction from the fact that Ma's murderer was dead, he would have it.

Still, the thought of telling him pained her. When her grandmother had died, Katya hadn't even been able to speak the news. Starbride had done it for her. Well, a little voice inside her said, couldn't that happen again? Starbride would watch her stumble and then step into the breach. That was what she did; that was the love she offered. Katya would do the same for her if it came to that.

No, she couldn't be a coward. Her father would hear it from her lips while the two of them were alone. Then he could fall to pieces. Oh spirits, she'd never seen her father fall to pieces, didn't know how to begin to comfort him and would have to try while desperately wanting comfort for herself.

And she couldn't forget Reinholt. Childish brat that he was, he'd lost his mother, too. Katya scrubbed her face. She'd have to force it all down, draw on all the reserves of strength she possessed, be a comfort to her family, and then collapse into Starbride's arms.

CHAPTER SIXTEEN

STARBRIDE

Yanchasa whispered in Starbride's ear as she walked. If she wanted to be faster or stronger, she used flesh magic to change herself in little ways, unseen to those who followed her, those she quickly left behind. She cleansed the traps she'd left on the basement stairs. No good would come from letting her friends blow themselves to pieces.

Roland was still pinned to the floor of the cavern, screaming his lungs out. She'd decided to keep him that way. The remnants would never tire, and he couldn't command them anymore. He'd stay just as she'd left him.

"Can you feel him?" she asked, still preferring to speak aloud, no matter that Yanchasa could hear her thoughts.

"I can easily divide my attention." He strode at her side, though sometimes he flickered out of sight. Never out of her mind, though, his presence a comfort.

Starbride burst from the palace doors, knocking them wide in her haste. She wouldn't bother with the occasional street fight. The real fun lay outside the wall. The reason Einrich's army hadn't breached Marienne's gates was probably because they couldn't. Some design of Roland's wouldn't let them. Well, she'd change that.

She ran, speeding past packs of people who called out to her, but they were only blurs. She laughed with sheer joy, Yanchasa joining her in the freedom of movement. A group of people gathered near the gate, barring the way, and Starbride sensed two pyramids nearby, hypnotizing them.

"Clumsy." Yanchasa shuddered. "Those pyramids are like—"

"Junk." Starbride cleansed them with a thought. Some of the gate guards staggered or blinked at one another, laid down their weapons, and barked questions. Others held their ground, mind-warped into utter obedience. Starbride stopped near one of the confused who stared at his weapon as if it were the strangest thing he'd ever seen.

"A halberd," Yanchasa said. "Take it."

"I don't know how to use it."

The wielder blinked at her. "What?"

Yanchasa chuckled. "I'll show you."

It was as simple as images flashing through her brain, showing her how to move, how to use flesh magic to build up the muscles in her arms and back, how to strengthen her hips and legs. She grabbed the halberd, ignored the astonished man's protests, and gave it a few experimental swings before twirling it around.

"Marienne, to me!" she shouted. "We take the gate for the king!"

Some rallied to her charge. Others turned and ran. When the first of the mind-warped engaged her, Starbride cut him down with hardly a thought. She dodged through their ranks, slicing, jabbing, and cleaving any caught in her path. When they finally took the massive gates, she heaved one of them open, bolstered by the gifts of the flesh.

She had to stop and stare as the two hosts clashed against one another in the field before Marienne. Night was falling, the field bathed in gray shadows and white snow trickling softly from the sky.

King Einrich's troops fought what had to be the entire population of the countryside surrounding Marienne. Katya had told her that Roland had stripped the country holdings bare, making corpse Fiends of the dead and mind-warping the living into being his army. The humans would have to give way to the dark, but that wouldn't stop the remnants from slashing through their ranks.

And then there were the holes in Einrich's army, rivulets of dead cut down by what she'd known as lesser Fiends, Yanchasa's created children.

"My misguided young." Yanchasa rested a flickering arm on Starbride's shoulder. "You know what to do."

Starbride focused through the pyramid in her chest and felt the call go out like a pulse. This was what had given her crippling pain that morning. Roland's twisted call had been summoning the blood of Belshreth, but he hadn't done it correctly.

Hers was a proper call, blood to blood, promising what the children wanted. The ranks of Einrich's army closed as the children abandoned the field. Spindly, horned things, their skin mottled blue and white, all long talons and huge milky eyes, they leapt over friend and foe and crowded around Starbride, stroking her skin and adoring her.

"Go." She pointed at the backs of Roland's mind-warped forces.

As she strode in the children's wake, she called all the remnants to do her bidding, and then all that was left to kill were the mind-warped humans. She supposed she could break their conditioning, if Roland had left anything of their old selves, but Yanchasa waved a gauntleted hand.

"Be fearsome, daughter."

She set her halberd swinging. Yanchasa's memories filled her to the point where she could feel the heavy armor across her shoulders.

From the corner of her eye, she saw Yanchasa's shimmering form mirroring her movements and soon lost herself in combat.

When there were too many, she held out her left arm, and fire bloomed, melting flesh and cracking bone. Spheres of infinite black blossomed among her enemies while great booming explosions shook the earth, flinging men, women, and horses into the sky. She didn't have power, she *lived* as it.

Yanchasa crowed beside her. "Long has it been since I could test my skills, daughter. I haven't fought in my meager human form since, well, I can barely count the ages." Yanchasa's memories swelled, how good it felt to leap and stride again, to swing a weapon, to command those under her, and to see an enemy cut to pieces.

By the time Starbride reached Einrich's army, her gore-covered hands stuck against the wooden haft of the halberd. Sweat ran down her face. She breathed hard, but she knew she could fight the same battle again if needed. Allusian and Farradain faces stared with open-mouthed horror even as she and her children dispatched their enemies.

In the light of their torches, she cleansed the blood from her face and bowed. "I am Princess Consort Starbride. I've come to see the king."

They glanced at one another and then at the halberd. Starbride cast it away. She wouldn't need it to kill them, but they hadn't seemed to realize that. Several escorted her to the heart of the army while her children took the rest of Roland's forces.

Einrich stood in the middle of a host of guards, mounted and shouting orders. Several of those guarding him sported wounds, and Starbride bet the enemy had reached him several times. Even Lord Vincent had a set of five cuts across his arm. It had to have been one of Yanchasa's children who'd scored on him.

Einrich sat forward on his horse, peering at her in the gloom of falling night. Lord Vincent moved between them, and Starbride laughed in his face.

"Starbride?" Einrich asked.

She pointed toward Marienne. "Majesty, I've come to offer you your city back."

Countess Nadia approached from Einrich's side, her own leather gear spotted with blood. "Are you all right, Princess Consort?"

"Better than all right, Countess. Roland is my prisoner."

Einrich's face ran a gamut of emotions before he settled on straight-lipped caution. He dismounted and looked out over his army as the children and the remnants turned the tide. "I see we have much to talk about."

They all stared and stared and stared as Einrich led the way to his command tent. Starbride couldn't decide whether to laugh or rage at all the eyes on her. They watched her forehead or over her heart and both her hands. They stared boldly or from the sides of their eyes. Lord Vincent displayed the same calm, dangerous aura as always. Starbride returned his stare with one of her own and dared him to say a harsh word to her.

"Kill him if you wish," Yanchasa said.

Starbride cocked her head and thought it best to reply in her mind. *I thought you would urge me to caution, hoard my power and bide my time.*

"I am not your lord, nor queen. I am here to help you come into your own power. My time upon the world is done."

Starbride saw the truth in that but wondered if it was really so. Maybe after her struggles were done, she could see what might be done for the council of Belshreth.

The ghost of a caress kissed her cheek. "Sweet daughter."

Both of Einrich's grandchildren waited in the tent with their nannies. Starbride should have expected it with Vincent so nearby. Good. That would save time. They were young, but they had to be told of all they had lost. Better to learn pain early.

"Something's happened," Einrich said when they were as alone as they were going to be. He looked her up and down. "Something terrible."

"Terrible and wonderful, one after the other." The image of Katya cut through the haze of power, and Starbride lost her breath. So much of her life would never happen again. She stumbled, and Einrich reached out to her. His concern shook her to the core. Tears started in her eyes, and the roaring in her ears drowned out Yanchasa's voice.

Einrich gasped and turned her hand over, staring at the pyramid as if that was all he could see. Had he meant that a terrible thing had to have happened in order to bring her into her new power, or was he calling the power itself a terrible thing?

"Small minds," Yanchasa said. "You've delivered them vengeance."

And that was what mattered. "Katya…" Even with all her power, she couldn't say it.

He grasped his heart as if he might fall. "No."

Starbride stammered, trying to get the words out, but they wouldn't come. She went the easier route. "And the queen has fallen."

"Fallen?" Vincent said, shocked beyond decorum. "In battle?"

"Of course," Starbride said, glaring at him. "Bravely and fighting, using the gifts given to her."

Einrich went pale under his beard. Vincent helped him sit. Both children started to cry. Even if they couldn't understand what had happened, grief hung heavy in the air. Einrich's breath came harder. "You said Katya," he said. "Please, spirits, don't tell me Katya had to kill her mother."

"No," Starbride said, "Roland killed her, but Katya…" Why couldn't it pass her lips? It hurt, but she had fixed it. Roland was her prisoner, and now the power to change the world filled her to bursting. Starbride could make all of Katya's dreams for her kingdom come true.

"Katya what?" Einrich said. He'd gone completely still, and she thought her next words could shatter him like glass.

"She…" The core of her seemed to vibrate, as if something deep inside was screaming. "She is…"

"Dead?" Vincent asked.

Einrich took a shuddering breath.

"Yes," Starbride said, and if Yanchasa's power hadn't been holding her up, she would have fallen.

Einrich gathered his grandchildren into his lap. He held out an arm to Starbride, inviting her into his grief.

She staggered back. "No!"

His arm dropped. "Please, all of you, leave us."

Vincent jumped up to haul the nannies outside. When he began to shoo Starbride from the tent, she almost lit him on fire, but she didn't want to make enemies in her own camp.

Outside, the snow continued to fall, muting the world in a gray and white haze outside the torchlight. Starbride turned her face up, only mildly surprised when the flakes rolled down her cheeks without melting.

"Why don't you weep?" Vincent said.

She lifted an eyebrow. "Why don't you?"

"Because I don't. But you do."

And when had he ever seen her weep? Or did he just assume she did because she was a woman? Maybe it was because she was human, and he was above such things. "Reinholt is alive," she said, trying for some reaction.

He only cocked his head, and Starbride grew bored with him.

The others found their way to the command tent soon enough: Maia, Brutal, Freddie, Hugo, Scarra carrying Castelle, and then moments later Reinholt and a few of his friends from Dockland. They met in a whirlwind of weeping and hugging as tragic news passed from group to group. Reinholt stared at Vincent, who returned his look calmly. Without a word, Reinholt brushed past him and entered his father's tent, Maia on his heels. Starbride stayed back from them all, at a loss for what to do now that the fighting was done.

"There are many tasks ahead of you, daughter," Yanchasa reminded her.

The city would need seeing to. Luckily, Starbride wasn't sleepy. And after Marienne had been set to rights, Einrich wouldn't want to rule without her input, not once he'd found out all she'd learned about the world. She had access to insurmountable power, the kind that would keep any future Rolands from even thinking of taking the kingdom. Einrich would be the king—Starbride had no wish to strip him of his title—but she would be his strong right hand, his hammer.

"Miss Starbride?"

She turned to Freddie and Hugo. They'd been a great help to her. She had a sudden thought about sharing laughter with them in her hideout, together with Dawnmother.

A chasm threatened to widen under her feet, but she filled it with power. Loss hurt, but the power muted it, made her calm. Funny, she'd thought she'd loved them more than that.

"Tell us what happened," Freddie said.

"I'm so sorry, Miss Starbride." Hugo wept, but for Katya or Dawnmother? How could he weep while she couldn't?

She shrugged. "I had a chance and I took it."

"You left Roland screaming on the cavern floor," Freddie said. "Kill him and be done. This isn't you."

"It is now."

"You had to take power where you could," Hugo said. "I understand, but now that it's over, you can put it back, as you once did with the princess." His lips pressed together until they turned white.

Yanchasa was right. These were small minds. "I have no need to put it back, Hugo. I am in complete control. Katya was only given ferocity, all that Yanchasa would give to any Umbriel." She told them briefly of Belshreth, of Yanchasa's act of revenge when the Umbriels had summoned him to do their bidding, before they knew what a complex person Yanchasa was and not a beast to do their slaughter.

They frowned, and Starbride pitied the fact that they were not pyradistés or adsnazi. Then she could have given them a taste.

"You're not acting like yourself," Freddie said.

"I'm better."

He bent close to her face. "Not mourning the love of your life is better? You used to be so afraid for her, and now that she's dead, you can't—" He turned his head, blinking away tears as he cleared his throat.

"You'd rather me be inconsolable? Reduced to a crying puddle on the floor?" She stuck her lower lip out. "You want to take care of me, Freddie?"

He sneered, and she knew his reaction would have hurt her before.

"Katya would want me to be strong," she said. "She would want me to create a legacy for her, to protect her family, to kill Roland, and make sure nothing like this ever happens to her homeland again. So that's what I'm going to do."

Katya would be so pleased. She wouldn't want Starbride to cry; she never had.

Hugo wrung his hands. "Miss Starbride, you can't—"

"Leave her alone, Hugo," Freddie said. "She doesn't want our help." He pulled Hugo away, Hugo stammering and objecting, but Freddie just frowned and stared at her as if he didn't know her.

"That won't be the end," Yanchasa said. She lounged against the side of Einrich's tent, arms clasped behind her.

"I know. But time is the enemy of pain."

"I must learn all of these fabulous Horsestrong sayings."

Redtrue could have taught her, if she hadn't died, or Dawnmother.

Starbride looked to the snow again. The soldiers had propped up torches among the remains of their army. Someone had set a bonfire in the field near the gate. People trickled in and out of the city. Einrich would move soon, or maybe he'd decide it was safer out here, just until they'd cleared the last of Roland's forces from Marienne. Everyone would wait until the morrow to reclaim their dead, after the snow had covered them in white and frozen them solid.

CHAPTER SEVENTEEN

KATYA

Katya thanked all ten spirits that she could walk nearly upright, though she wondered why the builders had never gotten around to digging out and reinforcing the rest of the tunnels.

"We're still headed toward your capstone," Redtrue said as they stooped.

"Good." Maybe the tunnel builders had been hoping to climb the pyramid, seize the capstone, and harness its power. They could have been early Farradains trying to unearth what they needed to keep Yanchasa at bay. When this path proved too difficult, perhaps they'd dug the higher passages that Katya was used to. After all, there was no need to uncover the entire pyramid when they just needed the capstone. "We can climb out."

When they stopped to rest, Redtrue fidgeted constantly as if the stone floor pained her. As soon as she moved, she grimaced and rubbed her ribs. Katya sighed in sympathy. She'd had a cracked rib before, knew how painful it could be. No matter what Redtrue did, she'd never be comfortable on stone.

After the fourth time she shifted and grimaced in the great pyramid's direction, Katya took pity on her, hoping to distract her from the pain. "Do you have questions? About the parts of the story you haven't been able to worm out of anyone else, that is."

She sniffed. "I don't want to know."

"And yet you keep mentioning it," Dawnmother said. "If you had a servant, she would say…"

Redtrue muttered something in Allusian.

Dawnmother smiled at Katya, who cocked an eyebrow. "My life for you and also the truth?"

"I would never keep a servant," Redtrue said.

Dawnmother shrugged. "Then you would be poorer for it."

They fell to soft bickering, and Katya watched Dawnmother work her magic. Lost in argument, Redtrue's fidgeting stopped. But as Redtrue and Dawnmother lapsed into Allusian, Katya's own fears came squirming back: Roland and Starbride, the safety of her friends, of her family.

Ma.

Katya closed her eyes and tried to drift, summoning other images, quieter thoughts, but she kept coming back to that hallway. The tilt of Ma's chin as she stood beside Roland, resolute, unwavering, a queen that would rather die than give the monster beside her the satisfaction of her fear. Katya's mind whipped through the death, a scene that would live in her nightmares. She didn't settle again until she could see her mother's body unmoving on the floor, Hugo's coat over her face.

Spirits above, she'd have to get married without her mother by her side. How could Fah and Fay be so cruel?

Thoughts of the spirits led back to the carvings in the depths of the dead city. Fah and Fay hadn't treated this place so kindly either. The luck spirits were notoriously fickle, cursing as often as they blessed.

Maybe the people of this land had forsaken the spirits and made their worship immoral or illegal. That would make the tunnel builders part of some ancient cult who knew what they were looking for, rather than exploring Farradains. If her people had made the tunnels, they wouldn't have bothered to hide them or seal the way down.

Keener minds than hers would have to work on this puzzle. "Let's get moving."

Redtrue grimaced again. Katya couldn't help a bit of prodding to quiet her own weary head. "Is all that grimacing for your ribs, or are you still afraid?"

"Who said I was afraid?"

"You did," Dawnmother said, "by your every action."

"You needn't fear Yanchasa," Katya said. "It's asleep, and it'll stay that way as long as my family stays in power."

"You bargained with the creature," Redtrue said.

Katya disregarded her arch tone. "Not exactly." In fits and starts, she told Redtrue some of the story. Her ancestors had summoned Yanchasa, took in its essence to recapture it, and now the Umbriels bore the curse in order to keep it asleep.

"But not you," Redtrue said. "I would have felt it."

"No, not me."

Dawnmother wisely kept silent.

"If your ancestors had not summoned the creature—"

"If they had never come to this land in the first place," Katya said.

"I won't do you the discourtesy of quoting Horsestrong's saying about 'ifs,'" Dawnmother said.

"Are you trying to suggest that I must hold your family blameless for the deeds of your long-dead ancestors?" Redtrue asked.

"I don't see how blaming anyone helps anything."

"As long as you have known of the existence of the greater Fiend, you have done nothing to rid yourself of it."

"Like what?" Katya turned to glance at her in the cramped passage. "Let it out, give it a bag for its things, and point the way home?"

Redtrue gave her a withering look. "What can be summoned can be banished, or did your tutors neglect logic?"

"No one passed down instructions on how they summoned it."

"Because they wanted to keep the creature," Redtrue said.

"Or to keep anyone else from summoning another," Dawnmother added.

They emerged into another large room. As she turned to the others, Katya worried that Redtrue's frown would peel the lower part of her face away.

"How many could there be?" Redtrue asked. "These great Fiends?"

Katya shrugged. "How many glaciers are there in the high mountains?"

Redtrue didn't seem as appalled as Katya thought she'd be. "Maybe they could be cleansed."

"You said something like that before. How can you cleanse something into not existing?"

Redtrue shook her head. "Something about the energy, when I feel the capstone's energy spike—"

Katya's head snapped up. "What did you say?"

"The energy feels—"

"No, you said the capstone energy spikes. Is it doing that now?"

Redtrue nodded slowly. "Several times since we fell down here."

Katya scrubbed at her hair so hard it pulled. "And you didn't say anything?"

"Is it not normal? You and your family are surrounded by circumstances I would consider very odd, yet they seem ordinary to you."

Katya stared down the dark tunnel. If only she had Crowe or Starbride to tell her what it meant. "Roland must be trying to use it. Spirits help us if he succeeds."

"He can tap into this power?" Redtrue asked.

Katya had to lift her arms and drop them. "I couldn't tell you all the things he's capable of."

"Are you sure it's him?" Dawnmother asked. "Perhaps there's another explanation."

Katya barked a laugh. "I suppose it could be Yanchasa waking up." Her insides went cold as soon as the words left her mouth. They stared at one another and then at the walls as if Yanchasa might come tearing through them any second.

"Just how big is this Fiend?" Redtrue whispered.

"Big," Katya said.

"*How* big?"

Dawnmother hissed at her. "Do you think anyone has measured it?"

"Big enough to tear away a chunk of the palace if it decides to stand up," Katya said.

"Perhaps then you can measure it," Dawnmother said, "sew it some trousers."

"I was only trying to—"

"Enough!" Katya barked, cringing at the noise.

Dawnmother cleared her throat. "We've been speaking in normal voices for hours. If the giant monster *is* waking up, our whispering is not going to keep it restrained."

"You're right," Katya said. "There's nothing we can do but keep going."

They began walking again, but Katya knew they all stepped more carefully, and no one seemed as inclined to speak as they had before.

When they found more writing, Katya was loath to stop and study. Time slipped away, though it was impossible to tell how late it had gotten underground. Her body cried for rest, though she knew they should keep pushing forward. The way out couldn't be far.

Being down amidst the stone and Yanchasa's presence wore on Katya as much as her fear for Starbride and her grief over her mother's death. The few supplies Dawnmother had stashed in her bag kept them going, but soon Redtrue plonked down in one of the rooms and refused to move again.

Katya bit her lip and looked to where the tunnel continued. They could leave Redtrue and send help later. If they could light one of the old torches, they wouldn't need a pyramid to see.

"You're exhausted," Redtrue said. "I see it in your face and the way you stand. You need rest as much as I do."

"For once, we are agreed." Dawnmother sat against the opposite wall. "We must try to sleep."

Katya shook her head and tried to tell herself that every muscle didn't ache. "Starbride and the others will be worried."

"And how much more will they worry if we blunder into something we're not ready for? Or do you intend to try to break into this capstone cavern without my help?" Redtrue asked.

Katya sighed as she sat.

"We'll have clearer heads after a few hours' rest," Dawnmother said.

Katya shrugged out of her coat and used it as a pillow. As soon as she laid down, the stone floor seemed like the most comfortable featherbed she'd ever slept in. Her eyes slipped shut before she'd even realized, and the events of the day played over her mind and locked in an indecipherable jumble.

Ma perched on the edge of a settee and raised a teacup to her lips with practiced elegance, her delicate features serene.

"You're not dead!" Katya wept, so happy she'd been mistaken.

Ma smiled and patted her knee. "Tell me about your day."

Six years old again, Katya crawled into her mother's lap. "I'm fighting Roland, and then I'm going to marry Starbride."

"How nice. Have you seen your brother today?"

A loud knock came from the door. Ma frowned at the noise. "Tell them to go away, Katyarianna."

Katya hopped down and ran for the door, growing as she went until she could answer the knocks as an adult.

Her father stood there, beaming. "Do you have the crop report, Katya?"

"No, I—"

He pushed past her, Roland and Crowe following on his heels. "You were supposed to have it done," Crowe barked.

"You'll bring shame on our house," Roland added. "Einrich, you told us she could do it."

Crowe sneered. "Always neglecting your duty."

Katya looked back and forth between them. "I don't know anything about crop reports. It wasn't mine to do." But she knew it was. They'd assigned it to her months ago, and she'd forgotten. "I'm sorry!"

"Well, we'll have to take something in its place." Roland glanced around the room before his gaze settled on Katya's mother. "That'll do."

He moved toward her. Katya tried to follow, but her feet were frozen. "Wait!"

Roland lifted Ma from the settee, and she just kept drinking tea. "One crop report for one mother, that's fair," he said.

"Da," Katya shouted, "make him stop!"

Crowe waggled his finger in her face. "It was your duty."

Da was staring at Roland, and Katya took one shaky step in his direction. "Da, don't let him. Do something."

"I'm sorry, Katya, it's too late."

Roland stepped around them, Ma still in his arms. "I'll just throw this out back, shall I?"

"He's your brother," Katya screamed, her words barely discernable, even to her. "Why didn't you stop him when you had the chance? Why didn't you kill him? You let him murder my mother!"

Ma wilted in Roland's arms, her life snuffed out by Katya's words. The edges of the room turned dark.

"No," Katya whispered, "no, no, no."

Roland looked down at the burden in his arms. "You did this, niece."

"No."

"All your gifts," Crowe said, "wasted."

"Katya?" Da asked, and he held Ma's lifeless body, too. "How could you let this happen?"

Katya tried to look away, but Ma was everywhere: sprawled on the settee, crumpled on the floor, slumped over in the chair, even hanging on the wall. Crowe, Da, and Roland were asking her what she'd done over and over. Reinholt and Maia stumbled over Ma's body and shrieked in horror. Little Bastian and Vierdrin wept and tugged on Ma's skirts, asking why she wouldn't play with them.

Katya tried to run, but her legs wouldn't obey her. She put her hands over her head and howled.

"Katya!"

Katya kicked up from the floor, pulse pounding in her ears. Her shoulder smacked into the wall, sending waves of pain down her spine. Her wound ached, and her shoulder and hip throbbed from where they'd been resting on the floor. She fought to control her breathing as spots danced before her eyes.

Redtrue knelt at her side, one arm outstretched. "What in Darkstrong's name is the matter with you?"

"Tactless," Dawnmother said, glaring at Redtrue as she stepped past. "Can't you see she's had a nightmare?" She touched Katya's shoulder lightly. "Deep, even breaths, Princess. Focus on the now."

Katya's dream faded, all but the bodies and the weeping. "How long were we asleep?"

Dawnmother rubbed her arms. "Difficult to tell down here. Long enough to grow very sore. A few hours?"

Katya pushed off the wall and tried to ignore the shaking in her legs. "Let's get moving."

Dawnmother and Redtrue shared a glance, but Katya told herself she'd continue even if she had to feel her way in the dark and claw her way out of this place. She would not close her eyes again anytime soon.

CHAPTER EIGHTEEN

STARBRIDE

Starbride sat atop the wall overlooking Marienne, content to watch the city ebb and flow. With the gates thrown wide open, people trickled in and out. A few packed knots of men and women moved with armed purpose, led by a shouting commander. They ferreted out the last of Roland's troops or patrolled the streets. Most wore the blue uniforms and chain shirts of the city Watch, but others wore the king's colors.

In the field beyond the wall, darkness reigned. Out among the snowy tents, a few campfires burned low. Einrich himself had yet to reenter Marienne. He seemed content to let his soldiers or those belonging to his nobles make sure the way was safe. Most of the Allusians stayed with him, though Starbride had spotted a few darker faces amongst the crowd. Maybe the bulk of her people felt the Farradains would need time to get used to them.

The city was alive with torchlight, people moving through the night hours, most celebrating, others weeping. A few carts had gone past, bearing heaps of dead. Deeper in the city, she heard strains of music and a few drunken roars.

Yanchasa lounged on the other side of the walkway, his back against a support, one armored leg dangling over the side. "All this could have been prevented."

"Did you try to convince Roland that there was an easier course?"

"He barely heard my voice, daughter. I could only give him scraps."

"He always claimed he wanted his people to be happy, that he had a better plan for ruling. Do you believe that?"

Yanchasa crossed to her side of the wall and leaned far over the edge. "I think he believed himself." He gestured at the battered city. "If he could even understand me, he certainly didn't listen."

"But what about—"

"Who's up there?" someone shouted from below.

Starbride glanced down. Captain Ursula stood below, lifting her torch high as she tried to peer through the gloom.

"The only soldiers assigned to the wall are over at the Dockland side," Ursula called, "so either get going, or get your ass down here."

Starbride held her utility hand close to her face, casting pale light over her features.

Ursula's eyes widened. "Princess Consort?"

"Do I still have to get my ass down there?"

"What are you doing?"

Starbride pushed off the side and dropped. Ursula shouted a warning and darted forward, but Starbride used flesh magic to make the impact ripple through her body as she landed on her feet.

To her credit, Ursula's mouth snapped shut quickly. "I'd heard you'd changed."

"Like I've developed a sunnier outlook on life? Well, I suppose I have."

Ursula's eyes found the pyramid in her forehead and over her heart.

Starbride lifted her hands. "Here, too."

"So I see."

"Are you wary of me now, Captain?"

"I'm wary of everyone."

"I should have expected that answer from you," Starbride said. "But you know enough to be warier of some people more than others."

Ursula's eyes turned to flint. "Ballantine. Is he still here?"

"Don't know and don't care."

This time, Ursula's mouth stayed open a little longer. "You stepped between us earlier. You do care about him, or I'm the king of thieves."

"To care is not a crime," Yanchasa said, "as long as it does not turn a strong heart to weakness."

Horsestrong couldn't have said it better. Starbride pictured Freddie sprawled dead on the ground or gone from her life forever. She would miss him, she decided, miss his sense of humor. Of course, he hadn't been laughing lately.

She'd have to help him remember how. "I don't want you to kill him."

"When it's lawful, it's called execution," Ursula said.

Starbride gave her a cold look. "Killing Freddie won't be lawful while I'm—"

"Are you about to say, 'in charge,' Princess Consort?" She cocked an eyebrow.

"The king is in charge. I'm just..." But what was she without Katya?

Ursula stepped forward. "Are you all right?"

"I'm fine! Why wouldn't I be?"

"Your face just, well, crumpled."

Starbride wrenched away. She couldn't seem to catch her breath as the world tilted. She sank to her knees as words abandoned her. The ground shifted, or was she falling? Dirt slid through her fingers as she caught herself. Ursula's voice gave way before the roaring in her ears. She reached for Yanchasa but felt nothing. Abandoned again. All she could see was a vision of the slender bit of metal that marked the place Katya and Dawnmother had died.

She'd died there, too, leaving a power-filled corpse, just like the rest of the remnants.

Starbride slapped the ground, and it shook, the force pulsing from her destructive pyramid reverberating through the street.

Ursula shook her shoulders, shouted in her ear, and Starbride wanted her to stop, wanted it all to stop. The power had seemed like enough, but oh, it wasn't, wasn't, wasn't.

"Enough, daughter."

The world faded to quiet, and a white void passed over Starbride's eyes, reminding her of the time she'd been blinded. Katya had taken care of her then. She could live in that memory, let it carry her away.

"Stop."

The memories of Katya froze and faded until all she could see was Yanchasa. Pain and loss faded to a dull, tolerable ache.

No pity or anger marred Yanchasa's face, only steely resolve. "Seek your sympathy or your rage elsewhere. Remember what little training the Farradains gave you. Remember what I taught you. Unless you'd rather be alone?"

The pain beckoned again, a world without love; a bleak, purposeless future.

"No!" Starbride grabbed for the adsna and let it flow through her. She fed her emotions into it, letting the river of power carry them away. The white void faded, and she realized she'd folded into a ball.

Awkward hands patted her back in endless little circles. "Can't leave her alone to go get help," Ursula mumbled. "Where's Rhys when I need him? Maybe I can carry her."

Before she could try, Starbride said. "Did you find Sergeant Rhys, then?"

The motion on her back ceased. "Are you back with us?" When Starbride didn't answer, Ursula said, "Found Rhys late this afternoon. He'd been hypnotized, but when we broke the pyramid, he came back to himself."

"Good." Starbride unfolded and sat up.

"We should get you inside," Ursula said. "You're cold to the bone."

"I'm fine."

"I'm sorry I called you Princess Consort. I shouldn't have done that."

Starbride got to her feet. "Who told you?"

"Rumor. I hoped it wasn't true, but after I saw that you're not together, and you…" She gestured to the cracks radiating out from where Starbride had fallen.

"Carry on, Captain." Starbride strode away, ignoring Ursula's questions, focusing on Yanchasa's presence, and letting nothing else enter her thoughts.

❖

The idea of sleep bored her, so Starbride strolled through the city. Some voices greeted her, but most gave her a wide berth, especially once they saw the pyramids. A few saw past them and clapped her on the back. One drunk woman swung her around by the arms, and Starbride let herself be pulled into the dance until the drunk woman fell to the ground.

Master Bernard and the few pyradistés left in the city gathered around the academy, clearing the courtyard of rubble and filth. He waved Starbride over and blinked at the pyramids glinting from her skin. Instead of horror, she saw a bloom of curiosity on his face that made her want to throw her arms around his neck.

"Are you planning to work until dawn?" Starbride asked.

"We were just about to call it a night," Master Bernard said. "There's nowhere to sleep inside the pyramid, and the dorms might not be safe, so we thought we might go back to the warehouse."

"The hideout? Haven't you had enough of that place?"

He shrugged. "We won't have to be on our guard there."

Her fellow pyramid users hiding in the dark, afraid of riffraff? The very idea offended. "I can keep you safe."

"Thank you, my dear, but we don't need a forest of traps."

"I wasn't talking about traps." She pushed through her flesh pyramid and put out a call. The chill in the air peaked, and she sensed Yanchasa's children hovering at the edge of the light. "Rest here or wherever it pleases you. You will be guarded."

Master Bernard and the others glanced around. Whether they could sense the children or not, they would detect the more ominous chill. "There's something in the shadows," one of the pyradistés squeaked.

"Guarding, not harming," Starbride said.

"You've *turned* them?" Master Bernard asked.

"Something like that."

"With?" He pointed to his own forehead and then hers.

She chuckled, and Yanchasa did the same. "Rest now," Starbride said. "Knowledge comes later." The pyradistés hurried off to one of the dorms, and Starbride commanded the children to watch over them. "I always liked him. How much can we share with them?"

"Enough but never all, daughter. I learned the lessons of Belshreth, so you won't ever have to."

The lessons of Belshreth served her well the next few hours. She settled several disputes, broke up a number of fights, scared away looters, and finished collecting all the remnants. She knew she'd have to do something with the hollow things soon. Their presence disturbed the populace more than it comforted them. Still, they were useful at the moment. She set them to watch the city as they'd done for Roland, only now for Einrich.

"I hope he appreciates you, daughter," Yanchasa said.

She tried to join in the revelry, but it never seemed to last long around her. Those so drunk they could barely stand welcomed her presence for as long as they stayed awake, but many seemed wary or too curious. She didn't want to repeat her story over and over.

Soon after dawn, as she lingered near the palace, she spied her opportunity to find out just how much the king had come to appreciate her. Einrich rode into the square with a contingent of guards, several nobles, and a handful of Allusians by his side. He gave the lean numbers that turned out to cheer him a royal wave.

From the steps of the palace, Starbride could read the tension in the line of his back, the sorrow in his shoulders that threatened to stoop with every step of his horse. His eyes softened when they fell on her, and she shifted from foot to foot. She hadn't realized she was so ready for him to be angry or imperious with her.

"Majesty," she said as he dismounted. She threw in a bow.

"Starbride." He grabbed her shoulders, greeting her as a relative even though she wasn't, would never be.

"Be easy, daughter," Yanchasa said.

Einrich bent to her ear. "I am grateful for everything you've done for me, for all of us, and for my kingdom. Please, always think of me as family."

Starbride felt tremors begin in her body but could do nothing to stop them.

Yanchasa said, "Focus inward," just as Einrich said, "I will always consider you a daughter."

Starbride wrapped her arms around Einrich and pressed him close. She heard the gasps, and the crowd murmured to itself. One did not embrace royalty in public, but she trembled so; she needed something to hold on to.

Einrich hesitated, and she was about to push away, but his arms closed around her, and he patted her back. "There now."

"Starbride?" several voices asked.

Starbride pulled away to see her parents coming from Einrich's pack, and there was Brutal, Maia, and Hugo, hope in their eyes.

Starbride turned away, letting the adsna flow. She showed weakness, and they were glad of it?

"They will be glad again of your strength soon enough," Yanchasa said.

Starbride stepped farther away. "Majesty, if you have any need of me, I am here."

He nodded once, and she thought she saw him tremble, too. "I'd like to see my family."

The dignitaries and Allusians remained in one of the ballrooms under the watchful eyes of Countess Nadia. Starbride's parents tried to press toward her, but she hurried away, leading the king along with Brutal, Maia, and Hugo. When Einrich didn't speak, the rest seemed inclined to silence. Starbride welcomed it and didn't look at them.

She hung back as Einrich lingered over his wife's body where it lay in the corridor. He didn't remove the coat from her face but bent close and whispered something. Maia knelt by her uncle's side, and Starbride stared at the floor. Maybe they'd feel better if she burned the queen's body to ash. Would they grieve less with nothing physical to mourn?

Had that helped her?

If she could only set the adsna roaring through them, it would wash away their grief. "The people of Belshreth must have never felt sadness," she whispered.

"You will feel all again one day, daughter, when the pain is less. Let the adsna be a balm. And for them," Yanchasa said, pointing at Einrich, "there's always mind magic."

She cocked her head and wondered what Roland's vision of eternal happiness for the kingdom would look like in the hands of a master.

At last, Einrich signaled Brutal to bear the queen away until she could be seen to. Some of the servants had already returned to the palace and some of the housekeepers as well, everyone eager, it seemed, for their lives to return to normal.

Starbride let Maia and Hugo take the lead as they ventured into the dark basement and then the caverns beneath the palace. Being this close to the capstone, to Yanchasa's physical body, made power hum in Starbride's ears, and she felt the comforting presence surround her, blocking out pain. They stepped over the bodies of fallen remnants, no one giving the poor dead things more than a glance.

At the bowl-shaped divot in the cavern floor where his daughter had been obliterated, Einrich stayed silent. More of the cavern had come down during the fight, and the floor was littered with stone. Starbride let the adsna flow until it screamed, and she felt hollow.

"I don't know if this cavern is safe, Majesty," Hugo said.

Maia clung to Einrich's arm. "Perhaps we should come away, Uncle."

Einrich pressed his palm to his mouth. Starbride thought he might collapse, but he exhaled and straightened. "You said you captured Roland, Starbride."

"Yes."

"Show me."

She led the way, her belly warming in anticipation of his gratitude.

Roland's screams had become a wheeze. Maybe the pyramid inside him kept him from healing. When he saw his brother pinned to the cavern floor, one-armed, sweating and writhing in agony, Einrich stopped mid-stride. "What have you done to him?"

"Less than he did to your wife and daughter, Majesty."

He turned a cold eye on her at last, and she welcomed it. When he turned back to Roland, she saw rage pass over his face. She thought he might stride forward and kick what little life remained from his brother, but he held himself rigid, fists curled at his side. Maia and Hugo approached their father with a myriad of expressions on their young faces.

"Why have you left him alive?" Einrich asked.

Starbride shrugged. "For the pain, and for you, of course. I thought you might want to have a hand in his death or at least witness it."

Einrich put his arms across Hugo's and Maia's shoulders. "I am not such a man. But he is too dangerous to keep captive for public execution."

At his feet, Roland opened his eyes and shrieked, "The pain!"

"End this torture," Einrich said.

Starbride dropped to Roland's side and opened his belly to remove the pyramid. The others gasped as they watched.

"How did you...and why?" Hugo asked.

Maia pressed her mouth as if she might be sick.

Starbride looked between their stricken faces. Roland had caused them such pain, and they felt only horror at seeing him tortured. She felt as if she would have understood that once.

"Do you want to do it?" Starbride asked.

Hugo and Maia didn't answer. Einrich's tendons stood out in his jaw. "I can't."

Starbride saw the problem: he had no weapon, and strength alone wouldn't prevail against Roland's Aspect. Very well. She would make it easier for him.

Starbride's flesh magic skittered along Roland's body as he sagged against the stone, still held by the remnants. He tried to speak, but she laid her destructive palm over his mouth.

His old wound called to her. The blow that had nearly severed his leg so long ago was still a part of him, the limb held in place only because he had merged with his Aspect. It made him slower than he should have been. The Aspect had caught him at the cusp of life and death, making him more corpse than man, the reason he'd needed his daughter to pass along the Aspect to others. If Starbride removed Yanchasa's gift, his leg might separate from his body.

Flesh held the answer, but Roland had barely scratched the surface of its uses. Starbride flexed her power and fused the leg back on to his body. Roland cried out against her palm, and she pressed down harder.

Einrich and the others shouted, wanting to know what she was doing, but she didn't bother to speak. They'd see soon enough.

When she was done with the leg, she searched him for other wounds but found only the missing hand. That she thought he should keep as a reminder.

"Ready to have some of your essence back?" she asked.

"What are you talking about?" Einrich asked. "What are you giving him?"

Yanchasa answered, "Ready, daughter."

Starbride focused on flesh again, on the rusty handle that lived inside all Umbriels and would turn them back into humans. She had cleansed one person of it before, had taken every ounce of Katya's Aspect and returned it to its rightful owner.

Starbride remembered Katya's energy as a ball of utter darkness, accessible only through Crowe's Fiend pyramid, but Starbride saw it in Roland for what it was: a collection of flesh energy nestled in the brain, spread from there throughout the body, and she had the siphon waiting in the center of this room.

Starbride tapped the energy, and it poured from Roland. He arched against the remnants' arms, his eyes rolling back in his head. Starbride used herself as a conduit, letting his power cascade with the rest of the adsna until it came to rest invisible in the capstone. When she'd drained him, he collapsed against the floor, blood leaking from his eyes, ears, and nose.

Yanchasa's laugh echoed inside Starbride like the peal of a golden bell. "The second gift you've given me, daughter!"

"The least I could do," Starbride said.

Roland lay still, unconscious but breathing, his cheeks pink with health beneath the blood, and his face never to hold its Aspect again. She sat back on her heels and commanded the remnants to withdraw.

"Miss Starbride?" Hugo said.

Maia fell to her knees. "Oh spirits."

Einrich grabbed Starbride's shoulder. "What have you done?"

She smiled up at him. "Made it easier for you." She looked to Yanchasa who was staring at the capstone, eyes narrowed. "What is it?"

"What do you mean?" Einrich asked.

"I think we should move away from here, daughter," Yanchasa said. "I have an uneasy feeling."

Starbride glanced at the capstone and reached out with her senses but felt nothing. Perhaps the adsnazi were entering the city. If they cleansed the capstone, she didn't know what might happen to the person who slumbered within. Yanchasa could be freed, she supposed, but it was just as likely that Allusian meddling would kill or hurt him in some way.

"Dearest daughter," Yanchasa said, face shifting between maternal and paternal smiles.

"Starbride? What have you done?" Einrich asked.

Starbride gestured one of the remnants forward, and it scooped Roland into its arms. "Shall we retire to the dungeon?" she asked. "Maybe you can have that execution you wanted."

They only stared at her, open-mouthed. She supposed she'd have to get used to that.

CHAPTER NINETEEN

KATYA

Katya stumbled through the tunnel, hardly seeing what was ahead. A few hours of sleep hadn't been enough, but Horsestrong and all ten spirits couldn't get her to stop and rest again. When she saw the shadow partially blocking the tunnel, she thought she'd finally become tired enough to hallucinate.

But Dawnmother said, "What's that?"

Katya pulled up short and blinked away fatigue. Something sat against the wall, large enough that they'd have to step over it. "Legs?"

"Attached to what could only be a body," Redtrue said.

Katya drew her belt knife as they crept closer. A musty smell washed over her, past the dry scent of stone and dust that had tickled her nostrils since she'd come to this place. As soon as light fell over the body, Katya put her knife away. This was one corpse, at least, that wouldn't be getting up to attack them anytime soon.

The skeleton had a few leathery patches of flesh still attached to its face, though its limbs were bare of skin, and its clothing had gone to rags. All had turned the same grayish brown as the surrounding stone.

Katya knelt in front of the empty sockets. She couldn't tell if this had been a man or a woman. It wore trousers and a shirt of an indiscriminate color, but the make was utilitarian and without adornment. A curved knife lay near the skeleton's outstretched fingers; the others curled in its lap.

Katya picked up the knife and studied the handle, but the plain, wrapped leather gave her no clues. She set it back down at the skeleton's side.

"There are more," Redtrue said.

Another skeleton lay stretched down the middle of the tunnel. An arrowhead stuck from its back, caught in a rib, and one hand lay pointed down the tunnel as if showing the way out. They stepped over it carefully and continued into the open space beyond.

Katya's heartbeat quickened at the scene of ancient slaughter. Skeletons lay scattered across the long room along with weapons and tools. Dawnmother knelt next to one and shifted a pickaxe out of its bony fingers. Beneath it was a rust colored stain of long-dried blood. Another slumped against the wall, its jaw and half its lower face missing, slashed away. A few more sported arrows or deep tears through the remains of their clothing, exposing nicked and broken bones.

"Someone killed them all," Katya said.

"Why were they left here?" Redtrue asked, turning a slow circle.

Katya shook her head, but she could guess. It would have taken a lot of effort to haul this many bodies through the tunnels. Perhaps whoever had killed them had thought them not worth the bother.

Another stain lay off on its own, a puddle so large she didn't think anyone could have survived its loss. "Someone was killed here and then moved." A friend of the attackers? If she had come down here with the Order, chasing someone, she would have carted off her own wounded and dead and might have left the rest.

As she took a closer look at the room, she saw that this space had never been someone's home or shop. The floor and ceiling were unfinished and choppy, the walls pitted and crooked. The tunnel makers had carved this from solid debris. "By the tools they're holding, I think these must be the tunnel makers. They must have retreated here during an attack."

"It didn't do them much good," Redtrue said. "Were these some of the original inhabitants of this land? Did your people not stop until they'd killed them all?"

Katya shook her head. "I won't let you bait me into a fight." Redtrue bristled, but Katya ignored her. "Besides, we've decided that this had to have happened a long time after my people first arrived. The stone here had to settle enough that these people could build tunnels."

But, she reminded herself, they'd also been drawn to rooms that had been important to the original inhabitants, and it was clear that the pyramid had always been their goal. Maybe whoever had made these tunnels were *descended* from the original inhabitants. They hadn't all been killed when her people took over. Some of them had probably survived, interbred, and remembered.

But remembered what?

Dawnmother poked her head into the continuing tunnel. "The tunnel ends here."

Katya shuddered at the thought that they might have reached the end of their hoped-for way out. If the way into these ancient tunnels had been sealed, they could be trapped under tons of rock with nothing but the dead to keep them company.

And Yanchasa, of course.

Katya gritted her teeth and stared at the dead-end. It was green-flecked stone that stood out sharply against the gray rock. By the steady light of the pyramid, she followed the new stone upward to a large hole above them. "Bring the light closer."

She stood on tiptoe. The tunnel continued above their heads in a gentle slope, following the green-flecked stone. Katya couldn't keep in a grin. "It's the pyramid. We've made it."

When she glanced at Redtrue, the tunnel wall caught her eye. Rust colored stains covered it, too, but these had been shaped into letters.

"Those are not Allusian," Redtrue said.

Katya shook her head. It was an older dialect, but one she still recognized. "They're Farradain."

❖

Before they began the arduous climb, Dawnmother insisted they rest, even if it had to be among the dead. They ate the last of their food and water. Katya sat and stared at the Farradain letters written in someone's blood. She couldn't make out all of them, but what she could gather gave her a good approximation:

"Do not seek the Fiend, or you shall die as these." Beneath it was a mark she'd studied under Crowe's tutelage.

The Order of Vestra hadn't always been as secretive as it was now. Always a shadowy group, some of her forebears had thought to give it an ominous reputation. Whenever they apprehended criminals or traitors, they left a mark, something to strike fear into the hearts of any traitors who might have escaped, a stylized O and V, linked together.

The mark in front of her wasn't as graceful as what she'd seen in books, but given the medium, she wasn't surprised.

"So," Redtrue said, "whoever made these tunnels sought Fiends as well as your spirits, just as I suspected."

Katya rested her chin on one fist. It certainly seemed as if the tunnel builders had been looking for the Fiend, or at least the Order had thought so. But what would they want with it? Their ancestors had seen the havoc it could wreak. Surely they didn't think they could control it if they let it out.

"Perhaps they thought it could be banished, and with it gone, the Farradains would have no power," Redtrue said.

"That's a long time to hold a grudge."

"The Umbriels were able to maintain a secret society since they first arrived here," Dawnmother said. "Why would you think no one else could?"

A secret order dedicated to pushing the Farradains out of Marienne? Hopelessly outnumbered, perhaps the tunnel builders thought Yanchasa was their only hope for victory. But if they knew how to summon Yanchasa, then the method wasn't as lost as Katya had originally assumed.

Katya peered up the tunnel that ran along the pyramid's side. Luckily, it wasn't a straight climb; the tunnel zigged and zagged in a series of ledges. If they were careful, they wouldn't need rope. "Shall we climb?"

Redtrue cradled her ribs as if the idea pained her. Dawnmother helped her bind them tighter, but Katya knew she'd be in agony before she reached the top.

"I could go alone," Katya said. "You command the light pyramid to keep glowing; I try to make myself known at the top."

"If there is no one in the capstone chamber, you would never be heard," Dawnmother pointed out.

"I can get us through the stone," Redtrue said. She glanced at Dawnmother. "But you could stay and wait for help."

Dawnmother tossed her braid over her shoulder. "And then who would help the two of you to the top? Off you go. I'll be just behind."

Katya stepped into the short tunnel, ignored the bloody writing on the wall, and wiped her hands on her trousers. Grabbing hold of the jagged tunnel lip above, she bounced a couple times on her toes and then used the side of the pyramid to push up. She found the first platform of stone, a little nook she could fold part of herself into, balancing on her knees. The tunnel resembled a stubby stairwell that more or less followed the pyramid's side. Katya pulled up into a new hollow and then had to turn and brace against the pyramid again. If she slipped, she wouldn't go far before banging into the next lip down. It was hard going, but at least the tunnel offered many chances to sink down in a crouch against the pyramid's smooth surface.

She had to wonder if the tunnel builders had hoped to make something more permanent, replacing this body-torturing tunnel with steps driven into the pyramid's side or a rope they could use to haul themselves up. But the Order of Vestra hadn't given them the chance. If they had managed to break into the capstone cavern, they would have been kicking themselves when they found the tunnels the Farradains had made for that very purpose.

She closed her eyes when she rested, imagining a sunny meadow or wide forest. As she climbed, she tried to think only of the top, but she had no way of knowing how high they'd progressed. No matter which way she turned, the rock waited only a foot from her face.

When Katya stopped to rest again, she closed her eyes and thought of the great Fiend that slumbered behind her back. Was Yanchasa ever restless? She'd felt the trembles as Roland tried to wake it, but did it always twitch slightly, something they wouldn't feel? Did it know she was so close? Maybe it could sense Redtrue as she could sense it.

Katya tried to shake such thoughts away. "How's everyone doing?"

Only the sound of breathing answered for a few moments. "Keeping up," Dawnmother called.

"Can we rest?" Redtrue said as a series of gasps.

"Lean against the pyramid if you can."

Redtrue mumbled something about trying to stay away from the pyramid as much as she could.

"A losing battle, no?" Dawnmother called. "I'm sure Horsestrong's wisdom is in there somewhere, but I can't think of it right now."

Katya didn't want to nag them to keep going. Redtrue couldn't be having an easy time. But grief and anxiety and fear were piling up inside Katya. If she didn't get out of this dark, close place, this city of the dead, she'd clap her hands over her eyes and scream.

"I'm going to keep on," Katya said.

She heard Redtrue grumble to a start again. Good. If she'd been forced to scream at the top and hope that someone would hear her, she might have gone mad.

Katya commanded her arms to grab hold of the next ledge. She told herself to turn, to brace against the pyramid and push up, and then turn again. She shut out everything else, only slowing when the light began to dim, and she knew Redtrue had stopped to rest. Then Katya braced her back, closed her eyes, and lost herself in the tingling relief of her resting arms and the protests from her thighs.

When the light came closer, Katya climbed, using raw, bleeding fingers to search for the next hold. Finally she turned, felt upward, and encountered only smooth stone.

"We're here," she called.

"Horsestrong be praised!" Dawnmother called.

Redtrue only mumbled something.

"Can you feel the stone?" Katya asked. She bent until she could see Redtrue's face just below her.

"Give me time."

Katya fought the urge to say that she wanted out of this cursed place now. She took a deep breath, counted to five, and let it out again. When she'd done this three times, the stone above her head shifted.

Katya watched it closely, picturing the whole of it crashing down. They wouldn't be able to make it down the tunnel before the entire place caved in. And even if by some miracle they did, where could they go?

The stone rippled, shifting away from the pyramid's side. Some of it trickled past, turned to sand, and Katya closed her teeth on a yelp. As the rock flowed, it left a gap just large enough to slide through, a way to wriggle between pyramid and stone.

Katya eyed the small gap and knew she couldn't do it, couldn't go where the stone would be pushing against her back and chest, cutting off her air.

"We need to go higher," Redtrue said, "before I can focus again."

Katya opened her mouth, but no sound would come out. She couldn't say what she wanted to, that she'd wait here for rescue. They could climb past her.

But the space was too small for that.

All of them could live here together! Redtrue would make a hole big enough for the people above to pass them food and water, and they'd be fine. She nearly laughed, but she knew how shrill and crazed she would sound.

Katya lifted her arms into the gap while her brain shrieked that she couldn't do this, she wouldn't. Her body would shut itself off in protest.

No! By all ten spirits, she would do her damned duty! She had hunted traitors, fought Fiends, rode at the head of an army, killed a dear friend, and watched her mother die. "I will not be defeated by a fucking hole in the ground," she said between clenched teeth.

The stone continued to shift above her head, and she wriggled upward, eyes closed so she wouldn't have to see the rock inches from her nose. Redtrue's ragged breathing followed. Dawnmother grunted as she climbed, no doubt pushing Redtrue upward.

Katya clutched the wall and gritted her teeth, tasting the dust, becoming one with it. She felt far above her head and finally encountered empty air.

She turned her head as much as she could, amazed at the soft glow coming from above instead of below. She launched herself upward but slipped, sliding downward a few inches. Redtrue cried a protest. Katya took a shallow breath, all she could manage with the stone pressing against her. She forced herself to calm before she inched upward and pulled into the toothy maw of the capstone cavern.

CHAPTER TWENTY

STARBRIDE

Starbride sat cross-legged in the dungeon while Roland slept on the floor. Einrich and the others had made excuses and left. She knew they were pained by the sight of their kinsman, though she couldn't say why. Roland wasn't fearsome anymore. Without the powers of flesh, he was less than nothing, just as she'd suspected all along. He was still a pyradisté, and the dungeon was full of trap pyramids, but without the flesh magic riding him, he couldn't retune them. He hadn't learned their secrets as she had.

Starbride felt over Roland with flesh magic and brought him awake with a start.

He gasped, eyes wide. When his gaze landed on her, he uttered a low moan. "What have you done?"

"Sorry, we've done that bit already." Einrich had kept asking it even after she told him.

Roland felt along his face. "You took the Fiend away."

"There are no such things as Fiends."

He glanced at her sharply. "You've taken it into yourself."

Yanchasa appeared behind him. "I can't stand the way they say that."

Starbride sighed. "He or she. There is no *it*."

Roland trembled, pale. She remembered Maia's first awakening in the strength chapterhouse after they'd rescued her: shock followed by crippling sorrow as she remembered everything she'd done. Of course, Maia had only been under the influence of Yanchasa's darker side for a few months. Roland had been living with it for eight years.

He curled around himself and sobbed.

"Crying won't save you now," Starbride said.

"I want to die!" He crawled toward her, all the way to the end of his chains. "I was trying to help everyone!" He blinked. "Or was I?"

Would Einrich thank her if she killed him? "Your time will come." She'd let Einrich decide. If he asked her to kill his brother, she would, but it had to be his decision.

"You can't let it control you." The stump of Roland's right arm grazed her boot. "Get rid of it before it's too late."

"*It* again," Yanchasa said. "Idiot."

"Just because you were afraid of power doesn't mean I am," Starbride said.

He laughed, hysterical shrieks echoing around the cell. When he stilled, he lay on his back, staring at the ceiling. "I kept some control. Even with the Fiend, I kept some of myself, but you're lost."

"I have more of my mind than you ever did!"

He shook his head, tears leaving tracks across his temples. "I wanted everyone to be happy, whether they wanted it or not. No crime, no traitors, just bliss."

"Happy to starve to death, to burn?"

"You won't care about anything. You'll remake us to suit your needs or just turn us to dust." His eyes drifted shut. "Dust."

"The loss of my flesh has driven him insane," Yanchasa said.

Starbride couldn't let it go so easily. "I am myself, you charlatan. Yanchasa's shown me more than you could ever imagine while you existed on scraps. You were brutal and petty, the only aspects of mighty Belshreth you could understand."

He laughed again. "You've killed us all."

"Come away, daughter," Yanchasa said.

Starbride stood to join him at the cell door when Roland called out.

"Have you found them all yet?"

Starbride paused. "Found what?"

"Me."

Her heart sped a little faster, and she thought of Alphonse, Roland's copy. "How many are there?"

He beat one fist against his forehead as if trying to remember. "I lost track. Please, don't let them hurt anyone else."

"Now you need my power? Where are these copies?"

"I sent them out for Katya!" He beamed at her like a child expecting praise. "That's where they must be."

She shrugged. "Then they're dead. I destroyed your army."

He breathed a sigh of relief. "Thank you."

"I don't want your thanks!" The adsna dulled, snuffed by a tide of anger. "You should burn, you bastard, die the way she did!" She thrust her arm forward, ready to call upon the same destructive sphere that had swallowed Katya and Dawnmother.

The adsna hit her with such force that she staggered. It swept away her feelings like a harsh winter wind. When she straightened, she couldn't even remember what anger felt like.

"Softly, daughter," Yanchasa said. "He could be useful. The more the king depends on your power—either to kill this man or wring information from him—the more solid your position will be."

Solid, yes. Everyone needed to believe she could finish what she started. Starbride strode from the cell and shut the door. "No good can come from losing my temper."

"Excellent, daughter. Everyone in the kingdom will benefit from your wisdom."

And if they wouldn't listen, she would not take Roland's path. She would show them she was right, carefully, calmly, and a good way to start was by continuing to help with city reconstruction.

When she reached the receiving room that guarded the way out of the palace, her parents were waiting. Starbride pulled up short, uneasy, the adsna fluttering in and out of reach.

"They are just two more people, daughter," Yanchasa said.

"You don't know them," Starbride mumbled. She could race around them, she supposed, but she'd have to confront them sometime. She steeled herself for their embrace.

Her mother got to her first, throwing her arms around Starbride and doling out both love and recriminations, as if nothing had happened in the time they'd been apart. They didn't stare at her pyramids, but she knew the questions would come soon enough.

When her father swallowed her in a hug, her world seemed to buckle as it had when Einrich had embraced her. Much as he claimed to care, though, Einrich wasn't her father, hadn't been the one to hold her when she was hurt, to sing to her when she was sick. She recalled spending hours on her father's lap while he plied his trade, lithe brown fingers bending silver or gold, working with tiny stones held in tweezers.

"Papa," she sobbed into his shoulder.

"It's all right, my lucky Star."

Starbride's mother harrumphed. "It is most certainly not all right. This place is a shambles. I've had to give no end of advice about how to set it straight."

Starbride laughed through her tears. "I'm sure you minded that a great deal."

"We'll have none of your lip, thank you."

Starbride pulled back to look at them both. Her mother had changed into one of the frothy dresses the Farradains favored. Her hair had been artfully arranged on top of her head, no doubt by Rainhopeful, who hovered just behind her. Her father wore flowing Allusian trousers, though her mother had forced him into an embroidered Farradain coat. It seemed a little loose, as if she'd borrowed it from someone, or maybe he'd just lost weight. His round face seemed gaunter than she remembered, and both of them had more gray mixed with their black hair.

Her father's servant, Lakeloyal, stood beside Rainhopeful, and Starbride nodded to both of them. Their nod back was hesitant, tinged with sorrow, and she knew why. Not for Katya, but for Dawnmother. All Allusians servants would be giving her that look now.

"I'm so sorry, Star." Her father cupped her cheeks, and she read in his eyes the grief she should have felt. She wanted to throw herself into his arms again, but Yanchasa's spectral hand hovered on her shoulder, and she knew they weren't alone. Other dignitaries, courtiers, and nobles lingered in the halls beyond, waiting to see what she would do.

Starbride fed her feelings into the adsna and let it carry them away. Her mother stepped in front of her father, breaking their contact. Her fingers passed over Starbride's forehead. "Tell us, daughter."

The words were too close to something Yanchasa might say. "I don't have time."

"Don't have *time?*" her mother said.

Her father wound his arm through hers. "Later, Star? Let us help you."

She smiled, so grateful she hugged him again. "Later, Papa."

"But where are you off to?" her mother asked.

Starbride wanted to say, "Anywhere but here." Instead she said, "Wherever they need me," and continued out the front doors. As she passed down the steps, the flow of people entering and leaving the palace gave her a wide berth, as if tales of her deeds had already spread. She didn't mind. It hastened her journey.

Before she could enter the city, she spied someone else waiting and watching the palace from the shadows of a counting house. As Starbride approached, the watcher stepped into the light.

Castelle had lost her hat somewhere along the way. At least she'd changed out of the blood-soaked rags she'd been wearing the last time Starbride had seen her. She still seemed pale, and Starbride bet she'd either argued her way out of bed or slipped away unnoticed.

"I didn't know I'd kept so many people waiting today," Starbride said.

"I'm told I have you to thank for saving me." Her voice was still distorted. The swelling on her face had gone down, but the flesh was still bruised, and the angry line of stitches holding her cheek together said she would have a scar running the length of her face. Starbride smiled, glad she'd let Castelle keep the wound. Maybe it would remind her never to break anyone's heart again.

"Is there something you wanted?" Starbride asked.

Castelle closed her eyes, and Starbride saw the glimmer of tears in her lashes.

"If you're looking for someone to grieve with," Starbride said, "you'll have to look elsewhere. I'm busy."

"I wish I could be busy."

"And why can't you?"

She shrugged. Maybe that's what their entire conversation would come down to.

"You can come with me," Starbride said. "There's a lot of wreckage and such to clean up, a lot of people to sort out."

After another shrug, she trailed in Starbride's wake.

Yanchasa showed her the trick of how to move the adsna through stone using utility magic. The Farradains had never discovered it because they *never* let the adsna flow. They always had to be in control. The Allusians had the knack, based on what Katya had told her, but they wouldn't let themselves recognize the scale on which it could be useful. Starbride mended buildings and hustled huge chunks of debris out of the street. People around her marveled while Castelle directed traffic, and several remnants cleared the streets of smaller detritus.

Even with all the work, Castelle didn't lose her downtrodden look. "Is this what we're supposed to do now? Stay busy?"

"Are you only now realizing you loved Redtrue?"

"I did. I know it. I loved her, and Katya…" Castelle stared at Starbride with haunted eyes. "I was jealous of you. No matter what had happened in the past, I thought she'd never be able to resist me. I thought you were lucky, now I just…Starbride, I'm so sorry."

"Save your pity for someone who needs it."

Castelle sank down in the dust, leaning against a storefront. She looked like someone had beaten her, body and spirit.

Starbride sighed. "I can take it away if you want."

Castelle blinked at her with witless cow eyes.

"Your memories. I can take Redtrue and whomever." She couldn't say that she could erase Katya, not so easily. "I can fill in the gaps with whatever you like or nothing at all. It'll be as if you lost your memory, as if you'd never even come to court."

"You can do that?"

Starbride nodded and watched the emotions play across Castelle's face.

"Would you do it, if you were me?" Castelle asked. "Don't you want to grieve?"

Was this the plan for the indeterminate future? Everyone wanting her to sit in a corner and cry with them? The dead wouldn't want that.

"No," Starbride said. "Decide, please. I have things to do." She crossed her arms. One more minute and then she'd walk away.

CHAPTER TWENTY-ONE

KATYA

Katya, Redtrue, and Dawnmother limped through the larger tunnels leading toward the palace. Katya gritted her teeth at their slow passage, at still being out of the sun and air. They passed smears of blood and dead corpse Fiends. The tunnels were littered with debris, especially the one Katya thought they'd fallen from. She saw the bowl-shaped divot in the dirt and frowned. Someone had thrown a disintegration pyramid, and she had no idea who might have been caught in the blast.

"Come on," she prompted them, and they leaned on one another as they sought the way out.

When they reached the laundry still unmolested or greeted, Katya didn't know what to think. They'd seen no sign that anyone had been digging for them, but the tunnels weren't crawling with enemies either.

They wound through the basement and climbed the stairs, and as Katya reached the top, she heard a shriek. She turned toward the noise and drew her knife but saw only the back of a fleeing woman in livery and a bundle of sheets left behind.

"Well, unless Roland has hypnotized people into doing the laundry, that's a good sign," Dawnmother said.

The return of servants to the palace could only mean one thing. "She's won. Starbride did it." She beamed at the others until even Redtrue gave her a small smile.

The reasons why no one searched for them could wait. They found the fastest way up and into the halls. Katya headed for the greatest collection of voices and found a large room near the entrance of the palace practically bursting with people. A few of them screamed when they saw her, and she pulled up short.

Countess Nadia rushed forth from the pack. "Highness! We heard you'd been killed!"

"By whom?"

"The usurper, of course." She looked back and forth between them. "You look as if you've crawled out of your graves."

Dirty, sweaty, bloody, she bet they looked exactly the part. "Where is Starbride?"

Nadia hesitated, and Katya resisted the urge to grab her lapels. "She is not dead," Katya said, putting force behind the words to make them real.

"No, no, I'm sorry. She's not dead."

"But she thinks you are." Brightstriving emerged from the crowd like a ship before the waves. She bowed, and her husband followed her. "Where have you been?"

Katya almost laughed at the archness in her tone, but she was too tired. "Do you know where Starbride is now?" Her heart ached at the thought of Starbride thinking her dead. Guessing at Starbride's fate while they'd been apart had been bad enough, but to *know* of her demise? It had to have been the disintegration pyramid. They'd fallen just as it went off. The whole kingdom probably thought she was dead, her father included.

"Starbride went into the city," Brightstriving said, "to help people."

Nadia gave her a sideways glance, though Katya couldn't imagine why. "And my family?"

"Your father went to look for your, well, I would say body, but we thought you'd been consumed by a pyramid, Highness," Nadia said. "I am so sorry to hear of the queen's death."

Ah, grief. It had given way to worry for a moment. "Thank you."

"I don't suppose anyone kept track of Baroness Castelle?" Redtrue asked.

When everyone shook their heads, Redtrue rolled her eyes as if to lament the fact that her problems were less significant than those around her.

"Countess," Katya said, "please tell my father I'm alive. I must find Starbride, and I know Dawnmother is as anxious as I am."

Dawnmother nodded, gratitude in her eyes.

Katya turned to Redtrue. "If I know Castelle and tragedy, she'll find the nearest bar." She gestured toward the doors. "Can you manage?"

Redtrue eyed the floor as if she might not have the will to put one foot in front of the other, but she nodded. Dawnmother offered a shoulder to lean on. Katya walked under her own power and tried to dust her clothes off, but it was no use. She would have changed into diamonds and silks if it would have helped her find Starbride, but she knew she'd be loved just as she was.

"Highness," Nadia said as she walked with them, "perhaps we could send someone looking in your stead?"

And leave her alone to pace and worry? "No, thank you, Countess. I'll find her."

"Perhaps someone could aid you? Fetch you some water, at least."

"If you want to send your own searchers, Countess, be my guest. As for the water, I'm afraid I can't wait." It would be nice, and so would a chair, but she felt as if Starbride's spirit pulled her along, and she couldn't resist or she'd break apart.

Nadia stepped in front of her, and Katya staggered. Yes, this was court, where everyone wanted to talk everything to death. "What is it, Countess?"

"Starbride is not quite as you knew her."

"What are you talking about?"

Brightstriving caught Nadia's arm. "Grief, that's all. Once Star sees you, she will be herself again."

Katya made for the doors again, even more determined. If Starbride had defeated Roland, no doubt she had to use some grief-filled rage to do so. But like Brightstriving said, all would be right once they saw one another again.

They headed toward the closest tavern, asking along the way if anyone had seen Starbride or Castelle. To Katya's surprise, everyone seemed to remember Starbride, at least. Still, there was no reason to worry. There weren't many Allusians in town, and Starbride was famous as the leader of the rebellion. Some of the townspeople still had her colors pinned to their sleeves.

As more people grimaced when they heard Starbride's name, unease tightened Katya's shoulders. The crowd parted, and Katya pulled up short, her body going cold. A gray-skinned corpse Fiend was digging through the rubble of an abandoned house. It shifted stone and wood into little piles with the same mindless exuberance she remembered from when its kind had tried to murder her.

Passersby gave the corpse a wide berth but seemed neither terrified nor blissfully hypnotized. Katya's hand twitched toward her knife, but the dead thing didn't seem inclined to hurt anyone. This had to have something to do with Starbride, with her being not quite as Katya knew her. The cold wind gusted, whipping right through her tattered coat.

"Castelle!" Redtrue cried.

Katya turned at the happy cry. Redtrue hobbled down the street toward where Castelle sat against a tumbledown building. Castelle blinked a few times, frowning as if she didn't know them.

As Redtrue came closer, she rubbed her eyes. "Red? Is that you?" She pushed up against the building, but when Redtrue reached her, they collapsed in a crying heap, arms entangled, both of them babbling.

"But where is Star?" Dawnmother asked.

Katya scanned the crowd but didn't see her. She moved to Redtrue and Castelle, sorry to interrupt their happiness, but she needed answers.

"You're all alive!" Castelle shouted. She grinned so hard, her slashed cheek began to seep around its stitches.

"Watch your—" Katya started, but Castelle sprang up and wrapped her arms around Katya, threatening to send them both to the ground.

Katya grunted, and Castelle staggered, unable to keep her feet. Katya put an arm out to steady her and looked hard at her pale face. "Are you wounded or drunk?"

"Can't I be both?"

Katya barked a laugh.

"How did the three of you escape from that disintegration pyramid?"

"We were never caught by it," Redtrue said as Castelle helped her up. "I shall tell you about it after we find a healer. There should be several in the Allusian camp."

Castelle embraced her more gently. "There are healers in Marienne."

"There are many things in Marienne," Redtrue said, eyeing the corpse Fiend.

"Have you seen Starbride?" Katya asked, the one question she wanted answered more than, "What is that thing doing cleaning up the street?"

Castelle's face held that same hesitation, that tiny bit of fear.

"What is wrong with everyone?" Katya asked.

"She did something with the pyramid, the one underground," Castelle said. "I'm not a pyradisté, so I don't know exactly what. She saved my life."

"And that frightens you?"

"I can't explain."

"Just tell me where you saw her last."

"After she gave that thing instructions, she took the side street."

"Gave it instructions," Katya echoed. Well, she could stand there and gawk, or she could get moving.

By the time Katya and Dawnmother had walked down the side street, Starbride was gone, and they were pointed in a different direction, back toward the palace.

"We should write this down," Katya said after a growl. "It'll make a wonderful farce."

"I should have stayed in the palace," Dawnmother said. "I could have gotten everything ready for her."

"I wouldn't rob you of the chance to find her," Katya said.

"If she had come home first, I would have sent all the servants out to scour the city and bring you back."

"Much appreciated." She put a hand on Dawnmother's arm as she spied another corpse Fiend, this one lifting a sagging porch with a wooden brace.

"Left!" a voice called. Katya's head whipped toward the sound.

Starbride still wore her black leather outfit, the one that hugged her curves, and even with her hair untidy, a few laces open at the neck, and dust sprinkling her from head to toe, she looked glorious, her profile standing out starkly against the pale building behind her. She had one fist on her hip, and the other waved in the corpse Fiend's direction.

"Star!" Dawnmother called. She ran forward.

Starbride turned, and Katya's breath caught. Starbride's beauty always affected her, but this was more: the tiny triangle glowing in her forehead, a similar glow above her heart. It was the oddest jewelry Katya had ever seen, but it didn't stop her from hurrying forward.

Dawnmother hit Starbride in a shambling run, but instead of both of them going down in a heap of limbs, Dawnmother bounced back as if Starbride were a marble column. Starbride had to fling an arm out to grab her.

"Dawn?" Even as Dawnmother threw an arm around her shoulders, Starbride looked past her. "Katya?" Her mouth wobbled and turned down before hardening and then turning down again.

Katya could understand. She felt so much, and she'd only had to fight Roland once that day. And she'd never had to face the fact that the love of her life was *dead*. Katya put her arms around Starbride and Dawnmother both. As Starbride's embrace settled around her, Katya was struck by her strength as well as the fact that she felt colder than the winter wind.

CHAPTER TWENTY-TWO

STARBRIDE

Dawnmother was alive. Katya was alive. Starbride's brain repeated those words until they penetrated the adsna. They were filthy, stinking of dirt and sweat. They trembled in her arms. If she wanted, she could pluck them both up and carry them down the street.

"Is this real?" she whispered.

"It seems so, daughter," Yanchasa said, though Starbride could barely hear him over the chanting in her mind. Dawnmother was alive. Katya was alive.

They were weeping, and she felt a tickle along her own cheeks. Why was she weeping? Because, a voice inside her screamed, Dawnmother and Katya were alive!

If Lord Vincent found out, would he be smug?

"I'm so glad you're all right," Dawnmother said, just as Katya said, "You are the best sight I've ever seen in my life."

They both laughed, and Starbride tried to join them.

Katya grinned through her tears. "Are you taller, or do you have new boots?"

"I was going to ask that later," Dawnmother said. They pulled Starbride into separate hugs without waiting for an answer. Katya's lips pressed to hers, and they were so *warm*. Starbride held her, relishing that warmth before she stepped back and wondered at the color in Katya's cheeks.

Katya took Starbride's hands and frowned at the palms as if she might ask about the pyramids, but she only smiled. "I'm so sorry I worried you, my love."

Starbride tried to feel the moment, but it wouldn't quite come. The adsna didn't want to be dismissed. She tried to make the world tilt as it had before, but all she felt was caution. *Are you sure this isn't a trick?* she asked Yanchasa.

"I can only be as certain as you are."

"Are you hurt?" Starbride managed.

"Tired mostly," Katya said. She couldn't seem to keep her hands to herself, and they burned wherever they touched. Starbride pinned a smile on her face. As she caressed Katya's side and settled on a hip, a memory half arose: Katya in the bath, wet hair streaming across her shoulders and breasts. A flush built in Starbride's cheeks and cascaded through her body. She met Katya's eyes and saw her feelings reflected there. Katya lifted her hand and kissed it, dirt and all.

"Let's put you both to bed." Starbride linked her arms through theirs and led them toward the palace, suffering their squeezes and hurried words. She could barely listen, desperate to explore the feelings Katya stirred within her. If she could just find the right balance of hot and cold...

"Hmm," Yanchasa said.

Starbride blocked out the voices of the others. *What is it?*

Yanchasa fell into step at Dawnmother's side. "I was just noticing the way they're all looking at her now."

Starbride glanced around. The townspeople who'd been so leery of her were smiling and bowing for Katya.

"As if she's the one who led their rebellion," Yanchasa said.

She is their princess.

"Well, then all their problems are solved! Dear Princess Katyarianna is all they need."

Fear wormed into Starbride, digging past Katya's heat. With Katya back, what use would there be for her? It would be parties and croquet and listening to dull nobles with boring problems. Worse, she'd be standing at the back with the courtiers again.

No! As Princess Consort, I'll be at the front of the dais.

"Yes, at Katya's side and just a little behind, and her behind the king. Unless the king gives the prince his position back, and then you'll be four people behind. Unless the children are in there with Lord Vincent."

Starbride fought the urge to shake her head. Even now, Katya and Dawnmother had little frowns on their faces.

"All that power," Yanchasa said, "forced to stand at the back."

Starbride couldn't believe it. They'd seen what she could do. No one would ever be able to dismiss her again, to leave her out, leave her behind, *abandon* her.

"That's right, daughter, not after you show them your power."

Yes, Katya couldn't match what Starbride had learned. Princess or not, she would accept the newfound power at her side, *just* at her side, no more standing behind.

They hurried past the people gathered in the palace entry and made for the stairs. "You'll want to see your father first," Starbride said, remembering her courtesies.

Katya gave her another of those doubtful looks that quickly transmuted to one of love. She ran her knuckles down Starbride's cheek. "Come with me?"

Katya needed her support. Starbride flicked her eyes to Yanchasa, who raised his hands in mock surrender. "I see how she needs you, daughter."

The king had taken up residence in the summer apartments. Perhaps Roland had left too much of his stamp on the winter ones, though now everyone had more need of the indoor rooms. Starbride imagined the summer balconies and windows would feel chilly for those ill-equipped to deal with them.

Stepping inside the king's informal sitting room, Starbride could feel the bubble of grief. From just outside the circle of friends and family, Lord Vincent turned. His gaze remained steely until he saw Katya, and then he bowed, his gray eyes widening.

Einrich, Reinholt, Maia, and the children formed a little huddle in the middle of the room. Past them, Hugo, Brutal, and Freddie gathered near the wall. Starbride let Katya go, and everyone converged on her, talking and crying over each other.

Dawnmother stayed at Starbride's shoulder. "How long were you outside, Star? Your skin is like ice."

She wasn't as cold as some. On the bed lay a cloth-covered body, probably the queen's. Starbride had to wonder how long they'd let her lay there. Once Katya left, would they all succumb to grief again?

Hugo and Maia pulled Dawnmother into an embrace, both of them avoiding Starbride's gaze. Freddie stared at her curiously over Dawnmother's shoulder as they hugged. After the initial questions were answered, Katya turned to Starbride with love in her eyes. The others might be wary, but Katya could see the physical changes and still believed the woman inside was the same.

Finally, the faith Starbride had been looking for. The happiness she thought she'd lost filled her somewhat, but she knew it should have been greater. She should have thrown herself at Katya the moment their eyes met. She tried then, letting Katya's arms enfold her while those around them cooed.

"We did it, love," Katya mumbled. "We're all together again."

Starbride cocked her head. Who was "we" who did "it" exactly? She remembered being alone on the battlefield.

But Katya had lost her mother. She had a right to be confused. But Starbride knew one thing that would cheer her more than having her family and friends back together.

"I caught him for you, Katya."

"Caught?"

"Roland. And now you don't need a Fiend to take revenge on him. You can do it however you please, and your spirit will be at peace."

When Katya still seemed confused, Starbride said, "I took his Aspect away. He's locked in the dungeon, waiting for you."

Katya didn't lose her frown, and Starbride wondered if she'd started speaking Allusian. Maybe she'd lapsed into ancient Belshrethen.

"No, daughter, she doesn't see the gift you've given her," Yanchasa said.

But how could that be? Before she could try again, Einrich cleared his throat. "Let us rejoice that our grief is not as great as we thought it to be. Darker matters can wait."

Darker matters? Revenge was a reason to rejoice, or had she been mistaken all this time?

Still, they seemed content to be near one another. She could feel their stares, particularly on the pyramids, but also on her face as if they were searching for something. Katya's arm around her began to feel stiff and awkward until Starbride couldn't stand it anymore.

"I feel like we should be doing something," she said at a gap.

Maia chuckled. "I know the feeling. We've been scrambling for so long. Sitting makes me feel tense."

"Why don't we split for a time?" Einrich said. "Or stay if you'd rather. We need to clean up, eat, and make arrangements."

Funeral arrangements, she supposed. Starbride stood at once. Katya had a quick word in Brutal's ear. He patted her shoulder, and she followed Starbride out.

"What was that about?" Starbride asked.

Katya sighed. "Averie. She...she died on a staircase nearby. I asked him to make sure her body was taken care of by us rather than mixed in with the others."

Starbride rubbed Katya's arm, trying for comforting. As they went toward Katya's summer apartment, she pointed down the hall. "Do you know what happened to those mind-warped guards we knocked unconscious?"

Starbride shrugged. "Probably dead by now. Those loyal to the crown have cleared the palace."

Katya seemed even sadder, though Starbride couldn't say why. Once behind closed doors, Dawnmother scraped together enough help to get them a bath before seeking one of her own.

"Star," Katya asked when they were alone, "what did you mean about Roland?"

Starbride stripped slowly, watching Katya do the same. The sight of her body, even bruised and bloody, caused ripples to pass through Starbride's core. "Are you sure you want to talk?"

Katya raised an eyebrow. "I suppose it can wait."

In the bath, they didn't have much room to maneuver, but Katya's clever fingers had never needed much space to work their magic. Starbride took the pleasure Katya offered and then gave her a taste of what their new life together would be like.

Starbride felt Yanchasa's eyes upon her, but the thought didn't disturb her as it once might have. With Yanchasa's whispered suggestions, Starbride used flesh and mind magic to take Katya to new heights until she arched over the end of the tub, gripping the sides, her eyes rolled up in her head, mouth open, and entire body racked with spasms of pleasure.

When Katya had reached her peak several times, Starbride released her, and she slumped into the water so hard, it splashed over the sides. Starbride had to lift her up lest she drowned.

"Star," Katya slurred.

"Shh." Starbride held her tight and finished bathing both of them. When they were clean, she used her augmented muscles to lift Katya from the tub and wrap her in a blanket on the settee. "You wanted to know what happened, love. I thought it best to show you."

Katya licked her lips before she tried to speak again. "You've become some mystic lover, and a super strong one at that?"

"I'll tell you a story." Starbride cuddled Katya close. "I thought you were dead, caught in the disintegration blast. Well, I didn't let myself think it at first, and then Freddie convinced me."

"I'm so sorry, Star. I thought you knew that I had fallen, that you were searching for us."

"I had to get Roland. That was the only thing that mattered. I had this idea that you would have no peace until he was dead. I didn't care if it killed me; I had to see him broken."

Katya gripped her fingers, but Starbride's feelings weren't as intense as her words. Katya wouldn't understand that, though. Starbride went on with her journey to the capstone and what she'd found out about Belshreth and Yanchasa. She ended with how she'd trapped Roland in his own skin for good.

During the tale, Starbride savored the feel of Katya resting against her chest, facing away from her. Katya was probably surprised, a little disbelieving, but that was to be expected. They'd lived with the idea of Yanchasa the monster for a long time.

"I am not offended, daughter," Yanchasa said. "Opinions can be changed."

And Katya deserved the benefit of the doubt. If anyone could see the necessity, the opportunity of power, it was her.

When Starbride finished, Katya sat up and faced her. "So, you can hear Yanchasa right now?"

It was almost past her lips that she could hear *and* see Yanchasa, but she decided that might be too much. "Yes."

"Star—"

"I know what you're going to say."

"Because you're reading my mind?"

Starbride frowned. "Don't be paranoid. I know because I know you. You're going to say something about power corrupting."

"As we've seen *every time* someone's been taken over by a Fiend."

"First of all, there are no such things as Fiends. Second, do I look corrupted to you? Third, I've already told you that Yanchasa passed on the worst Aspects of herself as an act of vengeance."

Before she could put up the rest of her fingers with arguments, Katya laid a hand over hers. "I heard you, Star. But how much faith are you putting in someone who would pass on such murderous instincts?"

"Acting on revenge, you mean? Isn't that what we've all been doing since Roland took over?"

"Funny, I thought we were trying to save a kingdom and the people we love."

Starbride rolled her eyes. "I suppose now you're thinking of letting Uncle go because he's not a threat to you anymore."

Katya stared at her hard. "You have made that a very difficult decision."

"What's so difficult? He's the same person who committed the atrocities."

"That's not true now, and you know it! I *despise* him, and even I'm confused about what to do!"

Starbride lifted her hands and dropped them. "Maybe he was corrupted by Yanchasa's ancient curse, if you want to call it that."

Yanchasa threw back his head and laughed.

"But that doesn't erase what he's done," Starbride said. "And the people of Marienne won't see it that way, either. They'll want someone to pay. Maybe after a public execution, this city will be able to heal."

Katya stared at her.

Starbride returned her look with a cool gaze. "If you ask, 'what happened to you,' I'm leaving."

"Then you must see the difference in yourself."

"The ways in which I'm stronger and more powerful? If anyone could see it, I thought it would be you. I thought love would help you see it."

When Katya could only gape, Starbride stood and wrapped a blanket around herself. "Dawnmother will have prepared some quarters for me. Why don't you find me when all of this has had a little time to sink in?"

CHAPTER TWENTY-THREE

KATYA

Katya scrubbed her fingers through her damp hair. This new Starbride had to be a trick, some cruel joke. She was still asleep in the dead city below the palace, and this was another nightmare.

All the times she'd envisioned Starbride's beautiful face—either worried, determined, or weeping with joy at seeing Katya again—she never imagined what she'd actually found. And it wasn't just the smooth triangles of crystal adorning Starbride's body. She was cold, outside and in. Neither the bath nor their lovemaking had warmed her. For all the pleasure Starbride had given, it made her smug more than anything. As for what Katya had given her, well, it seemed not to have affected her at all. Everything probably paled in comparison to the sensations granted by Yanchasa.

Katya shivered and drew her blanket tighter. She didn't care what Starbride said, she'd seen Yanchasa's effects. She'd felt them. Even if it was true that Yanchasa used to be human, or that it chose what it passed on to those who'd captured it, that still meant Yanchasa contained the cold, malicious killer Katya had come to know as a Fiend. A sliver of humanity couldn't erase the monster.

But how to get Starbride to see that?

Katya stood. The fight wasn't done, that was all. She had hoped Roland's capture would put an end to it, but there was one task left, one more hurdle. She could cope with that.

Katya dressed quickly, every movement reminding her of Averie. She could pick a thousand new maids, but never as wonderful a friend, no one with such good advice, such easy wit.

Katya would see to it that Averie was entombed in the Umbriel crypt.

Once she dressed, it was easier to plan. She'd need allies, someone who knew what it would take to convince Starbride to let Yanchasa's power go. A pyradisté? The only one who came to mind was Master Bernard, and Katya didn't think he knew much of Fiend magic.

Adsnazi, then. But Katya feared that going to Redtrue would only upset Starbride further. They hadn't started out as friends. Well,

Redtrue didn't start out friends with anyone, but she and Starbride had been hurrying toward antagonistic the last time they'd been together.

Perhaps the only testimony Starbride would listen to was from someone well-versed in Fiends, someone who could remember what it was like to merge with one. Luckily, they had the greatest authority on the subject sitting in the dungeon.

But Katya's feet failed her as her heart sped. She pictured the dungeon stones, the airless, lightless dark. She had to stretch her arms to prove that she had room; the walls weren't closing in. No, she couldn't go underground again, not yet.

After a deep breath, she calmed. She wasn't ready to see her uncle anyway. The man she'd thought of as Roland was seven years dead. The only thing left was the creature who'd stolen her home, enslaved her dearest friends, and killed her mother. He was the beast who'd hunted Starbride and forced her to fall under Yanchasa's sway. How could she see him as anything but that, no matter what he looked like? How could she speak to him without ramming her dagger down his throat?

Katya headed to Maia's room but paused when she arrived. Katya's fight wasn't over, but that didn't mean Maia's peace had to be interrupted. She could be with Brutal, claiming some fleeting but much needed happiness. How could Katya take that away from her?

The youngster Katya remembered would be eager to help. This new Maia—with the haunted look in her pale blue eyes—would she be so quick to throw herself into danger? Or would she still tell Katya not to be silly, not to hesitate when asking for help. They were family.

Still, Katya was about to turn away when the door flew open. On the other side, Maia jumped back, bow half drawn. Katya froze in shock.

Maia's arrow tipped toward the ground. "Sorry, I didn't know who it might be. Why didn't you knock?"

"I didn't want to disturb you." She tried to peer around Maia's shoulder.

Maia rolled her eyes. "I'm alone. Do you want to come in?"

Katya sighed. Starbride's predicament wouldn't wait. "I have to talk to you about something delicate."

"Spirits, please don't tell me it's Brutal. I've already said I don't want to talk about that over and over."

"You've just piqued my interest all over again, but no. It's Starbride."

Maia stood aside so Katya could slip past. "That was my second guess."

"She's merged with Yanchasa, I know it, no matter that she says it's some kind of teaching."

"And you want to know what merging with Yanchasa is like?"

"Will it do me any good? I don't want to dredge up old pain."

Maia relaxed on a divan. A glass and a nearly full bottle of wine rested on the table. Nice restraint on her part. Katya was tempted to drain a bottle by herself.

"Tell me what she told you," Maia said as she scooted another glass closer and poured for both of them.

Katya related the story as best she remembered. Maia sipped her wine and listened. At the end, she shrugged. "It doesn't sound like anything I felt. There were no whispering voices, no teaching or guiding, more like someone pulled a blanket over my thoughts. The most horrible actions seemed not only necessary but enjoyable, and I didn't question them."

Maia toyed with her wine glass and stared at the floor. "There was a desire, all the time, to hurt everyone, to find new *ways* to hurt them. I could fight it because going on a rampage didn't suit my purpose or my father's plans, but it was always there."

Katya remembered her brief time as a greater Fiend, when Starbride helped her stay in control. She'd thought of such murderous instincts as the essence of Fiends. That meant brutality lurked in the core of Yanchasa, no matter what the rest of it was.

"I saw Starbride's face," Maia said, "as she knelt over the tortured body of my father. She'd done something to him with a pyramid, and he was screaming and moaning, and she was smiling, Katya."

Katya drained her glass before she stood to pace. "We have to do something."

"Like she did for me." Maia shuddered. "Now I'm happy to be myself again, but when Starbride first freed me, I was miserable."

"Because you remembered."

Maia nodded and didn't lift her eyes.

Katya sat beside her on the settee. "You had no control, dearheart. You didn't choose to merge with your Fiend." Not like Roland had.

Maia wiped the corner of her eye. "I wasn't miserable just because of the memories, Katya. Spirits above, I *missed* it."

"The Fiend?" Katya asked, fighting to keep any inflection from her voice.

"The power. I know you remember a little, but once you've merged with that kind of strength." She flexed her fingers. "It felt as if anything was possible. I felt invincible. I think that's why I was so rash sometimes, why anyone with a Fiend is. Hurling yourself into danger is part of the thrill. And even though I wouldn't go back to that terrible state of mind, it was nice not to worry about consequences."

Like the penalty for killing people? Katya kept her mouth shut. It wouldn't do to go asking for advice and then judging Maia on everything she had to say.

Maia leaned her head on Katya's shoulder. "If Starbride has the power and the confidence, but Yanchasa is holding back the need for slaughter, the rashness, and the total dominion of its personality, I'd find it tempting to change places with her."

"That's what I'm afraid of. If she just had confidence in a power she trusted, that would be one thing, but she's *cold*."

"And ruthless."

"She's not the same person, but she claims she's better."

Maia shook her head. "Do you think we can convince her?"

"She still loves me. I saw it in her eyes. The real Starbride is in there somewhere. I just have to convince her to fight."

"I'm with you. If she turns us into pudding, we'll get turned together."

Katya laughed, tears stinging her eyes. "Do you think she'll listen to us?"

"Let me do the talking."

"You sound like me."

"At whose knee do you think I learned?"

❖

Katya couldn't lurk in the secret passageways. She wasn't any more ready for them than she was for the dungeon. And spying seemed the last way to get Starbride to trust her. Instead, she decided to accompany Maia to Starbride's room and let Maia take the lead in the conversation.

Weariness knotted Katya's shoulders and stretched the wound in her back. She couldn't sleep, though, even without the problem of Yanchasa. The chill of her nightmare lingered in her thoughts.

Dawnmother's drawn face said she hadn't gotten any rest, or maybe she was seeing the difference in her mistress, too. She would have to have been blind to miss it.

Starbride had changed into one of her Allusian outfits. This one had loose fitting trousers in deep blue silk and a shirt that fitted around her midsection and flared at the sleeves. Her smile held the same smug edge, but her mouth wobbled as Katya watched, as if the real Starbride was fighting for control.

"Hello again," Katya said.

Starbride set some papers down. "More questions?"

"Just seeing how you are." Maia plopped down beside Starbride as if nothing had changed.

"Fine. Just going over some reports from the city."

"My father's reports?" Katya asked.

"Your father needs his rest. I'm more than capable of handling a few things for him. I led a rebellion while you were gone, Katya."

"And you did it splendidly, love."

Starbride's new smile held a smidge of her earlier warmth. "Thank you."

"But reports," Katya pressed. "You've never shown an interest in them before."

Maia gave her a warning look, too late to put off Starbride's frown.

"I have the advice of someone who ruled a place far larger than Marienne for centuries," Starbride said. "I think I can handle a few missives. Unless you don't have faith in me?"

"It's not that at all." Maia frowned until Katya sank into a chair. "Katya's just being the worrier she was born to be."

They all chuckled. "I just wanted to know how you're settling in," Maia said.

Starbride gestured at the room. "Fine, and you?"

Maia stared at the floor and shrugged. Starbride touched her lightly on the wrist. "What's wrong?" She glanced at Katya.

Katya shook her head. "She didn't want to tell me. I made her come see you."

"What is it, sweet? Is someone bothering you?" The pyramid in Starbride's forehead flared.

"Nothing like that. I just wondered if you'd tell me what it's like. The power, I mean."

"Why do you want to know?"

Maia spoke so softly Katya had to lean in. "I had it once."

"And you miss it."

"A bit. I'm happy to be myself again, and I'm so grateful to you, Starbride."

Starbride smiled and chucked her under the chin. "Of course."

"But I didn't miss feeling helpless."

"I know what you mean." Starbride glanced to the side as if listening to someone else's comment. Katya squirmed. That had to be Yanchasa's voice.

"I don't miss the killing," Maia said.

Katya sucked in a breath. Starbride frowned. "Killing?"

"Yes, I killed people happily. I don't miss that."

Starbride looked away again. Katya glanced at Maia, urging her to press the point.

"It felt as if someone else was in charge of my thoughts." Maia stared into space. "Every decision I made was influenced by…"

"Yanchasa's Aspect." Starbride frowned, and Katya wondered how quickly Yanchasa was talking now. "You two should be resting."

"And you?"

"I'm not sleepy."

Katya cocked her head. "I always sleep better with you by my side."

Starbride seemed torn again. Her mouth quivered, and she took a breath so deep she shuddered. "Sleep here with me, then."

Maia started to stand. Starbride touched her arm. "No, you stay. I don't want you to be alone."

Maia glanced at Katya, and she knew they were thinking the same thing: it was more than a little awkward to think of sharing a bed, especially when Katya's and Starbride's bedtime often included more than sleeping.

"Right here," Starbride said.

When Katya glanced at her, the pyramid in her forehead flared again, and darkness slammed into Katya like a herd of wild horses.

CHAPTER TWENTY-FOUR

STARBRIDE

Maia slumped to the side, but Katya slid forward. Starbride leapt the short table between them and caught Katya before she could hurt herself.

"Will you straighten out Maia?" she asked as she laid Katya on the settee.

Dawnmother hurried to Maia's side. "What have you done?"

"Don't wake her. I just put her to sleep."

"They are not children, Star! Did you even think of how angry they'll be when they wake?" Dawnmother's face had that line between her brows that Starbride was coming to think of as her normal expression. "My life for you—"

"Dawn, please. How many times have you said that in the past hour?"

"I will repeat it until you listen. Your feet are set on a dark path, and if you don't turn back…" Her mouth worked before she closed her eyes and took a deep breath. "Star, you risk becoming the kind of person you have hated all your life, a selfish monster who cares only for her own ends."

Hurt battered through the adsna. "How dare you even think that about me?"

"How can I not?" She pointed to the two sleeping figures. "How can you not when you have done this?"

"Set their minds and bodies at ease, you mean?"

"Assaulted them, Star! Used magic on them without their permission, when all they had done was come to check on you."

"They came to tear a rift between me and Yanchasa."

Yanchasa leaned against the settee where Katya rested. "As I warned you," he said.

Dawnmother's face grew thunderous. "There *should* be a rift, just as when you befriended that tall girl when you were eleven, the one who tempted you to steal."

"I'm not a child anymore, Dawn. Yanchasa is not a young thief."

"Not young, I'll grant you." She gestured at the papers under Maia's shoulder. "But thief seems appropriate. That *thing* wants you to take over, and it's changing you from the inside. Why else would you think you know better than the king what to do with these reports, that you know what's best for the princess and her cousin even regarding their own bodies?"

Starbride's ears and cheeks went hot. She vividly remembered the brooch she'd stolen at her friend's insistence, the shame when Dawnmother had marched her back to return what she'd taken and apologize. She had pleaded with Dawnmother not to tell her mother, and Dawnmother had agreed if Starbride pledged never to speak to the tall girl again.

"I'm…" She couldn't get the words out.

Yanchasa stood at Dawnmother's shoulder, arms clasped behind him. "You're what, daughter? Sorry?"

"Well?" Dawnmother asked.

Yanchasa tsked slowly, a smirk on her face. "Still eleven, are we? I wonder if Redtrue lets people speak to her like this."

"Star." Dawnmother knelt in front of her. "Wake the princess and Maia, and we'll—"

Starbride tuned her out, eyes glued to Yanchasa as anger built within her. *Why mention Redtrue?*

"Well, no one speaks to her like this because she doesn't have a *servant*, wouldn't be burdened by one, from what you remember."

Starbride launched to her feet. "You'd throw her in my face?"

Dawnmother fell back. "Star?"

"I wonder if she'd hear me," Yanchasa said.

Starbride stepped around Dawnmother. "I thought I was your chosen one, and you mention another?"

"Gifts must be earned, daughter. I will not have mine squandered."

Dawnmother pulled on Starbride's arm. "Star, whatever the monster is saying, do not listen!"

"Just what *are* you saying?" Starbride asked.

Yanchasa gestured toward the scattered papers. "You've seen what must be done. Why linger? The kingdom needs you for more than these petty problems. Unless…"

"Yes?"

"Well, unless you'd *rather* immerse yourself in smaller problems." He smiled pityingly. "It's nothing to be ashamed of, daughter. Some people are just not made for greatness."

Starbride marched around the settee and gathered up her papers, ignoring Dawnmother's wails. They'd see who was made for greatness. It certainly wasn't Redtrue. She was afraid of power, and how could that ever make one great?

Dawnmother pulled on Starbride's arm, and Starbride grabbed her chin. "Do you need rest, too, Dawn?"

Dawnmother tensed as if she might jerk back, but Starbride held her tighter.

"No, mistress," Dawnmother said, an unknowable look in her eyes.

Starbride saw the look for what it was: one more petty problem she didn't have time for. Other feelings tried to surface, but she shut them down. "If anyone comes looking for me, I'll be with the nobles and the king. It's high time they convened the council." She glanced at Katya and Maia. Dawnmother would look after them, and they'd be safe, and she wouldn't have to concern herself with their welfare for the time being.

Yanchasa's proud look made Starbride's skin tingle. As she strode into the hallway, Yanchasa kept pace with her as if they were comrades.

"Of course we are, daughter. You always give me reason to be proud of you. There's no challenge or test that you cannot overcome."

Faith, just what was lacking in all her friends and family. She'd seen it briefly in Katya's eyes, but then that Darkstrong-cursed doubt reared its head. Didn't any of them see she could handle this power and Yanchasa's advice? She was in control, but none of them would believe that. Perhaps they were incapable. Perhaps they preferred her weak and vulnerable.

"Time, daughter, will let us see who can be convinced."

When Starbride was admitted to Einrich's formal sitting room, she found him meeting with several nobles, namely Countess Nadia, Baroness Jacintha, Viscount Lenvis and a bald, bearded man Starbride didn't know.

It rankled not to have been included, but she supposed she shouldn't have been surprised. Like Yanchasa said, they needed time.

And proof of her power, of course.

Baroness Jacintha beamed at her, but she was the only one. Starbride returned her deep bow with a gracious nod. She wasted no time showing Einrich the documents she'd been looking at, those from the Watch detailing crime or destruction in the city.

"I've already started restoration efforts," she said, watching surprise cross all their faces. "I've repaired some buildings, settled some disputes—"

"Did you loose those dead things on the city?" Lenvis asked.

Starbride stared at him hard. "I have put them to good use, Viscount. I did not create the remnants. The Fiend king did that."

"I have heard," the bearded man said, "that there are actual Fiends in the city, too. They'll need hunting down."

"Be easy, Count Mathias," Einrich said. "I believe our young Starbride has that covered, yes?"

She nodded, though she didn't appreciate his underhanded comment on her age. "They are now under my command."

Lenvis still looked at her strangely. "And how many will share that fate?"

Starbride considered hurting him, but she didn't think that was necessary yet. Jacintha stared at him with wide, appalled eyes, but she couldn't censure him because of his rank. At least someone else understood.

"Wise of you to spare him," Yanchasa said. "Strike too hard too quickly, and you'll find yourself with no one left to rule."

Countess Nadia sidled close. "Forgive Lenvis, my dear. He has yet to hear from his family on the coast, and he fears the worst."

Starbride nodded her away. Einrich was saying something about increased Watch patrols, and she needed to let him know she could handle things in Marienne. "The remnants can patrol the city. If you wish," she added as Lenvis glanced at her again.

They all grimaced. "Perhaps not," Nadia said. "They make people a little uncomfortable."

Small-minded people, perhaps. She'd seen the discomfort and hoped they'd get over it. Lenvis gestured at the reports she held, his face still holding open hostility. He seemed miles from the pretty young bauble Nadia had been pursuing before Roland had taken Marienne. "How did you come by those reports, Princess Consort?"

"Starbride developed many ties to the Watch in our absence," Einrich said, "as leader of the rebellion."

At last, a rational head. He saw how much she could do for the city. But Yanchasa's mouth puckered in a frown.

What is it? Starbride asked.

She shrugged. "Probably nothing."

Starbride tried to keep one ear on the other conversation as she thought, *Tell me.*

"The king said, 'in our absence,' as if now you won't be needed. With Countess Nadia's comments about the remnants, it's as if they're saying they don't need you at all."

"I can take over that project," Starbride said, interrupting something Countess Nadia was saying.

"Which project?" Einrich asked.

"City restoration. If you don't want to use the remnants, I can do it myself. I've already made a start."

"We were talking about crime," Lenvis said.

"I can help with that, too. A few criminals are nothing to me. Or have you seen the Fiend king lately?"

That turned him a little white around the gills.

"We weren't all hiding while the fighting was going on," Count Mathias added. "If it's criminals that need hunting down, I'll be happy to help."

"I'm sure you could aid the effort, Starbride," Einrich said, "but you're only one person, and we do have an entire city Watch. I think it would do the people good to protect themselves."

"And you don't want them hiding you away as some piddling commander of city forces," Yanchasa added.

Starbride nearly stamped her foot. *Be useful but not too useful?*

"Aim higher," Yanchasa said.

"I've got the lesser nobles and the courtiers pretty well organized," Jacintha said. "Some weren't happy about helping put the palace back in order, but I told them we've all got to lend a hand. If the queen were with us she'd be doing the same." She bit her lip. "I'm so sorry, Majesty. If I had known she was coming to meet us in the servants' quarters, perhaps I could have—"

Einrich touched her shoulder. "You could have done nothing, Baroness, but thank you for your condolences. Perhaps we can all speak again when I convene the council of nobles."

An uncomfortable silence descended. The others bowed and said their good-byes. "Starbride, stay a moment," Einrich said. He gestured for her to sit beside him. "Wine?"

She nodded graciously. He waited until after he'd poured to nod to the reports. "Why did you keep these from me until now?"

"I thought you might be tired."

He smiled kindly. "How considerate of you."

It was, wasn't it? She returned the smile for Yanchasa's benefit.

"I hope you don't think me a doddering old man just yet."

"I've always respected and admired you." She blurted the words without thinking but realized how right they were. Einrich had been her supporter from the beginning, or so Katya had told her. And he'd been willing to keep her as his family even after Katya had…died.

That was a mistake, she told herself as the wine threatened to come back up, a bad dream.

Einrich's light touch on her shoulder made her start. "That's kind of you to say. I try to do well at my job, all parts of it."

"You don't think I should have kept those reports from you."

"Running this city and this kingdom is my responsibility, no matter that I haven't been able to do it lately."

"I can help you."

"I know you can. That's why I asked the others to leave."

She clenched her fists, wondering if he was going to ask her to get rid of the nobles who were slowing him down.

"I need you to undertake a mission, one you're uniquely suited to. I want you to take these remnants and Fiends and go north to clean out the last of Roland's troops."

Starbride narrowed her eyes, teetering between intrigued and insulted. "What troops?"

"Countess Nadia has had word from some of the survivors in the north. Roland wasn't dragging people all the way back here to be hypnotized. He had a camp up there, where his minions were taking live victims so that they could fall under the influence of a pyramid. I need a pyradisté who can fight to seek this pyramid out, destroy it, free those who are simply under its sway, and eliminate those who've been warped to the point where they cannot be saved."

It did sound uniquely suited to her. None of the other pyradistés knew how to fight like she did. None of them had the power of the remnants or the children. And Einrich probably didn't want to haggle with the adsnazi or have them poking randomly around his kingdom.

Starbride waited for Yanchasa to speak, but she just stood there.

"What will Katya think?" Starbride asked.

Einrich seemed a little taken aback. She was, too. The words popped out without her permission. "She'll miss you, but she'll understand," he said. "I don't think she's quite ready for another fight."

Yes, Katya had been through a lot that day. "I'll do it."

"Splendid. You'll need some messengers."

But who? Not Dawnmother. The image of her face captured in Starbride's hand hovered in the front of Starbride's mind, and even the adsna couldn't banish it. From the depths of her memory, she pulled one of Horsestrong's tales, where his servant Birdfaithful said, "There are deeds one can never come back from."

Einrich cleared his throat.

"I'm sorry?" Starbride said.

"I said I'll find a few people for you. You didn't seem able to think of anyone."

"Thank you, Majesty."

"Thank you for taking this weight off my mind. Hard to start putting the city to rights if you've got another force massing outside your walls."

"True." And so much easier to think about than moldy old Horsestrong tales. "I'll be ready to go at first light."

He nodded, and she left, Yanchasa striding by her side down the hall.

"Well?" she asked.

Yanchasa flickered back to male with a shrug. "It's a start."

"I expected you to say whether you thought it was a good or bad idea."

"What do you think?"

"I'm the only one who can do what Einrich wants."

Yanchasa cocked his head and waited.

"Or it's a fool's errand."

"Or it's neither."

Starbride sagged against the wall. "Perfect."

"Did the king send you into the country as a clever ploy to get you out of the way, or does he genuinely need your assistance? Or is it both? You'll have to figure it out. Since Roland and I could not speak directly, I know nothing of his schemes. His mind is closed to us and prying into the minds of heads of state—especially Einrich's—will net you more trouble than you can handle at this point."

"But one can never be too accommodating?"

"Not at first, no. I would wait a bit to flex my muscles."

"I'll clear out his country problem, then," she said. "I'll build more of a reputation with him and with the people."

"And then those like Viscount Snotty won't dare oppose you."

She liked that plan. Now all she had to do was find something to keep her occupied until it was time to go. She could return to her apartment, but Katya and Maia would still be there.

"Best get some rest, daughter. You're being sustained by the adsna, but it can't keep you nourished forever. Find food and drink and somewhere to sleep."

Katya's apartment wasn't being used. Starbride headed in that direction, her heart already lighter.

Edette's slender fingers glided over the parchment. "More horns?" he asked.

Starbride studied the drawing of the beast, admiring Edette's handiwork. His skill in art was almost as perfect as his body. Starbride had to prevent her eyes from caressing that very shape as his brown skin glistened against Starbride's wine-colored sheets.

"Focus," Edette said, slapping her lightly with the parchment.

"It's fearsome. I like it."

"Like it?" He stuck his bottom lip out. "I was hoping for bouts of ecstasy."

Starbride slipped an arm around his waist, pressing their bare flesh together. "I can show you ecstasy."

"Dearest Chas, you've shown me twice today already. If I'd known you simply wanted to languish in bed all day, I wouldn't have brought my art box."

Laughing, Starbride rolled off the bed. She let the morning air cool her naked body, prickling her with gooseflesh before she called the adsna. It carried warmth up through her long legs to her buttocks and balls and on through her chest until she felt the heat creep up her neck like a warm bath.

"Look again," Edette said, "and tell me what you really think."

The creature on the parchment had four feathered wings, two sets of horns, spikes on the chin and cheeks, and a giant curved jaw filled with fangs. Starbride scrubbed through her short hair. "It's going to make Wallux shit himself."

Edette laughed and propped his chin on both hands. "I'm so glad you like it."

"Can I use a weapon with these claws?"

"You mean you need a weapon more impressive than the one you're already wielding?" He brushed the inside of Starbride's thigh.

Starbride chuckled deep in her throat. "I thought we brought our art box. Didn't want to languish in bed all day."

"I can't help myself around you. Are you going to meet this fearsome general as a man or a woman?"

"Who could tell past all this?" Starbride said, waving at the parchment and trying to picture her body in its fearsome form.

"Darling, no, no. Start out as human and change in front of him. Do you know if he fancies one sex over the other?"

"No idea."

Edette sprang up on his knees and put his arms around Starbride's shoulders. He was always so warm. "Then be both, darling, just to catch him by surprise. He'll spy a tantalizing pair of breasts and follow the line of your body down to a massive c—"

From behind them, someone cleared her throat. Starbride didn't have to turn to know it was Layess, clothed today in her scholar's robe of sky blue silk.

"I should have known I'd find you still abed," she said. "You called the war council, Yanchasa. I would have thought you'd be on time."

"You should have known better," Edette said.

"With you around, I suppose I should have." Layess stared at them, arms crossed. "Are you going to get some clothes on, or should I delay the meeting?"

"Let's all go to the meeting naked," Edette said. "It'll make it more interesting."

Starbride chuckled and pulled her trousers on. Edette wrapped a simple kilt around his hips, the only clothing they could ever talk him into besides the translucent silk ribbon he sometimes tied across his breasts.

Starbride slipped on a shirt and long coat and regarded the drawing again.

Edette moved the parchment away and stretched his body against Starbride's; he wasn't quite tall enough for them to fit together perfectly. "If the claws don't suit you, Chas, change them as you go." His full lips were so inviting. She had to taste them once more.

Layess cleared her throat again.

"Oh, master of patience," Edette said, "if you're not going to join in, go away!"

"No." Starbride started for the door, leading Edette. "We should all go before we're truly late."

Starbride opened her eyes with a gasp. She could still feel the gentle heat sliding through her body and Edette's lithe form draped around her own. Desire ran through her in rivulets, stemming from anatomy she'd never imagined she'd possess.

"All things are possible with the flesh."

Yanchasa stood at the foot of the bed. Her helmet had gone missing, showing off her short, spiky black hair. Starbride didn't know what to say. She'd never been a man in her dreams, though she'd sometimes wondered what it would feel like. She stopped the thought as her cheeks flamed. "What happened to your helmet?"

Yanchasa felt her own brow as if surprised to find it missing. "I'm not sure. Maybe you've made me feel more comfortable in your head." She flashed a winning smile.

Starbride frowned. She was grateful, but she didn't know how she felt about Yanchasa taking up residence.

"That was the first time I saw what you'd come to know as a Fiend," Yanchasa said. "Edette was a talented artist. I miss him so."

"Why am I dreaming your memories?"

"Oh." He shrugged, but those devious brown eyes held answers. "I guess I was remembering too loudly. I am only in your head, you know. It's not as if I can wander off and find something else to do."

That made sense, but she still didn't like it. "I like to dream my own dreams."

"I don't know if I should be hurt or not. Didn't you find it interesting?"

Starbride felt her face burn again. She wouldn't trade her own body for anything, but Yanchasa was right. It had been interesting to exist in another skin for a while.

CHAPTER TWENTY-FIVE

KATYA

S omeone was shaking her shoulder. "Princess?"
"Perhaps if we threw some water in her face," someone else said.

Katya heard a sputtered laugh. She knew the voices, but she couldn't quite place them. Spirits above, her head was full of sand.

"What about this other one?"

"Be gentle with her!"

"Darkstrong took gentleness when he decided to poison Starbride's mind. Katya, wake up!"

A shot of pain rolled down Katya's arm. Someone had pinched her, hard. She was betting on the impatient, imperious voice. Only one person did imperious like that.

"Redtrue?" Katya tried to say. Her eyes wouldn't open, held by lead weights.

"See? A little force is all that's needed."

"If you pinch her again, you'll feel my palm across your cheek!" That had to be Dawnmother.

"You wouldn't dare!"

"Ladies, please, allow me." Castelle's voice, that. "Katya, can you hear me?"

"Mmm." Her eyelashes could flutter, but it was so hard to get them to do more. "Up, up." The world tilted, and she knew she was upright, but she barely felt the pressure that kept her from toppling over. She'd never been so tired. Was she drunk?

Katya tried to control her flapping lids and saw a pair of brown hands lifting her head. "Try to stay awake, Princess. Can you not use a pyramid to help her?"

"This is precisely why *we* do not practice mind magic."

"I brought you here to help!"

"Then let me pinch her again."

"Katya," Castelle said sternly, "you have to wake up now. I need backup."

Katya tried to laugh. She tried to say, "You should try being buried alive with them," but it only came out as a long slur.

"What was that?" Castelle said. Her scarred face hovered in and out of Katya's vision.

Katya pushed Castelle back and tried to stand, but her feet wouldn't obey her. They all yelled at her to sit down. She couldn't remember drinking.

No, she'd been doing something important, speaking to someone. Starbride. Something was wrong with Starbride. Katya willed her eyes to stay open and saw Dawnmother, Redtrue, and Castelle kneeling before her. Maia was passed out on the settee behind them.

"What happened?" She licked her lips and worked her mouth, anything to try to stay awake.

"Tell her," Redtrue said.

"Starbride used magic on you, but she is not to blame," Dawnmother said. "It is that thing controlling her."

"She has surrendered to it," Redtrue said. "As I said must always happen."

"My Star is in there somewhere, and we must help her escape," Dawnmother cried.

Katya agreed, but she couldn't help the betrayal that burned inside. Starbride had used a pyramid on her, but there'd been no warning, no sign. She'd reached out and put Katya and Maia to sleep with frightful ease.

"Where is she?"

They were silent for a few moments. "I could not wake you," Dawnmother said at last.

"How long?"

"It's morning again. You slept the rest of the day and all night. I could do nothing to rouse you, and I had to wait until morning to fetch Redtrue."

"To ask Redtrue to come," Redtrue said.

"I thought, since she knew about Fiend magic…"

"We were happy to help," Castelle added.

Redtrue snorted, but she bent and peered into Katya's face. "I could only help wake you using non-magical means. I will help Starbride if I can, but I do not know what to do if she will not surrender this power willingly."

"Can you cleanse her?" Katya's head still felt as if it might float free from her body, but it was easier to keep her eyes open if she kept moving.

Redtrue shook her head. "Only the pyramids she bears. But you saw how she cancelled my pyramid in the hallway before. Could I even get close to her?"

"She's using the pyramids in some new way," Katya said.

Redtrue shrugged. "All your ways are new to me."

Perhaps the answers lay below. The ancient Allusians had worshipped the ten spirits, but their descendants might have been seeking the Fiend. They knew something about it, maybe about how the Farradains had summoned it.

She had no one else to ask about Fiend magic. Crowe was lost to her, and the adsnazi were reluctant to even discuss it. Maybe it was time to let Master Bernard into Crowe's office. Starbride had worked with him during the rebellion; she must trust him. Maybe he could figure out a way to shut off Yanchasa's connection to Starbride.

"I need to speak with my father."

"He can tell you where Starbride went," Dawnmother said.

Katya began to stand and had to sit again. "She's not here?"

"No, the king sent her on some mission. His servants told me not to worry. I thought perhaps Castelle could get answers where I couldn't, but now we have you."

"Can someone help me to my father's apartment?" She gestured toward where Maia rested. "And can someone else look after her?"

Castelle helped her down the hallway. Redtrue took the opportunity to rest in Katya's place, and Dawnmother looked after them both. Katya took deep breaths as Castelle guided her by the elbow. She tried to clear her mind of fog, but it felt as if Starbride had hit her with a hammer rather than magic. She'd had easier times recovering from concussions.

Luckily, it was early morning, and her father was still in his apartment. She knew he'd be meeting with the nobles' council soon, and she'd hoped to be there with him, but she didn't think it would look good if she kept falling asleep over his shoulder.

His aide admitted her, and Castelle waited in the hall. Katya told her father what she knew. Da rubbed his chin as he listened. He seemed even grayer than when they'd marched on Marienne. "I sent her away precisely because I couldn't predict what she was going to do, though I didn't know at the time that she'd put you to sleep."

Katya fought the black mood that fatigue had put her in. She was just happy her mother's body had been removed. She couldn't have coped with it just then. "Why else did you send her away?"

"We need room to think, Katya. She's taken it on herself to police the city. She took reports meant for me. No matter what else this connection with Yanchasa is doing to her, it's making her think she's in charge. Now, I am grateful for her help and am quite willing to reward her—"

"Da," Katya said with a laugh, "*Starbride* would have been happy just to have us all together, but Yanchasa wants something else."

"And how can we discover what that is?"

Katya told him of the underground city, that the ancient Order had thought someone was seeking the Fiend, and she knew they were looking for old places of spirit worship as well. Through it all, Da listened with eyes wide. He loved a good adventure story as much as he loved a good mystery. "That's amazing, Katya. I had no idea. And you think something down there might give us a clue about how to break Yanchasa's hold?"

"What do you think the native pyramid was made to do?"

He shrugged. "I haven't given it much thought."

Katya remembered Dawnmother's words about rulers never remembering history. Maybe they should have made more of an effort. "The people who built the tunnels would have heard of Yanchasa from us, after it destroyed their ancestors, but what if the people who already lived here knew about Fiends? I mean, we don't know how much work Vestra and her husband had to do to use the natives' pyramid against them."

Da sat across from her and leaned on his knees. "You think the answer is none, that the pyramid was already ready for that purpose?"

"Perhaps, but I once heard Crowe say that retuning a pyramid's purpose is all but impossible, though it didn't seem so for Roland or Starbride."

He rubbed his beard and stared into space. "We need more information."

"But who can we let down there?"

"Would you think less of me if I said I was sick of secrets?"

"Only if you'd think less of me for saying the same thing."

"Everyone knows about Fiends now, just not about us. I think we'd be safe letting the knowledge monks into this dead city of yours. As for what the pyramid is for, we'll have to take either the adsnazi or one of the few pyradistés left into our confidence."

"I was thinking about Master Bernard."

"Always a friend to the crown," Da said.

"And Redtrue already knows just about everything."

"I'll leave her to you."

"Lucky me." Katya yawned hugely. "Don't you need me at the council?"

"I have plenty of allies in Countess Nadia and a few of the others, and as much as Dayscout has his own people's interests at heart, I trust him not to stab me in the back. No, Starbride remaining attached to Yanchasa is a problem for the kingdom as well as her family. And it's one we have to figure out while she's gone."

Katya smiled softly. "Her family?"

"Of course, my girl. Don't you think I know how much you care for her? I know she'll be my daughter soon. Under the law, this time, not just in your heart."

"Thank you, Da. Ma said something similar before she…" She cleared her throat roughly.

"I believe it, my girl. We've discussed it many times, she and I. She always took longer to warm than I did, but she was getting there." He reached out, his large palms enfolding hers.

"I'll invite Master Bernard up for a chat."

❖

Master Bernard listened to Katya's story so closely she feared he might tumble out of his seat. She laid it all bare for him. If they had until Starbride's return to figure out how to free her from Yanchasa, there wasn't time to hold back.

He didn't look as strong as she remembered. He'd shaved his beard when he'd went into hiding, and it was only now growing back, a shade of its former bushy red self, and she noted more white streaks than before. He was thinner, too, but so was everyone who'd been left behind when the city fell.

"So much makes sense now," he said, "all the secret ways Starbride knew of combatting the corpse Fiends, how she was familiar with anti-Fiend magic and the Fiend king." He pointed toward his feet. "And the great Fiend is down there now? I thought all the talk of ritual and placating such a creature was a children's tale."

"It's down there, and it's awake."

He paled. "I saw the physical changes in Starbride, but I sensed others as well. I admit to a tremendous sense of relief when she took our *guards* away this morning."

"She's blind to the Fiend's malevolence."

Master Bernard tapped his chin. "And besides the anti-Fiend knowledge that Starbride imparted to us rebels, no one else knows Fiend magic?"

Katya told him what Starbride had told her, of the Belshrethen eventually becoming the Allusians, but how they seemed to have forgotten—on purpose, perhaps—the secrets of flesh or Fiend magic.

"Interesting. There must be something wrong with it on a fundamental level, some corrupting energy, or else why throw away such power?"

"It would explain why the adsnazi are so hesitant to use destructive magic," Katya said. "They see it as all stemming from the same source."

Master Bernard snorted. "I don't recall a fire pyramid ever urging me to kill my family, or whatever it is these Fiends do."

"You probably shouldn't get into a debate with Redtrue."

"Oh, I'll debate," he said, "as long as she wants."

Katya blinked. "You're hired."

He stared before he laughed, slapping his knee. "I'll look at this capstone whenever you're ready. As for the underground city, I'd love to see it, too, and I know just which knowledge monks to call on to help in our research."

"Urge them to keep quiet. Too many onlookers will get in the way. I'll get Dayscout to assemble some Allusian scholars, and Redtrue can gather more adsnazi. I'll meet you at the entrance to the royal quarters in an hour."

❖

Dayscout had to attend the nobles' council with Da, as did Leafclever, but the looks on both their faces said they were dying to get into the underground city. Redtrue brought along a couple of adsnazi, and Master Bernard brought a few knowledge monks who wrung their hands in anticipation.

The monks had brought laborers armed with shovels and pickaxes. After half a dozen deep breaths and self-assurances that she would see the sun again, Katya showed them the spot where she'd fallen during the fight with Roland. She called on Brutal and Maia to watch over the monks and make sure they didn't wander into the capstone cavern. She would have had Freddie and Hugo standing guard as well, but they'd ridden out with Starbride.

That had to have been Da's idea. Katya bet Starbride didn't think she needed help. Da had probably had to sell the idea under the excuse that she would need messengers, though she'd taken three other riders for that. Whatever the reason, Katya was glad that someone besides Yanchasa and a host of Fiends were watching Starbride's back.

Katya shook those thoughts away as she continued toward the capstone cavern with Redtrue, Dawnmother, Master Bernard, Castelle, and one other adsnazi. The other had elected to go down into the ruined city.

Katya chatted incessantly. She kept waiting for Redtrue to make a snide comment about that. She'd fought down her panic, but it threatened to come back every time she looked at the stone walls, or spirits forbid, the ceiling. It was as if she could feel the rock waiting to collapse and swallow her again.

"How are your ribs?" she asked Redtrue, hoping her voice seemed normal. Her skin felt far too tight from the inside.

"Sore. I don't relish being close to the capstone again."

Katya nodded, but she bet their reasons for discomfort were far different. Their time underground hadn't seemed to affect Dawnmother or Redtrue as it had her. When they passed the door and emerged into the capstone cavern, Katya's eyes snapped to the hole they'd climbed up, and she had to force the memories down. The cavern was wider than the tunnels, at least.

Redtrue glared at the capstone. "I don't know what else this abomination can tell us."

"Can you tell what purpose it was originally meant for?" Katya asked.

Redtrue pulled a pyramid out of her bag, but the look on her face said she was already out of her depth.

Master Bernard's nose nearly touched the capstone as he leaned close. "It's the same sort of energy I detected from the corpse Fiends but slightly different from the pyramids Starbride designed to hide us from the corpse Fiends' senses."

"Meaning that its purpose always had something to do with Fiends?" Katya asked.

"That would be my guess. But it sounds like Starbride has found a way to retune pyramids entirely, some new way of accessing pyramid magic."

"She said she was letting the adsna flow," Katya said.

Redtrue glanced at her sharply. "That is an adsnazi saying."

"I would love to hear all about it," Master Bernard said.

Redtrue stared at him as if doubting his words. The other adsnazi spoke first. "The adsna, the world spirit, is like a great river. It travels up from the world and all around us, and those that can sense the energy can let it flow through them."

"But," Redtrue added sternly, "we only work in harmony with the adsna and do not twist it to our own ends. Right, Riverwise?"

He shrugged. "Isn't using it at all twisting it to our own ends?"

Redtrue looked at him as if he'd grown another head. "Leafclever recommended you come with us."

"So?"

"How could he give me someone who spouts such nonsense?"

"Not everyone is as stubborn in their philosophy as you."

Katya found it hard not to adopt the young man on the spot. "And what do you think of our capstone?"

"It feels more like our magic than Farradain pyramids do."

"And what do you know of Farradain pyramids?" Redtrue asked.

He shrugged again. "I talk to people."

Katya had to chuckle. "If what Yanchasa said is true, and the Belshrethen became the Allusians, I don't think they all went to Allusia."

"You think some of them came here and brought their magic with them?" Master Bernard asked. "That sounds like a workable theory."

Redtrue harrumphed. "My people are not descended from Fiends."

Katya's eyes rested on the glowing capstone, and she pictured the monster trapped beneath their feet. "There are no such things as Fiends," she whispered, but she couldn't believe it. There were monstrous people in the world. Surely, they deserved a label all their own.

CHAPTER TWENTY-SIX

STARBRIDE

Yanchasa's children kept their distance, hidden among the trees as Starbride rode north through the forest to Roland's rumored hypnotization camp. Every once in a while, one of Starbride's companions would glance into the woods as if they felt the children's icy stares.

Starbride couldn't help but think of her companions as nursemaids. They weren't as bad as Dawnmother, but she felt Freddie's and Hugo's eyes on her all the time. They rode just behind her, the three messengers packed in tightly behind them, and the remnants loping a few paces around the entire party, just far enough away to not scare the horses.

Starbride was tempted to bark at her companions that if they didn't like the children's or the remnants' presence, they were welcome to return to Marienne. But she needed the messengers, and Freddie and Hugo would refuse. They couldn't spy on her if they didn't keep close.

Hugo nudged his horse next to hers. "I'm fine," she said before he could speak.

His mouth snapped shut before it edged open again.

"And no, I am not reading your mind. You're simply very obvious."

She was trying for insulting, but he beamed. "Always happy to oblige."

A tremor of guilt made her sigh. "Sorry, Hugo. I don't like being looked after."

"It's my pleasure to inquire about your health, Miss Starbride. You looked after all of us for so long, remember?"

"And now you think I need you instead?" she asked.

"That's not what I meant." Had his voice always grated on her nerves so much?

"Come and ride back here, Hugo," Freddie called. "You can ask me how I am."

Now that was more like it. If she couldn't have some actual combat, she'd take some verbal sparring. "Afraid I'll hurt someone, Freddie?"

"Yes."

She frowned. "I expected you to say no or comment on how I've changed."

"Starbride would know how she's changed. I won't play games with you, Yanchasa."

She wheeled her horse around. "I'm not Yanchasa!"

"Yeah? Prove it." He gave her a hard stare, and the others looked at her anxiously. The remnants skidded to a halt.

She gestured to her own body. "You have eyes, yes?"

"They're one of the senses I'm currently trusting."

"Well?" She didn't know what to say, searching for some way to refute his claim, though she didn't know why she bothered.

"Nor do I, daughter. Ignore him," Yanchasa said.

"Well?" Freddie asked. "Is that your entire argument?"

"I don't need to argue with you."

"I suppose you don't, Yanchasa."

Heat prickled her temples. "That is not my name!"

Yanchasa leaned against a tree just behind Freddie's shoulder. "Kill him, daughter, if he bothers you this much."

Starbride glared at her. "I do not need to punctuate my arguments with force!"

That seemed to shut them all up. Starbride turned her horse and kept going. As they journeyed farther into the forest, she rubbed her arms. She should have brought a cloak. It had started snowing again, and they might be traveling all the way into the hills.

No, she shouldn't be cold. The adsna kept her warm, but she couldn't quite reach it. The chill of winter wormed into her core.

"What's happening?" she whispered.

"Oh, are you talking to me?" Yanchasa asked.

"Why can't I…"

"What is it, daughter? Feeling the cold wind, are we?"

And it wasn't just that. She hadn't been on a horse in ages, and she was starting to feel a deep ache in her legs. The wind knifed through her clothing and turned her hands and face to ice. Her head began to throb, and the emotions that had tormented her before she'd found Yanchasa's peace, the sorrow she'd felt when Katya and Dawnmother had died, threatened to engulf her.

But they were alive! She should have rejoiced, but all she could remember was the power she'd lobbed around so casually, the suspicion of family and friends. They wouldn't want anything to do with her now. Even Freddie had become her enemy.

"Please," Starbride whispered.

"I am not your slave. You do not beckon me forward when you need me and dismiss me when you're through."

"I meant no disrespect."

"You do not shout at me, daughter. I am the one with centuries of knowledge. I am the one whose experiences can save you. I am the wellspring of your power." Heat flooded her, thrusting the chill away. As the adsna pounded in her veins, it banished her guilt, and she sighed as if relaxing into a lover's embrace.

"I do not like teaching you these lessons, daughter."

"I know. I'm sorry."

"You know that I love you." His affection coated her like honey.

"Me, too. I'm sorry." No one else could ever love her like this. No one could ever be so close, so intimate. Not Dawnmother, not even Katya. And Yanchasa's love was immortal. Starbride saw that now.

They camped for the night at an abandoned village. Starbride wished they could keep going, but her mortal companions couldn't see at night, and they felt winter's chill more keenly than she could. She left the remnants and the children to guard outside while she and the rest stayed in a large, abandoned tavern.

The others camped in the common room, Freddie and Hugo agreeing that would be safer. Starbride took the largest bedroom. There was another, but she didn't bother to mention it. If they wanted to stay together, they were welcome to each other. She wouldn't miss their accusing eyes.

She laid in the bed and stared at the ceiling. After an hour passed, she stood and snooped around. With her adsna-augmented eyes, she didn't need light. A knitted coverlet sat at the foot of a bed big enough for two, probably the tavern's owner and their spouse, unless the owner was accustomed to taking different people into his or her bed. A dresser sat across the room, a white doily masking the dark mahogany wood of the surface. Starbride pawed through the objects that dotted the top: a glass lamp, an empty bowl made of tarnished silver, and a jewelry box.

Starbride opened the box slowly, listening to the creak of the carved wooden lid. Her hands trembled, and she paused to marvel at them, thinking of all the times she'd gone through her own beloved jewelry. These objects were flotsam compared to what she was used to, but she could sense the love in the battered copper comb, the bronze pin in the shape of a sunburst, and the strand of glass pearls. She thought of Countess Nadia's string of perfect Lanaster pearls, something this box's owner couldn't even dream of. She could almost smell the crisp air on Nadia's balcony and hear her throaty laugh as Starbride asked her again for the naughty story that went with those pearls. They had time to tell that story now that Roland had been dealt with.

But would Nadia bother? Or would she invent some excuse to be elsewhere? Friends were hard to come by for the very powerful. How many friends did Einrich have, after all?

Starbride slapped the lid shut. She hadn't worn jewelry in a long time. Lack of adornment seemed the proper reaction to war. And when she'd led the rebellion she couldn't afford to draw attention to herself.

She supposed she could start now, adorn herself with some of her father's carefully crafted pieces or the consort bracelet.

Starbride rubbed her wrist as she sat on the bed. Maybe she shouldn't have put Katya to sleep. They could have gone on this mission together, shared this too-wide-for-one bed, and Starbride could have convinced Katya that her newfound power was a good thing.

"Sleep now, daughter," Yanchasa said. "Time enough for thinking in the morning."

And there was no room to be alone in her dreams. Starbride lay back and shut her eyes, but she didn't know how sleep would find her.

What a little prick Wallux was. He sat stiff-backed on his pony with his nose so high in the air that Starbride wondered if his upper lip was covered in shit, and his nose was trying to get away from it.

For all the grandeur of the army gathered behind him with its purple pennants flapping in the air, he was unimpressive, thin faced and homely, and by the length of his legs, he couldn't have been much taller than five feet.

He puffed up and heeled his mount to meet her when she rode closer with her honor guard. Their shaggy ponies weren't much different from the large elk her people rode, so much more sure-footed on ice and snow than the lowland horses. Maybe Wallux wouldn't have seemed so small if his pony wasn't so large. Overcompensation if she'd ever seen it.

"Hail, General Yanchasa, leader of Belshreth's mighty army," the man to Wallux's left said, as if Wallux himself was too important to speak to her. The aide's Belshrethen was good, and she wondered who had taught him.

But her grasp of his language was better. She'd had the best kind of tutor, the kind whose mind she could get into and rattle around in. "Hello to you, too."

Wallux glanced at his aide as if waiting for more. When the aide began another lengthy speech, Wallux asked, "Have you come to surrender?" in his native tongue.

"I would ask you the same question, but I don't care to hear the answer." She slid off her elk, and several of her honor guard did the same. She held her arms out and smiled at Wallux as the guard undressed her.

Wallux and his aides glanced at one another. An oily, superior smile broke out on Wallux's face. "This gesture isn't necessary. I will accept your surrender without the need for you to abase yourself."

"Sporting of you," Starbride said. They'd rid her of armor and weapons. Another was leading the mounts away.

As they bared her breasts, Wallux gave a start of surprise that quickly turned into a leer. Several of his aides looked away. "Of course, it would be rude not to accept such a superior offering as yourself."

As Edette had guessed, his eyes traveled down her body as her guard removed her boots and socks, then her trousers. He licked his lips as he stared at the cloth guarding her loins. When her guard whisked it away to reveal her manhood, Wallux reared back so hard his pony shied. She hoped he'd be thrown, but he managed to bring the animal back under control.

Starbride couldn't hold in a laugh. Her guards jogged back toward their mounts and left her naked in the middle of the field.

Wallux sneered. "We also have pyramid magic," he said with a snarl, "and we use it for more than just these petty tricks!"

"Good for you." Her voice roughened, the sound designed to pain human ears. Wallux flinched, but his eyes widened as he watched the horns slide from Starbride's brow.

The pain was exquisite. Claws sprang from her fingers and toes, and four crow's wings sprouted from her back in a flurry of blood. She pushed her jaw down, felt the chin and cheek spikes emerge as she relished the swelling of her muscles, the snapping of rearranging bone. She took her first step forward, and her vision faded to a red haze as she changed her eyes to black pools. As she walked, she called to the crystal that surrounded them, the bones of the mountains, the heart of Belshreth.

It thudded into her, drawing blood, and she made it part of herself, piling it around her until she was encased, shaping it until she towered over Wallux and his army.

She brought her foot crashing down, and he squelched between her toes. His mages hurled magic that died before it reached her, cancelled by her troops. She waded among the army, ripping, stomping, losing herself in a blood-drenched haze.

Starbride bolted upright. Power coursed through her, so much that her pyramids bathed the room in white. She could still hear the cries of the dying, their blood on her crystal covered hands.

The light began to fade. Starbride flexed her numb left arm; it had been caught beneath her while she slept. One leg was on the bed, the other dangling over the side. She must have been restless in her dreams. Her head throbbed, and between the pain and the power buzzing through her, she felt as if she hadn't slept at all.

A noise made her look to the open window. The shutters knocked into the wall as they moved lazily in the icy breeze.

"How did the window get open?" she asked.

No one answered. The adsna died down, the room went dark, and the cold became immediate. She pulled the coverlet around her. "Yanchasa?"

His voice seemed faint. "Breathe deeply, daughter."

"I told you I don't want your memories!"

"I only wished to show you the heights that power can take you to." He sounded as tired as she felt.

"I already know. I defeated Wallux's, I mean, *Roland's* army. Why do you sound so tired?"

Yanchasa's spectral form appeared on the edge of the bed, but she could see the dresser through his torso. His helmet was still missing, and now most of the armor from his arms and legs was gone, leaving only a few pieces, reminding her of how she'd felt in his dream. She barely felt his touch at first, then he flared, and his caress across her cheek felt as substantial as her own hand. As he pulled back, he faded, and she couldn't get over the feeling that he'd exhausted himself.

"What's happening to me?" she asked. "What's happening to you?"

"You are beginning to feel again, now that your grief is less."

But whose feelings, his or her own? "I don't want…" But she remembered the way the cold had seeped into her bones, the certainty that she couldn't go back to the way things were, not after everything she'd done. Yanchasa loved her, would always love her, perhaps was now the only person who *could* love her.

"No!" she said, burying her face in her palms. "Katya loves me."

"Of course she does, daughter."

"No, I mean it!"

The bedroom door flew open. "What's wrong?" Freddie stood framed in the doorway, one dagger out. When he spied the open window he went to it and took a quick look out. "Did someone try to—"

Starbride barreled into his chest, nearly knocking him over. She threw her arms around him as confusion wouldn't let her be, emotions pulling her back and forth, muddying the way to the adsna. "Katya loves me," she said.

"She does, Starbride," he said as his arms went around her. She heard his dagger clatter on the dresser top. "I've known her a long time, and she's never happier than when she's with you. She's never cared about anyone more."

Starbride sighed into that thought. Why did she need it so badly? Why was it so important to her? What was it compared to the power in her grasp?

"The power will make her love you even more, daughter," Yanchasa said.

Starbride turned his way, but Freddie dipped his knees until they were eye level. "Hey!" He snapped his fingers in her face. "Whatever it's saying, don't listen. Stay with me." In the moonlight from the window, his eyes seemed colorless.

"You don't understand."

He laughed harshly. "The temptation to do bad things? Oh, I understand, sweet."

"See where his mind goes?" Yanchasa asked. "Same place as the rest of them: power equals evil."

Freddie held her cheeks, capturing her face. "Remember when you had to try skulking?" he asked. "And again, when you wanted to go to a dive bar, what did you call it? A den of ill repute?"

She smiled at the memory. "It wasn't much of one."

"But you were so excited, remember? You were so desperate to see the seedy side of life. That's when I really started thinking of you as a friend."

"Dawnmother had too much beer." Tears rolled down Starbride's face, and she dashed them away. "Why am I crying?"

"Lack of beer has that effect on me, too."

She laughed. She'd told Ursula she didn't care if Freddie lived or died, but that was a filthy lie.

The cold of the room hit her so hard she collapsed. Freddie caught her arms and held her upright. "What is it, Star? Tell me how to fix it, and I will."

"Do you need to be fixed, daughter?" Yanchasa asked.

"The cold," Starbride said with a gasp. Her knees wouldn't stop trembling. She'd thought the adsna was weak before, but this felt as if someone had taken the floor away.

"Stay here." Freddie lowered her to the rug, and she heard him ripping the bedding from the mattress.

Yanchasa knelt in front of her face. "Cold again, daughter? You need only ask."

"Why are you doing this?"

"Stay with me, stay here with us." Freddie wrapped her in blankets and lifted her. He hurried from the room. "Hugo!"

They were both with her then, talking to her, rubbing her arms, their touch like brands.

"Is this better?" Yanchasa asked, her voice cutting through the clutter. "Do you like being weak?"

Hugo's face passed through Yanchasa's as if through fog. "Do you remember that time I followed you into the woods, and I kept staring at your legs?" Someone had lit a candle, and in the dim light she couldn't tell if he blushed or not.

Starbride tried to summon the memory, but it felt so far away.

"Remember when we first saw Katya in the hallway at the palace?" Freddie asked. "When she'd sneaked in after Roland, and we came in after her? You were so happy to see her."

"What would she say if she could see you now?" Yanchasa said. "You're supposed to be helping the king, not collapsing like an old wet sack."

Starbride sobbed as shame piled onto the thoughts writhing inside her. Why wouldn't her body work; why wouldn't her limbs obey her?

"Make them," Yanchasa said.

Starbride tried, but the others were shouting memories, and she couldn't think. Why weren't they helping her? Why were they just standing there, touching and talking to her? "Help me."

They claimed that they were, but they were just calling out memory after memory, one misery after another, so many *feelings* until she felt as if her head would split open.

Over their heads, standing beside the mystified messengers, Yanchasa waited. "You can do it, daughter."

And she felt it, a spark deep inside. She'd let it go, but she could get it back. "I'll help you if you need it," Yanchasa said.

No, she could do this. She could return to power. She'd lost it momentarily, but she was not weak. She grabbed for it, but it slipped from her grasp. She wailed, and they patted her more frantically. Freddie yelled at the messengers to saddle the horses. They wanted to take her back to Marienne as she was, weak and in pain. She'd have to admit her shame to the king, to Katya, and watch their eyes go dark with pity. They'd put her to bed and set a nursemaid to watch her, maybe several to fetch her food and drink, to dress and bathe her. They wouldn't think her capable of anything if she fouled up this one, simple job.

Katya's eye would stray to someone more capable, someone like Redtrue.

"No!" Starbride grabbed the adsna and yanked, making power roar through her, knocking back those around her and silencing them at last.

Starbride basked in the power as she stood. The blankets fell away, and she glowed again, secure. "Sorry to trouble you."

Freddie cursed. Hugo rubbed his face and looked as if he might weep. The messengers watched her closely as if they feared another emotional purge.

"It's not yet dawn," Starbride said. "Get some sleep." She strode outside, done with sleeping for the time being.

"I'm so proud of you daughter," Yanchasa said. Starbride was pretty proud of herself.

CHAPTER TWENTY-SEVEN

KATYA

Katya studied a drawing one of the knowledge monks had made of the hidden city's ten spirits. She'd commended his accuracy. She could almost feel the gritty dust drifting in the air and smell the dry stone.

Katya breathed deeply and stared out the window in her sitting room. She was no longer underground. She was high above the dead city and never had to enter it again. Whenever she thought about the cramped tunnels and the subterranean rooms, her palms began to sweat, and the shakes overtook her.

Eyes closed, Katya prayed to all ten spirits that this feeling would go away in time.

But which spirits? The images she'd known ever since she could remember, or those in the drawing? Ten spirits, five male and five female, each pair dressed exactly the same, features mostly the same, and worshiped by a people who'd had no contact with her own before the great battle that decided their fate.

Katya folded the paper until only one figure remained of each set of twins. Five spirits, each sharing a body with its male and female halves; five rulers of ancient Belshreth, each able to shift between man and woman. The natives hadn't brought spirits from Belshreth. They'd brought their rulers.

But if the Belshrethen had overthrown the council of five, why build a temple to them? She pushed the paper away and then pulled it closer as if the motion would give her the answer. "A *hidden* temple. You weren't supposed to remember them? Or maybe you weren't supposed to venerate them."

It must have been hard in those first days for the refugees of Belshreth. They'd had to flee their crumbling city after imprisoning its rulers. They were separated from the rest of their people either by accident or choice, and they arrived in a land foreign to them. Perhaps they met other friendly natives; perhaps they'd had to struggle through on their own. There had to have been those who'd lamented the rebellion, who'd wished a return to the good old days when they were safe and warm and comfortable. Some of them would turn the tyrants of memory into saviors who could perform miracles.

But the majority stayed true to the attitude that had led them to rebel, and those that regretted leaving their homes had been forced to meet in secret. They'd handed down their memories until the figures in them became legend, a hoped-for future.

Maybe those who'd constructed the capstone thought it would either keep their former rulers imprisoned, banish them if they managed to escape, or keep the populace from using flesh magic.

But her people had retuned it. Instead of keeping the Fiends away, the Farradains had called one of them.

"Oh spirits," Katya said. "Redtrue was right. We screwed everything up."

And after Yanchasa was imprisoned in the pyramid, the people who worshiped the council of five saw their chance to free him, but the Order of Vestra killed them before they had the chance.

"At least we did one thing right," she muttered, though there would have been no need for the Order of Vestra if the ancient Farradains had never messed with flesh magic in the first place. They must have realized the curse they'd condemned their people to right after they'd done it. After all, they hadn't passed the secrets of flesh magic to anyone but members of the Order. If the Farradains had known about other flesh magic—like the ability to reshape their bodies—would they have been so selective with its use? Or would they have turned Farraday into another Belshreth?

Katya rubbed her temples. It was all conjecture until someone could translate the underground writing, but how would knowing help them free Starbride?

Katya stood to pace, missing Averie again, both for the companionship and for someone to bounce ideas off of. Maybe she should go looking for Maia, but Maia was having a bit of fun exploring underground with Brutal. And Dawnmother was speaking with Starbride's parents. Da was in council. Katya could have joined him, but she thought her mind would wander as the nobles and commoners and Allusians went round and round in debate.

A knock on her door made her jump. She waited, but there was no one to answer it. "Come in."

Reinholt poked his head around the door. "Hello, Little K."

She stared at him. She hadn't seen him since she first crawled out of the dead city. Her father had told her that Reinholt had cried when he'd thought she was dead, but he hadn't bothered to visit since she'd proved she was alive.

Katya bit back the urge to bark, "Where in the spirits' names have you been?" and swallowed. "Hello."

He smiled, and it had a bit of the old Reinholt gleam. Gone was the bitter edge from the last time they'd had a lengthy conversation, just before he'd abandoned his duty and his children.

"Look," he said, "I'm sorry I was such a colossal ass."

That didn't begin to cover it.

Before she could speak, he held up a hand. "I know it's going to take a while for you to forgive me. I understand, I do. And I'll say I'm sorry as many times as I need to. I'll make everything up to you."

As if he'd just broken a lamp and blamed it on her. "Rein—"

"I met Appleton's family."

She sucked in a breath. "You what?"

"I did them the most damage, so I've spoken to them. It didn't go well."

"I don't expect so. You killed one of them. The city, Rein, the riots."

"I know."

"And then you left!"

"I know, Katya. You can't say anything that I haven't said in my own head." He scrubbed through his hair and paced, reminding her of herself. "That's why I sneaked into Dockland, why I tried to find out what happened to all of you, why I went along with Starbride."

Katya's eyes narrowed. "*Went along with*? She saved you!"

"Yes, I went along with her extremely smart, fabulous ideas. Happy?"

"If she hadn't taken you in, if Roland had caught you—"

"Like I said, nothing I don't already know."

She cocked her head. "What makes you think I'll ever forgive you?"

"Because I'm your brother. Because our mother's gone, and because I'll be standing with you at your wedding whether you want me to or not."

That same old Reinholt audacity. She had to admire it even as she wanted to kick him in the shins.

"And because," he said, "I wouldn't accept the crown prince's title even if our father fell over, cracked his head, lost his memory, and forgot what a total prick I am."

Katya sputtered a laugh.

"You've got better crown prince instincts in your right boot than I do in my entire body," he said.

Going a little far perhaps, but she bobbed her head side to side as if to say that was probably true. "I'm not the real heir anyway, just a placeholder for Vierdrin. You have been to see your children, yes?"

"Where do you think I've been since you miraculously returned to life? Even the reincarnation of my sister couldn't tear me away from their little faces."

This time, her smile was genuine. "And Lord Vincent?"

"Ah, that's a pricklier manner. I've burned my bridges there, committed the ultimate sin in his eyes."

"Dereliction of duty."

"Which is a shame because I was quite in love with him."

Katya's mouth fell open. "Did you *ever* love Brom?"

He gave her a dark look. "It is possible to love more than one person, Katya. Not all of us believe in that one, perfect, true love like you do."

"Starbride is all the woman I need."

"Hooray for you. Lucky for me, there are all kinds of people in the world."

She gestured for him to sit across from her. "If you love Vincent, you have to fight for him."

"Hopeless, romantic idiot," he said.

She did kick him in the shin then. He uttered a curse and scooted away. "Why are you here?" she asked.

"Seemed the right thing to do. You came back from the dead to see all of us." He glanced around. "Where is Starbride? I half expected to find you writhing all over each other."

"Must have made you wonder why I said, 'come in.'"

He shrugged. "Like I said, all kinds of people in the world."

"You're an ass."

"Granted. So, where is she?"

Katya crossed her arms, then unfolded them and let them lay in her lap. She needed someone to puzzle out Starbride's predicament with, and here was a pair of ears that claimed to be willing. But how could she share her most intimate thoughts with Reinholt? She didn't know if she'd have been able to do that *before* he was half responsible for nearly burning Marienne to the ground.

He hooked his hands under the settee. "I'm not moving until you tell me what's bothering you, so you might as well start."

"I could just leave."

"I could just follow you."

She narrowed her eyes. "I could kill you."

"Maia wouldn't love you anymore. I'm her favorite cousin now."

"Liar!"

He shrugged again. "Besides, there are only a few servants around, and I'm heavy. You'd never shift my body through the halls on your own."

Katya sighed loudly. "Have you heard any of the stories about Starbride?"

"I saw her outside Da's tent. She's gone pyramid wild or something."

Katya spilled everything to him, and to his credit, he didn't make as many pithy comments as she expected. She glossed over some details, their most intimate conversations, their lovemaking, but she got her point across.

"I don't know what to do," she said at last.

"Must be new to you."

She searched his face for sarcasm but found none. "I do like to have a plan."

He steepled his fingers and stared at the table. Katya left him alone in his thoughts and marveled at the change in him. Before Brom had betrayed them, he'd been her sarcastic but lovable brother, a man who liked to tease and wink at life. She was a little ashamed that she'd never thought much of him, even though he'd be king one day, and if she wasn't too old to go adventuring, she'd still be leader of the Order, reporting to him as she did her father.

That had never seemed real, and not just because her father seemed immortal. When Reinholt had revealed himself to be a spoiled brat, oh, she'd thought of him more often, but nothing good. It was as if the jovial personality he'd always displayed had been some kind of mask.

Now she saw the truth: he'd never grown up before the trouble started. If he'd become king, he would have been loved, a golden god the populace could cheer, but all the work would have been done by those around him, advisors and the royal pyradisté and the Order. A committee would have done the job of one king.

And now he could see he wasn't right for it. What he *was* right for, exactly, Katya had no idea, but he seemed to be trying to figure it out, and she was a little touched that one of the places he'd started was with her.

He sat up so suddenly, Katya started. "Well," he said, "it doesn't seem like you can convince her to give the power up. Did Master Bernard say he could help?"

Katya shook her head. "Flesh magic is new to him. He only learned a little, and Starbride taught him that."

"Is there any way you could sneak up on her and knock her out?"

Just the thought made Katya's insides roil. "I couldn't hurt her, Rein."

"There are people for that."

Katya shuddered.

"It'd be for her own good, Katya." When she didn't speak, he sighed. "Well, if someone could knock her out, maybe that would give the adsnazi or Master Bernard room to work."

"She defeated an entire army singlehandedly. If her Fiend guest didn't rip your throat out, you'd probably find her skin hardened like steel and end up making her angry."

"I wasn't nominating myself to do the dirty deed."

She opened her mouth to say, "No, you wouldn't," but she kept the words inside. "Any other ideas?"

"Trick her? You must have some way of making her vulnerable."

"This is the love of my life you're talking about, Rein."

He barked a laugh. "I suppose this is why you keep an infamous murderer in your group, Little K. Someone's got to think nasty thoughts for you."

"Pennyn—Freddie is innocent."

"Still, didn't you always say he and Crowe did the dirty jobs for the Order? There must have been a reason they were nominated."

She waved, not willing to get into that. "I'll think on it. If you come up with something solid, let me know."

He nodded, but she could see his exasperation in the way he fought not to cross his arms. He could make hard decisions as long as they didn't jeopardize his own skin.

"Have you heard about Roland?" she asked.

"Maia told me on her way to your underground city. Nice find, by the way."

"Thanks."

"What are we going to do with our mad uncle?"

"How do you feel about him?"

He shrugged. "Sorry for him."

Katya sat bolt upright. "Sorry? For the man that poisoned your wife against you? That started this whole ugly business that even now isn't finished?"

"The Fiend did all that, Katya, not the man."

She could see by his confusion that he believed that, something she couldn't bring herself to do. She didn't know how she'd speak to Roland without cutting his throat, but Reinholt seemed nonplussed. "Come with me," she said. "I've got another job for you."

Katya led the way into the dungeon, though they needed Reinholt's Fiend to penetrate to the deepest layer. Katya turned her lamp up as high as it could go and fought not to think about the stone walls pressing in. She had to close her eyes several times in quick snaps, picturing an open field, a forest, the wide blue expanse of the ocean.

She repeated over and over that these walls were steady; they weren't coming down, and they didn't house a giant Fiend, only what remained of one.

"I'll stay behind you in the shadows," Katya said. "I don't want to talk to him."

"You just want me to see if he's crazy? If he remembers what he did as a Fiend?"

"He remembers. I know he does. I just want to know…" She couldn't finish, didn't even know why she'd led Reinholt down here.

"If he's sorry?" Reinholt asked.

"If there's enough of him left to be sorry."

He didn't argue. She could have kissed him for that. Did it matter if Roland was sorry for what he'd done, what the Fiend had made him do? Would that make everything better? Why did she care enough that she wanted to hear it?

If she could forgive him, then anything Starbride did wouldn't matter. Katya locked that thought away.

Soft whimpering came from Roland's cell. Starbride had spoken about Maia's transformation, how she'd wanted to die, how Dawnmother and others had held and comforted her. Katya felt a twinge of sympathy for anyone left alone in the dark with his sins.

When Reinholt pushed open the cell door, the whimpers ceased. "Is that you?" Roland called.

Katya slipped into the shadows while Reinholt lifted the lantern toward his face. "It's me, Uncle."

Roland blinked at him. "Nephew? Is that you, Reinholt?"

He was filthy, his hair and beard in tangled knots. His shirt was torn and smeared with blood. As a child, Katya had worshiped her uncle, leader of the Order, a strong, intelligent, fearless man. She'd hung on his every word, an annoying little burr stuck to his side whenever he'd been in the palace.

As this Roland held up his stump to ward off the demons in his mind, Katya knew her beloved uncle was as dead as she'd thought him to be.

"Stay back," he said. He rolled, wrapping himself in his chains until he was flush against the wall. "I don't want it to hurt you."

"How could you hurt me now, Uncle?" Reinholt asked.

"Yanchasa." Roland's lip quivered. "I hurt everyone I love." His stump slashed through the air as if scraping at the words. "I tried to fight back. Anytime I could slow myself down, I did. The Fiend, it likes to play with people. It likes to hurt them. Anytime I could play cat and mouse with Katya and the others I did. I thought I was enjoying it, that the Fiend was enjoying it, but now I know I was trying to slow myself down!"

Killing Ma was meant to slow them down? Katya ground her teeth together so hard sharp pain slid along her jaw.

Reinholt knelt on the stones. "Yanchasa can't hurt you anymore, Uncle. Starbride saw to that."

"He's got her. He'll get everyone eventually. You have to guard yourself, nephew. Guard your children." He sucked in a deep breath and stared at nothing with horrified eyes. "I tried to kidnap your children."

Reinholt snapped his fingers. "That was the Fiend, Uncle, don't you remember?"

"They're going to kill me. And they should. Kill me before I hurt someone else, before I have the chance. Choices are *terrible*, nephew. Don't let anyone tell you differently."

Reinholt glanced over his shoulder, asking if Katya had seen enough. She started to edge out of the cell.

Reinholt paused before he followed. "Uncle, you were in the palace while the armies were fighting outside the wall."

Roland stared at him blankly.

"You said you knew you were toying with Katya. Why abandon your own army in the field to play with her?"

"I was with the army."

"No, Uncle, you were in the palace, remember?"

"Not me! *Me*! There were many of me with the army. They could take care of things. I would have won."

Reinholt just stared, but Katya remembered the host of attackers all speaking with her uncle's voice. *Hello, niece.* He'd left his copies in charge while he'd come into the palace to kill her. From what she'd heard of the battle outside the wall, he was right. If Starbride hadn't come along, he would have won. Katya hurried from the cell before the urge to strangle him overtook her.

Roland looked to the small movement, his eyes wide and terrified. "It's him! He's here!"

Katya kept going, and Reinholt followed on her heels, leaving their uncle shrieking in terror and rattling his chains.

CHAPTER TWENTY-EIGHT

STARBRIDE

Starbride watched the forest go by. Shame burned in her cheeks whenever she recalled the night before, but she didn't exactly know why. Because she'd succumbed to her weaker nature or because she hadn't fought harder against...

She couldn't finish the thought. Yanchasa crouched in her mind, and it was foolish to think he didn't know how she felt whether she let herself articulate her thoughts or not. Yanchasa stayed silent, though she thought she felt something from him. Satisfaction. When had she started feeling his emotions?

"Look ahead, daughter. Listen."

Starbride's gaze snapped forward. There was nothing to see along the road, but she heard rustling and the echoing crunch of cracking wood.

Freddie slipped off his horse with an easy motion. "I'll scout ahead."

Starbride almost called for him to stop, worry for his safety warring with her need to be the one who led the charge. She narrowed her eyes and fought to find her center.

Freddie jogged back moments later. "It's a whole hypnotized village."

"How do you know they're hypnotized?" Hugo asked.

"Regular people talk to one another as they work. They take breaks. These were just...blank."

"What was the snapping noise?" Starbride asked.

"They brought down a tree at the village edge. Probably firewood."

"Hypnotized or not, Roland wouldn't have wanted them to freeze to death," Starbride said. "How many?"

"Too many for the few of us."

"For you perhaps. Not for me, not for them." She nodded into the trees and put out her call, the adsna filling her with confidence. The children gathered in the nearest shadows. The remnants shuffled their feet, ready to attack.

She gestured one messenger forward. "Ride back and tell the king what we've discovered and that we're taking care of it." She waved four corpse Fiends toward him. "Make sure he gets to Marienne safely." She put mind magic behind the words, embedding it in the remnants' pyramids.

They gathered around the messenger, who grimaced as if he didn't know which was worse, staying here where he could feel the presence of the children or riding back alone with the remnants. "Yes, Princess Consort." He spurred his horse back along the trail.

"We'll circle around the side," Freddie said, "come at them from two different directions, but we should scout that way first."

Starbride shook her head. "Let's do what we came to do so we can get back."

He opened his mouth, but Starbride waved him away. "You circle around if you need to. We're going in." She kicked her horse forward, taking the children and the remnants with her.

A small cluster of thatch-roofed buildings sat in a clearing ahead. A stream wound near the opposite side, frozen over now, but during spring Starbride bet it flooded its banks time and again, the reason for the low rise of dirt near its edge.

People moved through the village with single-minded purpose, carrying wood or blades, and she heard the clang of a blacksmith's hammer. The people seemed a little worse for wear, their clothes ragged. Starbride could smell the dirt on them, and she was certain that the thatch would have been repaired if the villagers had been in their right minds. And there would have been children or dogs playing in their midst.

As she rode into the open, she sensed hypnosis pyramids in several of the houses. She let the adsna flow, changing them to wells of power. She'd expected the villagers to drop whatever they were holding, but the work didn't cease. They'd been mind-warped.

That shouldn't have been possible without a pyradisté working on them, and Starbride didn't think Roland had been out here recently. He'd had too much to do in Marienne. But he'd either made time, or someone else was working for him.

Starbride scanned the houses as she rode closer, looking for active pyramids. Something called from the edge of her senses.

One of the mind-warped villagers turned her way and gave a shout. His expression didn't change to fear or fury but remained placid, soulless as an alarm. The other villagers picked up weapons or tools, whatever they could reach, and charged. Starbride waved the remnants and the children forward. This would be a slaughter.

"Look out!" Yanchasa called, and Starbride's body lurched to the left. An arrow skimmed her arm, drawing a line of pain across her bicep. She hissed and sealed the cut with flesh magic before sliding down from her horse, making herself less of a target.

She spotted the archer along the tree line to the east and commanded two of the remnants to lope after him. He shot several arrows into them, but they didn't slow, and she didn't stay to watch them tear him apart.

She burned several villagers to ash. When a pyramid came flying at her from a cluster of buildings, she cleansed it with a thought.

"Stop, stop, we're on your side!" someone cried.

Starbride followed the pyramid scent and found the pyradisté between two shacks. She was young, probably thirteen or so. Her dirty blond hair had been cropped close to her head, and she hadn't lost the baby fat in her cheeks.

"My side?" Starbride asked. "Which side is that?"

"I work for the Fiend king! Don't you? You have the corpses!"

"Guess again."

The young pyradisté looked hastily left and right as she backed away.

"Princess Consort!" someone called from out in the press. The young pyradisté ran. Starbride was about to pursue when one of the messengers charged toward her on his horse. "Princess Consort, Lord Hugo and Master Freddie are trapped within the forest."

"Trapped?"

"By a gang of these." He gestured at the hypnotized people. "I was barely able to escape. They'll be overwhelmed."

Perhaps they should have scouted ahead after all. She cursed Freddie for getting himself and Hugo into trouble. She needed to catch the pyradisté. She started after the young girl without thinking.

"No," she said. "I need to go after Freddie and Hugo."

The messenger slid down from his horse. "Here."

"The pyradisté is a more pressing target," Yanchasa said, standing behind the messenger's shoulder. "If she escapes, she could create more problems for us."

Her body felt wrenched in two directions. "Freddie and Hugo could die!"

The messenger stared. Yanchasa's eyes narrowed dangerously. Starbride felt the adsna roar through her, threatening to steal her feelings.

"No!" she cried. The power pulsed, forcing the messenger back a step.

"You don't want your mission to succeed?" Yanchasa asked. "Did you enjoy your time last night?"

Before she could reply, the power drained away, and the cold crashed over her like a wave. Her legs threatened to buckle. No! She wouldn't give in this time, wouldn't sag to the floor and beg for help or surrender to the power that stole her emotions. She stumbled toward the horse.

The messenger had to help her up, and after she was astride he swung up behind her. "Take me there."

He aimed the horse in the right direction, and she barely held on. She tried to call for the children or the remnants, but that power wouldn't obey her.

Starbride heard the shouts echoing off the trees long before she saw the fight. Hugo, Freddie, and the last messenger tried to use the forest to keep a mass of mind-warped villagers from surrounding them. As she watched, the messenger went down beneath a wall of swinging blades. Freddie stayed ahead of the strikes, trying to get to Hugo who swung his rapier with wild abandon.

It wouldn't be enough. They'd have Hugo soon. Freddie would never reach him in time. Starbride flung her destruction hand out to summon fire or an earthquake or even a flash bomb, but the power felt sluggish, disobedient.

"Hugo!" Starbride cried. He couldn't look toward her, and she knew of only one way to help him. "Get down," she said to the messenger. Once he was clear, she rode into the fray, her horse knocking villagers to the side. Some turned toward her, weapons raised. "Hugo," she called again, "your Fiend!"

A blade dug into her thigh, turning her voice into a howl. Her horse reared as the villagers chopped at its hide. One of Starbride's feet slipped from the stirrup, and her arms couldn't hold. She slid to the ground, the impact sending shockwaves through her knees. The booted feet of the villagers converged on her.

Yanchasa was there, waiting to help, but hatred for her own cowardice reared within her. A club thudded into her ribs, driving her breath out, and an acid sting rolled all the way to her core as someone buried a knife in her back. She opened her lips to call Yanchasa's name.

A warm spray bathed her from head to toe, and the booted feet flew away as if before a hurricane. Her body folded in pain. The knife that had bitten into her dropped to the crimson-smeared grass. She lifted her head to look beyond it. The forest was a ruin of blood and body parts. The messenger was a retreating dot in the distance, and his horse lay in three tidy, oozing pieces.

Freddie perched in a nearby tree, watching with a look of awestruck horror as Hugo tore the last villager's head off. His eyes had become pits of light blue. The spike jutting from his chin moved up and down as he breathed hard. Crow's wings had torn the back of his coat wide open, and as he turned to look at Starbride, he bared his fangs in a snarl.

Starbride struggled to her feet with the aid of a small tree. She curled her free hand over her ribs, and her foot squelched as blood from her leg filled her boot. More flowed down her back. Hugo took a shambling step toward her.

Starbride reached for the adsna, but it eluded her still. Freddie slipped down from his tree, too far away to help her. Hugo took another step, and Starbride reached through her flesh pyramid in a way she hadn't since she'd first felt the adsna.

She sensed Hugo's ability to become human again—that rusty handle inside all Umbriels—and yanked on it. The magic still felt sluggish, but it grew stronger as he stalked toward her. By the time he broke into a run, it flowed again. When he neared her, she felt the rusty handle give, and he collapsed mid-step, falling into her arms and making her cry out in pain. She managed to guide him to the forest floor without dropping him.

"I can't find the medical kit," Freddie said

He tugged her upright, making her stutter a cry. "What are you doing?"

He was tearing cloth. "I have to bind your wounds, but the horse with the fucking medical kit is gone!"

"Shouting's not a good idea." The pain beat at her, and she knew it should have been excruciating, undeniable, but she was slipping away. Hugo had almost died, and half of her still wanted to go chasing that pyradioté, but she was so tired. She sank to the ground, and Freddie went with her.

"Everyone else is dead." He pressed something against her numb back. "I can't stop this bleeding."

Starbride gasped as the adsna filled her. "You don't have to." He jumped back with a curse when her wounds mended themselves.

Yanchasa stood amidst the trees, the bare amount of armor over her clothing. "What have you done, daughter?"

"I saved my friends."

"I never expected betrayal from you, someone who claimed to know it so well."

Guilt tried to worm into her, but she stopped it with a thought. "That's a shabby trick. I betrayed no one."

With a blink, Yanchasa stood just in front of her. He laid a spectral palm on Hugo's head, and Hugo came awake with a start. "I understand the connection he must have for you, daughter. He carries my flesh; he must call to you."

"He's my friend."

Hugo staggered upright but would have fallen again had Freddie not caught him. "What's going on?"

Freddie shushed him, his eyes fixed on Starbride. She glanced at him, but her words with Yanchasa couldn't wait, and she didn't care to keep them in her head. "You're working through me."

Yanchasa leaned back, an unreadable look on his face. "Sometimes you lack the necessary skill."

That made sense. Still, she'd learned so much. She felt the adsna waiting, ready to carry her feelings away, but she didn't want to bury her disquiet. She knew Yanchasa could make it worse, could make the cold feel like a thousand knives; he could make her wounds reopen. And she'd let him in, embraced him.

She didn't want to rid herself of him, not completely. There was knowledge and power in those bottomless eyes. And as today had proven, Roland's forces were still at work. Surely they could come to some compromise.

"Stop working through me," Starbride said.

He cocked his head.

"Teach me what I need to know, and let that be that." Images reared in her mind, her doing or his she didn't know: the awful way she'd treated Dawnmother and Katya and Maia. Starbride fought the feelings down, but one image wouldn't go away, the shutters fluttering in the breeze. Had he been using her body while she slept?

"Don't bother telling me that you're all I have," Starbride said, "Instead, consider this: I *am* all that you have."

His eyebrows lifted. "Marienne is filled with your kind now."

"And which of them will have you? Redtrue? Think again. Her very nature would make her turn tail from you and run."

Yanchasa smiled, and she saw respect in his gaze. "Do you seek to become my teacher, daughter?"

"No. Horsestrong knows you have more wisdom for battle and strategy, but I can't let my friends be sacrificed."

"Sacrifice is sometimes necessary. Katya knows this."

Starbride screwed her eyes shut. "And please stop digging through my memories. I am not Katya. I am me, and I will not sacrifice my friends!"

Yanchasa held her hands up in surrender. "As you wish. From now on, if you want my help, you must ask. I will be but a shade lingering in your mind."

Yanchasa was annoyed, but Starbride would take irritated over imperious and commanding. When she blinked again, Yanchasa was gone. Starbride glanced around, unable to remember the last time she hadn't been able to find him when she looked.

"Starbride?" Freddie asked.

She'd forgotten he was there. "Are you wounded, either of you?"

"A bit," Freddie said just as Hugo said, "Not after transforming."

With a thought, Starbride healed Freddie's cuts and bruises. As Hugo said, he was whole, even if he did look a little drowsy.

Freddie cleared his throat. "What happened?"

"Put your necklace back on, Hugo," Starbride said. "We should find the messenger, and then I need to round up the chil...the others."

"What happened?" Freddie asked again as he tried to keep pace with her.

"Think you and Hugo can find the rest of the horses?"

He stepped in front of her. "Is it like a children's story, and I need to ask three times?"

Starbride took a deep, steadying breath. "I cannot begin to explain."

"Because I'm too stupid to understand?"

"If it gets you out of my way, yes." She stepped around him.

"I think my horse went that way," Hugo said loudly.

Freddie slashed a hand through the air. "I'm not leaving you alone until you give me some clue about what in the name of Ellias's big balls is going on!"

"And I'm sure your horse went that way!" Hugo yelled.

"Both of you shut up." Starbride didn't know what she could say. Her feelings were still a jumble. She was annoyed and amused at Freddie and Hugo, ashamed and proud of herself. It was like having two minds, but she couldn't feel Yanchasa however she turned. "Let's finish the job here, let me work a few things out, and then I will try, Freddie, truly I will." She let some of the adsna back in, letting it calm her. It was a difficult balance, like figuring out how to work a stubborn sluice gate. How much to let in and how fast determined what she felt and when. She had to keep the cold at bay, at least.

Freddie's lips mashed together so hard they turned white, but at last he lifted his arms and then dropped them. "Come on, Hugo. Let's go find the horses."

CHAPTER TWENTY-NINE

KATYA

Whatever she did, nothing led Katya any closer to figuring out a way to free Starbride from Yanchasa's influence. Maia had been overwhelmed by the merest trace of Yanchasa's personality. Roland might have had closer contact with the Fiend, but it had only driven him more insane.

Redtrue consulted Leafclever about the capstone, and he agreed that they couldn't cleanse it on their own. It would take all of the adsnazi working in concert to change such powerful magic. And they couldn't say what would happen to someone attached to that magic, like Starbride, and all those who carried a piece: Katya's father, Reinholt, his children, Maia, Hugo, and now Brutal. They could be cleared of the Fiendish taint, or they might be killed.

Katya nodded when she heard. "Keep studying. We can't act on the capstone until we know everyone will be safe."

Redtrue frowned. "What if the only conclusions I can draw are ones you won't like, those that will only serve the greater good?"

"I suggest you don't speak such answers out loud." She slid her thumb along her rapier pommel, and Redtrue left her alone.

Maybe all of Katya's troubles would blow over, a voice inside her suggested. Yes, and maybe tiny winged spirits would deliver her dinner. The world was full of ifs, and as Dawnmother would say, every one of them was a hole in the road.

Katya decided to wander, her solution to so many problems in the past. She wasn't surprised when her feet took her past the council chambers. With so much to fret over, it was no wonder her brain tried to find yet *another* set of problems.

What she needed was something to put her sword to. By the raised voices in the council chamber, she thought her father might appreciate that.

Before she reached the door, it flew open, and nobles boiled out, faces thunderous. A few nodded as they stomped past. Only Count Mathias and Countess Nadia seemed calm. Leafclever and Dayscout brought up the rear, and they seemed just as agitated as the others.

At least they offered a smile before they wandered off, heads close together.

Katya found her father in his usual seat at the head of the long council table. He rested his chin in one fist and stared out the row of windows lining one wall.

"I won't ask how it's going," she said.

The lines under his eyes were deeper, purple-tinged. "This isn't a council. It's a giant millstone, and I'm the donkey trying to keep it going round. Most of the nobles are dead set against a parliament. They see it either as the catalyst for the capital's fall or knuckling under to the demands of the peasantry."

"Did they catch the part where a madman was actually the catalyst, and that the peasantry helped reclaim the kingdom?"

"Call it selective memory. I think their backs are up because of the Allusians. I tried to press upon them that the Allusians are only here to look after their own interests, but some don't believe me. I've told them we could learn from our neighbors, but you can guess how well that went."

Katya slipped into a seat beside him. "As welcome as a bad smell."

Da rubbed his chin. "Maybe if I push the Allusians on the nobles more, they'll better buy into the parliament idea, clinging to their fellow Farradains, no matter if they're poor."

"But using the Allusians like that would alienate them, yes?"

He shrugged. "They like the parliament idea. If I can get Dayscout to go along, perhaps we can perform a routine to get everyone looking the way we want."

"I don't envy you."

He sighed. "I miss Cat."

Katya's heart thudded. They hadn't really talked of Ma since the day they'd all been reunited. "Me, too. She always had clarity."

"My thoughts exactly."

They chuckled before bowing their heads in the face of all they had lost. Katya watched her father struggle with emotion even as she did. "When will we have the…" She took a deep breath. "The funeral."

"Tomorrow."

"So soon?"

"Not soon at all, my girl, as these things go."

Katya couldn't help but remember her grandmother's funeral, when events in the capital had come to a head, spurred on by Roland. She wondered if the glass carriage used to carry the royal coffins was still in one piece.

"We'll gather quietly at the crypt," he said. "Family, friends, and a few nobles waiting outside. I thought you'd want to inter Averie at the same time."

Katya hiccupped through a nod. It was probably best to avoid a show of wealth when so many people in the city had lost someone. They couldn't all have a state funeral, and it was best not to remind them of that fact.

❖

When Katya emerged from the palace early in the morning, she stopped cold. The glass funeral carriage rested at the bottom of the stairs, empty but polished and ready. Reinholt stood beside it, and Katya just kept herself from lunging at him. Their father had come up with a simple, effective way to keep the populace from resenting the royals anew, and Reinholt stomped all over it.

When he saw her, he grinned. "I did consult him, Little K."

She skidded to a halt and forced herself to look at the noticeably empty carriage. One glass side had been left out. "What's going on?"

"This isn't for Ma. My friends and I have been circulating through the town, telling everyone this is a day of mourning." He looked up at the sky. "Come on. We're late."

He climbed up into the carriage's seat and waved her aboard. She climbed up slowly, giving him a sidelong glance. The remaining side to the carriage rested beneath them. "Where is Da?"

"He'll meet us at the crypt."

Katya kept her frown as they drove through the streets. When a woman stepped forward from the meager crowd and set something in the open side of the carriage, Katya watched her warily. She wiped tears from her cheeks, glanced at Katya, and nodded.

She stepped back, and Katya saw a rag doll, one button left in its dirty white face, sitting upon the velvet lining inside the carriage.

As they continued, more people came forward to lay objects in the carriage until they had to stop and put up the side. Even then, people put their keepsakes on top. Sometimes they just touched the carriage as it rolled by, darkening the glass with fingerprints. A day of mourning; she finally understood. Reinholt invited the populace into their grief instead of hiding from them. It let them know that their monarchy mourned with them, that their leaders had lost people, too.

"Clever, Reinholt," Katya said.

"Not all of us are thinking with our *crowns*, Katya. People need this." When she stared at him, he returned the look, but his held a hint of defiance. "I'm serious. Of the two of us, who is more in touch with their feelings?"

Bad feelings, she'd give him that.

When the carriage was overflowing, people started laying things behind the driver's seat or at Katya's and Reinholt's feet. Katya put them beside her, but soon she had to walk in order to make room, and by the time they reached the graveyard south of Marienne, Reinholt walked, too, leading the horses.

A crowd followed them to the graveyard gates and stopped. Maybe they thought the less people to disturb the dead, the better. The gravediggers had been operating overtime. Unclaimed bodies now rested in a mass grave near the back, and that was where Reinholt steered the glass carriage. They paused before a large pit, gaping black like a wound in the earth. Da waited with Maia and Brutal. Off to the side stood Countess Nadia, Baroness Jacintha, Dayscout, his servant, and a few others. More townspeople gathered at the fence to watch.

"Today we bury the dead," Da intoned, "so that the living might continue." Old words, said at gravesides since Marienne's beginning, only not by loved ones, not by the king. The gravedigger said them before he cast in the first shovelful of dirt.

"Come on," Reinholt whispered in her ear.

Katya helped him lift the glass carriage from its wooden base. Brutal, Jacintha, and some of the others carried it to the large pit, and the gravediggers attached it to a pulley, just as they would a coffin. Maia and Nadia led the others in gathering the loose keepsakes. They placed them in the grave as the carriage slowly descended.

The glass funeral carriage that had cost a fortune was soon entombed in dirt. The people along the fence moved away in little groups. Katya and her family trekked toward the large crypt where scores of Umbriels slumbered, the stone and marble square guarded by the statue of an immense hawk that peered at them with suspicious eyes.

Captain Ursula met them just inside the iron doors, standing guard over two bundles, both swaddled head to toe in linen and tied with cloth-of-gold cord. The smell of flowers and rosewood oil permeated the air, and Katya spied plant stems woven through the shrouds.

She grabbed at her side for a hand that was not there, might never be there again. Tears threatened to choke her, and she feared her feet might not carry her farther. Maia caught her right hand and Reinholt her left as they followed Katya's father deeper into shadow.

"Captain," Da said, "thank you for guarding my family." His eyes were so soft and sad, Katya wanted to put her arms around him, but she feared letting go of Maia and Reinholt.

Ursula bowed and stepped out. Katya saw a shadow waiting in the back, the man who would entomb her mother and Averie. There were already two niches waiting in the wall, and plenty of bare space for the rest of them.

Da touched Ma's forehead. Without a word, he turned and left, cloak flapping behind him. Maia approached the bier on shaky legs. She laid the ghost of a kiss against the fabric shrouding both bodies and then followed Katya's father.

Reinholt gave Katya a squeeze, but she wouldn't let go. "I killed Averie," she whispered. "I let our mother die."

Reinholt bent to her ear. "The monster did, not you."

She shook her head wildly, and the crypt blurred. "You don't understand. I—"

He gripped her hand so hard shocks of pain traveled up her arm. "I do understand, and I'm still right."

Had Castelle told him what had happened to Averie, or was he just trying to make her feel better? It didn't matter. He let go and then bid farewell to their mother. Katya realized she'd never been so happy that Lord Vincent kept the children away. She didn't want to think of them seeing their relatives fall to pieces.

Katya sank down beside the bier. She and her mother had already said good-bye, once in life and again in death. What words could comfort her now? She couldn't rid herself of the image of Averie's terrified face the night Roland had captured her, long before he'd turned her into a weapon.

One touch and then the smell of flowers was too overwhelming, the crypt too close. She staggered outside and tried to block out the sound of the gravedigger mixing his mortar.

Da tried to take both his children and his niece in his arms and ended up squashing them until they protested. They chuckled at that, the fragile mood cracking like an egg.

"At least it's stopped snowing," Reinholt said.

Katya knew they should have been thankful the ground hadn't frozen. If they'd waited any longer to bury their dead, they would have been waiting until spring. "I think I'll walk back to the palace."

The others put up a mild protest, but she declined. She wanted to hoard her grief, to lament her loss and not have to endure that of others. She waved at her family's carriage and enjoyed the crisp air on her warm cheeks.

As the wind gusted, she shrugged forward in her coat, sticking her fingers under her arms, a pose which blended with others who hurried past. The dark gray day promised snow, and everyone wanted to be out of the cold, their grief either forgotten or better seen to indoors. Maybe she would go to a tavern, become Lady Marchesa Gant for a few hours, but that would put her in the center of others' sadness again, and she couldn't afford a flood of tears.

Before she passed a dark alley, Katya moved toward the center of the street, the cautious spirit of Crowe always with her. Her gaze darted back as a shadow peeled away from the others and followed her.

Katya sighed. Maybe with the Watch's increased patrols, thieves were getting desperate enough to attack in broad daylight. Well, hadn't she been looking for a problem to put her sword to?

She sighed again. It just made her more tired.

Katya scanned the street before she turned. Her stare brought the footpad up short. He was older than expected, probably her father's age, and his dark hood would have screamed thief had it not been cold enough to warrant it.

Katya rested her hand on her rapier. "It's not worth your life, fellow."

He grinned, showing yellowing teeth amidst his salt-and-pepper beard. "Perhaps it is and perhaps it isn't."

Katya cocked an eyebrow. "A philosopher thief, eh?"

"When you get to my level, they don't call you thief anymore. You labeled me usurper."

"No." Her breath came quicker. "You can't be." The army was dead. She had a flash of Roland yelling, "Not me! *Me!*"

The thief cocked his head and gave her that *same* grin. "Hello, n—"

Katya drew her rapier and leapt. She jerked to a halt when the thief whipped a pyramid from his coat pocket. Others in the street only hurried faster if they noticed at all.

"So many dead, niece," the thief said. "Do you want to make it a few more?"

"He's finished. *You're* finished. Why won't you just die?"

"I'm thorough. You always admired that about me."

Katya gripped her rapier so hard that either she or it had to shatter. "You I can kill."

"Does that mean the other me is still alive somewhere?"

She circled, looking for a way to limit his throwing range. What kind of pyramid? That was always the question. And would he throw at her or other people? There weren't many now. If it was flash or fire, she could dodge, but destruction or explosive could catch her in a blast even if he missed.

"Are we going to stare at each other all day?" she asked.

"Well, I had hoped to get a little closer."

One of the people who'd seen them might be running for the Watch. She could wait for help, but that would give him more targets. She feinted forward, trying to get him to throw.

He backed off a step, but she darted toward his side, forcing him to twist. His arm dropped. She lashed out with her rapier and cut a line across his shoulder, tearing into his coat but not his skin.

He brought the pyramid around, but Katya batted it out of the way, knocking it from his grasp and sending it sailing across the lane. It hit the side of a shop and burst into flames. Screams started around her, and people shouted, "Fire!"

Katya put the cries out of her mind and ran her uncle's puppet through. As he sank to the ground, the light fading from his sky-blue eyes, she heard the clatter of booted feet around her.

Someone said, "Princess, what's—"

Katya's eyes were fixed on the thief's face, his *smiling* face. Alarms jangled in her mind, and she put her arms out, catching hold of several people and pulling them away. "Back, get back!"

Luckily, everyone seemed to listen lately when someone called for them to watch out. The body lay still long enough for her to feel foolish, for those around to ask what had happened, but then it blew skyward, the force of an exploding pyramid sending shockwaves across the street and raining gore on top of them.

Katya put her arms over her head, waiting for the macabre shower to stop. She looked into Captain Ursula's shocked face.

"I thought it was over," Ursula said. "By all ten fucking spirits, I thought this was over!"

Katya shared her sadness if not her disbelief. At least this was a problem she could deal with. She smiled wryly. And now she knew another way the Farradains could come to see the Allusians as allies.

She grabbed Ursula's coat sleeve. "Come on." Katya led her away, but not toward the palace this time, toward the main gate and the adsnazi camp.

CHAPTER THIRTY

STARBRIDE

S tarbride had called the children and the remnants back to order, but the longer she stared at them, the more wrong they seemed. She could see why they didn't sit well with people. The remnants were reanimated with adsna into a mockery of the lives they'd once led. Still, they were better than the children, who were pure adsna given breath.

With a wave, Starbride banished the children to the mountains where they belonged. Best to let them flock around the glaciers that held the rest of the council of five. They loped away without a word, but she could sense the sadness drifting off them. They'd been designed to miss her.

No, not her. Yanchasa. She couldn't forget that again.

Yanchasa stayed silent, even as Starbride drained the magic from the remnants, and they dropped to lay with the rest of the bodies. As their reclaimed power filled her, she stretched her neck and relished the surge of warmth. Yanchasa was right, power did feel good, and the more she had, the better she felt, both in body and spirit.

"We couldn't find the other messenger," Freddie said.

"It's no matter. He knows the way home." She looked to the woods surrounding the village. The pyradisté who'd been helping Roland was still out there, and they couldn't leave her to run amok through the countryside.

Freddie gave her a cold look. "*She.*"

"What?"

"Alecia, the other messenger. You climbed up on a horse with her, Yanchasa. You didn't realize she was a woman?"

Starbride swallowed her anger. "I didn't notice, and don't call me that."

"Didn't bother to notice, you mean. Do you know the name of the one who got killed?"

She looked back and forth between Hugo's and Freddie's faces before she mounted her horse. "No."

"Starbride would have bothered to find out," Freddie said.

"I am Starbride," she said through gritted teeth.

"Starbride would also have bothered to find out if any of the villagers had been hypnotized instead of mind-warped," Hugo said, not looking at her.

Starbride clenched a fist. "They weren't. None of them seemed bewildered when I cleansed the pyramids. They were definitely warped."

"You didn't check inside the buildings. Those things just killed everyone."

"And I just dispatched *those things*."

"And who is I, exactly?" Freddie asked.

Starbride wanted to shout that she'd saved their lives, but of course, *Starbride* would never throw such a thing in their faces. "I did what I felt was right." She pulled in a bit of adsna to cleanse her anger. They must have seen the change come over her face; they nudged their horses away.

"I am Starbride," she said calmly.

"Starbride would have yelled at us," Freddie said.

Starbride wanted to snap all his bones and then knit them together again. "Nothing makes you happy!"

He smiled, and she wanted to throttle him. "I can see why Ursula hates you." She turned her horse, following the weak signal of the pyradisté.

"Perhaps you went too far," Hugo whispered, but Starbride heard him clearly.

Freddie made no response, but Starbride could almost feel his satisfaction.

❖

In the middle of the forest, the pyramids called to Starbride like a beacon. It said something that the pyradisté didn't abandon them even though Starbride could track her. With her footprints in the snow, maybe she thought it didn't matter. Perhaps she feared being defenseless. She was alone, and Starbride's attack had given her no chance to grab food or water. On foot, her lead dwindled, and many creatures in the woods would be hunting her. Wolves and other predators slinked through the trees, unseen, but Starbride felt their heat, could sense their pulses in the deadened landscape. It wasn't deep enough into winter for them to be starving, but they wouldn't pass up an easy meal.

Late in the day, Starbride pulled up before a small copse. The trees had thinned out during the afternoon, and the undergrowth had been battened down by a fresh layer of snow. It was eerily silent except for Hugo's chattering teeth.

Starbride sensed that the pyramids had stopped. She could feel the pyradisté's body heat behind one of the trees.

"I know you're cold," Starbride called. "Why keep running? The farther north you go, the colder it will be."

Freddie eased his horse close and pointed. Starbride looked ahead with augmented eyes and saw a plume of breath right where she'd known it would be.

"Why would anyone ever work for Roland willingly?" Starbride called.

"Willingly?" The pyradisté stepped out from behind a tree. Her face was red from exertion, but Starbride could see her shivering. "He has my *family!*"

Starbride eyed her up and down. She was thin as a rail, barely more than a girl. Her ears and nose were bright red with cold. She was lucky Roland hadn't strung her with trap pyramids from head to toe. "He won't be hurting anyone's family now."

The pyradisté's eyes widened. "What do you know about it?"

"I captured him. Marienne's no longer his."

Hope flared in the pyradisté's eyes, and she stumbled forward. "Oh, spirits above." She staggered to a halt, and her face grew suspicious again. "Don't care about no Marienne. Do you know where my family is or not?"

Hugo nudged his horse forward. "We can help you find them."

Starbride lifted an eyebrow. The girl's family was likely dead. All Roland would have had to do was hold the promise of their release. No good could come from saying that aloud, though.

The pyradisté bit her lip. "Why would you help me? I thought you were going to kill me after everything I did."

Was that how everyone thought? How Katya thought? "Don't you think a person needs to pay for her crimes?" Starbride asked.

Freddie hissed at her.

"What? Isn't that something *Starbride* would do? Make people answer for their actions?"

"For *Roland's* actions," Hugo said.

Was that right? With the adsna roaring through her, it was hard to tell. She sacrificed emotion in order to let power in. Now she couldn't always see right from wrong, but Hugo could. Maybe she should just ask his opinion before every action. It made her chuckle to think of it.

Starbride sent the adsna tearing through the girl's pyramids, cleansing them before she could react. She clutched her coat and fumbled her pyramids out into the open. When she saw three wells of adsna, she fell to her knees in the snow. "Oh spirits." Her eyes were so wide, Starbride expected them to drop from her face. "You did beat him, didn't you?"

Starbride nearly laughed, but thought that Hugo wouldn't do that. "What's your name?"

"Bea. He said I was powerful. He said I had to do what he wanted to the people, or he'd hurt my family. He had my brother across his saddle the last time, and oh spirits, Finny cried so bad."

Hugo dismounted and went to help her to her feet. "There now, it's all over."

"Did he get you from the academy?" Starbride asked.

"Never went to no academy. I lived with my family in the woods." Tears began in Bea's eyes, and she swiped them away, seemed offended that they'd appeared at all. "He said he sensed my potential. Are they all dead?"

Starbride didn't know if she meant her family or the villagers, but one answer would probably do for all. "Yes."

Bea clenched her fists, but she didn't give in to tears again. "I felt what you did. How did you do it and so fast and all at once?"

Her eyes were hard, revenge-seeking eyes. They wouldn't be put down easily. And Roland had been right. Power flowed through her like a river, not just the power to warp minds, but other schools as well, though none as strong as her potential for mind magic.

Starbride held a hand down so Bea could climb up behind her. "Come on. We'll take you to Marienne."

"What about the villagers? You're sure none are left?" Bea asked as she climbed aboard.

"We can do nothing for them," Starbride said, but the thought that echoed through her head was, "Wolves and bears have to eat, too." Perhaps that was Yanchasa's thought, but it made her smile all the same.

❖

They rode as hard as they could toward Marienne but were forced to stop before they reached the tavern where they'd bedded down the first night. Starbride was glad of that. She didn't think she could go into that room again, face that empty bed and well-loved jewelry.

They took shelter at an abandoned farmhouse. Well, all of them were abandoned around that part of the woods. It had just two rooms, so Starbride went into one and shut the door. She didn't care if the others had to share or that they barely knew Bea. She needed to be alone.

All afternoon, Bea's arms at her waist had been tentative, and when the horse had slowed, its footing sure, Bea had let go. Starbride felt her leaning away. As evening fell, however, she'd shifted closer, her small hands on Starbride's back and waist, seeking warmth.

Starbride had tried to ignore the little childlike touches. Her mind had been drifting to Katya, to what she'd say when they saw each other again. She teetered between guilt and anger at that guilt. She'd done so much for everyone, why should she feel guilty?

Because she'd put Katya to sleep without permission. She'd treated her like some kind of doll. She'd said she knew best and then just forced her magic upon the woman she loved. That couldn't just be forgiven. Birdfaithful had been right about that.

But Katya had needed sleep. First she'd been fighting and wounded and grieving. She'd had the hardest day anyone could have short of dying. At least those who'd died didn't have to keep putting one foot in front of the other. And then Katya had been fretting about Starbride and working herself into a lather. She'd needed someone to take the reins.

That didn't make it right.

Round and round in her head she'd gone, waiting for Yanchasa to have an opinion, but true to his word, he stayed silent. Starbride had nearly called on him a few times, ready for an outside opinion, someone to solve the matter once and for all, someone neutral.

Toward the end of the day, the tension in her shoulders pulled on the muscles in her neck, setting her up for a screaming headache. She'd let the adsna smooth the pain away, and the power had also taken her guilt, so she could finally think clearly.

That was when Bea had begun to lean in. The girl had been drawn to the adsna like a beggar to gold.

Starbride stood and went back into the other room. Freddie was lighting a fire in the fireplace and glanced at her curiously.

"There's a bed in there," she said.

He blinked at her and glanced at Hugo.

"I don't need it," she added before they could think whatever they were thinking. "So, I thought you could drag it out here. Or I could stay out here, and you three could have the bed."

Now they all looked confused, and Hugo seemed a little uncomfortable.

"I'm just...I don't want..." Starbride waved at them. "Does anyone want the bed?" How come every time she tried to do something nice lately, it turned out like this?

"The floor doesn't bother me," Freddie added. "Is his lordship too high and mighty for the floor?"

Hugo grinned and chucked something at him. It might have been a spoon. The place didn't have much. The bed she'd offered was nothing but a straw mattress on a rickety wooden frame. Starbride wondered if Roland had stripped the place of supplies or if it had been someone else, some enterprising looters who'd taken everything of value. Of course, if they'd stumbled onto Roland's encampment, they were now stiffening in the snow.

"Right." Starbride went back inside the bedroom.

"Miss Starbride?" Hugo called before she could shut the door. "Thanks for the offer."

She nodded. Everything she did seemed odd or wrong or not like it used to be; feeling nothing had been worlds better than this.

The adsna waited. She plucked just a touch and curled it around herself, taking the edge off her discomfort. The room seemed softer then, the bed more inviting. Maybe it was good that she'd kept it. She didn't need to keep vigil, sitting against the wall and waiting for daylight. She could sleep, and in the morning she would feel better. Wasn't that what Dawnmother said, that everything seemed better after a good night's sleep?

A soft knock on the door stopped her before she could sit on the straw. Fear seized her that it might be Hugo or Freddie. "Come in?"

Bea's small face appeared in the gap, lit by a candle held under her chin. It brought her cheekbones into sharp relief and made her seem much older, sinister even. Starbride shook the thought away.

"We found some candles," Bea said.

"So I see."

Bea slipped inside as if afraid she already took up too much space in the world. She shut the door softly, though Starbride doubted that Freddie and Hugo had already fallen asleep. It might be possible. Starbride had no idea how long she'd been reveling in the adsna.

"I thought you might like one."

Starbride blinked. She'd gotten lost in herself again. "One what?"

"A candle, silly." Her smile faltered. "I'm sorry. I know you're someone important, and I shouldn't…I'm sorry."

"Do you know who I am?"

Bea's face froze like a naughty student's on test day. "No, Miss."

"You already know my name."

"Yes, Miss Starbride. You're Allusian. I've never met an Allusian before. And you're the most powerful pyradisté in the whole world."

Starbride cocked her head. "And how do you know that?"

Bea stepped closer and lifted a hand as if to push against Starbride's chest, but her palm hovered a foot away. "I can feel it, Miss, coming off you like…" She burst into a delighted giggle and seemed very young indeed. "It's not like the horrid man, the Fiend king."

"Roland. He's just a man."

She shrugged as if she doubted that. "He never said his name. He felt as dead as those corpses he raised. What happened to your corpses, Miss? That's why I thought you were with him."

"I let them die."

Bea nodded as if this was just what she wanted to hear. "You're comforting, Miss. I'm sorry if that's a stupid thing to say. Thank you for freeing me. I'm sorry I attacked you. It was only because I didn't want to die, and I was thinking about my family and what he'd do if I—"

Starbride stepped away, halting the flood of words as she frowned. Roland never trusted anyone he couldn't manipulate. He mind-warped people into submission. She'd told herself that over and over, and history had proven her out. The only pyradisté Roland had let roam on his own had been Alphonse, and that was just Roland wearing a different skin.

And Starbride couldn't check for that. Bea's mind was as closed to hers as it would have been to Roland. The question was, had he had time to do to Bea what he'd done to Alphonse: hollow out her mind and lay his over the top, preserving her abilities and taking control of her body? Or did he think the threat of hurting her family was enough?

"Tell me about Finny," Starbride said, "about the rest of them."

Unshed tears danced in Bea's eyes, but she did as she was told, telling stories about her mother and father, her brother, laughing about a time they'd eaten too many berries and made themselves sick.

Starbride watched her, wondering just how good an actor Roland was. In the past, he'd always revealed himself. *What do you think?* she asked in her mind.

Yanchasa slid into the room from the corner of Starbride's eye, her eyes locked on Bea. "I couldn't say. This child doesn't seem like the vague impressions I got from Roland."

"But now that I've met you, I'm sure you can free my family," Bea said. "You're more powerful in every single way!"

It was hard not to be flattered. "Some part of me did admire his sense of purpose, even as I called him a madman."

"What was his purpose, Miss?"

"To rule the kingdom."

"Is that your purpose, too? Are you the Fiend queen?" She said it as if she didn't care one way or another, as if such things were outside her sphere, and Starbride guessed they had been, most of the time. That was until a lunatic had visited her village, enslaved her, and then either killed or mind-warped the rest of the population.

"Does it bother you, what you did?" Starbride asked.

Bea dropped her head. "I feel bad for the people, and even more so now that they're dead, but he made me do it, I swear."

It seemed a child's excuse, but Bea was little more than a child. She'd probably just reached the age where she'd have been tested by those that searched Farraday for potential pyradistés. Her own people had no such process. They'd left her out in the cold.

"I believe you, child," Starbride said. "You don't have to worry about the Fiend king. I've taken care of him."

"I knew you had, Miss, first time I felt your power."

Starbride smiled. Awe and admiration were nice after all the confusion and accusations. "You should get some rest."

"I was wondering if I could rest in here with you, Miss." Her eyes were needy, like a child asking to be let in after a nightmare.

"Sleep. I'll watch over you."

Bea climbed into the bed and squeezed into a corner. "There's plenty of space. I used to share with my brother, so I'm good at not snoring or flailing about."

"Fine," Starbride said as she settled against the wall.

"Do you think my family is all right?"

"Anything is possible."

"Finny will be eight at spring's start."

"You can always look for them."

"Can you help me look?" Bea said softly. "Can I stay with you when we get to Marienne? And we can all look? You and me and Freddie and Hugo?"

And all the royalty of Farraday. She didn't think they'd take too kindly to one of Roland's former helpers moving into the royal wing, never mind that she'd helped under duress. "I live in the palace."

"The palace has serving rooms, don't it?"

Starbride sighed. "There's a place where every pyradisté in Marienne goes to learn. That's where you'd be safest."

Bea shifted on the bed, making the battered old frame squeak. "Can't be safer than near you."

Well, that was the truth. And Starbride didn't really want to let someone so powerful out of her sight. "Where's that quiet sleeping you're famous for? We can decide everything when we return to Marienne."

Whether Bea accepted that or not, she quieted down, and Starbride leaned her head against the wall and closed her eyes.

Her feet thudded amongst Wallux's army, but the screams were faint to her ears, tall as she was. The wind roared around her, coming down off the glaciers and whistling past like the shrieking of some giant beast.

Another soldier exploded beneath her foot. This form was fearsome and unstoppable, but it was also slow. She pushed the adsna through the crystal that made up her body, and the ground quaked beneath her. Jets of fire spurted through the chasms in the ice and stone and incinerated her foes.

Still, some of them were getting away. Her army could only pick off those she left behind, or they risked getting trampled.

Starbride grabbed a hunk of her own crystal and ripped it from her body, molding it into a smaller version of the fearsome beast she now was. The caressed crystal took on shape, and she pulsed through that with flesh magic, setting an unnatural heart to beating and a low, animal brain to thinking. She poured bits of her own psyche into it, making a tiny, brutal copy of her more malevolent instincts.

It grinned at her with needle-like teeth. She commanded it to leap into the army's midst. She shaped more, made them brutal, fast, and cunning, with just enough wit that they wouldn't get themselves killed straightaway. Most importantly, she tied them to herself, her malformed little children, making them extensions of her own body that would obey her call of flesh.

Starbride woke up gasping. Night still reigned outside, and there was something else out there as well, a nearly imperceptible uptick in the chill.

She tried to remember what it had been like to create life, so different from what she'd imagined. But she'd not only created life; she'd controlled it. What if she'd called the children in her sleep, countermanding her earlier orders? She searched for Yanchasa, but he was still hiding.

No, the children were gone. She'd just been thinking of them as she'd drifted to sleep, and that must have summoned Yanchasa's memories. She felt through the flesh pyramid, but there was only Bea sleeping peacefully, and Freddie and Hugo slumbering in the next room.

Starbride laid her head back against the wall. It was only a dream. But something pricked at her memory until she lifted her head and stared at the light dusting of snow on her boots.

CHAPTER THIRTY-ONE

KATYA

Katya strode through the palace halls, happy to be delivering some good news for once. Groups of adsnazi, aided by Master Bernard and Captain Ursula, had tracked several of Roland's copies by the pyramids they carried. They'd managed to neutralize the pyramids, but so far, all of the copies had either forced the Watch to kill them or had killed themselves. Still, it was progress.

Katya knocked on the door to her father's study and winced at his bleary, "Come in."

He bent over a sheaf of papers and rubbed his temples much as she always did.

"Da," she said softly.

He lifted his head and blinked at her. "I wasn't asleep."

She grinned. "How's it going?"

"More of the same. You seem in a chipper mood, my girl. Good news on the Starbride front?"

Well, at least she could *end* their conversation with something positive. Nothing said they had to start there. She sat and told him what she knew but also that it had led them no closer to a solution.

He shook his head. "It's a bit beyond me, really, all this pyramid stuff."

"You're working on juggling three political factions who all want disparate things. Nothing is beyond you."

"I can do human things, ordinary, non-magical things. For all this other business, I had Crowe. It's why kings and queens have always had pyradistés all their own. This is quite a pickle."

Katya burst out laughing, but there was no humor in it. Her good news paled in comparison to all the bad, and she suddenly felt as if she'd accomplished nothing. Worse, she felt as if she'd been wasting time chasing Roland copies when she should have focused on Starbride.

After the battle had been won and Roland had been taken care of, they were supposed to have run away for a little while, just a day or two, maybe to the small cabin they'd met in before Katya had infiltrated the palace. No danger, only the bliss of each other's arms. Then she could have happily thrown herself into prickly government issues or rebuilding Marienne or comforting the populace or burying the dead.

When Da laid a hand on her shoulder, she realized he'd come around his desk to perch on the front. "We'll work it out, my girl."

"How?" She willed the tears roughening her voice to stop, but they hovered in her eyes. "All I can think of is how things should be, how nice it would be if problems solved themselves, but every time I think of Star…" She swallowed past the fist that had grabbed hold of her throat. "Da, what if I've lost her? What if we went through all this, city taken and retaken, Roland captured, my love still alive, but still *lost*?" She dissolved as Da put his arms around her. She balled her fists in his coat and wept so hard she couldn't manage any sound past her choking.

"That won't happen, my girl, it won't."

She couldn't force her voice to work, so she just knocked one fist against his chest.

"I don't know how," he said, "but I'm a king for spirits' sake, my wishes must count for at least twice a normal person's."

She couldn't even laugh.

"If our finest magical minds can't figure it out, I don't know what I can do," he said, "but I'm willing to put my thoughts to it."

Katya stood and tried to step away, stumbling over her chair. She steadied herself on the arm. "You've got a government to run, Da." She wiped her face on her sleeves.

He knocked her arm down and gave her a handkerchief. "Your mother would be appalled."

She breathed through a chuckle and then took another breath and another. She blurted out the news about the Roland copies just to get a little distance.

He praised her too much, the exaggerated pride reserved for small children who had accomplished simple tasks, but a knock on the door saved her from having to confront him on it.

A messenger waited outside, one of those who'd gone with Starbride, and Katya sank into her chair to listen. Starbride had found her objective, hadn't foreseen any problems, and the messenger had been able to return to them unharmed due to his corpse Fiend escort.

After the messenger left, Katya rubbed her chin and stared at a spot on the floor, desperation threatening to choke her again. "She'll be back soon." She laughed again without humor and wondered if she'd forgotten how to do it correctly. "We've all got good ideas about why certain solutions won't work for the Yanchasa problem. The best idea I've heard so far is to sneak up on her and bash her over the head before letting the adsnazi try to cleanse her."

Da looked thoughtful. "I suppose Starbride could use magic to cleanse any kind of poison you might give her."

"I'm not going to let anyone hurt her, Da!"

"A sneak attack might be the only way, my girl."

She just kept staring.

He returned her look with one of glacial patience. She bet it had set many a noble's teeth on edge. "No one's saying they would *really* hurt her," he said.

"Because hitting her over the head will just tickle."

He exhaled slowly. "There are people who know how to do such things better than others. Your Pennynail comes to mind, though I guess he's Freddie Ballantine now."

Katya cocked her head. "That didn't surprise you at all, did it?"

"I knew Crowe far longer than you. I knew he had a son."

Katya blinked slowly. "Freddie Ballantine is Crowe's son?"

"I guess there's no particular reason to keep that secret any longer. I don't know where young Freddie got that Ballantine business. Perhaps it was his mother's name or one of his friends. I know that when the Dockland Watch tried to hang him, he had help escaping."

"Crowe helped a convicted murderer escape execution? Rule-abiding Crowe?"

"Oh, he didn't tell me what he had to take time off for, but I figured it out. Crowe always liked to imagine he was smarter than me or more observant, and I was happy to let him think so."

"He said he kept secrets from us for our own good," she said.

Da shrugged. "And I believe that he believed that. It was enough for me that Crowe trusted Pennynail or that he knew his son was innocent. He had a certain sense about people. I trusted that. And he liked Starbride, which is why I think we should go to any lengths to help her back from wherever she's gotten to."

And they were back to this again.

Da patted her knee. "No maudlin thoughts. We'll figure out a way."

Katya thought of Freddie sneaking up on Starbride. She winced as she imagined Starbride's eyes rolling up, face going slack. "She's tougher now. Stronger. If she senses what Freddie's up to, or if the first hit doesn't work…"

"Her guard will need to be down."

"Spirits above."

"As Crowe would say, all for her own good, my girl."

Katya thought of Redtrue, of evil begetting evil. Starbride had been so mad with grief she'd sought Yanchasa to defeat Roland, and now they were considering another dark path to cleanse them of that evil? Yanchasa would be bouncing among them like a croquet ball.

She needed to talk to Freddie and Hugo, find out what they'd observed during their trip. And she needed Redtrue, their evil detector. "As soon as Freddie gets back, it will be easier to plan."

"It might be best to recruit Brutal to strike her as soon as she arrives, while she's tired and thinks she's safe."

Katya didn't know whether to shout, run from the room, or just sink to the carpet and weep. "Da, I can't."

His nod was slow, his gaze steady.

"I know that look," she said. "You gave Castelle that look before you had her bash my head in, when you kept me from coming back to Marienne to look for Starbride!"

His gaze drifted away. "I am sorry about that."

"Make it up to me by not planning to ambush Starbride behind my back. I can figure this out, Da, and I will. Promise me."

"Yes, yes, I promise. And I hardly need to remind you that I must put the needs of the kingdom above my own, my girl, and above my family's."

"You don't have to remind me," Katya said, practically through her teeth.

On the day Starbride returned, Katya greeted her at the royal stables. She grinned at the sight of her love no matter the circumstances. To her surprise, Starbride smiled back with a tired but sincere energy, and Katya's heart sped. All the talking and planning, she wouldn't have to use any of it. Starbride had come back to herself all on her own!

Then Starbride's head turned as if listening to someone, and Katya's stomach shrank into a black pit.

Still, Katya hurried down the stairs to greet them. Only when Starbride slipped down from her horse did Katya realize she wasn't riding alone. "Who's this?"

"Princess Katyarianna Nar Umbriel," Starbride said tiredly, "may I present Bea, a pyradisté Roland threatened into working for him."

Bea nearly fell in her haste to get down. She was a clumsy, tiny girl, the furthest thing from a pyradisté in Katya's mind. "Welcome to the palace. Shouldn't you be at the academy?"

Bea just stared, open-mouthed.

"Can she speak?" Katya asked out the side of her mouth.

"Bea, go with Freddie. He'll find a place for you."

Freddie led her away. As soon as they were gone, Starbride sank into Katya's arms. "Are you okay?" Katya whispered into her hair.

"I don't know what I am."

It was a start. "Want to talk about it?"

"Not here."

"Would you like to go through the halls or the secret passages?"

Starbride thought for a moment. "One of the messengers died. The other is missing."

"Oh. I'm sorry."

"I don't know who the one who died was. The missing one is a woman named…" Her eyes misted over. "I can't remember."

Katya pressed her close and started leading her through the secret passageways, thinking she'd like that better than falling apart in the halls. "It's all right, dearheart. I'll find out who they were. Their families will be informed. What are you going to do with young Bea?"

Starbride sighed miserably. "I don't know yet."

"All right."

"Is that all you have to say?" She jerked to a halt. With the light of the pyramids in her body, they didn't need a lantern.

"I can see you've had a difficult journey."

"Difficult?" Starbride laughed, and the sound made Katya's ears burn as much as a peal of Fiendish speech. Though she'd have to start thinking of it as Belshrethen, and the pain it brought as another Fiendish weapon. "I feel like I'm tearing apart, Katya."

Katya licked her lips. Oh, this was delicate, like the finest wisp of silk. Could she bring up Yanchasa now? Starbride's mood changed like lightning strikes. "Tell me how to help you, my love, and I will do it."

Starbride's cool palm caressed her cheek. "And if I asked you to fetch me the moon?"

Katya leaned into the touch. "I'd run to get a ladder."

Starbride tumbled forward, pulling Katya close. Her forehead thudded into Katya's collarbone. "You're my strength and my weakness."

Katya held her and didn't know what to feel, thinking that one description was Starbride's opinion and the other Yanchasa's. "I'm whatever you need me to be."

"That's very accommodating."

"I'm good at accommodating." She remembered their time in the bath and shuddered. It had been one of the best and strangest experiences of her life. She suddenly understood strength mixed with weakness.

Starbride leaned back, her eyes dry. "Why aren't you angry with me?"

"Do you want me to be angry with you?"

"I put you to sleep without your permission, you and Maia both. There are some deeds a person can't come back from, Katya."

"Well…"

Starbride's eyes narrowed. "You're not angry because you didn't think that was me. You think Yanchasa did it, not me."

"So, you *do* want me to be angry?"

"That's not the point!" She started walking again, and Katya had to jog to keep up with her. "I did it, me. If you're going to be angry with anyone, be angry with me. I take responsibility."

"All right."

"Stop saying that!" Starbride rounded on her.

Katya took a deep breath. "Did I like being put to sleep like an errant child? No, that was very unnerving. Did I like having Redtrue pinch me awake?"

Starbride's eyes narrowed. "What was Redtrue doing there?"

The quick change of subject left Katya floundering. "Dawnmother fetched her."

"Why?"

"I guess she thought that since she couldn't wake me, someone who knew pyramid magic might be able to."

"And did she use pyramid magic on you?"

"No, I told you—"

"Pinched you." Starbride slid her thumb along her chin, other hand on her hip. Her face swung between calculating and furious. "She shouldn't have touched you."

"Dearheart, she didn't hurt me."

"You would have awakened in your own time."

Katya fought the urge to say, "All right." "Thank you?" she tried, but Starbride wasn't listening.

"Are you angry with her?" Starbride asked.

"Well, I'm always a little angry with her."

"But not with me?"

"Well, she's infuriating, and I love you."

Starbride leaned her head back, mollified but still suspicious. "You've been angry with me before and still loved me. Is Dawnmother angry with me?"

"What is this obsession with having people be mad at you?"

"Obsession!" She huffed. "I only want everyone to be normal. What's wrong with that?"

Katya almost said, "Look who's talking." Instead, she gestured down the hall. "Shall we go to my apartment? You obviously have a lot on your mind. If you won't tell me exactly why you want me to be angry with you about the past, I'm sure I could work up to it in the present."

Starbride started walking again and didn't stop until they were safely in Katya's sitting room, then she whipped around. "You should blame me for what happened because I am not Yanchasa!"

"And you think that I think Yanchasa put me to sleep, not you?"

"Finally!"

Katya watched her pace. "Okay, then. You shouldn't have put me to sleep."

"But you needed it."

Katya's mouth dropped open. "That still didn't give you the right!"

Starbride nodded as if this satisfied her somehow. "Is that all?"

"Do you want me to storm away in a huff?"

Starbride shrugged. "Do what you like."

Well, hadn't Katya offered to do or be whatever Starbride needed? And for some reason, Starbride needed to feel guilty and angry. She kept insisting she wasn't Yanchasa, and maybe this bizarre turn was part of that. Yanchasa wouldn't feel guilty. Starbride wanted to feel like herself again.

"Fine," Katya said. "Why don't you meditate a little on why I'm so angry? Maybe then you'll see my point of view. What you did was a violation of trust, Starbride, and I'm not going to forgive it lightly."

When Starbride turned, chin wobbling, Katya wanted to hold her arms out and swear that all was forgiven, but she made her court mask drop into place.

"I'm sorry," Starbride whispered.

Katya hesitated. Was it too soon to forgive? "I need a little time to cool off before we speak again."

Starbride's eyes widened. "If that's my penance, I suppose it'll have to do."

Katya just wanted out of this conversation before she did something else wrong. "Then I'll see you later?" When Starbride nodded miserably, Katya let her face soften. "Get some rest, my love."

Starbride's face shone with gratitude, and Katya almost pulled her in for a hug, but she turned toward the door that led into the hall. She froze when she saw the spill of papers on Katya's low table. "What's this?"

Katya rubbed her hands together and stepped forward as lightly as if she were sneaking up on a hare. "Reports from the underground city." Was she still supposed to be angry, or did this change of topic suggest something else? When Starbride didn't respond, Katya said, "With their rock shifting technique, the adsnazi are plowing through the city, uncovering one house after another. The ones I found were all cleaned out, but you should see some of the artifacts the adsnazi have discovered."

Starbride whirled around, and Katya resisted the urge to leap away. "These are about summoning Yanchasa."

"Um, any of the council, I think, is what the cultists were hoping for. According to some old writings we found, the leaders of the old city constructed the capstone to keep any flesh-magic users out, but these cultists started to retune it to summon one. The knowledge monks think that some of the cultists might have even collaborated with the ancient Farradains to summon one of the council, but their plan backfired when they got—"

"Yanchasa," Starbride said. "In his beast form, he was out of control." Her head tilted again, and Katya resisted the urge to shake her. "If they'd summoned one of the others, things might have gone differently."

Katya nodded slowly, this time taken aback by the *lack* of emotion in Starbride's voice. "We can thank the spirits, well, thank someone for that."

Starbride blinked, and her eyes turned back to normal, even with the tears. "You'll always forgive me, won't you?"

"I'll always love you, dearheart, that I can promise. Blame my temper for anything else."

Starbride choked out a sob, and before Katya could reach for her, she bolted for the door and was gone.

CHAPTER THIRTY-TWO

STARBRIDE

Starbride felt like an idiot. "What is happening to me?" she asked as she raced through the halls. "What in Darkstrong's name came out of my mouth?"

"Are you talking to me or to yourself?" Yanchasa said, keeping pace beside her.

"Both! Neither! I went insane somewhere along the line, and no one told me."

"It's hard to be comrades with your lovers, I should know."

"Katya is more than just a lover. She's my *true* love."

"I think monogamy is the death of a species." Yanchasa shifted to female with an unpleasant look on her face. She wore only her breastplate for armor now. The rest of her was clad in dark trousers and a long, burgundy coat. A silver torque around her neck glittered in the pyramid light.

"But you loved the other members of the council?"

"Oh yes, some more than others."

"Edette."

She nodded. "And some of his opinions on affairs of state were infuriating."

"Katya couldn't understand how I feel, but maybe I wasn't putting it right. There's so much going on that I don't have words for."

"Isn't that always the way? I've found deeds speak louder than words."

But there were some deeds one couldn't come back from. "I should do something for Dawnmother to apologize for manhandling her."

Yanchasa sighed. "She is your servant, yes?"

"It's not like that. You've been in my memory, you should know." But knowing didn't equal understanding. Starbride thought of the ultimate servant's apology and knew the right course of action. When she burst into her apartment, Dawnmother started up from a pile of mending.

Starbride staggered forward and fell to her knees at Dawnmother's feet. "I'm sorry, Dawn!"

Dawnmother patted her awkwardly, and she had a right to be confused. Such apologies normally went the other way around. "Star, it's—"

"Don't you dare say it's all right!" She kept her arms locked around Dawnmother's knees to hide her rage.

"Star."

Starbride climbed to her feet and pulled Dawnmother into an embrace. "If you're not angry, say you were and that you've forgiven me."

Dawnmother's arms went around her. "My life for you and also the truth."

Starbride whirled away. "Why does everyone always want to talk and talk? I'm only asking for a few simple words!" She reached for the adsna, calming herself. "I'm sorry I grabbed you, Dawn. I'm sorry I threatened you."

Dawnmother smoothed her rumpled shirt. "I have forgiven you."

Starbride exhaled long and loud. "Thank you! At last. Everything is fine now, Dawn. Yanchasa and I have reached an understanding."

"Good. I'm glad." But her tone was carefully neutral and not at all Dawnmother.

Starbride sighed. That was probably the best she could hope for. "Katya said she would forgive me later."

"You've seen the princess already?"

"She met me at the stable." Starbride let the warm feeling flow with the adsna as she sank into a plush chair. "She loves me."

This time, Dawnmother's smile seemed genuine. "How could she not?"

Better. Normal. "See, everything's going to be wonderful, just as I said." She scratched her palm idly. The pyramid tingled a bit. "What have you been up to while I was away?"

Dawnmother turned back to her, and her eyes went to Starbride's palm. "You're bleeding."

Starbride looked down. She'd picked the skin away from the pyramid in a neat little triangle, as if trying to dig it out. She let flesh magic seal the wound. "Thank you for telling me." Maybe she should go see Katya now. But everything she said or did came out wrong. Even the adsna wasn't helping as much as it could.

Maybe this was what Yanchasa had mentioned before, about how she'd feel again one day. She'd thought of it as something to look forward to, but it made her long for the imperious distance the adsna had provided before. She'd acted badly, but at least she hadn't had to deal with the consequences.

Starbride knew that thought should make her feel horrible. She should have been glad that hurting another could make her feel guilty. *That* was what everyone had been so upset about! She hadn't minded killing Roland's mind-warped soldiers, and everyone had thought she should.

The idea only angered her more.

Dawnmother's touch on her wrist brought her back to herself. "Star, your *hand*."

She'd dug a trench around the other pyramid this time, smearing blood across the glowing triangle in her palm. She sealed it again. "I'm sorry I upset you, Dawn." But the adsna was raging through her so that she couldn't feel the emotion behind the words. "I don't know what to do."

Dawnmother's lips moved so close that her breath tickled Starbride's ear. "Give the power back, Star. You did not have these problems before."

Starbride nearly howled with laughter. Did she think Yanchasa wouldn't hear her if she whispered?

No, another part of her insisted. She had to listen. She hadn't had problems sorting her emotions like this before. When she'd thought Katya was dead, she'd needed this emotional distance, but Katya was alive. Dawnmother was alive. She could relax, let the power flow back into Yanchasa's capstone and let all these infuriating emotions rest.

But what if they weren't the product of Yanchasa's presence? If she gave the power back, what if the emotions stayed, but the calming adsna went away? What would she do then? Continue to bob from one feeling to the next, always sorry and angry?

And useless. She couldn't forget that.

Starbride clenched a fist. She wasn't useless. She'd led the rebellion, and she hadn't had anyone sharing her head.

But she hadn't caught Roland alone. What would the kingdom do if another threat like him reared its head?

Starbride's eyes slipped shut, and tears trickled down her cheeks. She felt Dawnmother's fingers wiping them away. If she spoke these thoughts, she knew what everyone would say: if trouble came again, they would deal with it. She envisioned the disintegration pyramid that had almost claimed Katya's life and knew she couldn't accept that.

Dawnmother hugged her, arms warm around her shoulders. Starbride disentangled from her and stood. "I'm sorry, Dawn." But for what she didn't know. She was apologizing a lot lately. "I have to go."

"Where?"

"Outside. I need to think."

"I'll come with you."

"No." She smiled to take out the sting, but she couldn't be sure if Dawnmother accepted it or not. "I'll be back soon."

❖

She decided to take the secret passages, wanting to avoid the stares, at least until she sorted her feelings out. "Did this ever happen to you?" she whispered to the dark. "As your power grew, did your confusion grow also?"

Yanchasa walked at her side in the darkened passage, so close that they would have knocked into one another had he been real. "I came to it more slowly than you did."

"And you were living on top of the crystal your whole life."

"The only issue of the mind I ever had to deal with was the odd case of cowardice from one of my troops."

Was that what was happening to her? Fear? If she couldn't master this power, she'd be less than useless. She'd become a liability. She stopped in the passages heading out of the palace and changed direction, heading for Katya's apartment. If anyone could give her a rousing speech about bravery, it was Katya.

"I used to get lost in these passages all the time," she said.

"I know the way."

Starbride winced. But Yanchasa lived in her head, why did it matter if he sometimes riffled her memories? At least he could see what she remembered and not become confused by it. She paused outside the secret door, her Darkstrong-cursed doubts rising again. She let the adsna flow until she felt surer of herself and lifted a hand to knock.

Yanchasa's spectral touch brushed her shoulder. "Wait, daughter. Listen."

Starbride pressed her ear to the wall and used flesh to augment her hearing. Several voices. It took a moment to make them out.

"I don't want to do it this way." That was Katya, her voice moving as if she was pacing.

"Something happened while we were out there." Freddie's low rasp. Starbride's cheeks burned as he told them of her weakness at the abandoned tavern and then their words in the woods. "She's changing, but I don't know if it's for the better. It's as if she's fighting Yanchasa one minute and being it the next."

"She seems a little better," Hugo said, her stalwart supporter. "More in control, warmer."

"But unpredictable," Freddie said. "I think sometimes the Fiend is speaking through her."

Oh, that *again*.

"Maybe all she needs is time," Katya said.

That was what she'd been saying all along!

"Time to go crazier," Freddie said. "Fantastic. What if we give her time, and the Fiend just takes over? Your brother's plan might be the only way, Katya. I can do it quick. She'll barely feel it."

Starbride's belly went cold.

"I just don't think we're there yet," Katya said. "I don't want to hurt her."

Starbride tried to swallow past the lump in her throat. "Yet?" she mouthed. Yanchasa put a finger to her lips.

A knock sounded on the door, and Starbride heard several of them talking at once, making out the addition of Dawnmother's voice.

"What happened?" Katya asked.

Dawnmother broke every confidence and told them how Starbride had whined and cried and picked at her pyramid. Shame and anger and the harsh tang of betrayal filled Starbride's mouth.

"We thought they needed time to adapt to you," Yanchasa said, shaking her head sadly, "but now I see they never will."

"Where is she now?" Katya asked.

"Gone into the city to collect her thoughts. I waited until she had time to make it out of the palace before I came. She might return at any time."

"Make a decision before this goes any further," Freddie said.

"I don't want to see Miss Starbride hurt," Hugo added.

Katya sighed loudly. "We need Redtrue. Doesn't this plan fall under the fighting evil with evil banner?"

Starbride's fingers dug furrows in the stones at the sound of Redtrue's name.

"We are ultimately talking about freeing Starbride from evil's influence," Freddie said. "I don't see how Redtrue could disagree. We're not using dark magic."

No, Starbride thought, just Freddie doing something to her that was quick so she could barely feel it. Did he plan to bash her brains in or shove a knife through her ribs?

"I think you're the only one who can make this decision, Princess," Hugo said.

"We all care about her," Katya said.

Starbride tried to give her a scathing look through the wall. Who conspired against someone they cared about?

When Katya spoke, Starbride barely heard, even with her augmented senses. "All right." Those damnable words again.

Starbride stepped back as if the words shoved her before she leaned in and listened to their plan. They were going to collect a few more of their friends and then ambush her as soon as she returned from the city. Freddie volunteered himself and Brutal to hurt her. Katya simply mumbled assent.

Starbride sneered. Crowe had been right. None of the Umbriels liked to do their own dirty work. Where would Katya be during all this? Standing off to the side, waiting for Redtrue to strip Starbride of her power, and then she'd rush in to pick up the pieces?

Starbride's feet were moving, though she barely felt them. She wanted to beat her fists against the stone, to make it quake, to shake Farraday to its bones. Trust was all she'd asked for, a little faith. She was making a transition, couldn't they see that, and all she needed was time.

But no, they wanted Starbride to put the past behind her just like that, to take the grief and terror and anger of the past six months and return to her chirpy, helpful, normal self, the woman who'd been happy to stand in the back and be invisible. And that was if they didn't manage to kill her by attacking her in the hall. The very idea that they could overpower her proved that they *still* underestimated her.

"It's an outrage, daughter, truly."

"I led the rebellion!"

"You were practically abandoned."

"I brought Reinholt to heel, I invented a way to avoid detection by the corpse Fiends, I helped free the monks, and I helped so many of the citizens."

"You captured the enemy and stripped him of his power!"

"Exactly!" Acid burned from her mouth to her stomach.

"Where is the gratitude?"

Starbride slapped her own hip so hard the pain traveled down her leg. "Your guess is as good as mine!"

"If it were me, daughter, well…"

"What?"

"I don't want to compare my past to your present."

Starbride thought swiftly of the peasants conspiring to bring down the council of five. "You think that if they can't cleanse me they'll find some way to imprison me?"

Yanchasa waved around her. "If the Belshrethen had attacked the council when we were together, things would have been different. But you have no one to help you. Everyone has turned against you."

"Everyone but you. I'm so sorry I tried to push you away."

Yanchasa smiled softly. "I'll help you all I can, daughter. You could flee."

But as she fled, her connection to Yanchasa might grow weaker, and she wouldn't feel the flow of the adsna as greatly. "No. I need as much power behind me as possible." And she knew where she could get it. If they wanted to attack her, let them try when she was at full strength. She'd go to the…

Starbride blinked. She was already on the path to the capstone cavern, but she couldn't remember turning. The snow on her boots flashed in her mind's eye.

"We have to hurry, daughter," Yanchasa said.

Starbride shook her head and felt a tingle within her chest. She could put out a call. There were still a couple of children within reach. That was good. She'd need their strength.

"Already done," Yanchasa said.

Starbride snarled. "I am in control here."

"Of course, daughter, of course."

"We need more allies, or did you already think of that, too?" Starbride focused through her mind magic and sought a power the adsnazi had shown her: the dream walk. They used sleeping, restful minds to be less intrusive, to admit speaking, the sharing of emotions, but nothing else. Starbride didn't have time for that. She thought first of Master Bernard.

"No," Yanchasa said. "He is hungry for knowledge, but he's known Katya longer."

That was true. She remembered how quickly he'd turned against her at Lady Hilda's trial. Instead, she aimed for Bea.

The girl was resting, and Starbride felt her mind jump awake at a touch. "Starbride, where—"

"Below the palace."

Shock thrummed down the line. "How are you—"

"Just listen. Because of the Fiend king, the crown has decided to leash all the pyradistés, starting with us."

Her mind was guarded, shocked. "Truly?"

"Why would I lie?"

"Oh, there are many reasons for a good lie," Yanchasa said.

Starbride waved to stop him from making her laugh. She sensed that Bea believed her, but something else lurked in Bea's thoughts: the desire for revenge. A royal had hurt her; now she would hurt them. Still, she wouldn't be enough. "We need to get to Crowe's old office." She changed direction, telling Bea how to meet her in the secret passageways.

"Why?" Yanchasa asked.

"If I can get the pyramid that Crowe used to commune with the capstone, we can drain your energy into it."

"And go where?"

They'd be spotted slipping out of the castle, and Starbride didn't want to unleash wanton destruction, not yet. "The Belshrethen attacked the council separately?" Her mind flashed back to the pages she'd seen in Katya's room.

"Oh, daughter, are you thinking—"

"You agreed we need more allies."

His delight filled her. "There is one more who could aid us," Yanchasa said.

Starbride nodded. They had to stop by the dungeon.

CHAPTER THIRTY-THREE

KATYA

Katya paced when she wanted to run. She supposed it didn't matter which she did as long as she stayed out of sight. Brutal and Dawnmother waited in the hall near Starbride's apartment. Freddie and Hugo lurked in the secret passageways. They had both routes covered, and now they only needed Starbride to return.

Maia and Castelle shooed servants and guards away, leaving Katya and Redtrue nothing to do but wait. Redtrue had invited more of the adsnazi into the palace, but Katya didn't want them getting too close. They couldn't have Starbride sensing their pyramids.

Katya rubbed her temples. "I can't go through with this."

Redtrue frowned at the wall. She'd had the same look of constipated anger since she'd arrived.

"No words of wisdom?" Katya asked. "No assurances that this is the path we must take?"

"The capstone feels different."

Katya's heart turned to flint. "Different how?"

"Fainter, maybe." She shook her head. "Is there something in the way, or has she done something to it?"

"I don't know what you're—"

"Would you stop chattering?"

Katya sputtered a moment, but Redtrue didn't look at her. "Something's not right. I felt it when I first entered the palace, but I can't tell quite what."

"You've known something was wrong with the capstone since you arrived, and you didn't say anything?" She clenched her fists to avoid putting them around Redtrue's neck.

"I didn't want to say until I was certain! Where are you going?"

Katya strode away without answering. "Dawnmother, Brutal!" she called. "Fetch Castelle and Maia," she said over her shoulder to Redtrue. "And someone go get Hugo and Freddie."

When they were all in the hall again, speaking over one another, Katya said, "Something's gone wrong, something with the capstone."

"How do you know?" Freddie asked.

"I can feel it," Redtrue said, "but whether it is Starbride or—"

"It has to be her," Brutal said.

Maia nodded. "Who else?"

"But she said she was going into the city, why go to the capstone?" Dawnmother said.

"Something changed her mind?" Freddie asked.

Katya ground her teeth into her lip. "Or she knows what we're up to."

"It could be Yanchasa making her go there," Castelle said.

Hugo threw up his arms. "We're not even sure she's there!"

Katya shifted from one foot to the other. They could venture into the city, search for Starbride, search the palace. Maybe they were wrong, and Redtrue's feelings had nothing to do with Starbride.

The Crowe in her gave her a stern look. There were no coincidences, not with this.

"It's her," Katya said, feeling the surety in her bones. "It's her, and she knows I've turned against her."

"Can she hear through walls?" Hugo asked.

Katya strode to her apartment, the others keeping on her heels. She went to the mirror that guarded the secret passageway and toggled the switch. When she stepped inside, she didn't know what she expected to see, a note perhaps. She didn't have an ounce of pyradisté talent, but she knew Starbride had been standing here, listening while they plotted. On some level she'd known the entire time. She'd wanted to get caught.

Or maybe she was just imagining things. As she stepped out, a gouge in the stone caught her eye. No, several gouges, spaced apart like fingers, something only the strength of a Fiend could do.

"What do we do?" Brutal asked. "Katya?"

"We have to go down there."

"Without the element of surprise?" Freddie asked.

Katya nodded. Better to take Yanchasa head on. "You don't have to come." She could feel their scoffs as much as hear them.

"We're going to need the other adsnazi," Redtrue said. "We dare not confront her without them."

Katya pictured all the people surrounding her laid out on the floor, hypnotized or dead with one wave of Starbride's hand. "Go, be quick." Everyone but Castelle and Redtrue stayed with her, counting off the minutes. "Maybe I should go, try talking to her again."

"Should we tell your father?" Maia asked quietly.

Katya shook her head. Her father was in council, and what could he do besides pace and wait with them? But what would he do if their plan didn't work?

Katya knew she couldn't strike Starbride down, no matter what, not even if Starbride had wholly taken on Yanchasa's Aspect. When

Katya had become a Fiend, Starbride had embraced her. How could she do differently?

But would Yanchasa force them into a conflict? Freddie and Hugo had told her that Starbride seemed to defy Yanchasa in order to save them. "Maybe I should just go," she said again.

Brutal's large hands settled across her shoulders. His fingers dug in deep, making her gasp before the pressure spread across her muscles, soothing them. "You can't let go of hope," he said.

"Hope that we can beat my love into unconsciousness so we can finally help her?"

"All we have to do is distract her. The adsnazi will do the rest."

"They won't be able to hypnotize her, Brutal."

His fingers kept up their work, and Katya could feel herself relaxing. "They can cleanse her," he said. "We just need to give them time."

"So the plan is to let her beat on us until they have room to work? I'd hug you if this massage wasn't so wonderful."

"I know the feeling," Maia said.

Katya wanted to demand details, but she kept her mouth shut. She'd leave the prying to Starbride after all this business was done. Her ferreter of secrets would be all the spy she'd ever need.

"Did she keep any corpse Fiends?" Katya asked.

Hugo shook his head. "She killed them all and let the wild Fiends go."

"You saw them leave?"

Freddie and Hugo glanced at one another, and Katya could tell that was a no. "She might have kept some."

"Can't the adsnazi take care of them?" Brutal asked.

"We're putting a lot on adsnazi shoulders."

"What's the alternative?" Maia asked. "Summon the Guard?"

There weren't that many of them left. "We need Lord Vincent."

Freddie snorted. "He's a good fighter, I guess."

"Will he leave the kids?" Brutal asked.

"I'm going to convince him." Katya strode from her apartment without waiting for acknowledgement. It was movement, something she needed, and if the others wouldn't let her go after Starbride alone...

Vierdrin and Bastian squealed when Katya entered their apartment, running for her at full speed. Reinholt rose from a settee, his face confused but welcoming. "Katya, what's going on?"

She must have forgotten how to use the court mask while she'd been away. She glanced at the children.

Reinholt knelt. "Why don't you two go into the nursery and play with Vincent?"

"Actually," Katya said, "it's Vincent I need to talk to."

"Ah, then I'll go into the nursery. Funny, we both watch over the children, but not from the same room anymore." He led the children away, and Vincent came out. Katya wondered if he'd had his ear pressed to the door.

"Highness." He bowed. "I'm at your service."

She told him a little of what had happened, adding that she might need his strength against any errant corpse or wild Fiends.

He listened with his usual lack of expression, but he cast a pained look at the nursery door. His duty was clear: as champion, he guarded the youngest heirs, but Katya was a member of the family he'd pledged his life to serve.

Before she had a chance to speak, Reinholt emerged alone. "They're fine," he said as Vincent took a step toward him. "You should go, Vincent. Go and help my sister."

"You won't be leaving the palace," Katya said. "Not really."

"And I'll stay here," Reinholt said. "There's a secret door nearby, and if anything happens, they will be in my arms and away in a flash." He chuckled. "If there's one thing I'm good at, it's running away and hiding."

Vincent didn't argue, but Katya saw the hesitation in his eyes. Dereliction of duty went against his soul, and she could tell he didn't trust Reinholt to do the right thing.

But this wasn't a Reinholt Katya knew very well, neither the charming prince nor the spoiled brat. This one was trying to reinvent himself, and he'd made it clear he wanted to start with responsibility.

"I believe him, Vincent," Katya said.

He cast another look toward the nursery door, past Reinholt, this glance full of love.

"The sooner we finish this business, the sooner you can come back," Katya said.

After a tiny sigh, he bowed. "Highness, my sword is yours."

Redtrue arrived with a host of people in tow. Even Leafclever walked beside her. Katya cocked an eyebrow. "Shouldn't you be in council with Dayscout?"

Leafclever shrugged. "Dayscout knows my mind. This seemed more important."

"Thank you." But now that they'd arrived, Katya couldn't get her feet to move.

Maia touched her elbow. "We should hurry."

Katya cleared her throat. "Anything different with the capstone?"

The adsnazi focused, some of them with eyes closed. "It's odd," Redtrue said. "I can barely sense the capstone's energy. Perhaps she's shielding it somehow."

Katya shifted her weight from foot to foot. They stared at her, waiting. If she kept them long enough, she wondered if they'd start wandering off.

"Basement is probably better than the passageways," Brutal said.

"Definitely less cramped," Hugo added.

Their tone screamed, "Normal conversation." Katya had to smile. "Let's go."

They trooped into the bowels of the palace again, scaring whatever servants they happened upon. Katya assured everyone that they were on official business of the crown, but she knew her movements would get back to her father. News would travel on the wings of gossip, as Dawnmother said.

That enticed her to hurry; she didn't want her father and the Guard involved. She couldn't take the chance that some overzealous guard might seize the opportunity to stab Starbride in the back, thinking that might be his way to glory.

When they passed into the stone of the caverns, the crushing feelings descended on her. She could do this, she reminded herself. Hadn't she done it already? When she'd taken the secret passageways with Starbride, she'd barely registered her surroundings. This was no different.

The thought almost made her laugh. Venturing into the caverns to see if Starbride would try to kill her, if she'd be forced to do the same was anything but normal.

Katya drew her rapier, thinking of corpses or wild Fiends. At her side, Brutal drew his mace, and the others readied weapons, the adsnazi drawing their pyramids, scanning the way for traps.

Déjà vu hit Katya hard. This was searching for Roland all over again. She wondered when the barrage of pyramids would start and clenched her teeth around a scream. No, that wouldn't happen. Starbride wouldn't want to kill her, couldn't—

"This doesn't feel right," Brutal said.

Katya glanced at him.

"I agree," Freddie said. "Starbride's smart. She wouldn't be down here alone. We should have encountered resistance by now."

"Traps. Fiends. Something," Hugo said.

"You're right." Katya didn't hear any noise coming from the adjoining tunnels, the places where the adsnazi had burrowed through the rock. The place should have been crawling with knowledge monks and Allusian scholars.

Redtrue cursed. "She couldn't have hidden the capstone's energy so well. It feels like nothing's there."

Katya broke into a run, not caring if it was reckless. She stumbled through what had been the cavern door into a well of complete blackness. Her heart hammered in her ears, and that clawing, suffocating feeling came back. It was the dead city all over again, tons of rock pressing down on her, killing her.

Light blossomed around her, pushing back panic. The top of the green-fletched pyramid poked out of the stone, and Katya breathed a sigh of relief that the capstone was still there, but even she sensed the difference. No light emanated from it, no feelings of restless energy. It was as dull and lifeless as a giant paperweight, all of its magic gone.

CHAPTER THIRTY-FOUR

STARBRIDE

Starbride clutched the pyramid that now held Yanchasa's remaining essence. Behind her, Roland and Bea planted traps in the tunnels that the adsnazi had burrowed through the rock. It wouldn't slow Redtrue down for long, but once Starbride got to the room detailing how to summon the council of five, she wouldn't need long.

Would that chamber look like the rest, she wondered? Walls the same uniform grayish brown with hints of colors long faded? As she moved, she glanced into what had once been buildings, homes or shops, their purposes lost to time. Piles of detritus had been cordoned off and showed signs that the knowledge monks had pawed through it. Dusty cloth that shredded upon touch, ruins of wood or clay, what did they hope to do with it? Study it, she supposed, for all the good it would do them. Well, hadn't the monks' forays done her some good in the end? Hadn't they found the very power she needed to finally make her feel—

What? Safe? Loved? Accepted at last? Starbride took a deep breath of dusty air and used flesh magic to cleanse it once it was inside her. Maybe after she had the wisdom of the combined council members, she'd know exactly what it was she wanted.

A lantern came toward her down the hall, yet another knowledge monk wandering the corridors of the dead city. They were everywhere, dividing their teams into shifts to work day and night. This one opened his mouth in what was probably a greeting. She put him to sleep, and he sagged at the bottom of the wall.

"You have to show me how you do that so quickly," Bea said, awe in her voice. "No one can ever make you do anything you don't want."

After Bea's ordeal with Roland, the ability to not be pushed around seemed a goal close to her heart. "Did you enjoy it, then? The mind-warping you did?"

Bea was silent a few moments. "Does that make me a bad person?"

"I won't judge you."

"None of us can judge one another," Roland said. Starbride glanced back at him, surprised to see him shift the monk's lantern far enough away that the man's robe wouldn't catch fire. When Roland straightened, he didn't look at her but stared at Bea. He'd done so ever since the three of them had joined forces.

Bea had glared and leapt for his throat. Starbride had expected her to demand the return of her family, but she'd just punched him with her small fists, making cries of inarticulate rage. She'd agreed to work by his side only after Starbride commanded her to. It had helped when Starbride whispered in her ear that after their trials were over, he'd be hers to kill.

"Once we summon the council, you won't need either of them, daughter," Yanchasa said.

Starbride shrugged and continued down the hall. Five of the children trailed them, their comforting cold sliding over Starbride's skin. Bea and Roland were probably chilled by the children's presence, but they'd have to take care of themselves. Yanchasa walked just ahead of the children as if leading them.

Ever since Katya's betrayal, Yanchasa had been ever-present, in mind if not in sight. While Starbride focused on pyramid work, Yanchasa guided her body, the height of convenience. Funny, but she seemed to recall it had bothered her not that long ago. Or had it been days since she'd thought about it?

"Well, after all this is sorted out..." She didn't know how to finish. After what was sorted out? The betrayal by her friends and family? By Dawnmother and Katya?

"Once we take care of the adsnazi, you can make them see the truth, daughter. It seems the only way."

Acid bubbled up Starbride's chest, and it took her a few seconds to cleanse it. "You mean mind-warping them."

"There is no turning back now," Yanchasa said, and she knew it was true, but how had it all gone so wrong?

"Isn't there some way?" She glanced to the side and saw Bea looking at her curiously, eyes suspicious. In a snap, Bea's expression changed to one of admiration. "Don't worry," Starbride said. "I'm not talking to myself."

"I guessed." Her eyes shifted to Roland, and Starbride could feel her seethe. "That's not a very powerful trap."

Roland stood from his work and then jogged to catch up. He didn't respond to Bea but held her gaze steadily.

"You'll have to give him time," Starbride said. "Without flesh magic, he's weaker than he was."

Bea sneered. "He's pathetic and frail."

Starbride shrugged, not caring if they got along as long as they obeyed. When she'd first come into Roland's cell, he'd shrieked and backed into the wall, chains rattling. She had to seize his body with flesh magic to still him. She tried to be kind, make him calm enough to listen. Finally she'd said, "I'll give you back your Aspect if you help me, your *Fiend*."

He'd stiffened like baked clay, watching her intently.

"Though I've already told you," she'd said with a laugh, "Yanchasa's no Fiend."

"No less a monster," Roland said.

Starbride had stepped close to him and let him go; he kept his feet and looked her in the eye. "One you want back. The strength, the power." She smiled. "The freedom from guilt."

His eyes had squeezed shut, white around the creases. "Spirits forgive me."

"You can feel his touch again."

He'd rolled his lips under, and she'd thought he might cry. She used flesh magic to make the dirt and old sweat slide from his skin. He shuddered, already smelling better, and she imagined he felt better, too.

"Yes," he'd whispered, and she smiled. She'd use him up and then cast him aside. It was what he deserved for everything he'd done.

A little voice asked what she deserved for everything she'd done.

As they came to a three-way junction, Starbride shook the thought away and tried to remember what she'd seen in Katya's notes.

"I remember the way," Yanchasa said. He turned her body in the right direction, the others setting traps as they went.

A gaggle of knowledge monks ambled down the hall, talking excitedly among themselves. Starbride put them all to sleep, all but one. An Allusian man in their center stared at the others in shock before he dropped to one knee, shaking their shoulders and asking what was wrong. When he spied Starbride, he called for help.

"Adsnazi," Starbride said. She slowed. If she couldn't use mind magic…

Yanchasa flickered at her side and laughed. "Fire or destruction or your bare hands, daughter."

Starbride glanced at her palms. She'd been scratching around the pyramids again, smearing them with crimson.

"Let me," Bea said.

Roland caught her arm. "It's not your place."

"Get off me, you pathetic wreck!"

"Daughter?" Yanchasa gestured toward the adsnazi. "Well?"

The adsnazi stood slowly, eyeing them. "Wait," Starbride said in Allusian. He paused. She stepped toward him, letting the pyramid rest in the crook of one arm. "The monks are only asleep."

"Your doing?" He glanced at her forehead, her bloody hands. "Why?"

"Yes, why are you taking the time, daughter? The others will soon be on our track—"

"I need to get past," she said. He was her age, maybe a little older.

He licked his lips. "I'm not stopping you."

"You cannot leave him behind to set the hunters on our track!" Yanchasa said.

Starbride's arm lifted, though she didn't command it to. She felt heat gathering in her palm, and a buzzing pain built behind her eyes. "Wait," she croaked. "I want to know his name."

Fire bloomed, and the adsnazi screamed. He writhed on the ground, and Starbride felt a pulse from the pyramid over her heart. One of the children loped forward and tore the screaming man's throat out in a rush of fiery blood.

Starbride pushed at Yanchasa, fought for her body, but it was like pressing back the tide. She grunted as she shoved and felt a tiny pop in her left eye as Yanchasa's presence subsided. At last, she could lift her own arm. "I wanted to know his name!"

"What does it matter?" Yanchasa asked.

Bea peered into her face. "What happened to your eye? The white bit is all red."

She used flesh magic to fix herself, or at least she hoped so. She'd have to look at it later. "Come on."

As they continued past the corpse, Starbride tried to find her center. How much of what she'd been doing, what she'd been feeling lately, was her own? Yanchasa's shadowy form disappeared, and his voice seemed fainter. It tired him to possess her. She wondered if he seethed inside the pyramid.

"My apologies, daughter," Yanchasa said. "It's been so long since I've prepared for real battle, I've forgotten my place." He laughed then, and the sound set Starbride's teeth on edge.

CHAPTER THIRTY-FIVE

KATYA

Redtrue stared at the darkened pyramid so long Katya was tempted to shake her. The other adsnazi spread out through the capstone cavern, searching, but for what? Starbride wasn't there.

"This isn't what I felt," Redtrue said at last.

Katya waited for more, clenching and unclenching her fist.

"We should search the palace," Brutal said. "She couldn't have gotten far." They made plans, search patterns for the corridors, the city. Katya kept staring at Redtrue. There was more to this story. They just had to figure it out.

"The energy was still there, muted, but still there," Redtrue mumbled.

"And you didn't sense the capstone energy coming up into the palace," Katya said.

Without sparing her a glance, Redtrue shook her head.

"We could get more allies from outside the wall," Castelle said. "Count Mathias, the Allusian nomads. There's no place Starbride can go that we can't track her."

"She's still here," Katya said.

"How do you know?" Dawnmother asked, and Katya realized she hadn't leapt into planning with the others. She called for them to hush, and they crowded around.

"The energy from the capstone is still here," Redtrue said. "I feel it more strongly now than when we were upstairs. It's still down here."

"But they weren't in the tunnels," Hugo said. "Where else could they...Oh, spirits."

The dead city. Katya could see the thought cross all the faces like a river jumping its banks.

Maybe Starbride had intended for them to run around like headless chickens, searching the palace and the city. More likely, she'd gone below because she was looking for something. Katya closed her eyes and tried to keep the past from washing over her. Close, dark spaces; air filled with dust, clogging her nostrils and scraping her throat raw; and the tons of stone hanging over her head, waiting to fall and keep her in silence forever.

Just as when she'd inched out of the ground to freedom, a voice inside her said she couldn't do it. No one could expect her to be so strong. Nightmares about her mother's death had merged with tableaus of stone crushing the life out of her, her family and friends being swallowed by the hungry earth.

Katya's eyes slid open. She'd feared being trapped underground with Yanchasa, but that had been her imagination running wild. Starbride suffered that very fate at this moment. "I have to," she whispered, never mind the fear that wanted to root her to the spot. Whatever might happen below wasn't the issue; she knew she'd die of shame if she stayed above.

She tried her best to shut off the squealing, fear-ridden part of her and gathered the adsnazi. Starbride had to have taken the new path down into the dead city. It was the only thing that made sense.

"Lead and we will follow," Leafclever said.

Katya started away. She couldn't talk about it too much or she feared she'd run, taken over by terror.

At the top of the path, a sloppy combination of stairs and slope, she didn't pause but nearly leapt the length of it. Speed was her only ally now. It wasn't until Redtrue hauled back on her arm that she even thought to listen to those around her.

"There is a pyramid ahead," Redtrue said, her tone betraying that she'd already said so more than once, and Katya had shut out her voice.

"Easy enough to cleanse," Leafclever said.

As Redtrue called for him to wait, the floor of the tunnel blew upward, knocking Katya to the floor. This was it. Now she would fall again, or the stone would crash down around her, or she'd wake up in the dead city to find that she'd never left.

Brutal hauled her upright. Her ears rang, and she choked on dust. She grabbed hold of his wrist to keep from following the shrill voice in her mind and sprinting upward.

"It's a special kind of pyramid," Redtrue was yelling. "One designed to explode if you try to cleanse it."

Katya coughed and tried to control her shaking. "How many more are there?"

"Two that will explode. Several that will not." Redtrue frowned. "Those that won't will hardly do anything."

Something leapt through the swirling dust, over the trap pyramids. Katya ducked, pulling Brutal down with her. She heard the screams of those behind as a creature landed in their midst.

Katya caught a blast of cold wind and well-remembered dread. She was afraid to turn and see what she knew was behind her but forced herself. She glimpsed mottled skin and huge eyes.

How would they fight a wild Fiend without Ma's Fiend to distract it? She began to call for Hugo to take his necklace off, but Vincent appeared before her.

He and the Fiend traded blows so quickly, Katya was afraid to blink. The Fiend scored a hit on Vincent's thigh. Vincent's sword carved a deep groove in the Fiend's arm. It all happened in the space of a few breaths before warm light and the scent of summer rain flowed from the adsnazi.

The Fiend shrieked and turned away, but Vincent stood between it and escape. He sliced, backing it into the glow. Katya grinned as the thing slowed, hampered by adsnazi power. She stood to join the fight, but the creature tottered and melted into a pile of molten rock.

They stepped away as it oozed down the stairs. As the adsnazi cleansing light gave way to normal light pyramids, the puddle hardened until the steps were encased in crystal.

Katya stared at the glimmers of light that ran along its twisted, beautiful surface. She couldn't tear her eyes away. "Disable the pyramids you can. The others we'll set off from a distance."

"What if the tunnel collapses?" Leafclever asked.

Katya looked to her companions, the determination on their faces. "Fiends are really just animated puddles of crystal." She had to laugh and watched confused smiles cross a few faces. "If the most powerful creature we've faced is no more than that, everything else is easy. If the tunnel collapses, we'll make a new one."

CHAPTER THIRTY-SIX

STARBRIDE

Adsnazi magic wafted down the hall like volcanic air, threatening to smother Starbride's chill. They were coming for her.

She'd never been so tired, but the thought of stopping brought no refuge. She knew what lay behind her. All she could do was keep going forward.

Tingloo ran up her arm, and she knew she'd gouged her palm deeper. The pain had become like a tiny needle passing over her skin. If she focused on it, she could think a little more clearly, but she didn't see how that could help her.

"What will they do, the other council members?" she asked. "Will they lay the kingdom low?" Did she want that? It was so hard to remember.

Yanchasa seemed distracted as she answered. "Whatever you wish, daughter."

But she'd bring them here in their own forms. They'd have the free will to do as they wished, become Farraday's rulers, perhaps.

"Who better?" Yanchasa said. "And then all your dreams for the safety of these people will be recognized."

"Your people didn't end up very safe."

"And what is the alternative, daughter?"

Seized by those she'd once thought of as friends, stripped of her power and imprisoned. Abandoned by Katya and everyone who claimed to love her. Yes, she knew all that, but it was hard to care. The fuel of her anger had been swallowed by the adsna along with everything but fatigue.

When she emerged into the summoning chamber, her breath caught, and natural curiosity rose up inside her. She should have been down here since they'd discovered this place.

A long space held aloft by ten marble columns in two rows. Colorful mosaics ran along the peaked roof and down the glossy green floor. With just a glance, Starbride knew what they depicted, tales of the council of five whose stories had somehow found their way to Katya's ancestors and provided the basis for the ten spirits.

Writing covered the walls, packing them from top to bottom. Pyramid users had made this room into a living book, set in stone to preserve its words. Starbride felt as if generations of people stood behind her, urging her to complete their dreams: *Summon the council. Destroy these invaders and return Belshreth to its place among the world.*

They would do wonders, and she would be one of them, joined together with Yanchasa the Mighty.

A wave hit her, but there was no water. She staggered, trying to keep her feet. Power roared through her, shards of pure adsna trying to carry away what she was, steal her power, and turn her into a well, just as they had every pyramid they touched.

"Adsnazi," she snarled. She pushed back and felt several of them crumple, their pyramids turned to junk. "Bea, Roland, throw your pyramids." She gathered the rest of the children around her, drawing on their strength. One of them crumbled to crystalline dust, but she felt the power of its destroyed body flow through her, strengthening her.

Starbride turned to the wall, letting Yanchasa study the writing while she fought the river of adsna. The cavern shook and bucked as Bea and Roland took up the assault, but she couldn't let that distract her.

"Very clever," Yanchasa said. "They planned to use the capstone and retune it to summon flesh magic instead of repel it." Starbride felt his grin take over her mouth. "They needed such a large pyramid because they hadn't learned how to be one with flesh magic, not like you and I, daughter."

But they couldn't perform the magic while the adsnazi hammered at them. "Open your mind to more of my power, daughter."

She let a bit more of Yanchasa's essence trickle in, and her vision dimmed. He began the call, flesh to flesh. She felt the glimmer of an answer, saw it in her mind's eye. In the depths of the mountains to the north, high among snow-packed glaciers, something stirred.

CHAPTER THIRTY-SEVEN

KATYA

Someone was shaking Katya's shoulder, and she could taste blood and dust. "Princess," someone hissed in her ear. She snarled at them. She was in her grave, couldn't they see that? She'd died and earned her rest.

"Wake up!"

Katya smeared the dirt from her gritty eyes. "Dawnmother?"

"You have to get up. We're here."

The last few moments whirled to life in Katya's mind: what they'd come down here to do, how the ceiling had collapsed. The buried city. Dead and buried in the ancient city.

No. She shook her head and stood, rubble falling from her. Someone had thrown an explosive pyramid. It was fighting Roland in the caverns all over again. Swords clanged nearby, and the unearthly shriek of a Fiend made her close her eyes again. Some of the adsnazi turned the thing to a crystal puddle while the others stared down the path, their faces masks of concentration.

One of Vincent's arms hung unmoving, but he'd kept his feet. Dawnmother was trying to get the others up, and if they wouldn't wake, she pulled them away from the combat. Castelle was still down and Hugo. Brutal, Maia, and Freddie stood and shook their heads.

"She's too strong," Redtrue said.

"Keep moving forward," Katya said.

They did, inch by inch, the adsnazi trying to cleanse the pyramids that were thrown at them, but most of the time, the best they could do was leap out of the way. Katya caught a glimpse of the pyradistés chucking magic at them and saw the young girl Starbride had brought back from the north and a hooded man who kept his face out of the light.

Freddie flung a knife, and Maia shot an arrow, forcing the duo farther down the tunnel, into a large columned room. Near the back of that room, someone turned.

Katya stared as Starbride's beautiful face contorted into a snarl. "Whatever you're doing, Redtrue, keep it up," Katya said.

"You don't understand! She's taking us one by one."
Katya glanced back. Adsnazi littered the floor.
"You have to kill her," Redtrue said. "She's lost to you."
"No."
"You must! If you don't, I'll have to—"
"No!" Katya roared, and in the room, even Starbride took a step back. Katya grabbed Redtrue's shoulders. "If you lay a finger on her, I will end you."

Redtrue's eyes went so wide, Katya could see her own reflection, and she knew Redtrue felt the truth in her words.

Katya turned back to where Starbride waited and saw the pyramid cradled in her arms. "Attack that. Or use it if you can." Before Redtrue could preach to her about using evil, Katya added, "Do it, or you won't get out of this alive."

A handful of the adsnazi shrieked in unison, and Katya thought even she could feel the power being traded back and forth. One of the wild Fiends at Starbride's side writhed and turned into a pile of molten crystal.

Starbride's face went from hatred and determination to fear and wounded betrayal. "Push them back!"

Fire blossomed along the ceiling as a pyramid caught a lip of stone and shattered. Katya dropped, but with nothing to catch, the flame puffed out, leaving the air hazy with smoke. More of the adsnazi cried out. Redtrue snarled, and the pyramids that the girl and the hooded man wielded flared bright white. They dropped them to the ground as they backed away from the entrance, leaving the way clear.

Katya darted toward Starbride, Vincent and Brutal at her side. The remaining Fiend blurred toward them, but Katya kept true.

Starbride backed up a step as if she didn't know the woman who loved her. She clutched the pyramid like a little girl with her doll. "Stay away from me. How can you do this?"

"Star, I only want to help you."
"You were supposed to love me."
"I do love you, more than anything. You're my heart, Star."
Starbride slashed a hand through the air. "You abandoned me."
Guilt cut into Katya like a knife. "Never. I went because I had to, Star, but you were always first in my head, always."
"Why?"
"Why? Because I love you!"
"I always have! It was you who gave up on me!"
Katya was lost, but she suspected what was happening. "Don't listen to it, Star!"

CHAPTER THIRTY-EIGHT

STARBRIDE

Katya advanced with a murderous look in her eyes. The colors of the mosaics seemed to shift, everything distorted by the adsna hammering at Starbride and the power she used to keep it at bay. This couldn't be happening. Katya wanted to murder her.

"Stay away from me," Starbride said. "How can you do this?"

"You have to die, Star. It's the only way."

"You were supposed to love me."

Katya's smile turned pitying as well as dangerous. "Is this because I left months ago? I came back, didn't I?"

Starbride slashed a hand through the air. "You abandoned me."

"You're not worthy of my affection. I only pretended you were."

"Why?"

"It amused me. Besides, if you really loved me, you wouldn't be causing all this trouble." Her lip pouted out. "*Do* you love me, Star?"

"I always have! It was you who gave up on me!"

Her vision grew hazy, and it seemed there were two Katyas, one who mocked her and the other who cried, "Don't listen to it, Star!"

Everything was falling apart. She reached for the children, but the cursed light from the adsnazi had washed over them, turning them into nothing, as they'd turn her into nothing. "Katya, please." There had to be something she could do. She didn't want to kill her beloved. She couldn't.

But then she'd be free. No more waffling back and forth, no more uncertainty. There would be power and the means to use it. Every path would be clear. It was Katya and her friends who muddied the way.

"No, they're my friends, too."

But were they? It had been Katya they loved from the beginning. They'd all betrayed Starbride in the end, even Dawnmother. Their part in her life was just over.

A deep well of loneliness opened inside her; she was so tired of fighting. She felt as if she hadn't slept in days, as if the only rest she'd been able to get was a fleeting dream. "I don't know what to do."

And there was only one person who had the answer.

"I need time," Yanchasa said. "We're so close, but I need more energy to bring them here."

Starbride was too busy flinging adsna at the adsnazi. She felt another one fall, hammered into unconsciousness by raw power, but it wouldn't be enough, not without Yanchasa's help. They were staggering from Bea's pyramids, but Roland's were missing their mark.

She darted away from Katya and jerked at his arm. "What's the matter with you? You're supposed to be helping me."

He laid his stump on her shoulder. "I am." He'd retreated so much that Bea's back was to him, and while she focused on the adsnazi, he flung a fire pyramid at her.

She howled as fire bloomed around her, and she dropped to the stone to roll. When she came up, her face was a blistered mask of rage. "You pathetic mongrel! You turn away from even scraps of power now."

Roland sighed and seemed wistful. "I was very good at being a monster."

"And now you're just a tool. Why did you let this happen to us?" Bea cried. Her face was a mask of inhuman rage, and she didn't seem to care about the pain, reminding Starbride of not-Alphonse and his bloodstained teeth.

Starbride laughed. "Part of me knew, you know. I knew you were just a copy of him, but I didn't care as long as I could use you."

"Use this!" Bea flung a pyramid, but it bloomed with light before it reached them. Starbride didn't know if it was her or the adsnazi. She sent another pulse of power through her pyramids and knocked an adsnazi down.

"Give me what's left of the capstone," Bea said. "You're not worthy of Yanchasa's power. None of you are! It was me he wanted!"

Roland drew another pyramid and advanced. Starbride looked to where Katya was creeping up on her.

"What do I do?" Starbride asked, the power of the adsnazi still trying to take her breath away.

"I cannot help you and summon allies, daughter, not without a deeper connection between us."

"What about your body slumbering under the capstone? What of its tremendous power?"

He sighed. "I've expended too much power trying to communicate with Roland and then with you. That body can no longer wake. But there is one thing we can do."

With pyramid-augmented sight, Starbride could see the gold and silver ribbon that attached her to the pyramid in her arms and the great consciousness within. What if she fed that ribbon, helped that consciousness come out further?

What other choice was there? If she was to survive this onslaught long enough for her allies to arrive, she needed to hold the adsnazi at bay.

Starbride opened herself to power and felt her consciousness fade before Yanchasa's mind.

CHAPTER THIRTY-NINE

KATYA

Whatever Katya said, Starbride didn't seem to hear. Worse, she seemed to hear someone else's words, and Katya knew who was to blame. At least Starbride's allies were fighting each other. Katya watched as the slim girl went down under the weight of the hooded man and the adsnazi assault. When the hooded man straightened, Katya's breath left her in a rush.

"Roland?"

He had the decency not to say, "Hello, niece." He tossed a bloody pyramid down at the slim girl's side. When he approached, she raised her blade. He stopped and mouthed something like, "I'm sorry."

Starbride stiffened, clutching the pyramid in her arms.

Redtrue rushed forward. "No, you cannot let her!" She grabbed at Katya's coat like a drowning woman. "We have to kill her now. She will become the Fiend if we don't."

"You heard what I said." Her eyes shifted between Starbride and Roland. When had it become so difficult to tell who the enemy was?

"Are you blind?" Redtrue cried. "The power of that pyramid is flowing into her, and she's doing some other magic I know nothing about." She gestured to the walls around them. "You know what this room is for. She could be summoning another *Fiend*."

"A council member," Roland said. "You can stop her, Little K."

Katya snarled at the beloved nickname. "I don't need you to tell me that."

Redtrue flung her arms toward where Starbride stood transfixed. "She has succumbed."

"Then get me in her mind. Use dream magic."

Her mouth worked soundlessly. Leafclever strode up behind her. "She cannot, Princess, and you know it. We must kill Starbride before it's too late."

Katya was tempted to turn her sword on him, but instead, she gripped Redtrue's hand. "Please, Red. Please."

Redtrue's eyes bored into Katya's. She nodded once. Leafclever sucked in a sharp breath. "You know what this means?" he asked.

She nodded again. Katya didn't know what they were talking about and didn't much care. Her friends, still groggily shaking their heads, gathered around her. Katya pressed a knife into Dawnmother's grasp and spoke in her ear. "If anyone interferes, you know what to do?"

Her gaze never wavered. "Yes."

Katya cut her eyes at Roland. "Watch him especially."

Roland stepped closer and drew a pyramid from a bag at his side. Katya let the point of her rapier rest against his heart. "Don't."

"Let me help you, niece."

She looked from his pyramid to Redtrue, who could cleanse it with a thought.

"I know more about Fiend magic than anyone here, save Yanchasa. Whatever they're doing, maybe I can slow it down."

"I should kill you for what you did to my mother."

He sighed as if the idea made him happy, but he also had steel in his gaze. This was the only man who could ever stand toe-to-toe with Katya's father during an argument, who could match him volume for volume, with the same passion, when each believed his cause was just. "I'll help first, and you can kill me after."

This must have been where Reinholt got his sense of humor. Katya gave Redtrue a glance. She nodded as if to say she'd keep an eye on him.

With her friends forming a barrier around them, Katya sat at Redtrue's side, just in front of Starbride's feet. Redtrue pulled her dream walking pyramid from her bag and closed her eyes. Katya closed hers, too, shutting out the heated words between her friends and the adsnazi. Seconds passed before she felt as if the hard ground dropped away, and she was pulled through the air.

The world faded to a white void.

Cavern gone, friends and family, gone. Even Redtrue was a hazy silhouette. "Starbride?"

Katya had never been able to see anything in these visions before. She'd always had to concentrate on Starbride's thoughts and emotions within the darkness of her own mind. This time, air rushed around her, and Starbride popped into view. The pyramids no longer marred her skin. She was dressed in the outfit she'd worn when Katya had asked her to be the princess consort: dark blue trousers, shirt and bodice, jewels around her throat, but her hair lay in tangled knots over her shoulders.

"Katya?" Starbride asked. Her eyes were the same milky white as the void. "I can feel you, but there's so little room in here. Did I pull you into the pyramid with me?"

Katya started for her, but a shadow stepped from the void behind her. She wore a metal breastplate over a knee-length coat, leather trousers covering her long legs, and tall black boots studded in metal. Her black hair was short and spiky, and her reddish brown skin was the same hue as Starbride's. She radiated strength and confidence along with beauty and charisma. As Katya watched, she shifted to male and then back to female before she laid her hands on Starbride's shoulders.

"Is that you?" Starbride asked.

Yanchasa bent to whisper in Starbride's ear. Starbride frowned. "You abandoned me."

"Never in my heart, beloved," Katya cried. "They forced me to leave Marienne, and I hated them for it."

"You could have come back for me."

"I did! You don't know how badly I wanted to run back to you as soon as I awoke."

Starbride's frown deepened, and the ghostly light of a pyramid shone from her forehead. "But you didn't."

"Monster!" Katya shouted at Yanchasa. "She knows the truth. It's only your poisonous words swaying her."

Yanchasa whispered in Starbride's ear again. "You want me to be weak."

Katya put all the force of love behind her words. "I want you to be whatever and whomever you like, my love. I adore every part of you."

Starbride shifted, color blooming in her eyes before fading. "I'm afraid."

Katya stepped closer. "Then lean on me, dearheart. I will help you as you've helped me. We're better as a couple than we could ever be alone."

Starbride tried to reach out, but Yanchasa laid his hand over hers.

"I don't know how to stop it," Starbride said.

Katya knew they didn't have much time. They were in some dream world of Starbride's creation, but Katya knew only one way to fight. She concentrated, and her rapier appeared in her grasp. "I think it's time you face *me* for a change, Yanchasa."

CHAPTER FORTY

STARBRIDE

Starbride's vision was hazy, but she felt Yanchasa's comforting presence, his words in her ear. She could hear Katya, but the sound came from the end of a long tunnel. Still, Starbride could feel her emotions as if they existed in the same head. She'd pulled Katya into a dream.

Had it always been a dream? Yanchasa's focus shifted, and Starbride could see Katya's hazy form coming closer and then sharpening, a rapier in her grasp.

But not aimed at Starbride. No, she pointed at Yanchasa. His attention split too far, some on Katya, some on transferring his essence from the capstone into Starbride, and even more trying to pull in one of the council members, a long process, but Starbride could feel a form beginning to solidify. She bet the adsnazi felt it, too.

Yanchasa's power filled her head with white noise, but as Katya leapt, Starbride felt that river slow. A longsword appeared in Yanchasa's hand, and she batted Katya's attack away. Undeterred, Katya came on again. This time, Yanchasa parried and slashed at Katya's arm.

The blow tore through Katya's bicep as if she were made of smoke. Katya gasped and backed off, her arm not bleeding, but blinking in and out of focus. She may not have been physically present, but the blows would take a toll on her psyche.

With a laugh, Yanchasa charged, and Starbride felt his control slip again. She'd had a dream, she remembered, in the hideout while Roland still controlled the city. She'd been running, trying to escape the castle, and Katya had left her behind. It had been buried deep, but part of her had always thought Katya had abandoned her.

Her waking mind had never believed that, especially after she'd gotten in touch with Katya, when their love had been easy to feel. Lately, it had been Yanchasa plumbing her subconscious and fanning the flames, but she couldn't realize it because he was *inside* her mind.

That shouldn't have been possible. She was a pyradisté. No one could invade her thoughts, not unless they used the same method as Roland and obliterated her brain before ransacking it.

"I believed you," she said. Grief had made her vulnerable, and she'd let him in, and then, Horsestrong forgive her, she'd believed everything he'd said. He'd turned her emotions as if cranking a handle, the adsna letting him control what she felt and when.

Yanchasa's sword rang against Katya's, but she cast one look over her shoulder. "I didn't have to lie to you, daughter."

Most of the time that had been true. Yanchasa had found every insecurity, every doubt. Starbride struggled against the power that coalesced around her like a web.

Yanchasa staggered, and Katya delivered a stab to her thigh.

"Keep fighting, Star!" Katya called.

Yanchasa's rage blew Katya away like an autumn leaf, and she tumbled out of sight in the void. "Fool, you're nothing without me, can't you see that?"

And it was so. No one could give her power like Yanchasa could, no one could ever be so close, so intimate. Yanchasa appeared before her and cupped her face in his icy fingers. "I can be everything to you, daughter. Embrace me fully, and you'll need no one else. I can watch from within your mind, and sometimes, if you're tired, I can use the body while you rest."

And she was tired, very much so, and the power filling her felt so warm and comforting. How bad could it be to—

"Get the fuck away from her!" Katya yelled, charging out of the white.

Yanchasa and Katya traded blows again. Starbride shook herself back to thought.

"Star, I love you," Katya called. "You can't doubt that, not ever." Her feelings leapt the space between them and wrapped Starbride like a warm blanket.

"Keep her busy!" Starbride yelled. She pushed against the power and held on to one truth: Katya loved her, and she loved Katya. Even if Yanchasa sometimes spoke the truth, that didn't make him any less of a betrayer.

She repeated that to herself as she tried to close the flow of power, but she feared it was too late. Yanchasa howled and blinked from sight, but Starbride knew the fight wasn't over. The ribbon of power doubled and smacked into her like a hammer.

"It would have been easier if you'd accepted," he whispered in her mind. "But I can steal your body if I have to."

"No more promises of love?" Starbride asked. In response, pain cascaded through her skull, and she cried out. Katya's arms went around her.

"More difficult," Yanchasa said, "but I can manage."

His power filled her. Her arms and legs jerked in their sockets, and she willed them to still. Yanchasa cut into his council-summoning efforts, and the excess power surrounded her.

"Fight it, Star!" Katya cried.

"I'm trying." It wouldn't be enough. Yanchasa's feelings of victory rose inside her, coupled with contempt for the beautiful woman in her arms. Farraday was a kingdom without ambition, but all that was about to change. "You have to kill me."

Katya held her tighter. "Everyone keeps saying that, but I'm not going to listen. Redtrue, can you bring us closer?"

Redtrue's hazy shape sharpened, and the edge of Katya's form slipped into Starbride's. Katya pressed their foreheads together, into each other, and Starbride felt the force of Katya's iron will. Yanchasa's power waned, but they were still two young minds against an ancient one, one that had been plotting, waiting. Yanchasa had grown tired of wasting time with amateurs like Roland and wasn't about to give up the prize she'd been given.

Starbride felt a sliver of affront, and a fourth consciousness brushed her own. Roland's power crackled alongside them. He'd been a strong pyradisté *before* merging with his Aspect. No wonder he'd always seemed leaps and bounds ahead of everyone.

"This is twice everyone has turned against you," Starbride said. "Now I know why *I* felt so rejected, Yanchasa. You were feeding me your own fears. Even Roland has turned on you. How did you think of him? Amateur? Puppet?"

Roland's angry power flared, free to do as he wished, no longer under Yanchasa's thumb. She knew the feeling. Yanchasa gave a hair's breadth of ground.

"It's like trying to move a boulder with a spoon," Starbride said. "We can't stay like this forever, Katya." All of them would tire before Yanchasa, bodies that needed to eat and sleep.

"Try harder!" Katya screamed.

Starbride didn't know if they could. Katya eased deeper into her until Starbride couldn't separate Katya's thoughts from her own. Both wanted the other to live as much as each wanted to go on living. One consciousness, bearing both sword and magic, they were invincible, unstoppable.

Yanchasa's grip weakened. "Think of the power, daughter!"

She and Katya had all the power they needed. They fought as a single force, aided by Roland and Redtrue and now the adsnazi, forcing Yanchasa back into the capstone. Starbride thought of her real parents, the love of her father, her mother's determination. "I am not your daughter."

"I will not be refused!" A pulse roared through them, and Katya nearly jerked from Starbride's grasp.

Roland's magic spiked in response. Starbride grabbed for Redtrue's power and forced her and Katya back together, their minds merging with such a rush that they emitted a pulse all their own.

Yanchasa screamed and gave way, and they intruded on her psyche the way she'd plagued Starbride's, saw her fears laid bare: that she would spend eternity imprisoned, never to feel the sun upon her skin again, never to see Edette or the other three, never to taste a pear or feel the rush of blood from a defeated foe.

"Get out of my mind!" he shouted.

"You're just as scared as the rest of us," Katya-Starbride said.

And they weren't alone. Redtrue followed them, and she pitted her own considerable will against Yanchasa's. Roland's power hammered on the pyramid, keeping all the precious ground they won. Katya-Starbride sensed the adsnazi pushing Yanchasa toward his prison as gently and unstoppably as a leaf being carried down a river.

Yanchasa jerked and struggled and screamed in dual voices, but they forced him down, cramming his consciousness into the pyramid and sealing the way out.

CHAPTER FORTY-ONE

KATYA

It felt so right. Each wanted to stay joined with the other. They could be Katya-Starbride always, sustained by love.

But in whose body?

"Making love will be easier and more difficult at the same time." And with that thought, they were separate again, though Katya still reveled in Starbride's affection.

"That was you," Starbride said. "Trust you to break us apart with a thought like that."

A ping of exhaustion traveled through the void like a vibrating harp string. Redtrue.

"We have to leave," Katya said. Still, she didn't let go of Starbride's spectral form, not trusting that Yanchasa wouldn't spring back between them. "Let's go together."

Redtrue was lying on the floor, her head cradled in Castelle's lap. Next to them stood Riverwise, the young man who hadn't been afraid of the capstone or its magic. Roland knelt by the large pyramid that had tumbled from Starbride's arms, the one that held the capstone's energy. He heaved as if he'd just run a race, and Hugo and Maia were at his sides. Around all of them stood a half-circle made up of Brutal, Freddie, Vincent, and Dawnmother.

And Starbride was in her arms. They stood together.

Katya heard a crunch at her feet. Four tiny pyramids littered the ground, leaving Starbride's body unmarked. Katya kissed her forehead over where the smallest pyramid used to be. "I'm so sorry, Star, if you ever felt anything less than loved."

Starbride put her arms around Katya's neck. "Deepest fears from my most inner self," she said. "Nothing I ever truly thought. Katya, I'm so sorry. I can't, I can't even tell you…" She sagged as if her legs wouldn't hold her.

Katya squeezed her hard and held her up. "I love you, Star. I always will. Just breathe for now and think on that." She cleared her throat. "It's done," she said loudly, making the others turn toward them.

Leafclever and his adsnazi stood arrayed before them, pyramids out. "Then, at last, can you stand out of the way so that we can deal with the monster that still lives inside that pyramid?"

Brutal didn't move. "Redtrue said you can't cleanse it yet, not without knowing what it might do to those still connected with Yanchasa."

Leafclever frowned. "We will not harm someone through magic, you know this. But we can take possession of that artifact in order to insure no one else *is* harmed."

Brutal looked back to Katya. "Let them through," she said. She worried that Starbride remained silent, but she knew that shame and guilt had to be hard at work in Starbride's mind. Katya bit her lip, unsure of the right course. She'd never had to tend to someone who'd just regained their humanity. As if reading her mind, Maia appeared at her side and helped her guide Starbride out of the way.

"Can you still hear its voice?" Katya muttered in Starbride's ear.

She shook her head. "Katya, how will I ever apologize?"

"They know it wasn't you. I know. All we need is…" She'd been about to say time, the thing that Starbride had asked for with Yanchasa sharing her head. "All we need is rest."

Maia pressed in close, and Katya heard her whisper, "Welcome back." Dawnmother pressed to Starbride's side and wouldn't let go. Two of the adsnazi lifted Yanchasa's pyramid carefully and walked it from the room.

They all tread carefully, nursing wounds. Katya sent Vincent ahead to have his arm seen to. Brutal and the rest of the adsnazi stopped to help their unconscious comrades and to check on the sleeping men and women they'd passed on their way to the fight. At the sight of a charred corpse, Starbride turned her face into Katya's shoulder.

"Wait," Starbride said. "What happened to Bea?"

"You mean me," Roland said.

Katya paused. She couldn't see him as wholly man or monster, but she couldn't say that aloud, not with Starbride so near and vulnerable. An inner voice asked how she could forgive one of them and not the other. Katya frowned so hard it threatened to become a snarl. Starbride hadn't killed Ma.

When Katya turned to Roland, his face shifted through several expressions, and she worried he might have another fit of madness.

He breathed deep. "When you offered me the Aspect again, I knew what I had to do. There was nothing left of that girl. When I saw her, I remembered. I had to stop me."

Starbride sobbed a laugh. "You're a very good actor."

"As leader of the Order, you have to be."

Katya had said that a few times. She clenched her jaw and fought the urge to identify with him. He held his pyramid out, and Katya plucked it from his palm.

Hugo put an arm around his shoulders and led him away.

"Bea told me a story about eating too many berries with her brother," Starbride said.

Katya had to swallow bile. "That's one of my father's stories, when he and Roland were children." Before Maia could follow Hugo, Katya caught her arm. "Roland has to go back in his cell." Maia's face hardened, but Katya shook her head. "You can stay with him or bring him something to make him more comfortable, but he cannot go free, Maia. You know that."

She nodded and followed on her brother's heels. Freddie replaced her, joining those clustered around Starbride. "You can't blame them," he said. "Both Maia and Hugo always hoped their father could be saved."

"But there are some deeds you can never come back from," Starbride said. "I should know." Katya hugged her closer.

As they began the climb up the disorderly steps, Katya noticed Redtrue, Castelle, and Riverwise stayed with her rather than go with the adsnazi. "What did Leafclever mean?" Katya asked. "About you not knowing what it meant to help me?"

Redtrue looked away, but Riverwise sighed. "By choosing forbidden magic, we are no longer adsnazi."

Katya stopped and half turned. Even Starbride looked at them with wide eyes. "Wait, you're not..."

"You're exiled?" Starbride asked.

"No one can bar me from Allusia," Redtrue said with a sniff. When Katya continued to stare, Redtrue stiffened, a challenging look on her face. "And just because I cannot call myself adsnazi does not mean I will conform to pyradisté ways."

Katya knew anger covering grief when she saw it, and she sensed that now wasn't the best time to thank Redtrue for what she'd done. Maybe there would never be a good time for that, not if it meant reminding her of what it cost. Maybe she could have a word with Leafclever later, or maybe Da could.

"I think I might learn Farradain magic," Riverwise said.

Redtrue stared at him as if he'd just lit himself on fire. "You will remain close to me," she said slowly. He grinned into her glower, and Katya thought she might have met her match, or at least had someone who might distract her from her current predicament. Either way, Katya put it out of her mind. She had Starbride to take care of first.

CHAPTER FORTY-TWO

STARBRIDE

Starbride tuned out the conversations around her. She kept seeing the burnt corpse in the hallway, kept imagining the hundreds she'd killed outside the city walls. She'd let Yanchasa out. How could she have been so stupid?

She knew what Katya would say: "Place the blame where it belongs."

Could she ever experience the adsna anymore? She couldn't bring herself to try. She'd have to practice magic the way she had before, with a different pyramid for each task, as blind and deaf to the flow of the adsna as any other pyradisté, unless the adsnazi could teach her differently. They might refuse. She wouldn't blame them if they did. Horsestrong preserve her, she'd hurt so many people!

Now she understood what Maia had told her about missing the Fiend's power. Not the desire to kill or the imperious coldness, but the freedom from consequence.

Starbride felt a tug at her consciousness, and it took her breath away. Yanchasa's voice was too faint to hear, but she knew what he wanted, what he could give her, the promise of power. She could be free again. All was not lost.

She thought of what Roland had done, his denial of power. The path to redemption began by saying no to the thing that had first led them astray. Starbride brushed Yanchasa's lingering essence away and tightened her grip on Katya.

Maia and Brutal caught up to them at the door to Starbride's apartment. He reported that none of the sleeping monks or adsnazi appeared to be seriously injured. He didn't mention the one she'd killed, but the image wouldn't leave her mind. Maia wrung her hands, seeming much closer to the young girl she'd been before the troubles started. When Brutal finished speaking, she flung her arms around Katya and Starbride both.

They staggered, and just as Starbride began to put her arms around Maia, Maia kissed both their cheeks and stepped back. "I didn't want you to think I was angry with you, Katya, because of my father. I just wanted you to know that I love you. That seemed important to say right now."

Starbride had to smile, and she bet Katya did the same.

"And," Maia said, "life's too short to keep secrets. I'm pregnant with Darren's baby."

Starbride felt Katya stiffen. She didn't think she'd heard complete silence before that moment. She knew that particular secret, and she was still surprised.

"Um," Katya said, and Starbride thought she did rather well to get anything out at all.

"You don't have to say anything," Maia said. "We'll work it out."

By the sweet smile Brutal gave her, Starbride knew two things: she'd already told him, and she wouldn't be a parent alone.

"Since we're all telling secrets," Freddie said. "I was once convicted of murder and hanged."

They all breathed out a not-quite laugh, the tension deflating. Starbride tugged on Katya's arm. "And we're going to get married."

Katya slid her thumb across Starbride's chin. "We haven't had a year of consortship yet."

"Darkstrong take propriety. We'll marry whenever we want."

Dawnmother hugged her other side. "Horsestrong couldn't have said it better." She waved at the rest of them. "Rest. Eat."

Starbride was stumbling by the time they got inside the sitting room. Once inside the bedroom, Katya had to half-carry her, and she passed out fully dressed on top of the covers, barely aware of Katya undressing her and putting her between the sheets.

❖

Starbride's eyes flew open, and panic gripped her heart until she reached out and found Katya asleep beside her. She'd been dreaming of snow-capped peaks and the screams of dying men, but they didn't have the clarity of Yanchasa's memories. Just another nightmare she'd have to live with.

She eased back into the pillows, watching Katya sleep by the light of the moon streaming through the window. Stars sparkled in the clear night sky, the snow done for the time being.

Idyllic really, and she knew she should relax into it, keep the calm while she could, but now that she was awake—her heart still pounding—she itched to be up. Even though she'd gotten no rest with Yanchasa, she felt as if she'd slept for far too long.

She dressed in the dark and tiptoed from the room. Dawnmother had left a bowl of dried figs and nuts on the table next to a lantern, just in case. Starbride smiled, and her stomach growled. She hadn't needed to eat much with Yanchasa around. She bolted a few pieces of fruit and put more in her pocket before she sneaked from the room, careful not to wake anyone.

Once out, though, she was lost. What were her choices? Walk the halls like a ghost, fully immersed in the wrongs she'd committed? Venture out into the cold, but to do what? She suddenly craved someone who understood, who'd felt this restless energy, the fight between wanting to do something good and wanting to collapse into a puddle and wallow in guilt.

Roland would know. Whether he could offer advice or not, he would know her feelings as well as she did. But how to get through the dungeon door without a Fiend?

She paused in the dark hallway, torn. She supposed Yanchasa might have left enough residue on her soul to get her through, but she'd hate to take the long walk only to have to come back unsatisfied. She kept picturing Roland's face as he turned on Bea—no, *himself*—in order to help her. He'd resisted the temptation to reclaim power long after it had been stripped from him. It had been easy to do when she'd been exhausted, but later, if it ever happened again? She needed to ask him how he'd managed it.

Starbride hurried to Hugo's room. He answered the door while clutching a robe around himself. "Miss Starbride?" he asked cautiously.

She breathed a laugh. "It's me. I need your help. I need to see your father."

"One second." He made as if to slip inside but eased back out. "To do magic?"

It hurt, but she couldn't blame him. "No, I promise. I just need to talk to someone who, um…"

He nodded and threw some clothes on before joining her in the hall. They didn't speak for most of the trip, but she couldn't help glancing at him from the corner of her eye.

"I'm sorry, Hugo," she said softly, just before they reached the dungeon.

He sighed a laugh. "You knew I'd forgiven you before you said that, right? There's little I wouldn't forgive you for."

She was tempted to ask what but squeezed his hand instead. "You are one of my dearest friends, I hope you know that." Tears threatened to choke her, and her vision swam.

He clutched her fingers and leaned in, planting a quick kiss on her lips. "I hope you will do me the honor of letting me escort you on your wedding day."

She wiped away the few tears that had managed to make their way out. "Let them try to stop us." The words sounded too close to something she would have said with Yanchasa sharing her head, and she shuddered.

When they found the dungeon door ajar, Starbride paused. Hugo glanced at her, and they stepped through together. Soft voices led them to Roland's cell. Einrich stood over his brother, a dagger in one hand, and Starbride wondered if that was revenge or mercy in his rigid shoulders.

Starbride waved Hugo back the way they'd come, but he stared at the dagger. Starbride pushed until he waited by the door.

"Did a part of you want to help Starbride and get your Fiend back?" Einrich asked.

"You should kill me," Roland said.

"For what you've done, or because you might do it again?"

Roland's face jerked up, and his eyes pinned Starbride to the wall. Einrich didn't seem to notice the glance. Maybe he thought Roland was staring at shadows.

"You're awake because you miss your wife," Roland said.

Einrich let out a slow breath. "Yes."

"I killed her, my own sweet sister-in-law. I killed a lot of people. But now I'm free." His eyes seemed to plead. "Free to die. I abandoned my duty for power. Everything I've done since doesn't matter."

Einrich knelt and brought the dagger close to Roland's throat. "Did you let it in, Roland? Did you invite it? Do you want it back?"

"It's not like that," Starbride said softly.

Einrich stood and whirled, face thunderous with a hint of panic. Starbride had never seen his emotions so naked. He held the dagger up as if to fend her off.

Starbride held her hands up so he could see her empty palms. As she stepped inside, she waved to Hugo to stay where he was. "Yanchasa saw everything I ever wanted or ever felt insecure about. Every slight became a monument to insult. And that was with the *thinking, reasoning* human behind the power. What you have, what Roland had, is the most monstrous side of Yanchasa's personality. You don't invite that in so much as it barges in and takes over." Both Roland and Einrich stared at her now, and they looked so much alike. She'd thought so before, but it was easier to see without Roland carrying Yanchasa's Aspect. Now Einrich was the more dangerous one.

"You've seen what happens when one of your Aspects emerges on its own," Starbride said. "When Roland merged with it, the cruel monster filled in all the bits of his mind that it could."

"And even the rest was under its sway," Roland said, looking at her as if she was the spirit of wisdom. "But the knowledge remains."

"And the guilt," she said, "because the power does feel good. Horsestrong forgive me, but it does."

"You're not telling me anything I don't know," Einrich said softly, and she could tell he was waiting for an excuse, but was it to kill his brother or spare him?

She pointed at the dagger. "Both sides of the blade carry mercy and cruelty. Killing him spares him the pain of guilt but leaves him no room to make amends. And you would have to live with the fact that you'd killed him."

"And if I spare him, I make him suffer the guilt, but he gets a chance to atone?" Einrich asked.

Starbride smiled. "And you'd have to live with that, too."

Einrich stared at his brother. "He asked me to kill him."

"Maia asked for the same."

"And you?" Einrich asked. "What are you asking for?"

Starbride thought of the residents of Marienne and the villagers she'd killed. What would make it right? To send herself to prison? Yanchasa was already there. If she held herself blameless, she had to hold Roland the same, didn't she?

"To make amends," she said. "To marry your daughter and make her happy. I want to live, and I want him to live to prove it can be done."

The silence stretched on until Roland raised his head. "What could I ever do? There aren't enough good deeds in all the world. A person could spend his whole life searching for them."

Starbride smiled softly. "Yes, a person could."

Einrich put his dagger away. He didn't embrace his brother. He might never be able to, but the look he wore didn't carry the hate it had when she'd first spied on him. He moved past Starbride, out of the cell. She sat face-to-face with Roland, not quite close enough to touch.

He folded his fingers over his stump and could hardly look at her. "Do you forgive me?" he asked.

She thought long before she answered. "No, not yet, but I understand you. I'm sorry I tortured you."

"I'm sorry I didn't give you any other choice."

"Tell me about your time with Yanchasa. I want to hear it."

After a deep breath, he began to speak.

CHAPTER FORTY-THREE

KATYA

Katya sneaked into the secret passageways before Portia could find her. Her new maid had arrived in Katya's apartment in a tizzy six weeks ago, days after Starbride had been cleansed. She'd stayed permanently abuzz ever since. It had only gotten worse as Katya's wedding approached. The week before the event, she'd checked and rechecked Katya's wedding clothes, her jewelry, and the plans. Now that they only had one day left, Katya expected her to be floating three feet above the ground with excitement. Anyone would have thought it was her getting married.

Katya had told her she wanted to sleep in on the last days before her wedding, and Portia had enthusiastically agreed. She'd promised to put together a large breakfast that Katya could have in bed if she desired. Katya didn't see the fun with no one to share it. It had been the job of the wedding escorts to keep Katya and Starbride apart for five days before their wedding, and they'd done a miraculous job. If Starbride was still in the palace, Katya had no idea where.

Katya had struggled to find her the first two days, and her escorts had been delighted to watch her try, particularly Reinholt, but after she couldn't even bribe the servants, she'd given up.

That didn't mean she couldn't hope to see Starbride where she was going, though the chances were slim. As she took her first step into the dark secret passageways, she shivered. Nearly three months since her ordeal underground, and tight spaces still unnerved her. Maybe they'd hidden Starbride in a closet. That would guarantee Katya couldn't go in after her.

She hurried toward the capstone cavern, giving a quick hello to the knowledge monks who teemed around the large portal into the underground city. They were still discovering its secrets, including the pyramid and its ominous capstone. If people had thought Yanchasa a myth before, they knew the truth now.

Katya grinned and knew it had an edge of malice to it. The bastard wouldn't be a problem much longer.

As she stepped into the capstone cavern, the lights of many tiny pyramids greeted her. The adsnazi had placed the pyramid that Starbride had transferred Yanchasa's essence into near the old, dead capstone, the easier to work with both at once.

Near the center of the cavern, Leafclever nodded to her. Katya returned the gesture and headed to where Redtrue stood apart from the adsnazi, Riverwise at her side. Katya didn't point out the distance. The adsnazi might be working with her this day, but afterward, they were going home without Redtrue among them. That didn't mean she'd be alone, if Castelle had anything to do with it.

Riverwise smiled and bowed, Farradain fashion. He'd chopped off the long lock of hair all adsnazi sported and seemed to be letting the rest grow out. "Highness. Some of the others are calling this your wedding present."

Redtrue sniffed. Except for the long lock, her head was freshly shaved. The adsnazi could say she was no longer one of them, but that wouldn't change who she was in her heart. "The magic is done today because we have now finished our research."

"I love it when you get romantic," Castelle said, hugging her from the side.

"It's a perfect wedding present, Riverwise, thank you," Katya said. "How long until we're ready?"

"Shouldn't you be preparing your suit of diamonds for the ceremony?" Redtrue asked.

"Alas," Katya said, "the emerald-studded venue I ordered isn't ready yet, and my sapphire-encrusted horse is too heavy to walk, so they're putting it on wheels."

Redtrue cracked a smile.

"Besides," Castelle said, "Katya and Starbride are getting married Allusian fashion."

"Mostly," Katya added.

Redtrue sniffed. "I'll believe it when I see it." She looked past Katya's shoulder to the capstone. "They're ready."

Redtrue didn't speak to any of the adsnazi as she joined their circle, and Katya read in her stiff back and shoulders that she still pretended it was a matter of pride between them, that she didn't regret her choices. Castelle's pitying glances told a different story, one Katya could guess: Redtrue's banishment cut her to the core. She could return to Allusia, but Katya bet she wouldn't, not until the adsnazi welcomed her home.

Katya had always thought that pyradistés lacked ritual. Whenever the Umbriels had Waltzed, Crowe had simply chained them to the floor and let them transform, commune with Yanchasa, and then he'd cared for their unconscious bodies afterward. The whole thing could have done with a bit more pomp.

Evidently, the adsnazi agreed with Crowe. There was no chanting or dancing as with a feast for one of the spirits.

The council of five, an inner voice corrected. Katya contained a shiver. Best to consider them the spirits for as long as she could. Of course, now that the people of Marienne were learning the truth, Katya had to wonder if even spirit worship would change.

The adsnazi sat and linked hands, each with a pyramid resting in his or her lap. Some stared at the capstone and some at Starbride's pyramid. Redtrue blinked twice and then not again. All around the circle, they wore calm faces and breathed in unison. Katya couldn't fathom the battle that was raging, and she was suddenly glad Starbride wasn't there to feel it.

Seconds passed, minutes. Sweat stood out on adsnazi foreheads, and some of their eyelids sagged or slipped shut. All the pyramids pulsed with white light, first slow and then as quick as the beating of a sparrow's heart.

The capstone and the smaller pyramid flared, so bright Katya had to shield her eyes, and then both faded, going dark. The adsnazi let go of one another and came back to themselves slowly, their pyramids the only source of light. Redtrue stood on shaky legs, always the first to get to her feet.

"Well?" Castelle asked.

"It's done," Redtrue said. "Yanchasa is now back where she belongs." She beamed, and Katya saw what Castelle must have seen in her. "There will be no more need for Fiends."

No more need for the Waltz, at least. Da, Reinholt, Maia, Hugo, and Brutal still possessed their Aspects, all carefully locked by pyramid necklaces. If all went as planned, Bastian and Vierdrin would never need to carry pyramids. They would never Waltz. The adsnazi hadn't wanted to risk draining the Fiends and giving Yanchasa a boost of power, but there was no reason to pass the Aspect to future generations.

Katya sighed. The end of an era. The end of secrets. Well, the end of Fiendish secrets. Who could say what the future would hold for the Umbriels without Yanchasa beneath their feet?

CHAPTER FORTY-FOUR

STARBRIDE

Starbride felt him go, Yanchasa's howling presence flitting past her mind's eye. When he'd been forced from Starbride's mind, he'd still had hope. She could feel him under the palace, waiting for another chance, seething with the need for revenge. He could wait centuries if necessary. Now he knew that he would never walk free again.

Starbride bet he was shrieking under the original glacier that had held him, trapped in his useless body, crying out impotently to his fellows. She wondered if they were happy to feel his presence again.

Dawnmother touched Starbride's shoulder. "Is it the ritual?"

"Funny that they'd call it that. There's not even any singing or dancing." She looked around the room where her wedding escort had hidden her that day, a place even Katya didn't know about: Pennynail's tower. Cleared of most of its shabby furniture, it was nearly presentable, and they had the master of sneaking himself bringing them food and drink.

Her several attempts to escape had left her lost in the secret passageways. She'd given up then and just gone where they'd led her. Thankfully, Freddie knew some beautiful places in the palace where no one else went, like the roof, with stunning views of Marienne and the countryside.

Still, nothing could compare to the sight of Katya, who'd been denied to her for five days. "What do you think she's doing right now?"

"None of that," Dawnmother said. "These Farradains think we can't play their games and keep the two of you apart, but we can."

"You sound like my mother."

"And may I point out that the Farradain games have kept her out of your hair for the past five days as well?"

"True." Though she did miss her father's easy presence. Starbride touched her gown where it hung before the mirror. "Is it nice outside?"

"The sun is shining. Hopefully, that will continue into tomorrow. It should melt the snow just enough to make things nice and soggy. Honestly, Star, spring is just around the corner. You couldn't have waited?"

"No." The king, the nobles, and the Allusians had finally reached an accord, with only a few outstanding details to iron out. What better time? "I wonder what she's doing now."

Dawnmother sighed. "Horsestrong save me from people in love."

Starbride sighed heavily and acted as if she might faint on Freddie's couch. "Fantasizing about Katya is all that's left for me."

"Perhaps not all." With a sly smile, she took a pyramid from her pocket and pressed it into Starbride's grasp.

Starbride didn't need to fall into it to sense what it did. Redtrue had been teaching her the knack of Allusian magic. "A dream pyramid? Is this for tonight?"

"In a few minutes. My wedding present to you. Well, mine and Redtrue's and Castelle's. As the latter pointed out, all the custom says is that you can't *see* each other."

"Clever Castelle." She slid her thumb up the pyramid's smooth side. She still couldn't use a pyramid without thinking of Yanchasa and all the people she'd killed. She'd used them only when she had to, and thankfully, that hadn't been often. Master Bernard, the pyradistés, and the adsnazi had taken care of any emergencies and cleared out the rest of Roland's puppets and traps.

Redtrue had been teaching her how to feel the adsna without letting it overwhelm her. She'd hoped to speak with the other adsnazi, but they refused to have anything to do with her. Their cold, polite rebuffs had hurt, enough that Katya had threatened not to work with them, but Starbride had insisted she should, for the good of the kingdom. Redtrue and Riverwise had been good enough teachers on their own. They could keep her from murdering anyone else.

"Star," Dawnmother said, "I know that look. Stop."

"I can't forget, Dawn, I—"

Dawnmother wrapped her hands around Starbride's, around the pyramid. "Remember what you've learned from your conversations with Roland. No nightmares are waiting for you here."

Starbride shuddered and leaned back on the couch. It was just a dream pyramid, nothing that could hurt anyone. She fell into the pyramid and waited.

It wasn't long until she felt Redtrue's pyramid linking with hers, and then Katya was there like a stampeding horse.

"Have five days ever felt so long?"

Starbride laughed, losing herself in the dreamy haze of Katya's love but not completely. The Farradain repetition of fives made her think of the council and Yanchasa's banishment.

"It went smoothly, no problems," Katya said.

"I'm, well, I don't think happy would begin to cover it."

"I can't wait to see you tomorrow."

Starbride squirmed in delight. "I'll take your can't wait to see me and offer a can't wait to hold you."

Katya chuckled, and the low sound made Starbride's insides warm. "If we keep going this way, you'll find out everything I have planned for you."

"Oh, you have plans?" Starbride asked. "So do I."

"Do tell," Katya said, and the desire Starbride sensed matched her own.

"You'll have to wait and see. But will there be time for all our plans?"

"Hmm, we'll just have to make sure we leave right after the wedding and get straight to the sex."

Starbride laughed deeply, and it felt so good to do so. She'd been billowed by emotions after the loss of the adsna, but they'd been cleaner than any she'd suffered under Yanchasa's influence. She was finally getting used to not having every emotion tinged with sorrow.

The next morning, Starbride was torn between waiting patiently for things to happen and pacing. Dawnmother finally told her it was time to dress, though Starbride would have been ready from dawn onward if anyone had let her. Even after she dressed, it seemed an eternity before Freddie came to fetch her with Hugo in tow.

"Miss Starbride," Hugo choked out. "You are so beautiful."

"And you, both of you, with your Allusian finery." Both wore loose fitting trousers and shirts, but each had an embroidered vest that buttoned high on the neck and extended in long points past their belts. Hugo's was a mix of light and dark reds, while Freddie's mixed green with green. And both had red ribbons pinned above their hearts in an elaborate flower design, the Farradain answer to greenery in winter.

Dawnmother wore a dress to match Starbride's, mainly white, the Farradain color for love and passion, but she too wore a ribbon-made flower. Like Starbride's gown, her large skirt was held out by petticoats instead of layers of fabric. Her bodice cinched in the waist, unadorned and simple, reflecting her nature. She wore her hair in the same tidy queue as always, only it had a ribbon flower in it as well.

She draped a long white cloak over Starbride's dress before donning one herself, and then they were off, sneaking through the palace until they could get inside the carriage her parents had secured.

Starbride tuned out her mother's fussing voice as she watched the city roll past the window. Farradain couples were married under the eyes of Ellias and Elody, inside the chapterhouse of love and beauty, but Allusian couples were joined in nature, under an open sky—or a tent if it was raining. Starbride knew Katya was glad to adopt Allusian customs in this case. The idea that her spirits were actually the ancient rulers of Belshreth still didn't sit well with her.

Allusian couples rode on horseback to the place they would be married, surrounded by friends and family, even whole villages. Farradain couples entered on foot with just their escorts. Starbride was glad of the carriage this time as it drove outside the walls of Marienne, close to the forest. If she'd had to walk or ride, she would have been chilled and spattered with mud.

She spied Katya's carriage on the other side of the huge crowd that had gathered to see them wed. A hard knot formed in her, desire to see the marriage through, anxiety for it to begin, and a bundle of nerves that whispered about the possibility of tripping in front of everyone.

Her father whispered in her ear. "Your mother could barely contain herself last night. She kept saying, 'A bride at last!'"

Starbride snuggled close. "I'm also lucky, Papa, just like you wanted me to be."

He kissed her temple. "You make your own luck, my Star. And I have Dawnmother's word that the princess will treat you well, or she'll spirit you away in the night."

Dawnmother nodded sagely, and Starbride had to laugh. The carriage stopped, and Freddie and Hugo piled out. Her father caught her before she could follow.

"One last thing." He pulled a small box from his trouser pocket and pressed it into her hands. "Your neck looked lonely, so I thought I'd make it a companion."

Starbride opened the box and stared at a diamond pendant in the shape of a starburst. "Thank you, Papa." She tried to swallow her tears as he fastened it around her neck.

Her mother gave a satisfied nod before she got out of the carriage. After a wink, Dawnmother followed her. Starbride kissed her father on the cheek before she climbed out. She and Katya disembarked at the same time, and Starbride's eyes locked on the woman she was about to marry.

Katya wore an Allusian suit: her shirt and trousers a mottle of darker blues, and her vest a shining cobalt. Embroidered silver butterflies raced across it, and she wore Starbride's old butterfly hairpin on her vest, nesting atop a red ribbon flower. Her hair streamed loose around her shoulders, held back from her face by a silver diadem. She grinned like the summer sun, and Starbride's knees nearly gave way.

CHAPTER FORTY-FIVE

KATYA

As Starbride alit from her carriage, Katya wanted to fall to her knees and thank any spirits or even council members that might be listening. When Dawnmother took Starbride's cloak from her shoulders, Katya sucked in a sharp breath.

She wore white, a Farradain outfit to complement Katya's Allusian suit. The white skirt shimmered, adorned with tiny crystals, and the white silk bodice glimmered with gold embroidery. When she stepped forward, the wind fluttered some trailing fabric behind the gown, and Katya saw what it was meant to be: butterfly wings, tucked behind her, but as the wind lifted them she seemed to take flight.

Katya's father took her arm. "Best get your feet back under you, my girl."

She smiled at him, and the look he gave her was filled with pride. He, like Reinholt, Maia, and Brutal were dressed Farradain fashion, trousers and long coats, except for Maia who wore a petal-like turquoise gown with added room for her expanding belly. The dress was made from one of Katya's mother's gowns, and it made her feel as if her mother was walking on her other arm.

Reinholt took that arm instead, leaving Maia and Brutal to walk behind her as Freddie, Hugo, and Dawnmother did for Starbride, who had her parents guiding her.

They both seemed to need the support. Katya noted Starbride's white knuckles, and spirits knew Katya needed the arms lifting her. Or did she need them to hold her back? Katya wanted nothing more than to charge forward and take Starbride in her arms.

Farradain couples were wedded by members of a love chapterhouse, and Katya rated the supreme heads, a man and woman who stood before the crowd clad in white robes. Allusian couples were married by tribal or government leaders, so Dayscout waited beside them.

He clapped in joy, and as Starbride and Katya stopped less than an arm's length from each other, he said in a high whisper, "I love weddings!"

Katya laughed, and some of the magic around them abated, but she was happy for the reprieve. If she smiled any more, her cheeks would be sore.

All three officiators asked if they promised to love each other. The love and beauty heads asked if they would be faithful. Dayscout said loyal, and Katya liked that better. They promised before the spirits and their families and witnesses to depend on each other. The heads advised them not to keep secrets, and Starbride winked. Dayscout advised them to keep each other warm, and everyone laughed.

Starbride watched curiously as the heads bound their hands together. She'd told Katya that Allusians had no such ceremony. They only thing required at the end of their marriages was that the newly minted couple ride a horse together. The heads said over their bound hands that they were one, but that they should never forget the halves that made the whole. They cut the ribbon, leaving Katya's and Starbride's right hands encased in white with their fingers free.

When the other two looked at Dayscout for parting words, he just leaned in and said, "Good luck."

As Katya looked at Starbride, she knew they'd have to add more to the ceremony to make it their own. As all three officiators pronounced them joined in marriage, they leaned forward and kissed each other deeply.

Some people in the audience gasped. Perhaps they thought a royal wedding should have more decorum. At the front of the crowd, Bastian and Vierdrin jumped and cheered. As Dawnmother led a ribbon-bedecked horse forward, Katya practically vaulted into the saddle built for two. She reached down for Starbride, who scoffed and used the stirrup to climb behind her.

Starbride sat with one knee bent so her skirt covered her legs. "When you live somewhere long enough," she said, "you learn a few things."

Katya laughed as she guided the horse toward the crowd. The wedding escorts mounted their horses, ready to serve as honor guard. The guests turned and waited to trail them back to the palace.

"You know what to do," Katya said to Brutal and Freddie. She put her heels to the horse, charging into the forest. Only Brutal and Freddie stayed with them as the others called out. Starbride held tight to Katya's back and whooped.

Just inside the tree line, while the confused crowd was still babbling, Freddie said, "Hurry on. We'll lay a false trail."

"Where are we going?" Starbride asked in Katya's ear.

"One of many surprises to come."

Katya guided the horse in a roundabout route to the cabin where she'd rendezvoused with Starbride on a night that seemed a lifetime ago, before they'd invaded the palace in a last push to unseat Roland. Starbride gasped and squealed as she grabbed Katya's shoulders.

"I love it!"

They swung down from the horse and hurried inside. Katya's helpers had decorated with swaths of white silk and red ribbon flowers over the windows and ceiling. The large bed Katya had required had been squeezed into one end and covered with white furs.

"Right to sleep, eh?" Starbride asked. "It has been a rough few days."

Katya shrugged and kept her tone light. "If that's what you want, I'm game."

Starbride's eyebrows rose. "Oh? Shall we test your willpower?" She reached behind her and tugged, and Katya heard the smooth sound of Starbride's bodice-strings slipping through their eyelets. Her heart jumped.

"Shall we test yours?" Katya unbuttoned her vest slowly, loving the way Starbride's eyes watched her fingers.

Starbride licked her lips, and Katya bit her own. "What say, we just count to three and then jump on each other?"

"One," Katya said.

"Two."

They leapt at the same time.

EPILOGUE

I'm sorry I wasn't at your wedding."

Katya forced herself to turn to her uncle. He seemed sheepish, hardly looking at her. Funny, she'd never thought him even capable of fidgeting. When he'd been leader of the Order, he'd been powerful, someone to idolize, even worship. As the maniac who wanted to kill her, he'd been terrifying, hateful, and still powerful but driven mad by it.

She didn't know the person who stood before her now. He was so much smaller than she remembered, but she'd been twelve when he'd *died*. Maybe she'd just grown. Reinholt said he had trouble eating. Of everyone who'd spoken to him, Reinholt seemed most at ease, maybe because he was comfortable with those who'd gone mad, having gone part that way himself.

"It's all right, Uncle."

He smiled and seemed much younger. Of course, that might have been his lack of a beard. Katya's father thought too many people might recognize him with it. Even without it, he couldn't stay in Marienne; he'd done too much. Katya was just happy the people thought of Starbride more as a savior than a killer. They were happy to let Roland stay the villain.

"I'm glad you're happy, Little K," he said. She almost snapped at him not to use that name. The specter of the murderous Fiend king loomed large in her head, and she didn't know this man. Luckily, Reinholt—the person she'd actually come to see off—emerged from the palace and saved her.

"Special envoy to Allusia," Reinholt said, rolling the words around as if tasting them. "I don't know whether to be flattered or not."

"Father wanted you gone before you drink every tavern in Dockland dry," Katya said.

"I don't know why I keep having to repeat this: it's not my fault I'm popular."

She snorted a laugh, and even Roland chuckled before staring into space. He did that a lot.

Reinholt patted him on the shoulder. "Ready to go, Uncle?"

"Yes, yes. I packed last night." He trooped down the steps to where the horses waited.

"I better go look in his bags," Reinholt whispered, "make sure they're not full of butter or anything."

"Are you ready to care for our batty uncle full-time? You'll have the guards and a few servants, but it's mostly going to be on you."

"I can handle it, Little K. Batty uncles and unsavory Docklanders are my specialty. And now that Da's got the Docklanders in his pocket, it's time for a new task. Don't worry. I can deal with the Allusians. Charming people is my talent, remember?"

She blinked at him blankly. "No."

He nudged her. "Ass. How are you liking married life?"

"All two weeks of it? It's absolutely perfect."

"Where were you hiding for one of those weeks? Or do you have no idea except that it had a bed in it?"

"I'm not giving you any details."

"You cost me a lot of money when I couldn't find you, you know. And everyone who bet on me as well."

"Good."

He put on an affronted expression, but she could read the affection behind it. "I'm going to miss this place. I'm going to miss Vierdrin and Bastian."

"You'll come back soon and visit them. Allusia's not far by ship."

"And Vierdrin will be learning how to be a queen." He kissed Katya's temple. "Teach her all you know, yes?"

"It's a promise. What are you going to call Roland while you're in Allusia?"

"A distant cousin. He wants to help people. Maybe there he'll figure out how. And maybe I'll find an enticing Allusian to romance."

"Or several."

He tilted his head back and forth, mouth turned down, considering. "Anything's possible." He walked down the steps and mounted the horse that would take them to Lucienne-by-the-Sea and then by ship to Allusia.

When Roland and Da had parted, there had been a few tears on Roland's part. He'd never be whole, but maybe some time in Reinholt's company would make him into someone entirely new. Maybe then he'd be ready to visit his children again. He still didn't seem to know what to do in their presence.

Katya watched them leave, then turned to where Freddie and Hugo waited in the doorway. This parting would hurt. "That time already?"

"We thought it better to get all the good-byes out in one day," Freddie said.

Katya tried to smother the feeling that everyone was abandoning her. When Starbride stepped out from behind them, her heart lightened. There was no trouble that Starbride's presence couldn't make better.

"I don't want you to go," Starbride said. "You're breaking up our gang."

Freddie snorted. "Some gang."

"Toughest there is," Katya said.

Starbride sighed. "What if I burst into tears? Then will you stay? Come on, Katya, a few manipulative tears."

Katya laughed. "Ask your mother if you want those."

Hugo's lip might have wobbled, but with his head turned away, Katya couldn't be sure. "Please don't cry, Miss, ah, Princess Starbride."

She laughed and threw her arms around him. "Why do you have to leave?"

"Because Ursula will arrest me if I don't go," Freddie said. Before Katya could speak, he added, "And the crown can't forbid it, not without starting down the same road we were on nine months ago. I've tested her patience long enough. She told me to leave or go to jail. I'm picking leaving, and I've made sure she knows it."

Hugo shrugged. "I can't let him go alone."

Freddie leaned close to Katya's ear. "He's madly in love with me," he said, loudly enough for all to hear.

Katya expected Hugo to turn red or shriek a protest, but he'd aged a lot in so short a time. "I just want to be there in case you die," he said.

Freddie sputtered a laugh. "Don't worry. We'll come back for a visit. We'll just have to sneak into the city."

"Or we'll venture out to see you," Katya said.

"We'll send word from time to time," Hugo said. "In case you need us."

Tears started in Starbride's eyes, but she breathed them away. "And we'll work on Captain Ursula while you're gone. Maybe she'll give up the hunt."

Freddie shook his head sadly, and Katya knew there was a story there. Before Starbride had a chance to pry it out of him, Katya drew her into a hug. She couldn't stand long, drawn-out good-byes. "Well, get going before I call the Watch."

They paused long enough to hug her and Starbride, and then they too were on their horses and gone.

Katya drew Starbride into an embrace and kissed her long and deep. "Don't worry, my loving wife, we still have lots of friends left to care for."

"Dearest wife," Starbride said, "you always know just what to say."

"Then try this: I'm resigning as leader of the Order."

Starbride's mouth dropped open. "Shall I guess why, or will you tell me?"

"Maia's ready to be the leader, or she will be once she's had the baby. And she'll have Brutal by her side. I've had all the duty I can stand for a while."

"So, you'll just have your duties as crown princess and tutors to the heirs, then?"

Katya sighed a laugh. "It sounds like a lot when you say it."

"Well, I guess you won't be surprised that I've told your father I won't be the king's pyradisté."

"Really?"

Starbride nodded. "Your father can find another, or perhaps he won't need one with Yanchasa gone. I've decided to go back to my true calling."

Her impish grin put a similar smile on Katya's mouth. "Not boring old trade law?"

"With all the new agreements between Allusia and Farraday, I thought it fitting. The Allusian students will be starting at the Halls of Law soon, and I will be joining them."

Katya drew her into another embrace. She couldn't help herself lately. "Well, what shall we do with all our free time?"

Starbride stood on her tiptoes for a kiss. "I have a few ideas."

"For right now, I've had breakfast prepared."

"Hanna's Retreat?" Starbride cocked an eyebrow. "Are you planning to seduce me?"

"I'm kind of tired. I was hoping you'd seduce me."

Starbride drew Katya down and kissed her again. "I love you, scoundrel."

"And I love you, Miss Meringue." Arm in arm, they walked back inside the palace.

About the Author

Barbara Ann Wright writes fantasy and science fiction novels and short stories when not adding to her enormous pen collection or ranting on her blog. Her short fiction has appeared twice in *Crossed Genres Magazine* and once made *Tangent Online*'s recommended reading list. *The Pyramid Waltz* was one of Tor.com's Reviewer's Choice books of 2012, was a Foreword Review Book of the Year Award Finalist, a Goldie finalist, and won the 2013 Rainbow Award for Best Lesbian Fantasy.

Books Available from Bold Strokes Books

One Last Thing by Kim Baldwin & Xenia Alexiou. Blood is thicker than pride. The final book in the Elite Operative Series brings together foes, family, and friends to start a new order. (978-1-62639-230-4)

Songs Unfinished by Holly Stratimore. Two aspiring rock stars learn that falling in love while pursuing their dreams can be harmonious—if they can only keep their pasts from throwing them out of tune. (978-1-62639-231-1)

Beyond the Ridge by L.T. Marie. Will a contractor and a horse rancher overcome their family differences and find common ground to build a life together? (978-1-62639-232-8)

Swordfish by Andrea Bramhall. Four women battle the demons from their pasts. Will they learn to let go, or will happiness be forever beyond their grasp? (978-1-62639-233-5)

The Fiend Queen by Barbara Ann Wright. Princess Katya and her consort Starbride must turn evil against evil in order to banish Fiendish power from their kingdom, and only love will pull them back from the brink. (978-1-62639-234-2)

Up the Ante by PJ Trebelhorn. When Jordan Stryker and Ashley Noble meet again fifteen years after a short-lived affair, are either of them prepared to gamble on a chance at love? (978-1-62639-237-3)

Speakeasy by MJ Williamz. When mob leader Helen Byrne sets her sights on the girlfriend of Al Capone's right-hand man, passion and tempers flare on the streets of Chicago. (978-1-62639-238-0)

Venus in Love by Tina Michele. Morgan Blake can't afford any distractions and Ainsley Dencourt can't afford to lose control—but the beauty of life and art usually lies in the unpredictable strokes of the artist's brush. (978-1-62639-220-5)

Rules of Revenge by AJ Quinn. When a lethal operative on a collision course with her past agrees to help a CIA analyst on a critical assignment, the encounter proves explosive in ways neither woman anticipated. (978-1-62639-221-2)

The Romance Vote by Ali Vali. Chili Alexander is a sought-after campaign consultant who isn't prepared when her boss's daughter, Samantha Pellegrin, comes to work at the firm and shakes up Chili's life from the first day. (978-1-62639-222-9)

Advance: Exodus Book One by Gun Brooke. Admiral Dael Caydoc's mission to find a new homeworld for the Oconodian people is hazardous, but working with the infuriating Commander Aniwyn "Spinner" Seclan endangers her heart and soul. (978-1-62639-224-3)

UnCatholic Conduct by Stevie Mikayne. Jil Kidd goes undercover to investigate fraud at St. Marguerite's Catholic School, but life gets complicated when her student is killed—and she begins to fall for her prime target. (978-1-62639-304-2)

Season's Meetings by Amy Dunne. Catherine Birch reluctantly ventures on the festive road trip from hell with beautiful stranger Holly Daniels only to discover the road to true love has its own obstacles to maneuver. (978-1-62639-227-4)

Myth and Magic: Queer Fairy Tales edited by Radclyffe and Stacia Seaman. Myth, magic, and monsters—the stuff of childhood dreams (or nightmares) and adult fantasies. (978-1-62639-225-0)

Nine Nights on the Windy Tree by Martha Miller. Recovering drug addict, Bertha Brannon, is an attorney who is trying to stay clean when a murder sends her back to the bad end of town. (978-1-62639-179-6)

Driving Lessons by Annameekee Hesik. Dive into Abbey Brooks's sophomore year as she attempts to figure out the amazing, but sometimes complicated, life of a you-know-who girl at Gila High School. (978-1-62639-228-1)

Asher's Shot by Elizabeth Wheeler. Asher Price's candid photographs capture the truth, but when his success requires exposing an enemy, Asher discovers his only shot at happiness involves revealing secrets of his own. (978-1-62639-229-8)

Courtship by Carsen Taite. Love and justice—a lethal mix or a perfect match? (978-1-62639-210-6)

Against Doctor's Orders by Radclyffe. Corporate financier Presley Worth wants to shut down Argyle Community Hospital, but Dr. Harper

Rivers will fight her every step of the way, if she can also fight their growing attraction. (978-1-62639-211-3)

A Spark of Heavenly Fire by Kathleen Knowles. Kerry and Beth are building their life together, but unexpected circumstances could destroy their happiness. (978-1-62639-212-0)

Never Too Late by Julie Blair. When Dr. Jamie Hammond is forced to hire a new office manager, she's shocked to come face to face with Carla Grant and memories from her past. (978-1-62639-213-7)

Widow by Martha Miller. Judge Bertha Brannon must solve the murder of her lover, a policewoman she thought she'd grow old with. As more bodies pile up, the murderer starts coming for her. (978-1-62639-214-4)

Twisted Echoes by Sheri Lewis Wohl. What's a woman to do when she realizes the voices in her head are real? (978-1-62639-215-1)

Criminal Gold by Ann Aptaker. Through a dangerous night in New York in 1949, Cantor Gold, dapper dyke-about-town, smuggler of fine art, is forced by a crime lord to be his instrument of vengeance. (978-1-62639-216-8)

The Melody of Light by M.L. Rice. After surviving abuse and loss, will Riley Gordon be able to navigate her first year of college and accept true love and family? (978-1-62639-219-9)

Because of You by Julie Cannon. What would you do for the woman you were forced to leave behind? (978-1-62639-199-4)

The Job by Jove Belle. Sera always dreamed that she would one day reunite with Tor. She just didn't think it would involve terrorists, firearms, and hostages. (978-1-62639-200-7)

Making Time by C.J. Harte. Two women going in different directions meet after fifteen years and struggle to reconnect in spite of the past that separated them. (978-1-62639-201-4)

Once The Clouds Have Gone by KE Payne. Overwhelmed by the dark clouds of her past, Tag Grainger is lost until the intriguing and spirited Freddie Metcalfe unexpectedly forces her to reevaluate her life. (978-1-62639-202-1)

The Acquittal by Anne Laughlin. Chicago private investigator Josie Harper searches for the real killer of a woman whose lover has been acquitted of the crime. (978-1-62639-203-8)

An American Queer: The Amazon Trail by Lee Lynch. Lee Lynch's heartening and heart-rending history of gay life from the turbulence of the late 1900s to the triumphs of the early 2000s are recorded in this selection of her columns. (978-1-62639-204-5)

Stick McLaughlin: The Prohibition Years by CF Frizzell. Corruption in 1918 cost Stick her lover, her freedom, and her identity, but a very special flapper and the family bond of her own gang could help win them back—even if it means outwitting the Boston Mob. (978-1-62639-205-2)

Edge of Awareness by C.A. Popovich. When Maria, a woman in the middle of her third divorce, meets Dana, an out lesbian, awareness of her feelings brings up reservations about the teachings of her church. (978-1-62639-188-8)

Taken by Storm by Kim Baldwin. Lives depend on two women when a train derails high in the remote Alps, but an unforgiving mountain, avalanches, crevasses, and other perils stand between them and safety. (978-1-62639-189-5)

The Common Thread by Jaime Maddox. Dr. Nicole Coussart's life is falling apart, but fortunately, DEA Attorney Rae Rhodes is there to pick up the pieces and help Nic put them back together. (978-1-62639-190-1)

Jolt by Kris Bryant. Mystery writer Bethany Lange wasn't prepared for the twisting emotions that left her breathless the moment she laid eyes on folk singer sensation Ali Hart. (978-1-62639-191-8)

Searching For Forever by Emily Smith. Dr. Natalie Jenner's life has always been about saving others, until young paramedic Charlie Thompson comes along and shows her maybe she's the one who needs saving. (978-1-62639-186-4)

A Queer Sort of Justice: Prison Tales Across Time by Rebecca S. Buck. When liberty is only a memory, and all seems lost, what freedoms and hopes can be found within us? (978-1-62639-195-6E)

Blue Water Dreams by Dena Hankins. Lania Marchiol keeps her wary sailor's gaze trained on the horizon until Oly Rassmussen, a wickedly handsome trans man, sends her trusty compass spinning off course. (978-1-62639-192-5)

Rest Home Runaways by Clifford Henderson. Baby boomer Morgan Ronzio's troubled marriage is the least of her worries when she gets the call that her addled, eighty-six-year-old, half-blind dad has escaped the rest home. (978-1-62639-169-7)

Charm City by Mason Dixon. Raq Overstreet's loyalty to her drug kingpin boss is put to the test when she begins to fall for Bathsheba Morris, the undercover cop assigned to bring him down. (978-1-62639-198-7)

Let the Lover Be by Sheree Greer. Kiana Lewis, a functional alcoholic on the verge of destruction, finally faces the demons of her past while finding love and earning redemption in New Orleans. (978-1-62639-077-5)

Blindsided by Karis Walsh. Blindsided by love, guide dog trainer Lenae McIntyre and media personality Cara Bradley learn to trust what they see with their hearts. (978-1-62639-078-2)

About Face by VK Powell. Forensic artist Macy Sheridan and Detective Leigh Monroe work on a case that has troubled them both for years, but they're hampered by the past and their unlikely yet undeniable attraction. (978-1-62639-079-9)

Blackstone by Shea Godfrey. For Darry and Jessa, their chance at a life of freedom is stolen by the arrival of war and an ancient prophecy that just might destroy their love. (978-1-62639-080-5)

Out of This World by Maggie Morton. Iris decided to cross an ocean to get over her ex. But instead, she ends up traveling much farther, all the way to another world. Once there, only a mysterious, sexy, and magical woman can help her return home. (978-1-62639-083-6)